My Sun and Stars

Published by Phaze Books
Also by L.E. Bryce

Cincinnati, Ohio

www.Phaze.com

My Sun and Stars

a novel of homoerotic fantasy by

L.E. BRYCE

A Phaze Production

Cincinnati, Ohio

Phaze Books
6470A Glenway Avenue, #109
Cincinnati, OH 45211-5222
Phaze is an imprint of Mundania Press, LLC.

To order additional copies of this book, contact:
books@phaze.com
www.Phaze.com

Cover art © 2007 Debi Lewis
Edited by Kathryn Lively

Trade Paperback ISBN-13: 978-1-59426-839-7
Trade Paperback ISBN-10: 1-59426-839-8

First Print Edition – October, 2007
Printed in the United States of America

10 9 8 7 6 5 4 3 2 1

Part One

My Sun and Stars

Chapter One

Adeja received his new orders with a professional silence belying his relief. A promotion from guarding the central hall of the palace to the quarters of the royal heir was nothing to scoff at. Zhanil was a friend of the army and often exchanged small talk with the soldiers posted to the royal household.

"The prince asked specifically for you," said Meden. "It's a great honor, if you want to call it that." The smile his commanding officer gave him was mystifying, one part conspiratorial and one part mocking. "As a post, it has its own risks and rewards. You might find it a welcome change—or not. Dinhal will take you."

In his three years on duty in the Rhodeen capital, Adeja had never been anywhere near the royal apartments, situated on the third level of the palace. Dinhal, who was Meden's personal message boy, was a dour guide, saying nothing and handing him over to the prince's chief eunuch without ceremony.

Adeja rarely trusted eunuchs. They all seemed to possess the same secretive, shifty eyes, a trait that came perhaps from being unmanned and having only food and gossip to console them. This particular eunuch was a dark-skinned Juvan with a prominent double chin and narrow eyes that were nearly lost in the fleshy folds of his face. Adeja disliked him at once. Still, he remembered his place and handed over his orders.

Unfolding the missive, the eunuch gave it no more than a cursory glance. "My name is Nakhet," he said, "and when you do not take orders from our master you will take them from me. Now then, the prince is waiting within and we cannot keep him."

From the foyer, Adeja followed the eunuch through a series of rooms, each more elaborate and richly furnished than the last. Several sleek cats lounged on cushions throughout the apartment, and servants were busy at their tasks. A few glanced up when he passed, returning to work only when Nakhet chastised them.

At last, they came to a terraced hanging garden with a view of the city and mountains beyond. Nakhet waved Adeja toward a reflecting pool tiled with blue mosaics. "Wait here while I inform Prince Sephil of your arrival."

Adeja, casually inspecting his surroundings, froze at the name. "I'm sorry, I didn't quite hear you. Surely there must be some mistake. I've been assigned to guard Crown Prince Zhanil."

Nakhet's laughter did not reassure him. Waving a plump hand thick with rings, the eunuch indicated the missive in his other. "I have your orders right here, soldier. You have been assigned to the household of the king's second son. Now, if there are no more questions, we cannot keep him waiting."

Once the eunuch was gone, Adeja knotted his hands into fists. Everyone knew the younger prince was a simpering fool who was not even permitted at court. No wonder Meden mocked him. This was not a promotion at all.

Nakhet returned with two other eunuchs and a young man dressed in clinging, pale green silk. Adeja made the requisite bow, formally presented himself for duty, and waited. If he remembered correctly, Sephil Brasides was nineteen years old with no military training whatsoever. His appearance certainly confirmed the tales: beardless and willowy, with pale skin and a mass of light brown hair that fell nearly to his waist. Had it not been for the apple bobbing at his throat, Adeja might have taken him for a girl.

"Is this the new sentry?" asked a low voice.

"Yes, my lord," replied Nakhet. "He comes highly recommended."

The prince now stood directly in front of him, in a cloud of costly fragrance that made his nose twitch. "What is your name, soldier?"

"Adeja ked Shamuz, my lord."

"Adeja," Sephil purred, drawing out the syllables as if tasting them. Adeja lowered his eyes to the pebbled mosaic that encircled the pool. He could feel the prince's gaze crawling over him, appraising him like a prospective buyer at a horse auction.

Sephil stepped back. "Yes, he will serve. That will be all for now. Nakhet, see to it this guard is properly stationed and that he knows the duties of the household."

* * * *

Adeja's shift lasted from sunset to dawn. Mostly it was quiet and uneventful, although the prince occasionally entertained. Musicians and dancers came in, and the guests brushed through the foyer in their finery and costly fragrances; Adeja could not fail to notice that most of them were young noblemen, probably the prince's friends. A few looked in his direction and smirked, making lewd comments about his physique. As they were usually drunk or high on *kif* when they jeered him, he ignored them.

On a few occasions he saw a eunuch bring in a youth for the prince's pleasure, and could hear the moaning and carrying on several rooms away. Adeja quickly learned that the prince had a healthy sexual appetite and apparently no taste for girls.

During the day, he went back to the barracks to eat and sleep. Most of his fellow guards had day shifts, but a few were in when he arrived. They lost no time in asking how well he liked being posted to a prince's apartments. "That one never leaves his rooms. He likes his parties, too, I've heard," said Hedir. "You must see some interesting things."

Adeja shrugged. He knew better than to complain about his employer or share gossip. Men got demoted or worse for engaging in such business. "It's really quite boring."

One night as he stood sentry duty in the foyer, he spied a figure moving through the shadows. It was not unusual for the servants to move about in the quiet hours, tidying up or going to and from trysts after the master retired. A palace never truly slept.

Even in the darkness from several feet away he could tell that this was neither a servant nor a eunuch. He tightened his grip on his pike, ready to call the alarm and strike if the stranger did not identify himself. "Who is there?"

In a swirl of silk, Sephil approached him. "Adeja, come with me to the terrace."

"My post is here, my lord," he answered.

"Are you telling me you like standing at attention for twelve hours at a time? You do not even have to use the privy?" Sephil's laughter was so disjointed Adeja could not help but wonder if he had been drinking or smoking *kif*. "I order you to come with me. You cannot very well guard me if I am elsewhere."

"My duty is to watch the door."

"You will not need that here." Sephil touched the pike, then, as Adeja slowly relaxed, eased it from his hand and leaned it against the wall by the door. "I gave you an order. You will accompany me."

The hanging garden was cool and quiet but for the soft splash of the fountain. During the day, the terrace afforded a commanding view of the city's western quarter and the mountains crowning the horizon. Stars spangled the night sky, and in the distance flickering torches delineated the ceremonial shrine of the pyramid of the Moon.

"Where do you come from, Adeja?" Sephil asked softly. "You are not a native of Rhodeen."

"I'm from Tajhaan, my lord."

Once again Sephil responded with that tipsy laugh. "Oh, you do not need to be so formal with me. You may call me Sephil. Tell me, is Tajhaan much different than Rhodeen?"

Even the most slow-witted prostitute knew the basic differences between the two kingdoms. Either Sephil was making inane small talk or he really *was* that ignorant. "Tajhaan is an oasis in the middle of the desert, my lord." Adeja gazed out over the city, bordered by the wide silvery ribbon of the river Khul. "This is a green land, not at all like home."

"Have you traveled far?"

"I've been many places and seen many things," answered Adeja.

Sighing, Sephil leaned against the terrace. "I would like to travel. I have never seen the desert or the ocean. I have never been much of anywhere. My father has a palace in Cassiare. When I was a boy we spent summers there and I saw the silk farms, but that was all."

Why the prince felt a need to confide in him, Adeja did not know. It made him slightly uneasy. "Traveling isn't as safe as it once was. Too many Turyar about," he said.

"I have heard about them. Are they very dangerous?"

"They're horsemen from the steppes north of the Sevaa wastes," replied Adeja. "They appear out of nowhere and attack without warning or mercy, and where they've been they leave smoldering ruins and piles of corpses. Men, women, children, it doesn't matter to them. I've seen them kill everything down to the village dogs. They have no cities and no kings, just scattered clans with chieftains whom you can't trust enough to bargain with. Stay behind your walls and be thankful you don't have to deal with them."

"Keep to my apartments and amusements like a woman and leave the rest to soldiers like you, is that it?" asked Sephil. Moving closer, he dropped his voice. "Tell me, soldier, what do you like in bed? Do you like boys?"

The question was so unexpected, so shamelessly blunt Adeja did not know how to answer. "Why do you want to know, my lord?"

9

"I will not dance around my reason for bringing you here," explained Sephil. "You see, I enjoy having handsome guardsmen on duty. I enjoy watching you stand at attention for hours at a time. You never twitch, never even blink. I cannot help but wonder what it would take to make you lose control."

This teasing was thoroughly inappropriate. No doubt the prince was drunk and would not remember any of it in the morning. "My lord, I am on duty, and my duty is to guard the door not to—"

"Not to pleasure me in my bed?"

"My lord, I think you are—"

"I am not drunk," answered Sephil, "and I do not smoke *kif*. I know what I am doing, and I hardly think you would refuse me if given the chance."

"I am a soldier, my lord."

Sephil laughed. "Oh, I have had soldiers before. They are insatiable. In fact, the last one could not get enough of my mouth." He leaned in close enough that their bodies touched. Adeja tried to move away, but Sephil hooked an arm through his and bent to his ear. "Bedez was uncut, and he once told me that all Tajhaani men were the same. I thoroughly enjoyed sucking him off."

Whether it was appropriate to rebuff a prince or not, Adeja broke away in horror. Of all the things he expected Sephil might say, hearing him confess such wantonness was not one of them. "My lord, I would never do such things with a member of the royal family. Your father would have my head if I did."

"Bedez said that, too, and the one before him, but I know enough about you soldiers to know you cannot get enough sex. I would not be surprised if you were hard right now, and picturing me on my knees in front of you. Besides, my father does not care what I do."

With Sephil's hands roaming his arms and chest, it was getting increasingly difficult to concentrate. "What happened to him, this Bedez?"

"He grew tiresome and started making demands. He wanted jewels and horses, and threatened to brag to everyone about how he pleasured me," answered Sephil. "I had him sent to Mekesh on the edge of the Sevaa wastes. There was nothing else I could do."

A chill knotted Adeja's belly at the prince's matter-of-fact tone. If he was not very, very careful, he could end the same way.

"If it's a plaything you want, my lord, you're better off buying yourself an *akesh*."

"What is that?"

"An *akesh* is a pleasure slave, a *pedith*."

"I have had plenty of those, but it is not the same. Having a slave who will do anything you command defeats the purpose. I prefer men like you."

Adeja carefully disentangled his arm and crossed both over his chest. "I don't go around bedding princes."

"Oh, am I that ugly?" laughed Sephil.

"One should not meddle with those above one's station," said Adeja.

It might mean nothing to you, but sooner or later someone will put a knife to my throat for daring to meddle with a king's son, Adeja thought. It was no wonder Brasidios barred his younger son from court. "Does your father know what you do?"

"I told you, as long as I do not create a public scandal, he does not care what I do."

However, that did not mean the king did not care what *Adeja* did. He found it extremely difficult to concentrate with Sephil pressing up against him, stroking his bicep through the thin wool of his tunic. Had the prince been anyone else, had he been an *akesh* or a *bakti* from the local brothel, his teasing would not have gone on this long. Adeja would have already pushed him to his knees and shown him exactly what soldiers did with whores.

* * * *

"What is the matter with him, Nakhet?"

At once, the eunuch moved to his side. "With whom, my prince?"

Sephil glanced in the direction of the foyer, trusting Nakhet's eyes to follow. The Tajhaani guard was off duty, but his presence hung heavy in the air, a thorn that refused to be pruned to fit Sephil's tidy little world. "He does not respond like the other ones."

"Give him time, my lord. These soldiers are rather dense, but once this one understands what is required of him I doubt he will be able to resist your charms for long."

"Yes, I think he will give good chase." Sephil slid his foot from his sandal to trace the fountain tiles with lacquered toes. *But I do not want him to be quite like the last one*, he added privately. Bedez had been good to look at and even better in bed, yet in their hours together something had been lacking.

In quiet moments, when Nakhet was not present to reassure him, Sephil wondered if perhaps he was mistaken in trying to repeat the experience. *I should send the man back to his barracks and forget the whole thing.*

Even as the thought formed, Sephil dismissed it. Adeja would remain, if only because he could not be trusted to keep silent if he left. Nakhet assured him otherwise, of course, but of late the eunuch's promises gave him no comfort. Adeja might stand wordless at his post, but who knew what he did or said when he was off-duty?

And I want him to stay, and learn to like me. I will be that much lonelier if he does not. Sephil drew his hair back from his face and bent over the edge of the fountain to try to catch his reflection in the water. *I am not ugly, so why does he resist?*

His eyes once again darted toward the foyer, where dull, stalwart Eumos stood guard, wishing night would come and Adeja with it.

"After tonight's entertainment," said Nakhet, "he may be better disposed to serve you."

"Is there to be *another* party?" sighed Sephil. Last night had been enough for him, and the thought of one more evening in the company of Ethurel and the other disaffected young noblemen who helped themselves to his hospitality held little interest. Once, they had been beloved links to an outside world he was no longer allowed to see; he had delighted in them, and let himself believe that his sentiments were returned. Of late, however, the emptiness of their interactions made his stomach roil, heightening his sense of alienation and growing despair.

I will never have true friends, or family, he thought. *Even Zhanil has no time for me.*

"Where do you find the money to afford all the wine and *kif* and pleasure slaves? Father keeps me on such a short allowance."

If he had expected a forthright answer, Nakhet disappointed him. "You know I have investments throughout the city," said the eunuch. "Do not trouble yourself anymore thinking about such things and trust me."

As he left, a servant came in with a selection of robes. Sephil, tempted to send the man away, regarded the embroidered silks with distaste. *That is the problem,* he thought. *I cannot trust Nakhet, but there is no one else.*

Chapter Two

Now would have been the ideal moment for Adeja to go to his commanding officer and request a transfer, but in order to have it approved he would have to divulge the reason for his request. Only a fool would tell the truth, and from the hints Sephil had thrown in his direction, he knew the prince would thwart the attempt.

For the next two weeks he remained at his post, pointedly ignoring the prince's increasingly provocative efforts at seduction. If he did not respond, perhaps Sephil would grow weary of the chase and send him back to the barracks. A demotion from the royal household would tarnish his career, but at this point it was better than the alternative.

Each night before bed, Sephil emerged from his bedchamber for what had become a ritual. Giving no thought to whom might be watching, he walked up to Adeja and ran his fingers over Adeja's ceremonial breastplate and sword belt, stroking a palm over the bulge in his leggings. Adeja drew a long breath and held it, determined to betray no reaction.

Sephil leaned forward to breathe in his ear, licking his earlobe before speaking. "If you want me, you know where I sleep."

Adeja stayed at his post and counted tiles, anything to take his mind off his erection and the tempting morsel laying in bed only a few rooms away.

After a few nights, Sephil's tactics became more aggressive. He sent a servant with a platter of long-stemmed mushrooms whose phallic caps were dipped in an opaque white wine sauce, and mounded pastries tipped with nipples of candied almonds. Toward midnight, Sephil came out, spied the untouched food and wine on the sideboard, and carefully speared a mushroom on a silver fork, suggestively licking off the sauce and drawing the purplish head between his lips before consuming it. "You could be enjoying a better feast than this," he said.

"I do not eat or drink on duty, my lord," answered Adeja.

"Perhaps I should have you exchange shifts with Eumos and invite you back when you are not on duty. Then you will not have such a ready excuse."

Eumos, the guard who had the day shift, was a pockmarked, middle-aged veteran obviously chosen by the king. As the man slept in a different barracks, Adeja did not know him, and Eumos had little to say to him, though at times he wore a sympathetic look that said he knew everything.

If I were old and ugly like him, my life would be so much simpler. Adeja never anticipated the day when he would think such a thing, but there it was.

Two nights later, Sephil brought a pleasure slave into the foyer and slowly made love to him on a pile of cushions he had ordered the servants to place there. With his mouth and hands he drove the youth to ecstasy before taking his pleasure, mounting him from an angle that allowed Adeja to watch his buttocks pumping and clenching.

The little whore wants me to fuck him right here. Adeja wanted to close his eyes, knowing it would probably be best if he did, but nothing could shut out the moans and gasps.

Once they were finished, Sephil gave Adeja a disappointed look and turned to nuzzle his partner. Shortly afterward, they withdrew into the bedchamber and throughout the night Adeja heard muffled sounds of ecstasy which he did his best to ignore. Had they remained in the foyer, he could not say what he would have done.

The pleasure slave left just as Eumos came on duty. Adeja greeted him, handed over the ceremonial pike and helmet, and hurried back to the barracks where he spent half an hour masturbating in the deserted privy. He could not endure much more of this teasing. Now was the time either to draw a brand across his face, request a transfer, or contemplate desertion. The alternative was unthinkable.

Meden was away, and a calmer assessment of the situation made desertion an unlikely choice. All he could do was show restraint on duty, though by now he was crazy enough with lust to forget propriety, to throw Sephil down on the floor and take him like the whore he was. He wanted to hear that seductive voice moaning his name, and yet at the same time he wanted to beat the prince bloody for playing games with him.

In his experience, sex and violence were not such divergent forces.

He went to his cot and slept for a few hours before he was roused by the call to the noon mess. Three coppers bought him a quarter of an hour with a youth from an establishment that catered to soldiers. The boy's rehearsed cries of encouragement did nothing to sate Adeja's hunger, and though he climaxed he went away disillusioned.

Evening found him in a sour temper which Sephil's appearance did not alleviate, especially when the prince made a point of commenting upon his restraint. "Hallisos was hot enough for two men last night. Tell me, have you ever had two mouths sucking you at the same time? Such a pity, you could have fucked us both."

Sephil obviously did not care that Nakhet and another eunuch stood within earshot. Knowing their proclivities for gossip, the entire court probably knew by now.

His apprehension only increased when Sephil left and Nakhet approached him. "Perhaps you have not noticed," commented the eunuch, "but there are many more opportunities in this household than elsewhere."

"I've never been an overly ambitious man," answered Adeja. "I'm curious, though. Is Eumos keen on the…opportunities here?"

Nakhet narrowed his eyes. "Eumos was recommended by the king, but sadly he does not, shall we say, qualify for advancement. Unfair though it may be to a veteran, the best opportunities come to those who are young and fit."

As the eunuch's gaze traveled up and down his body, Adeja wanted to ask him point-blank how he could get away with such shameless pandering. "I'm used to my soldier's routine."

"Life without change is dull, soldier," said Nakhet. "You would do well to consider your options while they are still available to you."

Uneasiness dogged Adeja through the next few hours. The eunuch's subtle prodding was more disturbing than Sephil's blatant overtures. He had endured enough. Tomorrow he would ask Meden for a transfer and take what menial post he could get. Even a colorless existence in Tajhaan held better prospects at this point.

Night fell on the city. By the quiet air of the household, Adeja could tell Sephil would not be entertaining. Later a musician might be summoned, or a pleasure slave, as the prince did not like to sleep alone, yet for now all was calm.

Twilight colored the foyer in shadows and deep cobalt. A light breeze stirred the hangings in the hallway beyond. Servants had not yet come to light the lamps in the prince's drawing room, and Adeja did not even hear their small movements.

"I sent them away," murmured a voice beside him.

Sephil, draped in a dark robe embroidered with lotus flowers, stood at his elbow.

"What do you want?" asked Adeja.

"To know why you keep saying no to me."

"Because you're a prince and I'm a soldier."

Sephil stood unbearably close now, his hands sliding across Adeja's middle to do things with his belt that should not be allowed. Adeja's breath hitched as those hands ventured lower, seeking his groin. He wanted to grab those hands and shove them away, and at the same time he wanted to pull them against his growing erection. "Why are you playing with me?" he gasped. "This is dangerous."

"It is just an innocent bit of fun, that is all," Sephil said sweetly, sounding like one who believed it. "You are always so serious. We are just playing. Nothing will come of it. And besides, how many other soldiers can boast of being in the mouth of a prince?"

His nimble fingers found the ties of Adeja's trousers and made short work of them, spreading open his fly to release his cock. Adeja felt a hand enclose the head, drawing him out with long, languorous strokes. He swallowed hard to stifle a groan.

"You are just like Bedez," Sephil purred in his ear. "I am going to enjoy this very much."

Still holding his cock, Sephil sank to his knees in a silken flutter. At the first touch of his tongue, Adeja nearly lost his grip on his pike. Now, as that tongue swirled around the head of his erection, pulling back his foreskin and darting into the slit, he clasped the weapon even tighter. Before he realized what he was doing, the fingers of his other hand tangled in Sephil's hair and he was rhythmically thrusting his hips.

Sephil made pleased noises in his throat. The hem of his robe was hitched up to his waist, and his hand was lost in the shadow between his legs.

The prince was skilled, there was no doubt, but his tricks were nothing a good whore did not know. Perhaps the threat of discovery or the knowledge that he was doing something so thoroughly forbidden made the encounter so delicious. All Adeja knew was he did not last very long. Trembling, clenching

Sephil's hair in a tight fist, his thrusts quickened and he came hard in that hot mouth.

He heard Sephil come, but did not look. His trousers still undone, his damp flesh softening between his legs, he rested his pike against the wall and sank down, breathing hard. Now he was at eye level with Sephil, who licked his fingers with a sated smile.

It was wrong, the whole thing was wrong and he should have rearranged his clothing and returned to his post at once, but he needed a brief space in which to catch his wind. "When," he gasped, "did you start doing this?"

Sephil gently touched his leg, encased in its embossed leather greave. Affection, however, played no part in this encounter, and holding each other in the afterglow would have been both awkward and inappropriate. Adeja made no move to touch him.

"I was sixteen," answered Sephil. "There was a guard assigned to these apartments who was quite handsome. One hot day I went past him into the garden to sit by the pool. I was wearing a thin garment, very thin. Perhaps you will say it was immodest of me, but these are my apartments and one never really pays attention to what the servants might be looking at. I saw his eyes on me then, and when I came back. I knew what sex was, and I knew the way this man was looking at me. It was insolent, of course, but I never felt so excited. He wanted me. I invited him in that night and asked him why he had looked me that way. Of course, he did not protest as much as you. In fact, he fucked me three different ways that night. I could not get enough of him."

"Where is he now?"

Sephil shrugged. "We carried on for a while, and then one day he was not there anymore. My father learned what I was doing. He confined me here and the man was posted elsewhere. The new guard was old and quite ugly, worse than Eumos. It was almost two years before I could get rid of him and get Bedez."

"So you just fucked him and packed him off like so much baggage?"

"You are insolent, soldier. I told you, I had nothing to do with his being sent away."

Adeja looked at him. "Maybe, but you don't seem to care very much about it. And as for insolence, you're a fine one to talk about that when you just sucked off a lowborn soldier."

"You were hard. You wanted it."

"Men do stupid things when they're hard. Did you really think I could stand that much teasing?" Adeja tucked himself back into his trousers and fastened the ties. "If your father finds out, I'll end up like all the others. Did you ever stop to think about that?"

"My father does not care what I do as long as I do not bother him or create a public scandal." Sephil gathered his robes around him and stood up. "But if you really do not want me," he said coldly, "then I will not bother you any longer."

He swept out of the foyer. Moments later, Adeja heard a door slam, then another. Getting to his feet, he retrieved his pike and returned to his post, but the rest of his watch was awkward.

At dawn, Nakhet entered the foyer and gave him a knowing look that Adeja did not return. The thought of the eunuch eavesdropping on him was repulsive.

"It is not wise to upset the prince," said Nakhet. "A guard should remember his place and be more cooperative."

"A guard's place is at the door."

Twice that day Adeja almost went down to Meden's office to apply for a transfer, but matters had gone too far for that. Should he make the attempt, someone on the prince's staff, probably Nakhet, might retaliate with the charge that he acted inappropriately. For all he knew, half a dozen eunuchs had been watching him with Sephil, all of whom could easily step forward and accuse him of rape.

Desertion became an increasingly appealing option. However, he did not have enough ready coin to see him out of Rhodeen. Another month or two and he might be able to pull it off, provided he could survive that long at his current post.

* * * *

Bedez had not done that, had not done or said those things at all. In fact, Sephil had put very little effort into seducing him, since the man had not cared beyond wanting to know how often they could fuck and how much trouble he would get into for bedding a king's son. Adeja, on the other hand, was proving to be more trouble than his good looks and hard cock were worth.

Sephil sat on the edge of his bed, toying with the tassel from the gilded draperies above. Acting the part of the amoral seducer did not sit well with him, or at least, it no longer provided the satisfaction it once had. *I only do it because it is what everyone thinks I am. If Father wants to call me a whore, I should at least try not to disappoint him as I do in everything else.* And yet, he realized, by acting the part he became that very thing he loathed. *For once, I would like someone to approach me, not because I propositioned them, but because they want to.*

"It might be best to cast about the slave markets for a strong, virile Tajhaani slave, if that is what you desire, my lord," said Nakhet. "Otherwise we risk a scandal."

"I am sure my father knows what I am doing. And you know perfectly well that he does not care," replied Sephil. "I do not want a slave." The pleasure slaves Nakhet procured for him were empty-headed creatures so willing to perform they were devoid of any personality. No slave, no creature broken to the lash, could be any different. Taking a slave to bed was nothing like having a real man, a pair of strong arms to hold him and keep him safe.

For all the difficulty he caused, Adeja *was* a real man. Sephil sighed, wrapped his arms around his knees, and pondered his next move.

Chapter Three

Sephil maintained a carefully studied silence, barely acknowledging Adeja's presence while showering lavish praise on a bewildered Eumos. His disdain might have been bearable if not for the ominous looks Nakhet threw in the direction of the foyer.

Adeja gave no sign that he noticed. Outwardly he continued with his duties, standing at strict attention while his mind wandered, formulating plans to escape the city. He would have no more than twelve hours, and he would have to go on no sleep at all, which he could counter by sleeping through the days before. Arranging a brief furlough would buy him an extra day or two and could easily be accomplished on the barracks end, but convincing Nakhet he was entitled to leisure time for whores and drink would be considerably more difficult. As the eunuch already spied on his master, it was possible he would have Adeja watched as well.

Twelve hours was probably all he was going to get. Speed and guile would be his only allies.

In the quiet attending his thoughts, he almost did not hear the soft footfalls on the marble floor. "Who goes there?" he growled, shifting his hold on his weapon.

The willowy figure silhouetted in the doorway belonged to Sephil. Adeja tensed, waiting for words of reproach or seduction, but the prince said nothing, only took his hand and gently tugged at him until he followed.

While Adeja had seen most of the other rooms, he had never been in the prince's bedchamber. A luxurious contrast to the barracks, in which his lumpy cot was one of several in a drab room, Sephil's chamber was floored with velvet-deep carpets and furnished with exotic woods and ivories. A sheer silk curtain, shimmering gold in the light of a single candelabra, draped a bed piled high with cushions.

Sephil turned and, undoing the clasp that held his robe closed, let the garment slide from his shoulders. Underneath, his naked skin glowed in the golden light. "Take off your clothes," he murmured. It sounded more like a request than a command.

Adeja tore his eyes from the prince's body to study the latticed screens against one wall. Behind them, anyone might be watching. "No," he answered.

Ivory fingers reached out to touch his cheek, his lips. "It is torture for me to lie alone thinking of you just outside the door," said Sephil. "Am I truly so terrible that you do not want to touch me?" His fingers slid down Adeja's breastplate in search of the fastenings. "Take this off and let me feel you."

Fear and desire quickened Adeja's pulse. He knew what peril he had entered into, and yet he could not deny that he wanted the beautiful young body that was being so freely offered to him. The need in Sephil's eyes was so earnest, so intense that before he knew what he was doing Adeja covered the prince's fingers with his own and helped him remove the armor.

Before he let it fall to the carpet, Sephil touched his lips to the breastplate and the sunburst that was the emblem of the royal house. "Do you know what my name means?" he asked softly. "*Sepha'il*. It is very old, and means 'little moon.' The Sun was my ancestor. Before he loved the mortal woman who was my foremother, he loved the Moon."

His fingers slid into the crease of Adeja's tunic, undoing the ties and kissing the bare skin underneath. "I want you to be my Sun."

They kissed as Adeja flung off the last articles of his clothing. Sephil was hungry for the touch of his lips, for slow lovemaking. Adeja found it difficult to accommodate him. Usually he did his business quickly, with boys for whom sex was merely another transaction. Now he found himself on a soft bed in a candlelit room with a partner who did not simply want to be mounted but stroked and fingered, caressed as if the encounter actually meant something.

Sephil was insatiable, skilled in arousing a partner's spent desire. Adeja rode him twice that night, but bringing him to climax was more work than pleasure. By the time the prince climbed off his softening member and lay down beside him, Adeja was too exhausted for the pillow talk Sephil clearly wanted.

"Do you do that every night?" he mumbled.

"You make light of my proclivities." Sephil turned over and propped himself up on his arm to gaze down at his lover. "Perhaps you think I should be doing more princely things?"

Adeja briefly closed his eyes. After sex, all he wanted to do was sleep. "I'd thought of that."

"You think I am spoiled, but you know nothing," said Sephil. "I am not my father's heir. I do not know how to do anything. I do not even leave these apartments. When my brother becomes king, I will never sit on his council. No one will ever ask me for advice or favors. This and my entertainments with my friends are all I have."

"If you want to play, do it with slaves. The man you sent to Mekesh is probably dead."

"Nakhet suggested I have his throat cut in some back alley, but I said no. Mekesh is very far away, and Bedez could be alive and well."

Opening his eyes, Adeja looked at him. The prince actually seemed to believe his own nonsense. "I doubt it. You don't know anything about being a soldier, and you don't know anything about life on a frontier like that. If you don't believe me when I tell you what shit holes places like Mekesh are, ask your brother."

"Bedez is a soldier," said Sephil. "He knows how to survive."

"That doesn't mean he wanted to be sent there. You shouldn't have played with him in the first place. I'm surprised you can even get away with it. Most fathers I know would kill their sons for bringing such shame on their families. At least, that's what they would do in Tajhaan. Maybe things are different here."

Sephil laughed harshly, but his eyes reflected deep hurt. "My father tried to kill me the first time, then he decided he did not care what I do. He does not care who my friends are or what I do with my lovers. He does not even notice me."

"And when he does notice you, what do you think will happen? You'll be lucky if he doesn't kill you, but I've got no illusions about what he'll do to me," said Adeja. "Did you ever think about that?"

Sephil evaded the question. "I want you to like me," he said softly. "Bedez did, you know. When we were together he used to call me his little *bakti*."

Adeja sucked in a gasp of disbelief. *You ignorant little fool.* "Do you even know what that means? Since you like Tajhaani men so much, you might at least learn the language."

"It was his pet name for me."

"No," said Adeja. "It means *whore*, because that's all you were to him, a little whore with a gilded ass."

22

"I do not believe you." But the strangled sound Sephil made in his throat told Adeja he did. "He *liked* me."

"You don't make men like you by rubbing up against their cocks and showing them your naked body like a bitch in heat. If a man wants that he can get it with far less risk in a brothel."

"Are you always this insolent?" Sephil asked sharply. "Why are you even telling me this? It would have been better had I not known."

Adeja sat up and began looking for his clothing. By the prince's tone, he knew in a moment or two he would be ordered to leave. "Because a boy who acts like a whore should at least know what he is in somebody else's language."

"Get out!" hissed Sephil.

There it was, cold and laced with venom, but under it Adeja discerned the voice of a child who would burst into tears the moment he was alone. He climbed off the bed and snatched his trousers off the carpet. "If you wanted somebody to flatter you, you'd have done better than to show your backside to a soldier. I can get a cheaper fuck elsewhere, and I don't have even to say anything to the whore."

An outraged shriek was followed by a cushion hurled at his head. Adeja dropped the clothing and bits of leather armor in his hands. Grasping Sephil's wrists, he wedged a knee between the prince's thighs and pinned him to the mattress. Sephil cursed him until, with a wide-eyed look of terror, he realized he was trapped. "Get off me!"

A scrape of leather soles against tiles behind one of the screens reminded Adeja that one or more of the eunuchs were watching. That alone should have instructed him to behave with greater caution, but he was beyond caring. "You wanted to be fucked by a soldier," he hissed in Sephil's ear, "and so I did. Maybe you'd like me to bring two or three of my friends in here to show you how we really fuck pretty boys when we sack a town?"

Sephil twisted and struggled. "If you do not get off me I am going to scream and—"

Adeja loosened his grip just long enough to slap him. "And then what? The guards are going to come running? You stupid boy, I *am* the guard." To his dismay, he found himself growing hard again, and he could see by the look on Sephil's face that the prince realized it.

"I did not do anything to you."

"You ordered me to drop my trousers and fuck you like some cheap whore," retorted Adeja. "You've got to be the stupidest prince in the world if you don't understand how dangerous that is. I'm probably going to be killed for all this, and none of it was my idea."

"I told you, my father does not—"

Adeja slapped him again. "Shut up. I don't care what you think your father will or won't do. Men like me are put to death for toying with princes like you." Shoving the prince away from him in disgust, he got up to find a towel and get dressed. "I don't really care to end up like all the others."

On the floor beside the bed he spied Sephil's robe. Picking up the garment, he flung it at the prince. "Cover yourself up."

The revulsion he felt now was the same he experienced when looking at the naked body of a whore with whom he had just finished, when the haze of need finally dissipated. His erection did not discriminate, his lust did not care what a willing woman or youth looked like under the garish paint, scent and shameless manner. It was only afterward that he felt remorse. A whore's life was nothing to envy.

Unlike those cheap women and boys, Sephil *was* beautiful. It sickened Adeja to picture him lying nude on a pallet in a squalid brothel, with a stranger's seed all over his thighs, and it made him angry. *If I were this boy's father, I'd strangle him for shame.* "You got what you wanted. I hope you're satisfied," he said tightly, and slammed the door behind him.

Chapter Four

A new tension filled the household. This time there was no waiting silence, no sense of anticipation, only the strain generated by two individuals who did not want to see or speak to each other.

At any moment, Adeja expected to be dismissed or arrested. Having sex with the prince was bad enough in its own right, but insolence was another matter entirely. Nakhet did not address the issue, which Adeja found odd, though there was no question that he knew about it.

Raucous parties filled the evenings. Sephil's friends called on him, oftentimes arriving with male or female pleasure slaves on their arms, and the sounds of sex occasionally drifted out into the foyer above the usual laughter, music, and carousing. Servants came just before dawn to lead dazed and drunken partygoers home.

One night, however, the young men left early, filing out of the prince's sitting room and muttering to themselves. The musicians followed them out shortly afterward. Something was not right. Adeja sensed a similar unease among the servants who were called in to tidy up, but as the matter did not concern him he gave it no attention.

The servants did their work, extinguished the lamps, and withdrew. Once again the apartment was silent, the prince and his eunuchs presumably having retired some time before.

It was not long before Adeja found he was mistaken. Sephil, a dark dressing gown wrapped over a linen shift, stepped into the foyer. "Adeja," he whispered. "Come with me to the terrace."

"I'm not going to fuck you out in the open," Adeja answered sharply.

"I am not here for sex." Sephil's voice was small, and he looked unusually pale. "I want to sit outside. Will you watch over me there?"

"My post is at the door, my lord."

"You do realize that if someone wanted to hurt me there are at least three other ways into this apartment, yes?" asked Sephil.

Adeja frowned. "My orders are to guard the door, not your person."

Sephil reached past him to touch the heavy wood. "I suppose it is worth more than I am. Come outside with me. The door will still be here when you return."

Outside in the hanging garden, the late spring air was cool and fragrant with night-blooming flowers. Sephil sat down on the rim of the reflecting pool and contemplated the dark water. "I sent them away," he murmured.

Adeja made no comment. If the prince wanted to talk to the empty air, that was his business.

Sephil apparently took his silence as a cue to continue. "I asked if any of them would still be my friends if I were not a prince. For once I was serious, but they laughed at me and said I was a terrible bore when I talked like that. I would have laughed, too, and forgotten about it. Then I had a strange moment. Do you know the kind, when you suddenly realize that everyone else is laughing but you are not part of the joke? I had a moment like that, and I suddenly thought of all the times when I was ill or sad and how they were never there."

He picked up a leaf that had fallen from an overhanging fruit tree and turned it in his fingers. "They only come here because it is a scandalous thing for them to do. They are not my friends. I wanted them to be, but they care nothing for me." As his head drooped, his loose hair fell forward to obscure his face. "It is such a terrible feeling to know you have nobody, that you are alone."

Adeja had no idea what to say. He did not know why Sephil even bothered to tell him this. "A man's family is all he needs," he finally answered.

"I do not have a family. I have been trying to tell you that all along. I have been shut up in these apartments for three years because of what happened with that guard. I have not seen or heard from my family since then. I am as good as dead to them. The only family I ever really had was Carran, but he is gone now."

"Who was that?"

Sephil pushed back a strand of his hair and sat up a little. "He was the eunuch who looked after me when I was small. My mother died when I was born. I had a wet nurse, and then Carran came. He used to play with me and tell me stories, and sometimes when I was afraid of the dark he would stay awake with me until I fell asleep. He always used to tell me what a fine,

26

strong prince I would grow up to be and he would praise me when I did things well. He died when I was eleven. I wanted to go to his funeral but my father said it was inappropriate for such a young prince to mourn so over a servant.

"Nakhet has no time for stories or games. He calls it nonsense. If I want someone to keep me company he calls for a pleasure slave." Rising, Sephil walked slowly to the edge of the terrace and stood contemplating the distant pyramid of the Moon. "I could not sleep. Would you stay in my room until I fall asleep?"

Instinct cautioned Adeja against saying yes. Who was to say this young man, with his wildly oscillating moods, would not shake off his melancholy and try to seduce him again? "I will stand just inside the chamber door, my lord."

Sephil took his hand and led him to the bedchamber, where a single oil lamp burned. He removed his dressing gown but kept on his linen shift as he climbed under the green silk coverlet. "You promise me, Adeja? You will not leave until Eumos comes?"

Adeja gripped his pike and went to stand by the door. He would have put out the light, but Sephil would not hear of it. The sheer gold hangings blurred his view of the prince, so he listened for Sephil's breathing and was relieved as it slowly dropped into the even rhythm of sleep.

His eyes roamed the chamber, lingering over the screens on the opposite side of the bed. There were too many shadows to see what might be lurking behind the intricate latticework, but he could feel the presence of another. *If Nakhet has the time to spy on his master, he certainly has the time to sit by his bed.*

Sephil's sleep was broken by a nightmare in which he thrashed and made little cries. Adeja made no move to go to him until it became apparent that he was half-awake and crying into the pillow. Propping the pike by the door, Adeja approached the bed and drew back the hangings. "Are you all right?" he asked.

A muffled sob told him no. Adeja contemplated the screen, the recumbent form on the bed and quickly stripped off his armor and boots, leaving the rest of his clothing on. He climbed onto the pillows to lie beside the prince but would not get under the coverlet even when Sephil drew it back in invitation.

"You're really too old for this," he said softly.

"I am not as brave as you, Adeja. I have always been afraid of the dark," said Sephil, "but I am more afraid of being left *alone* in the dark."

Adeja spent the rest of the night gazing up at the golden web swaying above his head, stroking the hair spilled across his chest and murmuring mindless words of comfort. When dawn began to lighten the space behind the screens, he gently disentangled himself from Sephil's arms, put on his armor, and went back to the foyer.

Eumos was already on duty. "I thought you'd left," said the man. Whatever else he might have thought—and his imagination probably ran riot at the sight of Adeja's disheveled clothing—he kept it to himself.

* * * *

"Oh, Sephil, you are *such* a bore when you talk like that," said Ethurel.

"So you would not visit me?"

Sputtering with laughter, the young nobleman exchanged glances with his friends before answering. "Everyone knows your father refuses to have you at court and that you are only a prince in name. Keeping time with you is such a *deliciously* scandalous thing to do because no one knows what you are about sealed up here in your apartments."

Sephil drew a sharp breath. "So you care nothing for me?"

"Oh, now you are being tiresome. You have such marvelous parties and—"

"That is not what I meant."

Afterward, Sephil did not remember throwing his guests out, only the smart of humiliation at realizing the life he had lived for three years was a lie.

Talking to Adeja brought him some measure of peace, even if the soldier did not quite understand everything he was trying to say. *He must think I am spoiled and selfish. Yes, I have been stupid, but what I want is only what everyone else wants.*

Seeing the truth was like being told someone had died. *But I am the one who is dead, do you not see? I thought I lived. Not until now did I understand that I really died all those years ago when Father confined me to these rooms and the world forgot that a person named Sephil Brasides ever existed.*

* * * *

The household became a somber place. Sephil hosted no further entertainments and had no visitors. Now that it was brought to his attention, Adeja began to notice how no communication passed between the prince and other members of the royal family. He knew Sephil had sent a message to Zhanil requesting his company, and that the Crown Prince sent back a terse reply stating he was busy with more important matters.

From Eumos he heard Sephil had a poor appetite and spent much time sitting in the garden reading or staring out at the city from the terrace. Sometimes the sound of weeping could be heard coming from the bedchamber, but Eumos offered no comment on this. Nakhet brought in a physician, who could not seem to find anything wrong with the patient other than he seemed out of spirits.

Each night, once the servants were asleep, Sephil came out wearing his dressing gown and a despondent look. Although the prince often wrapped his arms around Adeja and asked to be held, the gesture was anything but sexual. Whatever troubled him had smothered his libido.

Nakhet did not like the arrangement, which thoroughly puzzled Adeja. *So he doesn't care if I fuck the prince but all of a sudden he cares that I sit by his bed and hold his hand?* Had it been his place, he would have asked why *Nakhet* did not watch over Sephil or appoint someone to do it. A guard's place was at the door, not holding some frightened, womanish prince like a child.

As sitting with Sephil often required him to remove his armor, Adeja usually emerged from the prince's chambers in a state of disarray. Eumos greeted him with a raised eyebrow, but otherwise did not care what he did. "I had enough of that nonsense with the other one," he explained. "He rubbed my nose in it everyday."

Adeja adjusted his breastplate. As soon as he returned to the barracks he would be taking it off, but there was no need to arouse any suspicions. "What was Bedez like?" he asked. "I've heard tales, of course, but I'd rather hear it from you."

"Whatever you've heard probably isn't far off the truth. He might still be here if he hadn't confused his head with his balls."

Bedez certainly would not have wasted time in Sephil's bed unless sex was part of the bargain. Adeja did not know why he bothered, and the eunuchs probably would not have complained had he kept his post by the door and left a distraught Sephil to his sorrows. *That's what I ought to do. All this coddling isn't good for him.*

Adeja typically did not spend much time reflecting on things, but as he walked through the palace corridors, where servants bustled about on errands and officials gathered for the day's business, he could not help but wonder why Sephil clung so fiercely to him when he did nothing to encourage such interest.

The newly chaste Sephil made Adeja no more comfortable than he had been before. Desertion remained in his plans, which were still weeks away from fruition. By then, the prince would have shrugged off his melancholy, called his friends back, and taken a more familiar interest in his night guard.

He won't be my problem for much longer, though Adeja. Stripping to his tunic, he climbed onto his cot, still warm from its nightly occupant, and slept until the afternoon mess. After lunch, he beat two comrades at *keidu*, which no one in Rhodeen could seem to play with any skill, and added his small winnings to the sum he kept tied in a rag in his footlocker. Just before sunset, he went down to the common bath, cleaned up, and got dressed for the evening shift.

* * * *

Nakhet came in wearing an unreadable look. Rather than explain, he gestured to the servant who oversaw Sephil's wardrobe. "Find something suitable for the prince to wear out. No bright colors, and his hair must be pulled back."

"What is it?" asked Sephil. Watching the youth scurry for the clothes press, his anticipation turned to dread. Visitors no longer came to the apartment and Zhanil had rebuffed him. The response he received had been courteous but firm: *I regret to tell you that at this time there are many urgent matters requiring my attention at court, so any request you might wish to make will have to wait.* It sounded so formulaic that it might as well have been written by one of Zhanil's secretaries.

Not even a few moments to spare for your own brother? Sephil cherished such affectionate memories of him that only now did it occur to him that Zhanil might not share his sentiments.

Nakhet nudged him. "There is no time to waste, my prince." A length of black silk hung over his arms. "The king wishes to see you."

Sephil gazed in the mirror, at his long hair and girlish face. His father had always despised his appearance, and would like it no better now.

* * * *

Right away Adeja knew this evening was going to be different. No sooner had he appeared for duty than did a eunuch hustle him into the prince's bedchamber. "He's been asking for you," the man said.

"If he's sick, call a physician," replied Adeja.

"A physician has already come and prescribed a sleeping draught, but the prince says he won't take it unless you sit with him first."

"That is quite enough chatter, Jhadan." Nakhet's ponderous bulk filled the doorway. "You will not keep the prince waiting, soldier. We have already had to listen to his weeping for several hours."

Dressed in a rumpled shift, Sephil curled around one of the larger silk cushions, strands of his hair plastered to a face swollen from crying. Nakhet cleared his throat and made an announcement of Adeja's arrival that was not immediately acknowledged. The eunuch bent forward to jostle Sephil's shoulder when the prince stirred, looking up at Adeja with bloodshot eyes slow to focus. "Why did you leave?"

"I don't have the day duty, my lord." Adeja glanced nervously at Nakhet, wishing he would leave. "Now, what's the matter that you won't do as you're told?"

"All they want to do is make me sleep." Sensing now that they were not alone, Sephil lifted his head and ordered the eunuchs to get out. Nakhet gave a little bow as he closed the door. Adeja thought his manner entirely too smug.

Sephil let his head droop again. "My father sent for me today. He wants me to get married."

"Is that all? Getting married isn't bad news, unless the woman is old or ugly," said Adeja. He carefully set his pike on the floor and pulled a chair up to the bed. "So who is this maid?"

"A princess from Tajhaan," said Sephil, "but I do not want to marry."

"Don't you like women, my lord?" From what he observed, Adeja already knew the answer, but anything that kept Sephil from wallowing in his nauseating self-pity would do.

Sephil shook his head. "Not really. I tried to tell my father what an unlikely match I am, but all he did was to tell me what an ungrateful son I was to spurn such a beautiful princess."

"Any other man would jump at the chance to have a pretty wife."

"Adeja, are you married?" Sephil asked softly.

"No, but then most soldiers aren't married," he said. "There was a woman once, a widow I took up with before leaving Tajhaan. We had a good time together, but then she decided she didn't really want to be married to a young man or a soldier. Last I heard, she was married to a man with a little votive stand on

31

the Street of the Ancestors. So, is this princess of yours a daughter of the High Prince?"

Sephil nodded. "My father said her name is Terreh. All Nakhet can do is go on about how lovely she is and how many sons I will have." Groaning, he threw an arm over his face. "I saw the princess Zhanil married. Everybody said how pretty she was, and then when she came she looked like a horse."

A pretty wife might be just the thing to cheer you up, foolish boy. "I don't think you'll have to worry. Tajhaani women are known for their beauty. Having a wife would be good for you. She can give you sons who—"

"Who will see how unimportant their father is and be ashamed." Tears welled up in Sephil's eyes. "I am nobody, Adeja. Even my father said so. He told me he would rather marry this princess to a beggar on the street than waste her on me, but my father needs this alliance against the Turyar, and the High Prince of Tajhaan insists that she be married to a king's son. I always knew I meant nothing to him, that I was worthless, but I thought perhaps after three years he might have come to care for me just a little."

He lifted trembling hands to his face. "Adeja, nothing has changed. I wish I were dead. I am not just saying that. I sit and think all the time about dying. I wonder if anyone would even notice if I was gone."

Adeja could not help but glance back toward the door. For once, he rued Nakhet's absence. Had the eunuch been there to interject with some meaningless platitude, he would not have had to wrestle with his own awkward reaction. "You don't really want to die—"

"You do not understand what my life is like. Gods, why does no one listen when I try to tell them?" Sephil clutched the pillow and buried his face in the stiff embroidery. Adeja started to touch his shoulder, hesitated and gave in, gingerly pulling strands of the prince's hair away from his face.

After a time, Sephil looked up. His eyes were red, yet dry. "Nakhet thinks I sleep with the lamp because I am afraid of shadows. No, it is because I have terrible dreams. In one dream I am standing in my father's throne room but everyone has gone away, far away to some distant place, the entire city even down to the mice. They have forgotten me and I know it was deliberate. Then I have another dream. I am standing with my father and he takes me by the hand and presents me to the court.

He is smiling and says how proud he is of me and I can feel how much he loves me."

Adeja realized then that he was still stroking Sephil's hair. "I'd say that was a good dream."

The corners of Sephil's mouth turned up in a grim smile. "Then I wake up and it is not true."

* * * *

"My lord, you have a visitor."

Sephil preferred to stay in bed, but Nakhet insisted. Behind him, a servant waited with his dressing gown and a comb to straighten his hair.

Still bleary-eyed, wanting nothing more than to hide under his coverlets and forget the world, Sephil followed Nakhet out of the bedchamber and through the sitting room. "Who is waiting for me?" he asked. "If it is Ethurel or another false friend, I will not see them."

"You will see, my lord."

When he saw who awaited him in the foyer, Sephil stopped and choked back a breath. "Zhanil?" he croaked.

They had not seen each other in three years. Three years in which Sephil had forgotten what his brother looked like. At twenty-six, Zhanil was taller, broader in the chest and shoulders than he had been, and with his neatly trimmed black beard he seemed like a younger, more compassionate version of their father.

"You have grown, little moon," he said gently.

When he held out his arms, Sephil flew into them. Zhanil held him close, kissing his temple. "There is no need for tears. Father finally gave me permission to see you, so I came at once."

"He has not forgiven me."

"Yes, he has," said Zhanil.

"No, he even told me so."

Zhanil drew back. "It is difficult for him to show compassion, Sephil. Do not judge him too harshly. What he did, he tried to do for your own good."

"And letting me carry on with my parties and lovers is for my own good? Why did he not simply lock me in a dungeon somewhere?"

"He wanted you to learn the error of your ways, and you cannot learn anything shut up in a dungeon." Zhanil touched his cheek with a callused hand. "I think you have learned."

As usual, Zhanil did not understand. "Father is only releasing me because of this alliance with Tajhaan. I do not want to get married."

"I know, but princes must often do things they do not like." Once again, Zhanil embraced him, stroking his hair and making soft, hushing noises. "It will be all right, little moon. It will be all right."

Opening his eyes, Sephil peered over his brother's shoulder and saw Adeja at his post by the door. Adeja met his gaze and nodded his approval.

Chapter Five

Weighing the coins in his palm, Adeja counted them again. With a few more arrangements, he could leave Shemin-at-Khul forever, go back to Tajhaan or maybe farther south to Juva where the pay was good and the military strong enough to keep the Turyar at bay.

At this point, he should have been making preparations to leave, but something kept him back. It took him a few days to realize that it was Sephil. So fragile and childlike, not the brazen seducer of several weeks ago, this was the real prince behind the façade.

Gods, I'm no physician. The boy needs a healer or maybe a priest to look after him, not a plain soldier or a passel of shifty eunuchs. I can stand guard, fight off attackers, splint broken bones and sew up wounds, but I can't do anything for what ails him.

Days passed into weeks and still he did nothing. If he wanted to get to Tajhaan or Juva, he needed to leave now while travel was still feasible. At the height of summer, the desert could kill even the hardiest of souls. He had more than enough money hoarded, and his comrades were beginning to wonder why he spent none of it on drink or whores.

"Guarding the prince's household leaves me too tired for anything else," he explained. It was not entirely a lie. Watching over Sephil took almost as much energy as making love to him.

"Yeah, I can imagine," snorted Hedir. "I used to be posted in Bedez's barracks, and he was always boasting how sweet that boy's hole was."

"Bedez was full of shit," barked Adeja.

"They don't pack soldiers off to Mekesh for lying."

"They do if it's the king's son a man's shitting on."

Hedir snorted. "I heard you have to look hard to find a cock and balls on that prince. I certainly can't imagine him fucking anything with a cunt. Look, it's nothing to me if he likes to be rammed up his hole. So do you give it to him good?"

Adeja gave him a hard shove. "Trust me, if I was getting a piece of that sweet hole you'd know about it."

It was far too late to box Sephil's ear for allowing himself to acquire such a reputation. Given the situation, it was no wonder the king scorned the boy. A Tajhaani father would have cut his son's throat long ago, but Adeja could only guess Brasidios did not do it because it would have called attention to and given credence to the rumors.

* * * *

"I would like to go to the temple of Abh," murmured Sephil. "I feel like I am suffocating here."

Adeja gently combed his fingers through the hair spilling over his chest. Abh was the Rhodeen god of healing. "Do you want me to take you?"

"At this time of night I do not think I would be able to leave. I will have Eumos escort me tomorrow." Sephil ran his hands along the seam in Adeja's tunic where Adeja removed his breastplate and unbuttoned the garment. Although they lay entwined on Sephil's bed for close to an hour, nothing sexual passed between them. "If anyone asks, I will tell them I wish to purify myself before the wedding."

"Getting married is supposed to be a joyful occasion," said Adeja, "but here you're treating it like a funeral. This is a chance for you to make things better for yourself. Be a good husband and sire strong sons. I think you can do that."

Sephil gave a little sigh. "For most of my life I have been trying to please my father. It seems so futile to think anything can change now."

"My lord, you're not going to get anywhere by sitting here feeling sorry for yourself."

"Perhaps, but it is one of the few things I actually know how to do," said Sephil. "Adeja, I want you to know what I did before was not about you or those other men. I remember now. After my father punished me I was angry with him, so angry because nothing I did was ever good enough. I wanted him to open his eyes and *see* me. It worked, only now it is worse than it ever was before."

"I don't believe he hates you," said Adeja. "I know what you told me, but parents and children sometimes say or do things they don't really mean. My father had plenty to say when I told him I was turning my back on the family trade to become a soldier. I'd never heard such awful things from him, but in the end he wept and embraced me."

"You were not there when my father told me he wished I was never born." Sephil tightened his fingers in the folds of the tunic. "He meant every word of it."

"What does your brother say to all this?"

Sephil sat up in the middle of the bed with his back to Adeja. "Zhanil thinks I am too sensitive. People love him, so he cannot imagine any other sort of life."

On many occasions, Adeja saw crowds swarm Zhanil in the streets, all wanting to touch his hand or the hem of his garment as he rode past. "Sephil, you're no less worthy of being loved."

Turning, Sephil took his hand and bent forward to kiss him. His touch was soft, almost hesitant. "You should be my chief eunuch instead of Nakhet."

"Thanks, but I'd rather keep my balls."

"What I meant was I want you to stay with me always. I feel better when you are here." Sephil took one of his hands, lifted it to his lips and kissed it. "You are my Sun, do you know that?"

Adeja wished Sephil would not say such sentimental things. It made it so much harder to leave him.

"Will you stay here tonight?"

"You already know that I'll keep my post," answered Adeja, "same as I do every night."

"No, I meant—" Sephil bit his lip against embarrassment. "You would think that after all this time I might know how to do this, but somehow it feels different. All those other times, I felt bold and uninhibited. I might as well have been smoking *kif*. Now I feel more afraid than anything."

Adeja touched his cheek, running a callused fingertip over soft lips. "You want me to make love to you? I didn't think you wanted sex."

"If you do not want to, just tell me." Sephil kissed his fingers. His eyes were moist, shining in the golden candlelight. "Please understand, Adeja, I am not ordering you to do this. It is just that it means so much to me. For once in my life I want to feel what it is like to be loved."

Brushing his hair aside, Adeja cupped his face between his hands and kissed him. Sephil responded, twining his arms around Adeja's back and eagerly helping him undress, but his actions were not those of a promiscuous seducer. Once they were both naked, he lay back among the pillows and let Adeja take control of their lovemaking.

The next hour was a languid blur of kissing and touching in which the act of penetration seemed more an afterthought than anything else. Here, too, Sephil yielded, allowing Adeja to mount him however he wished. "I do not care," he said, "as long as you love me."

Adeja did not stop to ask what he meant, and his only response was a grunt. Now was when he usually turned a boy over onto his hands and knees to take him from behind. It did not occur to him until much later that he chose to make love to Sephil in the position that allowed him to fully embrace and kiss his lover while they arched and groaned toward climax.

Exhausted, lying sated and content in Adeja's arms, Sephil murmured, "It has never been that way with a lover before." He kissed Adeja's shoulder. "I should not keep you here. I know you want to leave."

"I never said any such thing."

"No, perhaps you did not say it, but I know it in my heart," said Sephil. "Some nights I feel you pull away from me, as if your heart is elsewhere. Since you came here, I understand things I should have known a long time ago."

Adeja did not know what to say. "You shouldn't pay too much attention to a soldier's rough manners, Sephil. Some things I said in anger. That business about Bedez and his pet name for you, that wasn't any of my concern."

"You said them because I deserved them." Sephil smiled up at him. "If a soldier cannot tell me the truth, then who can?"

* * * *

"I think it would be best if you resigned from my lord's household," said Nakhet. "You need not worry about future employment, as I can arrange a suitable post—"

"At Mekesh?" finished Adeja. He had scarcely reported for his post when the chief eunuch pulled him into a side room. "I'd hardly call that a promotion."

"It is not necessarily a death sentence. The garrison out there could use a man of your...prodigious talents."

Adeja watched the door, half-expecting Sephil to enter at any moment. The last time a guard was sent to Mekesh, the prince gave the order. *He said he knew I wanted to leave. He must have known I planned to desert him.* "Has he said he wants me to go?"

Nakhet's smile was so smug that Adeja would have liked to smash his fist into it. "Perhaps this explanation is above a common soldier, but certain inconveniences must be put out of the way for political expediency. My lord is a prince who is about to take a wife, and the king intends for the current state of affairs in this household to improve. Of course, your continued presence here is detrimental to that."

"I'm no threat to the prince's marriage and you know that," said Adeja. "I've been urging him to go through with it the same as you have."

"Ah, but we cannot have such an impressionable youth whispering words of love to a mere soldier, can we? My lord has always been high-strung and frail, and regardless of what he may wish, it is in his very best interest this business does not continue."

Adeja knotted his fists in his sword belt. "So fucking him is all right, but anything more than that isn't, is that what you're saying?"

Nakhet made a dismissive gesture. "If that is what you call it in your vulgar soldier's vernacular."

"Actually, we call it something much worse, and we usually say it about whores in the lower city," said Adeja. "And we have words for men like you, too, but I'm sure you already know what they are."

The veins in Nakhet's forehead and neck bulged with thinly constrained anger. "It is not for you to question what your betters do," he said tightly. "My duty is to keep my lord healthy and happy, and I have done so. In spite of your outrageous resistance, he was set on having you. He refused to send you away even after that unfortunate night you spent in his bed. Of course, had it been my decision, I would have had you sent away at once."

"Even though you were the one who arranged the whole thing?" asked Adeja.

Guards, borrowed from another garrison, came in at Nakhet's signal to take custody of Adeja. One demanded his pike and sword, which he was reluctant to hand over. Seeing his hesitation, Nakhet warned him against making a scene.

"The prince would not allow—"

"My lord is in no state of mind to decide what is best for him, and these men have been told that," said Nakhet. "You will be escorted to the city gates and from there taken to Mekesh. You need not worry about your belongings. They have already been collected from your barracks and your commanding officer has been told that you are being transferred. And you need not worry about this."

A small, threadbare bundle landed heavily on the desk; Adeja heard the familiar clink of coins within. "You are awfully frugal for a soldier," commented the eunuch. "One would think that you were saving up for something. You will find it is all there, plus a generous severance pay, though I doubt you will find much to spend it on at Mekesh."

Nakhet paused, lifting his finger to stop the guards as they stepped forward. Apparently he could not resist one more jibe. "I think," he said, "this might be a good time to caution you that the garrison commanders at Mekesh deal very harshly with deserters."

* * * *

Sephil found his chief eunuch hunched over the household accounts in the little study just off the foyer. "Where is he, Nakhet?"

Without looking up from his books, Nakhet gave a little shrug. "Who, my lord?"

"Do not feign ignorance with me. You know perfectly well who I mean. Where is Adeja? He should have reported for his shift by now."

"He has gone," answered Nakhet.

Sephil wanted to shake him out of his nonchalance. "He left the city?"

"I believe he is well on his way to Mekesh by now."

"*Mekesh?*"

"Yes, my lord," Nakhet replied irritably.

Surging forward, Sephil swept the books and papers off the desk. "Look at me when I speak to you! What have you done?"

"Only what is best for you, my lord."

"I did not tell you to do this!"

Without waiting for a reply, he raced out to the terrace. Night was falling over the city. The pyramid of the Moon hulked in the growing shadows, the distant mountains black against the last tendrils of sunset, and somewhere in that landscape was the one thing—no, the *only* thing—Sephil wanted, his sole comfort. Straining to see, to find Adeja, and knowing he could not, he uttered a long, low cry that brought the entire household running. "What have you done?"

Nakhet appeared behind him. "My prince," he said smoothly, "it is for the best. You are about to be married, and who knows what this marriage will do for your station? Your father's favor—"

"I do not *care* about that! You idiot, my father cares nothing for me and never will, no matter who I marry!" He sank to his knees, curled into himself and wept, not caring who saw or heard. "You knew—you *knew* what he was to me. How could you do this? *What have you done?*"

If one could physically tear hope from a living soul, Sephil imagined it would feel very much like the emptiness he felt now.

Chapter Six

Mekesh guarded the heights on the northwestern fringe of the Sevaa wastes, where the Khishtil Pass cut through the mountains and led down into the fertile Khul river valley.

Sevaa stretched over a swath of five hundred miles, running from the steppes populated by Turyar horsemen south to the mountain range that separated it from Tajhaan. Ancient kings had built fortresses to guard the heights, but after centuries of relative peace and prosperity, Rhodeen neglected its western defenses. The once-formidable strongholds had fallen into disrepair, and now only Mekesh stood between the Turyar and the fertile river valley on the other side of the mountains.

It was hard to believe anything could live on the plain. Heat shimmered off the earth below the cliffs on which the stronghold stood, and there was no vegetation beyond the pass. Scorpions eked out an existence in the waste, while from the walls one occasionally saw a black thread whipping across the dunes. At least one man a year fell victim to the *daku*, the deadliest serpent known to man. Given such dangers and the lack of water, it was small wonder that caravans went weeks out of their way to skirt the waste, taking the long southeastern route around the mountains toward Cassiare.

Supplies came from Shemin-at-Khul once a month, but never very much or of high quality. Rations were thin and the discipline harsh. Sentries were posted at all hours, drills were constant, and desertion was punished with mutilation and death. As he entered the stronghold, Adeja passed under a gate spiked with the heads of traitorous soldiers.

"We leave them tied out overnight for the scorpions to finish, though sometimes the *daku* get to them first. You can hear them screaming all the way back from the privy when it's the scorpions," said Radhar, under whose guard Adeja had come through the pass. "The snakes do quick work, but in the morning we've got to wear full armor in going out there to get the bodies. *Daku* can rear up and hit a man in the face if you get them angry."

A hard cot and footlocker were provided in a drafty room packed with eleven other cots. Armor and garrison-issue clothes, clearly secondhand, were also given to him; the tunic was too tight across the chest. "You'll not get a woman here to let it out for you," said a man whose broad face was splotched with broken blood vessels. "You'll be lucky if you see a woman once a year. They send a few whores once in a while, but by the time you get to fuck one she'll be worn out from the rest of us."

Over a meal of thin soup and ale, Adeja made discreet inquiries and learned that a soldier named Bedez had indeed served but took an arrow through the eye just three months before. "He had a pretty face," snorted Radhar, "until he got here. Did you know him?"

Adeja had been alternately curious and restive about his predecessor. "I served with him in Tajhaan. I'd heard he was here."

"He got in some trouble over a man's pretty son. What'd you do to get sent out here?"

"Nothing, really."

Radhar exchanged looks with Andias, the man with the splotched face. Both of them snorted. "Everybody's done something, otherwise they wouldn't be here," said Radhar. "You don't want to say, that's your problem, but I can tell you whatever you did there's bound to be somebody here who's done ten times worse."

Adeja sipped at his ale, the sourest stuff he had ever tasted. "I got in a fight with my commander over some woman. Bit his ear off," he lied. If he was going to be an undesirable he might as well be an interesting one.

"Is that what you did?" asked Andias. He glanced over at Radhar. "You owe me fifteen."

Adeja raised an eyebrow. "I take it you had a bet going?"

"We lay wagers on all the new arrivals," Radhar said quickly. "With your looks, I had you pegged for some trouble with another man's wife."

Adeja put the ale aside. Another swallow and he thought he might vomit. "I've fucked a few of those, but that's not what got me out here."

After lunch he was assigned a unit and entered onto the duty roster. Every man had a shift upon the walls or as lookout in one of Mekesh's three towers. His captain assigned him the evening watch on the north wall. His other shift was in the mess, scrubbing pots and tables with sand under the direction of a cook who promptly took Adeja aside and shook a work reddened finger at him. "I heard you bit the ear off your last captain," he grumbled. "You do that here and what the scorpions leave of you will end up minced and rolled into a meat pie."

Only in retrospect did he realize it was not the wisest lie he could have told. Adeja nodded obediently and fetched the sand bucket from the corner. Kaf wanted the grease stains scoured off the kitchen walls and he wanted it done quickly.

Seeing him, the two other soldiers already at work shifted over to make room for him. They were from his unit, the Jackals, and managed to introduce themselves before Kaf yelled at them to stifle the idle chatter. Jackals usually took the evening watch, while the morning and afternoon watches were allotted to the Scorpions and Vultures, the two other units. Rivalries were friendly, but in their frustration with the king and their hatred of the Turyar all three units shared common cause.

Attacks from the Turyar were sporadic. Already inured to a hard life on the steppes, the horsemen did not seem as bothered by the harsh environment and easily traversed the waste to fire arrows or launch baskets of scorpions at the men on the walls. One was occasionally picked off by a canny archer, and then it was cause for celebration, but most of the time their raids were too stealthy and lightning-swift to allow retaliation.

On his first night, Adeja crouched with his pike behind the crenellated wall and listened to a Turya raiding party fill the darkness with their eerie ululating cries. Off to the left, a brazier tempted him with its warmth, but Radhar cautioned him against standing too close to it. "That's the first place their arrows will go. Sometimes they throw pitch in, and if you're right there, well, that's not a pretty way to die. I saw a man go up like a torch just ten months ago. It took five days to get rid of the stink."

"How long have you been here?" asked Adeja.

Radhar shrugged. "Three years, I think. There's no point in counting. Once you come here, you never leave."

"New orders don't come?"

"Who's going to remember you're even out here? Oh, we've an unspoken rule that if you last ten years you can walk out of here and the sentries won't stop you, but nobody's ever lasted that long. Your friend Bedez, he lasted six months."

"I said I knew him," said Adeja, "not that he was my friend."

What he truly wanted to know was if Mekesh was such a forlorn post, with no hope of reprieve, then why did anyone stay? It was a question he had to phrase carefully, and prudence kept him from asking outright, but when he did the answer was not unexpected. "We still have families back in Rhodeen," said Radhar. "We're the only thing standing between them and the Turyar.

"It's not so bad up north in Khalgar. They still keep their defenses strong, so the Turyar can't get through the mountains there."

"What about the Dolmen Pass just north of us?" asked Adeja.

Radhar shook his head. "It's little more than a switchback trail. Foot soldiers might be able to get through, but it's too steep for an army of horses and supply trains. This far south it's treacherous going across the wastes, but once they get past us, the Turyar will find a clear path through the Khishtil Pass. It won't be long either, you mark my words."

Weeks slowly turned to months, and high summer came to the waste. Adeja did not envy the men on the afternoon watch as they returned from their shifts worn out by the heat and sun. Moist cloths and ale was often taken up to the walls, and in places awnings were erected, but the precautions were not always sufficient. In his second week, Adeja saw a man taken down who had collapsed from heat stroke; the sentry never came out of his delirium and died early the next day.

Burial rites at Mekesh were perfunctory. Elsewhere garrisons set aside a small room or two to act as a shrine, and the altar was cluttered with the gods worshipped by the many different peoples who served. Special care was always taken with the dead, especially when a man fell while executing his duty, and sometimes there was no outside family to take custody of the body. A man's comrades were his family, for they often knew him better than any wife or offspring. Units laid claim to certain corners of military cemeteries, soliciting donations and making the arrangements.

"It used to be better," said one soldier, as the sentry's body was carried out of the infirmary. "There are caves up in the pass where we could give the dead proper rites, but it means too many men gone from here for too long, and too much risk of desertion."

Adeja watched the corpse, sprawled haphazardly on a stretcher without even the dignity of a shroud, disappear around the corner. "You can't have been here that long," he said.

"No," replied the soldier, "but our stories outlast us. You know, when the Turyar come, no one will bury our bones, or tell our families how we died."

"Once a man gets sent here, I don't think it matters."

A heavily equipped detail was sent out to the edge of the waste to dig down into the hot sand, while archers and pikemen stood lookout for Turya raiders or agitated scorpions or *daku*. Digging a sand grave was difficult work, as the loose grains kept sliding back down into the hole and filling it, but at last it was deep enough for the corpse. The soldier's body, stripped of armor and clothing which were returned to the storeroom, was brought out on a tarp and laid in the hole. No prayers were spoken and no marker was left; the shifting sands would have buried it within a day.

"Sometimes we dig down and find another body, or the winds shift the sands and uncover the grave," said Andias. "The heat and sand dry them out. Sometimes we can even tell who it is."

"No prayers?" asked Adeja.

"What gods are going to listen to us out here?"

The arrival of a supply train from Shemin-at-Khul was reason to celebrate. Sacks of flour and onions, and jugs of ale were carted into the storerooms, while the unit commanders went about delivering mail. Adeja read out a few letters for men who could not read, and was surprised at the packet that arrived for him. Whoever wrote him had done so on good parchment, though he cringed when a caught a whiff of the expensive scent. No doubt some woman or whore had found out where he was stationed and was now trying to make his life even more difficult than it already was.

From the muttered curses some of his comrades made, he knew he was not alone. Such letters were a staple of barracks life, angry missives wanting money, claiming paternity or frothing with scorn for lovers abruptly vanished. Women knew nothing about the military. It was not as if a soldier had a choice of post, or when or how he was deployed.

Breaking the plain wax seal, he was surprised to find the letter was from Sephil. He sniffed the parchment, wondering why the prince bothered to write. It was such a silly, effeminate thing to do.

I miss you, Adeja. The Tajhaani embassy has arrived and my bride is in a palace on the other side of the city. I do not want to see her; I am afraid of what she will think of me. Yours is the only face I want to see now. I want you to know it was not my wish that you be sent to this place. I did not want to send you away at all, as you were the only thing that made my days bearable, but if I had to choose I would have had you posted to Cassiare. Nakhet arranged otherwise, and without my knowing. He said the whole affair was an embarrassment best left forgotten, never mind that it was his idea in the first place.

The other soldiers made catcalls at the fragrance oozing off the letter. "Oh, you had a wealthy one," said Javan. "I've heard they even put perfume on their—"

"Shut up and let me finish reading."

Nakhet says you asked for a transfer, but I do not believe him, and I have no way to get you out without further endangering your life. I know you wanted nothing to do with me. You told me the truth, but perhaps you thought what Bedez thought. I was shameless with him and with you, and I cringe to think of those times. I tried very hard to understand and to change. All I truly wanted was for you to care for me.

Adeja burned the letter on the kitchen hearth, where Kaf complained loudly about the smoke. Writing back was out of the question. Nakhet would only intercept his correspondence, and he could not afford to be so stupid as to put his sentiments down on paper, provided he could even obtain writing materials.

A second letter came a month later.

You did not write back, Adeja. I cannot blame you for despising me. It is my fault you are in that terrible place. I asked Eumos if anything can be done, but it would take an order from my father or brother to release you, and I fear they will send men to execute you instead. I would tell you to abandon your post and flee, except that Eumos tells me it is terribly difficult to escape Mekesh, and if you were caught you would suffer horribly.

I do not know what advice to give you because I do not know what to do. I can only urge you to be strong and ask you to forgive me for this.

I have seen this princess. There was a ceremony in the palace of the Sun. You were right: she is beautiful. Zhanil says he envies me, but I do not believe him. I smile as best I can because it is expected of me, but I feel nothing for this girl except pity. She is disappointed in me. Nakhet suggested I grow a beard, as this might make me resemble Zhanil more and please her better. I only wish she were not Tajhaani because it reminds me of you.

My father tells me to be grateful, that such a beautiful, royal bride is more than I deserve. He told me if I behave well my sons may be restored to the succession; he says nothing of me. On other days he tells me he will have one of my cousins consummate the marriage, as I obviously am not fit to do it myself. Zhanil has found a woman to teach me about pleasing a maiden but my heart is not in it. I am doing my best to obey, I truly am, but it is so terribly hard.

Adeja's companions chuckled. Javan flicked the corner of the scented parchment with a dirty fingernail. "That rich mistress of yours won't give up, eh?"

Sooner or later, he feared one of them would find out a young man was writing to him, and the king's son at that. Sephil needed to be a man and stop clinging to him for comfort he could not give. His world had narrowed to its harshest elements: searing sun, discipline as hard as the cot upon which he slept and the fear that rode out of the waste at night. His future was a hole in the sand, whether it came in a week, six months or three years from now. He had no more time for princes and their petty concerns.

* * * *

"I have said it before, brother: you are too sensitive. Of course she likes you."

Zhanil seemed not at all concerned by the murmuring and suspicious glances of the Tajhaani delegation. Smiling at them, he lifted his cup in salute and drank. Sephil did not note their reaction. It took every ounce of self control he possessed not to flee the hall in terror. In the three years of his exile he had forgotten what it felt like to stand among people and be watched by all.

"No, she does not," he whispered. "She is looking at Dashir."

All he could see of his betrothed was a slender column of orange and saffron silk topped by a gold-spangled veil. Almond-shaped eyes met his and quickly darted away to study the royal cousins.

During the ceremony, the princess approached the eldest cousin, bowed and offered her hand. The Tajhaani interpreter apologized for the error, telling the king that she had mistaken Prince Dashir for her future husband. While the court tried to smother its amusement behind jeweled hands and fans, Brasidios brusquely motioned to his younger son, who stood pale and nervous beside Zhanil. Sephil prayed the gods would make him disappear.

Naturally, the gods ignored him.

When the interpreter explained the situation to the princess, she gave her delicate hand to Sephil, but it was not with the same enthusiasm with which she had greeted Dashir.

Afterward, Dashir could not resist making light of the mishap. "I see the king has let you out of your gilded cage." Maturity had not blunted his cruelty. Not caring who saw, he plucked at Sephil's sleeve with rough fingers. "Pity, I thought you dead these last few years."

"I realize this is all very sudden for you," murmured Zhanil. "Had it been up to me I would have negotiated for a longer courtship, but you understand this alliance must be consummated as soon as possible."

"It has been explained to me," said Sephil.

Zhanil placed a reassuring hand upon his shoulder. "So your first meeting was not the success you wished it to be. These political matches often start cold, but once you become better acquainted with each other things will improve. Spend time wooing her. Perhaps you should learn a few words of Tajhaani to demonstrate your good intentions."

"If you think that will help," Sephil answered colorlessly. He did as he was told, trimming his hair and growing a beard to improve his appearance, while in private he did not think any amount of effort would win Terreh's interest. His brother and cousins were all so dignified, so masculine, he could never match them.

After the ceremony and reception in the palace of the Sun, Zhanil invited him to back his residence. Although their father approved the visit to the temple of Abh, going out remained a rare privilege. Sephil demurred at the invitation. Zhanil quickly realized what the matter was and took the matter in hand by speaking to Brasidios and the two eunuchs appointed as Sephil's minders.

Sephil envied his brother's ability to speak so easily to their father. When together, Brasidios and Zhanil seemed more like equals than ruler and subordinate. Even though he was once again received at court, Sephil knew his presence was not welcome. When addressed, he hesitated to meet his father's eyes and could not string together more than two words at a time. *What an idiot he must think I am.* He was not even capable of managing his own household, for when he attempted to evict Nakhet, the eunuch refused to go, and there was nothing Sephil could do to force him.

"Come," said Zhanil, tugging at his arm. "Let us go and forget diplomatic matters for a few hours."

Set in a garden surrounded by climbing vines and fruit trees, the gathering was small and informal. Zhanil's wife, housebound and heavy with her third child, welcomed Sephil with warm words, urging him to eat the delicacies her cooks had prepared.

"You look so pale," she said, "and I am certain the ceremony was exhausting." When he refused the food, she pressed strong red wine upon him and was not satisfied until he drank.

Two small boys came out with their nurses. It shamed Sephil to realize these were his nephews and he did not even know their names. Zhanil greeted them with unabashed paternal affection, setting them upon his lap while Sephil sat under a lime tree watching the scene. The tranquil bonds shared among these people did not encompass him, and he could not help but feel a sharp sadness at knowing they were strangers to him.

One small thing gave him hope. Swallowing his fear, he finally wrote to the garrison commander at Mekesh ordering Adeja's release. Although only his father or brother had the authority to make such demands, he decided he had nothing to lose by trying. His father needed this alliance and could not do anything to him that was worse than what had been done before. *If he locks me away again I will not have to marry this princess, and if he puts me to death it will be a welcome end to my troubles. As long as Adeja is safe and I have done something worthwhile, I do not care about the rest.*

A small smile escaped him at how confident and strong Zhanil was, how happy he seemed with his family. *I have no place in his world*, he thought. *I do not think I ever did.*

Chapter Seven

It began with a dark, thick object sailing over the wall and breaking open in the outer court.

Adeja did not see the incoming jar, only heard the crash of terracotta against the flagstones and the alarmed cries of the men standing nearby. Turning his head, he saw the sentries below scattering from a writhing mass of dark shapes that darted out toward them. He froze in recognition even before the men below shouted up that *daku* had been loosed inside the walls.

Another missile struck the stairs leading down from the walls, tumbled, and broke open. Radhar, his shield instinctively raised, had the post nearest the steps. He glanced down, shrinking back as he simultaneously slammed the lip of his shield against the ground to protect his feet. "Scorpions!" he cried.

The Turyar had chosen the perfect night for a raid. A new moon offered almost no light. Shapes scuttled through the shadows, but there was no telling how many gathered below the walls. Thus far the enemy operated in near-total silence, a marked change from their trademark battle shrieks.

More jars sailed over the walls, breaking on the stones. Pitch spattered out in all directions, catching fire from the braziers. Half the courtyard ignited in an instant, catching two men who did not move quickly enough out of the way. Their screams echoed up to the walls.

Men from the other two units were running out, some bleary with sleep and still struggling to get on their armor. One tripped over a *daku* and fell convulsing as it struck him. Another man speared the snake and flung the writhing body into the fire.

Adeja and the men on the walls dispatched the scorpions, using their pikes and shields to sweep them into the fire. The heat was now climbing toward the stairs, blackening the stones and threatening the nearest escape route.

Arrows whistled through the night, sailing over the walls like fireflies. Some glanced off stones, others found their mark. Shields went up, though not soon enough for some. Even as an arrow sliced through the first layer of his shield, Adeja saw Andias take one in the shoulder. With a cry, the man stumbled back, his arm falling to his side and exposing his torso to the pair of arrows that thudded into him half a second later. He twitched, made a gurgling sound, and lay motionless.

No one saw the first Turyar coming over the walls until the bugle of a tower sentry alerted them. Adeja turned into the onrush of two men. One he struck with his shield, delivering a backhanded blow that sent the man tumbling off the wall into the courtyard. The second he shoved back, where Javan gutted him with a sword. Beyond them, he saw more coming, a swarm of quilted armor and boar-tusk helmets, and now they were climbing up from multiple points along the wall.

"They've got siege ladders!" someone shouted.

Radhar and two others raced to push one of the ladders down. Radhar leaned out into the darkness that took off his head and sent it flying into the night. Spears made quick work of the other two men. Turyar surged up and over the wall, and there was no one to stop them.

Adeja smashed his shield into another Turya—a large man with wild eyes and pale braids as thick as a woman's wrist—who wielded the short sword typical of the steppes. Two blows landed in the center of his shield, the third augmented by the man's weight. Dropping his pike, now useless in such close quarters, Adeja unsheathed his sword and shoved the man back before jamming the point into his belly. Layers of quilted armor and flesh yielded, the man grunting as Adeja wrenched the blade out again. He fell, but Adeja was already turning, moving on without looking to see if the Turya was dead. Whether the man died instantly or bled out it made no difference as long as he was incapacitated. No one had time to be thorough in the heat of battle.

His thigh stung, and he felt a warm stickiness saturate his trousers. There was no time to stop and investigate a wound he could not even remember receiving. Someone was shouting orders, but it was not his commander, whom he had seen fall under a hail of Turya arrows. He could not make out what was being said, nor did he much care at this point. The stronghold was being overrun, and he knew that if he did not get off the walls he was going to die.

With nothing left to fuel them, the fire in the courtyard began to burn out. Stumbling over fallen men, his wound beginning to hamper his movements now that he was aware of it, he made it down the stairs and across the court. A dismembered *daku* twitched in the doorway leading to the mess, the half-charred corpse of one of its victims sprawled nearby. More snakes might be coiled in the shadows, but he could not afford to hesitate now.

Men occasionally ran past him, carrying weapons or searching for their superiors. No one stopped him. When he reached the barracks the place was empty, dark but for the flickering glow of flames coming through the window slat. A thin haze of smoke clung to the air, smelling of timber and pitch. The Turyar must have set fire to other parts of the stronghold.

Adeja got his money out of the footlocker. He shoved it under his belt, tied a cloth around his wound, and ran out again.

Turyar were now inside the main citadel. As he ducked into the mess hall on his way to the kitchen, he surprised two who were stripping a body on the floor. Killing them both, he started to step over the corpse when it twitched and a hand grasped his ankle.

Kaf had been stabbed in half a dozen places and now lay in a widening pool of his own blood. "All over," he gasped. "They...opened the gates...."

All Adeja could do for him was cut his throat. He did not stay to catch Kaf's last breath, but went for the kitchen and seized an empty skin from the shelf. Food, stored in the root cellar, would be harder to obtain and he did not have time to prize up the trapdoor. Thick shouts, growing steadily closer, reached him from the mess. Adeja dropped the skin, bent to pick it up, and saw the bloody tracks he made. He had stepped in Kaf's blood. *I should've cut his fucking head off while I was at it,* he thought savagely.

No time for food. I've got money and something for water, and that'll have to do. He seized the waterskin and fled out through a side room to the ledge leading to the midden. Darkness obscured the path, but under Kaf's unrelenting direction he had carried garbage this way so many times he could have gone blind.

The kitchen midden spilled over a rocky ledge overlooking the pass. On Adeja's first day, Kaf took great pleasure in informing him that many would-be deserters tried that route. The cook then motioned to the square tower overhead and with his finger made a cutting motion across his throat.

Gripping the edge of the wall with his hands, Adeja looked up toward the tower's black hulk. Everyone who could was running for the gates. Whoever was left above was either using their last arrows against the Turyar or holing up for a last stand. No one would be watching the pass, and even if they should somehow see him in the dark a friendly arrow in the back was better than being cut to pieces by the Turyar now ransacking the kitchen behind him.

A twenty-five foot drop awaited him. Shoving the empty skin between his teeth, he swung a leg over the edge, took a breath, and let go. Half a second later he landed heavily in a stinking pile. He gagged around the waterskin, not even wanting to know what he was crawling through.

The pile spilled down a steep incline toward a stone wall facing the pass. He slid and scraped his way down until he reached the crumbling masonry. How far down it was to the floor of the pass he could not gauge in the dark, but knew stakes had been driven into the rock wall to prevent enemies from scaling up. Putting out his hand, Adeja gripped one of the stakes; it pointed downward and was sturdy enough to serve as a handhold.

He felt his way down, using the stakes and digging into the rock with his fingers. Twice he nearly lost his grip, and by the time he reached the ground he was scraped and bruised. Behind him the night sky was alight. The sentry towers blazed, filling the air with heavy smoke. Distant shouts were smothered by the sound of falling timbers and masonry. Any Rhodeen who were still alive would soon wish otherwise.

He hugged the walls of the pass, listening for sounds of pursuit as he scrabbled deeper into the darkness. Once alerted by the rumble of hooves, he ducked into the shadows behind a boulder and watched from his hiding place as a band of Turya horsemen passed bearing torches. Up ahead he heard shouts and a startled cry. A short time later the riders reappeared, heading back toward the fortress. Six torches streaked by, throwing eerie patterns of light and shadow onto the walls before darkness reclaimed the pass.

Somewhere on the path ahead was a corpse. Adeja limped and crawled along, not knowing what he would stumble upon in the shadows. His limbs ached and throbbed, and the stench of the midden clung to his clothing. If the Turyar came this way again they would surely smell him. Two springs watered the pass, but they were far into the mountains and Adeja did not know the terrain well enough to be certain of finding them. The wound in his thigh had to be kept clean, and he needed to fill the skin.

When dawn came he went only a short distance farther before finding a hiding place well off the path, a shady hollow where he could sleep for a few hours before resuming his march.

Thirst and pain kept him half-awake, and a rattling sound stirred him. Opening one eye, he saw nothing by his head. The noise came from farther down, by his feet, and he realized he should have checked the hollow beforehand. He kept his breathing very even, his body very still and relaxed. Chances were the rattlesnake's fangs would not be able to pierce his thick leather boots, but he could not risk being struck farther up.

Around his head he had tied a cloth to keep off sun and sweat. Keeping his lower body as motionless as possible, he undid it and wrapped it over and around his left hand until it was thickly swathed. With his right he picked up a fist-sized stone. Slowly he sat up with his left hand extended. The snake coiled, gathered, and struck out, latching onto his hand. The right hand with the stone came down, crushing the serpent's head again and again until his instincts told him it was safely dead.

Flinging the dead snake away from him, Adeja quickly vacated the hollow and returned to the path. Adrenaline shuddered through him. He wanted to run, to put as much distance between him, the serpent, and the Turyar as possible, but his body would not obey him. He felt as though he had been wounded in a thousand places and his lips were cracked from thirst.

Two more snakes appeared on the path but no more Turyar. Adeja did not rest secure in that knowledge. Sooner or later, once they were finished plundering and razing Mekesh, they would enter the pass. Instinct cautioned him to travel at night, but in the darkness he ran a greater risk of running afoul of serpents or predators who hunted once the sun went down. He carefully chose his next hiding place, clearing it of a pair of scorpions before bedding down. A campfire would have reassured him, but he could not take the chance and so spent much of the night half-awake.

Six days saw him through the pass. On the second he found a spring where he could bathe his wound, scrub off some of the midden filth, and fill his waterskin. By then he was tormented by thirst, but he still possessed enough sense to wait until nightfall. There were too many hiding places above and around the spring, too many vantage points from which a Turya archer could take him. He had not ruled out the possibility that the Turyar were watching the springs hoping to lure survivors.

On a few occasions riders came down the pass. He hid from them, but they did not seem to be looking for him. They behaved more like scouts. Reconnaissance could only mean an invasion of Rhodeen was imminent.

Around this time Adeja discovered his money was gone. He remembered tucking it securely under his belt but could not recall where or when the bundle disappeared; the only likely scenario was that it fell out when he jumped into and then crawled through the midden. Now, left penniless on the eve of an invasion, he had to abandon his original intention of skirting around the Khul river valley and making straight for Khalgar. He would have to return to Shemin-at-Khul, file a report and face the wrath of a command that would blame him for the fall of Mekesh.

And when the attack comes, they'll stick me right in the front lines and you can be sure I won't have the same luck twice. The prospect was so glum he toyed with avoiding the city altogether and foraging his way to Khalgar, but a diet of insects and raw herbs was not going to get him very far. His belly ached with hunger and his wound needed attention.

The seventh day brought him down to Kesse, a village watered by a rushing stream where he did his best to bathe before approaching anyone. Nevertheless, his haggard appearance alarmed the villagers almost as much as the news he carried. Though they had no money to spare, they gave him food and dressed his wound, and the very next day a farmer offered him a ride in his cart to the next village.

Chapter Eight

"This is all the room I have right now," said Meden, indicating a rough pallet on the floor. "You ought to be down in the central barracks so they can assign you a new post, but on account of your wound and for old times I'll let it pass. Stay the night if you want, but in the morning you've got to go."

Adeja did not bother reminding him that he had already reported to the city's central authorities and been sent on to the palace to make a formal deposition. Had his wound not put him in so much discomfort he would not have troubled his former captain for a bed for the night. The officers who took his statement were far from pleasant, phrasing their questions in a tone that implied he was to blame for the current situation. The farther he was from the palace, the better.

His lost wages were not, they coldly informed him, their concern, and the best he could hope for at the moment was a new post. Tomorrow was soon enough to make an application. For now he simply wanted to lie down, close his eyes, and relieve some of the exhaustion that dogged him the past thirteen days.

Rest was more easily desired than obtained. Men constantly moved in and out of the barracks, and most of them wanted to know what he saw on the frontier and how he had been wounded. For the time being, he said nothing about Mekesh. His injury, he said, came from a minor skirmish, and since he was unfit for rigorous duty at the moment, he had been sent back to the city to convalesce. How many men believed his lie he did not know. It did not concern him.

Last of all, a man wearing the royal sunburst limped toward him, took his arm, and urged him into a private corner. "I've got some news for you," he said. "I think you might want to hear it."

Under the helmet, Adeja saw Eumos' lined, pockmarked face. "Did you just come off duty?"

"Yes, but not from where you think," answered Eumos. "I'm in Zhanil's household now."

"You got a promotion?"

Eumos shook his head. "I wouldn't call it that."

Adeja noticed how stiffly he moved. "You look like you were in a fight."

"You and me both," said Eumos. "I overheard the news about Mekesh. Zhanil and Brasidios are already calling their generals in, but they don't want to make it public yet. It's been nothing but dispatches coming in and out all afternoon. I heard somebody drop your name, so I asked around and found out you were staying here."

Leaning forward, Eumos dropped his voice. "I wouldn't if I were you, Adeja. I didn't do with the prince what you did and they were still going to execute me. If you've got any sense, get out of the palace and out of the city before the king starts looking for you."

"What happened?" asked Adeja.

"The prince got much worse after you left," explained Eumos. "Nakhet told him you were dead. I wasn't there for what happened, but the night guard told me he ordered his servants out of his chamber and cut his wrists."

Adeja took a deep breath. Only a desperate man opened his veins like that. *Oh, gods, you little fool.* "What happened next?" It surprised him how hard his voice was trembling.

"The prince didn't die, but he was very sick and wanted to go to the temple of Abh. I guess the physician they called couldn't do anything for him," said Eumos. "Nakhet wouldn't let him go. The prince called me in and whispered in my ear. Nakhet wanted to know what he said, of course, then turned me out when I wouldn't tell him.

"I went straight to Zhanil, just as the young prince said. I told him everything." Eumos reached out and put a hand on Adeja's arm. "You'll have to forgive me. I had to tell him about you, too, but you were at Mekesh. I didn't think it would matter."

His gaze roaming the barracks, Adeja knew he ought to leave the palace grounds immediately. "Go on," he urged.

"Zhanil stormed his brother's household. He arrested Nakhet and some of the others, and personally took his brother to the temple, but I don't know what happened to him after that. The king arrived at midnight and it was awful. Half the household was executed on the spot, including Nakhet, and the king was going to kill me, too, but Zhanil put in a good word. I got off with fifteen lashes. It hurts like cold death, but it's better than what I might've gotten."

Fifteen lashes were more than Adeja had any right to expect. For all he knew, the king's men were looking for him at that very moment. "I can't stay here."

Eumos nodded. "I know somebody in the city who can give you a bed for the night. Quickly, get your things and let's go."

In the corridor outside a sentry came looking for Meden. Adeja caught his arm. "What's your hurry?" he asked. "Shouldn't you be at your post?"

"On the walls," the young man gasped. "He's got to see this."

Emerging into the warm summer night, Adeja and Eumos saw people climbing to the roofs and walls. Soldiers, eunuchs, and servants gathered together, pointing and exchanging gossip. The stairs were too thick with people, so Eumos led Adeja along a back route to a sentry tower affording an unobstructed view of the city and fields beyond.

"We saw it around sunset," said one of the men on duty.

Where the mountains loomed over the western horizon, the tiny pinpricks of campfires blanketed the foothills. "There must be hundreds of them out there," said Adeja. He did not mention the Turyar. No one did, but they all knew. Only an army could support a camp that size.

Kesse would be a smoking ruin by now. If the people were smart enough to heed his warning they might have fled in time.

When they came down from the tower, Eumos handed Adeja a slip of paper. "This is the address of the friend I was telling you about. It's two streets down from the tax office. He said he'll wait for you till midnight, no later. Sorry I can't do more, but I'm taking a big risk as it is."

Adeja thanked him and made his way toward the palace gate. He got no farther. The sentries, seeing he was Tajhaani, stopped him at once, and when they saw his wound took him into custody. An attempt to provide a false name yielded a hard blow to the face, as one of the men on duty identified him. Bleeding from a cut lip, he was taken to a warren of rooms under the barracks and locked into one of the unlit cells.

The cell stank of musty air and stale urine. A bucket occupied one dank corner, and a stone slab in the other was the only place to sit or sleep. No blanket or pillow had been provided. Nor did anyone answer his questions, not even to tell him what he was being charged with. "You can't hold me unless you tell me what the charge is," he growled into the darkness.

Heavy footfalls and the rattle of keys answered his complaint. A face appeared at the door. "I do not need a reason beyond that you are contemptible," said a man's cold voice.

Through the barred slat Adeja saw the speaker. A thin golden circlet banded heavy brows above a face that conveyed dignity but very little warmth. "Look, I wasn't drinking or making trouble. I was about to find myself lodging for the night when those men grabbed me."

"This is the only lodging we have for deserters," answered the man.

Adeja strained against the chain that fixed him to the wall. "Who are you calling a deserter?"

"I am your king."

So *this* was Sephil's father, the man whose coldness had driven him to attempt suicide. Already irritable, Adeja suddenly felt far less cooperative than he might otherwise have been. "I don't care whose gilded cunt spit you out, I'm no deserter," he said. "I escaped that place with my life *after* the Turyar came over the walls, and I was wounded. I no longer *had* a post to defend. Didn't you read the fucking report?"

His face distorted by shadows and torchlight, Brasidios appeared to curl his lip. "On the contrary," he replied, "I have read and heard more about you in the last two weeks than I would have wished to hear in a lifetime."

Adeja sank back against the wall with a sigh. *Here it comes*, he thought. "You're not here because of what happened at Mekesh."

"My son was a frail, ignorant young man, and you took advantage of him."

Yes, it was exactly as he expected. The king had come on account of his son. "I did no such thing," replied Adeja. "I was forced to accept that assignment."

"Seducing him was *not* part of your commission," snapped Brasidios. "You have been the ruin of him, and now you will answer for it."

The king's choice of words strongly suggested that Sephil had died. "Do you really believe that? I was just the latest in a long line of soldiers your son seduced, and you know it, too." Adeja wanted to add that he had cared about Sephil, but he read the other man's hostility well enough to realize that claim would not get him very far. "If you want to punish somebody, go after Nakhet. He's the one responsible for the evil in that household."

Too late, he recalled that the eunuch had already been executed. Now, it seemed, it would be his turn.

"I did not come here to be subjected to your insolence," said Brasidios.

"Then why *did* you come?" asked Adeja. "Why didn't you just send somebody down here to cut my throat and be done with it?"

The shadow of a smile flickered across Brasidios' face. "Oh, you are going to be executed, as the one who opened the gates of Mekesh to the Turyar and brought war to Rhodeen."

"That's a lie and you fucking well know it!" Adeja surged forward, but the chains bit into his wrists, jerking him back. Death he expected, yet not under such pretenses.

"You want somebody to blame for what's happening now, for the Turyar and your son's death, blame yourself. Go ahead and kill me, but it's not going to change anything. Mekesh was lost decades ago. You neglected it just as you did your son, and now you've lost both. So go ahead, make me a scapegoat and execute me, but when the Turyar throw down your walls, skin you alive and stick your head on a fucking pole, you'll remember me."

Chapter Nine

The sound of a key rattling in the lock jarred Adeja out of an uneasy sleep. "What is it?" he mumbled. "If it's anymore of that slop you call food, you can fuck off."

"If you're complaining, that means your wound hasn't gone bad," said a familiar voice. "Get up and look lively. There isn't a lot of time."

Adeja's eyes watered at the lamplight streaming in through the slat. It took a moment for him to focus on Meden's face. "What are you doing here?"

"You'll see. Pessen, hurry up with the keys."

As he sat up, kneading sore muscles where he had lain on the hard slab, the door opened and two men entered. One of them grasped his wrist to unlock the chain. "It's a risk we're taking."

"The man we've got is Tajhaani enough to pass," said Meden. "Once they put the hood over his head and tie him to the stake nobody's going to notice the difference. Adeja, do you think you can get up and walk?"

Adeja had been given food and medicine for his wound, and informed that his execution was set for the day after next. What time he did not spend sleeping, he spent brooding and preparing for his fate. "I can manage. Are they that impatient to see me burn to death?"

"No, but we didn't think we should wait any longer to get you out. For now, just keep your mouth shut and follow me."

Meden stopped him in the narrow corridor, ordered him to strip, and gave him a commoner's threadbare tunic and leggings. Two soldiers shouldered past him into the cell, dragging a naked, unconscious man between them.

"All right," said Meden. "We're taking you to the gates. The man they just brought in, *that's* Adeja ked Shamuz. From now on, you're going to have to call yourself something else, at least until you're far away from here."

No one in the prison or at the entrance leading up to the ground level had been drugged or killed. The sentries simply let them pass. Adeja looked at them, then at Meden. "What's going on here?"

Pessen put a hand on his shoulder. "All they see is a commoner who got a bit drunk and disorderly with some soldiers the night before and is now being taken home. Our other prisoner is still in custody." He winked before giving Meden a nod and walking away.

"But if you really *want* to be executed," said Meden, "we can turn around and forget this whole thing, but I hardly think the little whore is worth it."

Even at this late hour the streets hummed with activity. People milled around, talking and conducting business. "It's been panic the last two days," said Meden. "The Turyar now have the entire western region and our lookouts say they're moving in this direction. Refugees started pouring in early yesterday with awful stories, and that started it. They wanted in and a lot of people here wanted out. Half the city is trying to run for Cassiare, but the king has closed the gates and declared martial law."

In that case, Adeja did not ask how Meden planned to get him out of the city. Presumably the man already had a plan. "What was that business before about the stake?"

"The king plans to have you burned alive as a sacrifice to the Sun to ensure our victory against the Turyar. It took some doing, but we got a condemned prisoner who looks a bit like you."

"Won't the king know the difference?"

Meden shouldered aside a vendor who got too close and put a warning hand on his sword when the man cursed him. "Not really. That is, how much of you did Brasidios *really* see in the shadows? Only the guards got a good look at you and they let you walk out of there."

They were almost through the bazaar, coming up on the tenements that faced the outer walls. Crowds were thick here, people and their carts loaded and ready to flee the moment the king relented. Lights blazed on the walls from dozens of braziers, and in their glow scores of archers stood ready to fire on the crowd if they turned to a mob.

Brasidios is an idiot, thought Adeja. *He should just open the gates and let these people go. Once the Turyar come, they're only going to get in the way.* "Why did they do it?" he asked. "Why are you going to all this trouble?"

"I told you before," answered Meden. "Things have been happening while you were rotting in that cell. The story's all over the city now, in every barracks and wine sink where soldiers gather. Eumos has been talking."

"Eumos is going to get himself killed."

"Not if Prince Zhanil looks the other way, and most of the men in the city take their orders from him. Mekesh was bad enough, and I haven't heard from a single man who thinks you're a deserter, not even the Crown Prince. Everybody knows you're being killed because of that whore."

Adeja seized Meden's arm and pulled him aside under the awning of a squalid tenement, where he had to wave aside two beggars before continuing. "That's a king's son you're insulting. Don't let me hear you call him a whore again."

Meden lifted his hand. "Don't chew my ear off," he said. "I'm only repeating what I've heard. Shit, if I didn't know you better I'd say you sounded like a man in love."

To that, Adeja made no answer. "It doesn't matter anyway, I suppose. What I really want to know is how you plan to get me out of the city when the gates are locked. Open them for one man and you're going to have a mob on your hands. I'm assuming no patrols are going out?"

"They're coming and going by the south gate," said Meden, "but that's a civilian-free zone and you'd be noticed. Besides, I know the sentries manning the walls over here. If you can manage a rope, they'll let you down."

As they neared the wall, Adeja saw sentries arranged along the stairs. Meden gave him a bundle to carry. "You just be silent and follow me like a servant, got that?" Clearing his throat, he roared up to the first sentry, a young man who shrank back at the imposing Juvan coming at him. "News is in from the south gate, and there's a package for Ondor. He's expecting us. Is he up there, or is he sleeping it off in some wine sink again?"

Too green to form a proper answer and seeing the captain's badge on Meden's arm, the youth just waved them through. Adeja, still holding the bundle under his arm, tried to look servile as he climbed up after Meden.

The walls were so thick with soldiers it was difficult to maneuver. No one on the king's war council seemed to have any sense, as these men would fall like scythed wheat once Turya archers started raining arrows down on them.

Meden steered him to the edge of the wall, which dropped forty feet to the dark plain below. Fires burned in the distance, a sea of lights reflected in the slowly churning river. Daybreak would see the Turyar ford the Khul and launch their attack. By this time tomorrow the gates would be thrown down and the streets choked with marauding warriors and corpses.

A dour-faced man came over to Meden. "We've sent emissaries to try to negotiate," he said, "but they keep coming back without their ears or hands." Adeja noticed his badge bore the royal sunburst, meaning he was under Zhanil's direct command.

"You're wasting your time," answered Adeja. "Get these men off the walls. They're perfect targets, clustered together like this."

Ondor gave him an appraising look. "So you're the one, eh? I heard you had a leg wound. Think you can climb a rope?"

"I can outrun fifty Turyar if it'll keep me from roasting alive."

"Good enough," said Ondor. "It's too bad you're not staying. We could use as many good men as possible."

One less man can't hurt your odds. You already don't have a crow's chance of holding this city. "I've seen as much of the Turyar as I care to see, but thanks."

A second man, also wearing the Sun badge over his armor, called out, gesturing Adeja over to the lip of the wall where a sturdy rope snaked down into the darkness. He took the bundle from Adeja's hands then, strangely enough, gave it back to him. Under his close-fitting helmet, his face seemed familiar, but Adeja could not be certain. "There is food and water here," he said. "There is also a letter of recommendation. They will accept it in Bhellin."

Adeja looked dumbly at the bundle before slinging it over his shoulder and across his chest. "You're sending me to Khalgar?"

"It's the best place right now," said Meden, coming up behind him. "I'd say go back to Tajhaan, but I've heard things aren't so good there these days. Khalgar doesn't have trouble with the Turyar, and they've a good strong army if you want to enlist."

A gloved hand pressed a pouch into his palm. Coins rattled inside. Adeja looked up and once again faced the man who handed him the bundle. "It is not much but it will get you somewhere safe," the man said. "Go north through the hill country of Ottabia to get to Bhellin. It is a difficult route but I do not think you will be followed."

Adeja took a moment to bid Meden farewell. Bending close to the man's ear, he murmured, "I wouldn't say this to any of the

Rhodeen men, but you're Juvan. This city isn't going to hold. Get out of here while you still can."

The only answer Meden gave was to place his hands on the rope to steady it. Adeja grasped hold, swung his legs over the wall and slowly began his descent.

Chapter Ten

From Shemin-at-Khul it took two weeks on foot to reach the Khalgari border. That first night, while darkness provided him some cover, Adeja stumbled and ran until his legs would no longer carry him. That day he spent curled in a ditch, watching the thin smoke that rose from the distant city grow thicker and blacker. By the second day, he could no longer see the western horizon.

Any soldiers left in the city would be the first to die. The royal family, nobles, and priests would be next. Sephil died just in time. Adeja did not like to dwell on what abuse Turya warriors would have inflicted on his body before killing him and hanging what was left on the walls.

It's the best thing that could have happened, Adeja told himself, yet in quiet moments he wondered why he continued to feel such a terrible ache whenever he thought of the prince.

Pursuit did not concern him once he left the Khul river valley. If Brasidios knew about the deception, if he was even alive, he no longer had the resources to go after a single man, and the Turyar had too much to do sacking and razing the city to care if a few stragglers got away. In fact, the Turyar often let some civilians escape to spread their fearsome reputations to cities and towns that might offer resistance.

He took his time, stopping in villages wherever he could to supplement his stores with nourishing food or purchase medicine. Two days he spent with a woman whose husband was away fighting for the king, and saw no harm in comforting such a winsome and accommodating wife who probably did not yet know she was a widow. Apparently he was a more considerate lover than what she was used to, as he left with extra food and a little pot of ointment to ease his itching wound. His discomfort was a good sign, she told him, as it meant he was healing.

The third week brought him to a stretch of low, dusty hills shaded by olive and oak trees. He soon found a road leading past villages where the people no longer had the light coloring or spoke the language of Rhodeen. This was, they told him, the province of Ottabia, the poorest of Khalgar's four principalities. Little could be spared for travelers, but villagers along the way gave him a place to sleep and pointed him toward a complex of buildings on a distant hill where he was told he might be able to find food or even work.

Weary from exertion and the heat, Adeja did not start out until midmorning, and so did not reach the hill until sunset. In the waning light, he paused before a rough stone image of Abh, god of healing and wisdom.

At the gate, he inquired if there was room for a tired man to spend the night. The man on watch, not even a proper sentry, lazily inquired if he had any weapons, gesturing when he saw that the visitor did not speak Khalgari. Adeja gave over his sword but kept his little knife. From there, he was directed down a path to the first building, where several rooms provided accommodations for pilgrims and other travelers.

No one else appeared to be staying, so he had the facilities to himself. A priest dressed in the pale yellow robes of the god brought water for washing and later a plain meal of flat bread and olives. "I speak the language of Rhodeen," he said. "If you come in peace, you are welcome here."

"It's good to see familiar gods again," Adeja told the priest.

"Where are you from?" asked the priest. "You have the accent of Tajhaan."

Parts of his story came out. He omitted most of the details, yet as he spoke the priest's narrowing eyes made him question the wisdom of having spoken at all.

"You deserted the army of Rhodeen, then?"

Adeja shook his head. "No, you have to have a post to desert and I had none. I was discharged fairly. I'm on my way to Bhellin, but I'm a bit weary and this wound of mine is still healing." Talking made him thirsty, and the ale brewed by the priests was very good. He paused to moisten his throat. "I've got a bit of money if you want it."

"We do not charge travelers for our hospitality."

"Well, then, I can work around here if you need it."

At this, the priest raised an eyebrow. "Are you asking for employment?"

"My father was a stonemason back in Tajhaan. He taught me and my brothers a bit of the craft, and I used to go around with him before I gave it up and tried my fortune in the army."

"What makes you think we need a stonemason?"

Adeja motioned to the darkness beyond the open doorway. "I saw some places where you've got crumbling mortar. I could patch it up for you. Or if you'd rather have a guard, I can do that, too, and probably do a better job than the one you've got watching your gate now."

No answer was forthcoming. In an empty room, Adeja went to sleep lulled by a mild breeze and soft cricket sounds coming through the window slat. Why he offered his services at a craft he had not practiced in at least fifteen years he could not say. *Perhaps I'm tired of being a soldier, of living it rough and fighting all the time, and spending my money on drink and whores. Maybe it's time to give it up, find a quiet place and trade, and maybe have a wife and sons, but that's not going to happen in any man's army.*

Rolling over onto his back, he gazed up at the ceiling with its chipping plaster. *Well, you're not going to find a wife here, either. These priests don't get married, and they're not going to let you keep a woman. Still, it'd be good to stay here a few months, just long enough to get some rest, before moving on to Bhellin.*

Morning brought two priests who questioned him at length about his military background. Finally, weary of their questions, he produced the letter of recommendation and handed it to them.

As they perused it, their disbelief only grew. "This letter is signed by the Crown Prince of Rhodeen," said one.

Taking back the paper, he examined it. Sure enough, it was signed *Zhanil Brasides* at the bottom. "I thought it was from my captain."

"So we are to take it that you never met Prince Zhanil?"

"No, and I don't know why he'd bother to write me a letter." Adeja's thoughts drifted far from the suspicious priests and the room in which they sat, going back four weeks to the night of his escape. He recalled the nameless man on the walls who handed him the money. Could that have been Zhanil? While he had seen the prince before, he could not recall whether the soldier had resembled him or not; there had been too much darkness and confusion. "Why would he do such a thing?"

"Why would who do what?" asked one of the priests, and he was abruptly reminded they were still present. At that point, necessity compelled him to confess more of his story. He left out all reference to Sephil except to say that he had been involved in a scandalous affair in Shemin-at-Khul and was sent to Mekesh, from which he barely escaped with his life.

"The king blamed me for losing the stronghold and opening the Khishtil Pass up to the Turyar," he finished. "He needed someone to blame for the horde at his gates, and he certainly wasn't going to point the finger at himself. It's true, I never spoke to Prince Zhanil, but the men who helped me escape told me he felt it was wrong to punish a soldier for doing his duty. He might have arranged the whole thing, I don't know."

When they asked if he had news about the city, he told them everything he knew. "What I saw didn't look good. I don't think the city held for half a day. I saw smoke from the walls that evening, and the next day you could see the whole horizon was dark."

That afternoon he learned why the priests asked. He was escorted from the traveler's lodge to another part of the complex, where yet another priest showed him around. "My name is Darinthes," he said. "I heard there was someone here who had news about the city. Is it truly as bad as my brothers are saying?"

"All I saw was the smoke," said Adeja. "I don't know anything else. I take it you're from the temple of Abh in Shemin-at-Khul?"

Darinthes nodded. He was a youngish man, his face reddened by sun and wind. "When the Turyar appeared below the pass we were ordered to evacuate with some of our patients. We have been waiting for word that it is safe to return, but now it seems we will have to stay here a very long time."

Adeja was tempted to ask about Sephil. He wanted to know if Darinthes attended him in his last hours or knew anyone who had. For the time being, however, silence was the wiser course. He gave his name as Shamuz and went to work that morning repairing part of a circuit wall. Although he had not touched a trowel or mortar in fifteen years, he still remembered enough to satisfy the priests.

The wall took two weeks to repair. Weeds had to be pulled away from crumbling mortar, old nests uprooted, and in some places entire sections needed to be knocked down and rebuilt. Adeja worked diligently, wondering what his father would say at seeing his soldier son return to the craft he abandoned as a youth. *He'd look at this wall and tell me what shit it was, that's what he'd do.*

Only the seasons hastened his work. Whatever was to be done had to be finished by winter, for the damp weather would ruin the mortar before it set. Summer turned toward autumn and gradually the days cooled, but it was still hot enough to make him wrap a damp cloth around his head before setting to work.

A job in a courtyard garden was just the thing for the last days of summer. Decades of weather and earth tremors dislodged some of the colored tiles from the walls. Adeja picked through the chipped pieces he collected from the undergrowth. While he soaked them in water, he scoured the wall where they were to be reset, loosening a few others in the process.

Standing back to survey the task, he saw most of the wall would have to be restored. The priests might like their natural gardens, but all that half-wild ivy and other vegetation wreaked havoc on the masonry, leaving deposits of mold that rotted the mortar and limestone used in the wall's construction. Fortunately, the pattern was simple enough that he could remove all the tiles, clean and replace them without having to be an artist.

He gathered the loose tiles in his tunic, which he removed in the heat, and turned to go when his gaze fell upon the two figures sitting in the shade on the other side of the courtyard. One was a priest whose name he did not recall, but the other was a young man with thin hands clasped in the lap of a novice's unbleached robe. His face was obscured by a fall of light brown hair, but the set of his shoulders was so familiar that Adeja dropped the bundle. Tiles rattled and spilled onto the pavement.

When the young man lifted his eyes to see what the source of the commotion was, Adeja forgot about the mess at his feet.

The youth murmured something to the priest and quickly averted his eyes. "Forgive him for staring," said the priest. "He thought you were someone he knew."

Shaking tiles off his feet, Adeja took a step forward. "Sephil?"

Dark eyes widened in a pale face. Sephil looked from him to the priest and shook his head. "No," he gasped. "I am seeing things."

The priest, whom Adeja now remembered was called Kalion, made reassuring noises even as Sephil began to hyperventilate. "There is nothing to fear," he said. "This is Shamuz, a stonemason who is staying with us for a while."

"No, my name is Adeja *ked* Shamuz," corrected Adeja. "Sephil, I thought you were dead."

It was now Kalion's turn to be puzzled. "Then you must be the soldier he told us about, the one who was sent to Mekesh and died."

"Do I look dead to you?" Once again, his gaze traveled from the priest to Sephil, whose eyes still reflected his terror. He looked thinner and paler than Adeja had ever seen him. "Yes, I went to Mekesh, but I got out of there when the Turyar attacked. When I got back to Shemin-at-Khul, I heard stories that the king's son was dead. Sephil, look at me. *I am not dead.*"

Kalion appraised them both. "It seems lies have been told on both sides."

"Sephil," said Adeja, cautiously taking a step closer, "I am *not* a ghost." He looked over at the priest. "Will you leave us for a moment?"

"Yes, but only for a moment. He is still my charge," murmured Kalion. When he rose to go, Sephil grasped his arm with a pleading look. "I will be just inside," he said.

Adeja took the seat he vacated. "I heard you were dead. They told me you'd cut your wrists and bled to death."

"I did," Sephil answered in a ragged voice, "but I did not die. I am inept at everything I do, you see. I could not even kill myself properly."

"Don't talk like that." Adeja wanted to put an arm on his shoulder, yet at the moment Sephil seemed to shun his touch. "Why would you do such a stupid thing? I wasn't dead and you were about to be married."

"I did it because I did not want to live. Nakhet said you had been killed and that it was best to forget about you. I ordered him to leave, but I found it was not so easy to be rid of him," Sephil explained. "As for the princess, I saw how she and my cousin Dashir looked at each other."

Adeja clenched his jaw, not knowing whether to embrace him or slap him. "What you did was selfish," he said, "and I don't mean your father's alliance. Tajhaan never would have sent troops in time."

"If I was a soldier surrounded by enemies, you would have called it honorable. I was a coward, but I was alone. I was not strong enough to do my duty, so I left it to those who could do better. Despise me if you want to, but know this: I was dead to my family a long time ago. Once you were gone, all I had before me was a hopeless future. There was no reason for me to go on living."

"For everything you've done I really ought to despise you," said Adeja, sighing heavily, "but I can't. Now tell me, how did you get from the temple of Abh all the way here?"

"Kalion told me some of the priests were ordered to leave the city before the Turyar attacked. I remember traveling in a wagon with them, but I was drugged for most of the journey. I know Zhanil gave the order." Sephil closed his eyes and when he reached for Adeja's hand his loose sleeve fell away, revealing the scars livid against the white skin of his wrist. "How did you find me?"

"Chance and the gods," replied Adeja. And perhaps Zhanil, if he had been the man upon the wall, played his own part. *He gave me money and told me which way to come. He knew I would find this place, and Sephil.* "Would you rather I left?"

"Why do you say that?"

"You seem afraid of me."

Sephil quickly covered his face with his hands. "I sent letters to you through Eumos, but you did not answer. I thought you were either dead or you despised me. Part of me does not believe you are real. I have been very sick, seeing and dreaming strange things. I do not want this to be just another dream."

"I'm not good with writing letters, and there weren't any materials at Mekesh," said Adeja. "Would you feel better if I showed you the wound the Turyar gave me?"

Sephil shook his head. "I am sorry about the letters. I complained so much, I would not have blamed you for not writing back."

"That's all right," replied Adeja. "The men thought I had a mistress in Shemin-at-Khul, and that I got sent to Mekesh for attacking my commanding officer. I never showed them the letters or told them anything about you."

Nodding, Sephil made a face. "I borrowed the parchment from Zhanil's wife; that is why it smelled like perfume. I could not trust Nakhet to ask him for writing materials. I sent another letter to the garrison commander at Mekesh ordering him to release you. I was too afraid to go to my father or my brother, but I waited too long. That night Nakhet told me he had spies at Mekesh who told him you were dead. Perhaps he intercepted the letter, or he perhaps simply said it out of spite. All I know is he told me it did me no good to weep for a mere soldier. Zhanil put him to death for everything he did."

At this moment, Kalion reappeared and gently informed them that it was time for Sephil to rest. "You can see each other later," he said, nodding to Adeja. "The prince has been gravely ill and has just had a terrible shock."

73

Once someone got around to telling him that Shemin-at-Khul had fallen and that his father and brother were dead, Sephil would have yet another shock. Adeja decided he was not going to be the bearer of that news, though he could well guess that when it did come he would be called upon to comfort Sephil afterward.

An hour later, the high priest summoned him. He was conducted to a plainly furnished office overlooking one of the complex's three gardens, where a tall, somber man awaited him. After introducing himself as Bedren, he promptly demanded to hear the entire story. "Had you told us in the beginning who you were, it might have spared Prince Sephil much pain."

"I had no idea he was alive, never mind that he was here," explained Adeja. "All I knew was he'd been taken to the temple of Abh to die. I just assumed that he had."

"Now that you are here you must stay," said Bedren. "At least until he is well enough to manage on his own. His brother urged us to give him the best possible care, and that is what we mean to do."

"Zhanil's corpse is probably feeding the crows by now."

Bedren frowned at his lack of tact. "Have you said anything to him regarding the state of his family or city?"

When Adeja shook his head, Bedren visibly relaxed. "Then you must continue to feign ignorance. What you say is likely to be true, but this is not the time for the prince to hear it."

Not that he liked having his life ordered for him, but as it was a tolerable situation Adeja did not complain. He now spent part of each day with Sephil, helping him take his exercise outdoors, keeping him company in the courtyard garden while he worked at repairing the wall and sitting with him at night until he fell asleep. Sephil spoke very little during their time together, but Kalion reported that his appetite and color improved.

At the beginning of autumn, word trickled in that Shemin-at-Khul had fallen to the Turyar, while a frightened populace in Cassiare, hoping for mercy, opened its gates to the conquerors. Turyar warlords seized control of both cities and set up their own tribal rule. News concerning Sephil's family was grim. Rumors were rampant that the males were put to death while all royal women of childbearing age were given to their captors to breed sons. Adeja had never known the Turyar to spare women, but in the case of a royal line it was not an inconceivable possibility for warlords wishing to establish their own dynasties.

MY SUN AND STARS

Zhanil fell early, said the informant, whispering his news near the circuit wall where Adeja knew Sephil would not come looking for him. "He rode out to meet them with five hundred men and never came back except hanging from a pole without his head."

In the square before the ruined pyramid of the Sun, the corpses of the king and his heir were stripped and hung upside down for the carrion birds. The informant went on to say that Zhanil's sons were flung from the pyramid terrace, and his unborn child hacked from his mother's womb. Other noblemen met similarly brutal ends.

"Some say Prince Dashir escaped," said the man. "The king made him Crown Prince when Zhanil fell, but he didn't stay to fight. I heard he escaped with the Tajhaani ambassadors and the princess."

If Dashir survived, it would not be long before the man turned up in the royal court of Tajhaan and proclaimed himself king of Rhodeen.

Adeja obeyed the priests and said nothing to Sephil, yet in the prince's somber demeanor he could not help but think Sephil already knew his family was dead.

* * * *

Such a strange irony, Sephil thought, *that the one member of the royal family least worth saving was the only one who had survived.*

No one told him anything outright, of course, but it was not difficult to understand the good intentions of the priests. They meant to spare his fragile nerves, but they could not prevent him from overhearing things. He knew his father was dead, and Zhanil. With that last realization, grief pervaded his numbness and he sat alone in his cubicle, aching at the memories of their final moments together.

Sephil, you did not have to do this. Through his drugged haze, he recalled his brother sitting on his bed, gently stroking his hands below his bandaged wrists. *You should have come to me. You should have told me how unhappy you were.*

I tried. You could not hear me. His lips formed words he could not utter. Tears of shame blurred his vision. *Zhanil*, he whispered around the sobs knotting his throat. *I want it to be over.*

And the end came, but the gods took the wrong brother.

Now that Adeja was here, seemingly resurrected from the dead, his heart should have been lighter. Instead, his relief felt bittersweet. No longer was Adeja a soldier with strict orders to stay with his charge. Nothing beyond his recuperating wound kept him at the sanctuary, as he made no secret of his distaste for what Sephil had done and had spoken openly of leaving once he was able.

It is for the best, Sephil told himself. *I have nothing to offer him. Yes, I will let him go.*

Not once did the priests approach him about claiming the throne of Rhodeen, and for that he was grateful. A man who could not govern his own life had no business leading armies or ruling others. His one small wish was to live out his days in this quiet, healing place and to forget he had ever been a prince.

* * * *

It was many weeks later, as a cold wind blew fallen leaves across the courtyards, that Bedren called Adeja in when Sephil received the news.

For the sake of the prince's nerves, most of the details were carefully omitted. At several points, Bedren asked if there were any questions, but Sephil was silent until the end, when he simply nodded and said he already knew.

Bedren and Kalion inquired if he wanted anything. Sephil took a moment to answer, looking down at his folded hands, then at Adeja. "I would like to be alone."

Alone meant Adeja was to stay. Sephil waited until the door closed before rising and asking Adeja to hold him. He neither wept nor spoke. Tears would come later, once the shock wore away.

Adeja hesitated to embrace him too tightly, for though he had put on weight Sephil still seemed too small and fragile. "There's one thing they didn't tell you," he said. "You're now the king of Rhodeen."

His face still muffled in the fabric of Adeja's tunic, Sephil shook his head. "I can only imagine what my father would say if he could see me at this moment."

"Forget about him," said Adeja.

"It is easier to say that than to do it. Zhanil should not have died. The gods are so cruel, to cut down those who most deserve to live," murmured Sephil. "I had no idea until it was almost too late how much he cared."

Drawing back a little, he gazed up at Adeja. "Even if I wanted, I could not possibly become king. Dashir is the heir to the throne."

"Dashir might be dead," said Adeja.

"I doubt it. He has always been cunning. If anyone escaped, I believe it would have been him."

"Your claim is just as strong as his."

Sephil slowly drew away. "Please, do not try to push me into something I do not want. I have no desire to take the throne of Rhodeen. I never did, and even if I wanted to, neither my cousin nor the Turyar are going to stand aside and let me be king."

Adeja cupped Sephil's cheek in his palm. Now that the prince did not have eunuchs to attend to his toilette, stubble shadowed his once-smooth face. "Darinthes told me Zhanil sent royal tokens with you just as he sent a letter with me. If you ask the priests, they'll take you to Bhellin. I will go with you. And if you ever decide you want to fight for your throne, I'll be the first soldier in your army."

"I would never ask you to do that for me," answered Sephil.

He turned his head toward the window. "You seem to want the throne for me much more than I want it for myself. Let it go, Adeja. It may sound strange to you, but I am at peace here. If I went to Bhellin, men would scorn me and try to kill me, either as an imposter or a legitimate threat. It is not worth it. If Dashir is alive and wants to take Rhodeen back from the Turyar and rebuild the dynasty, let him. I do not want to be king."

Sephil lifted his hands to touch Adeja's arms, his fingertips hesitantly ghosting along the rough wool of Adeja's sleeves as though the brazen prince of eight months ago had never been. "I want to stay here with you," he murmured. "What I did before was stupid and callous. If you walked out the door right now, I would not blame you. I have little to offer you, but would you stay if I asked?"

"Right now I have no plans to go elsewhere." With another lover, Adeja might have laughed to dispel the tension, but Sephil was in such earnest it did not seem appropriate.

Clasping Sephil's wrists, he turned them over and lightly stroked his thumbs over the scars. "You never really told me why you did this."

"I did not cut my wrists because you were gone," answered Sephil. "You would have left anyway. Nakhet told me you had planned to desert the army to get away from me. I knew in my heart it was no lie. I never gave you any reason to want to stay with me, and at least twenty reasons to want to leave. I did this because I loved you and I hurt you, and only when you were gone did I truly understand how alone I was. I did not want to go on living like that."

A lump formed in Adeja's throat. Women he had known made more impassioned speeches, weeping and tearing their hair, yet with them he had been as stone. "I won't lie to you, Sephil. Nakhet told you the truth. I *was* going to desert, but I stayed. And I'll stay now only if you promise me that you'll never do anything like this to yourself again."

Sephil bent his head to kiss the hands holding his. "Adeja, you do not have to stay. You do not even have to touch me if you do not want to. All those other times, you did it only because I—"

Adeja silenced him with a kiss. "I am not going to leave you, and I never said that I didn't want you." Lifting a finger, he traced Sephil's lips before kissing him again. "I never said that. That last time, when you asked me to love you, I did it because I wanted to."

"You truly wanted me?"

Adeja was surprised at the passion with which he was dropping kisses on Sephil's lips and eyelids. He pulled Sephil hard against him, nearly crushing that frail body with his need. "Didn't you once call me your Sun?"

Sephil's eyes widened and a little gasp escaped him. "Yes," he breathed, "and I meant it."

"Then I'll be that again, the Sun to your Moon." Adeja dipped his head to kiss the curve of Sephil's jaw and tease the delicate lines of his throat.

"But I cannot offer you anything."

Adeja uttered a short laugh. "Do you think I have any more or less to offer you? I've never understood what it was you wanted with a rough soldier like me."

Like a shy maiden, Sephil ducked his head. The first hint of a blush stained his cheeks. "Should I tell you?"

"I think you'd better, my prince."

Right away, Sephil placed two fingers over his lips to silence him. "Do not call me that anymore. I am just Sephil." He let his hand fall, sliding over Adeja's chest to cover his heart. "All I wanted were two strong arms to hold me, to keep me safe and to love me. That is all I want now."

"Then I can do that." Adeja bent his lips to touch Sephil's head. In the uncertain days to come, he could do that very well indeed.

Part Two

Little Moon

Chapter One

With slow, rhythmic movements, Sephil swept the courtyard. In late summer, apples and wild berries bloomed here. Now dead leaves dropped from the trees, and were caught in a swirling dance by the wind blowing over the sanctuary wall.

As he dragged the heather broom over the stones, Sephil did not mind that within the hour his work would be undone by windborne dust or the fall of brittle foliage still clinging to the trees. What he did was for the satisfaction of some small accomplishment against what was otherwise a bland existence.

When it grew too dark or the weather too harsh to work outdoors, he spent his time reading, puzzling over philosophical or devotional books the priests of Abh gave him to read, and trying to master the Khalgari language. From his earliest days with slate and primer, Sephil was a poor scholar, giving up when his efforts learned only scorn from his father and tutors. Now he wanted desperately to learn, yet because he did not know how to interpret religious texts he had to turn to Kalion, the priest who accompanied him on the journey from Shemin-at-Khul and now acted as his tutor.

"When Ulishban speaks of being unable to keep water from spilling out between his fingers, it is an analogy illustrating the futility of forming material attachments," explained Kalion. "The things men value in this world are in fact things which have no value at all, and the desire to possess them is a waste of spiritual energy. Do not grasp for more than what you are given. In this way one can accept the otherwise uncontrollable forces which rule his destiny and be at peace."

This Sephil understood all too well. As the only surviving son of the king, and regardless of what others might think, the throne of Rhodeen lay within his rights. *King* and *throne*, however, represented mere ideas, words rather than reality. It never occurred to anyone that the younger son might assume power, or want to.

Renounce the world, said the holy texts, *and renounce pain.*

MY SUN AND STARS

Through pain, he had tried to renounce the world altogether; the scars on his wrists reminded him that the gods were not yet ready to receive him. Forced to live, Sephil did his best to absorb the healing god's teachings and perform the meditations the priests prescribed for him; he felt a curious sense of calm, serenity as fragile as a cobweb. He wanted it to last, but knew somehow that, like all else he found comforting and good, it would eventually be torn from him.

And like his dream of calm, with each day his former life as a disgraced prince of Rhodeen slid just a little further from him, a persona that might have belonged to someone else. Sometimes, however, vivid recollections of his excesses, shameless words and deeds, shone through the haze, making him recoil in horror.

That cannot have been me, he thought, yet the priests encouraged him to embrace his shame in order to learn from it. Memories of wanton behavior, petulant scenes and selfish desires brought an agony of self-revulsion before he began to understand how loneliness and rejection could warp the soul. The person who had hosted riotous parties and cavorted with soldiers and catamites to spite his father and fill his empty hours was a distorted reflection of his true self.

Now Sephil was simply a novice who dressed in unbleached wool and tended the sanctuary grounds. His hands, their fingernails once bright with lacquer, were now roughened by work. Time became fluid, so when he turned twenty in mid-autumn he scarcely noticed.

Somewhere on the grounds, Adeja worked at repairing crumbling masonry. The man's presence remained among the few things anchoring Sephil to reality, and he could sense the man even from afar. Once lovers, they had not touched in six months, at first because Sephil was too fragile for such intimacy, then because he did not wish to encourage a practice he would most likely have to renounce.

A day will come when he must leave me. Adeja was a foreigner and a soldier. Not for him a monotonous life in a quiet sanctuary. One day he would crave a wife and sons, and more than Sephil could ever offer him. *He is not mine to keep.*

Finishing his circuit of the courtyard, he laid the broom against a stone bench and sat down to rest. Already a chill wind, smelling of wood smoke and dead leaves, swirled past him, scattering his efforts. Sephil watched with detached interest. Tomorrow he would return to complete the same task, and the next day. The elements merely acknowledged this.

Shuffling feet scraped the stones, drawing his attention to the end of the path. An elderly priest, half-blind and leaning on a stick, moved toward the bench. Like him, the man was a regular visitor, taking sun and fresh air to invigorate his spirits. Sephil stood, went to his side and offered his arm.

"Unniri, are you well today?" he inquired.

Unniri grunted and smiled, his mouth still showing most of its teeth. Kalion told him the old priest was nearly a hundred years old. "Young man," he said, lightly touching Sephil's arm with a brown, thickly gnarled hand, "why are you still here?"

The priest, who spoke the tongue of Rhodeen as well as Khalgar, often sat with Sephil and described his childhood in Bhellin and his life as a clerk overseeing the royal monuments, for he had not always served Abh. However, he could not seem to recall anyone's name.

"I was sweeping the courtyard," answered Sephil. "I wanted to rest before I go in."

Bobbing his head, the old man clucked his tongue. "But the world awaits you, young one. You will see mighty cities, and have a lovely wife and children to care for you in your dotage."

The thought was so absurd that Sephil could not help but smile. "Oh, no, not I," he replied. "I am not at all interested in marriage."

Unniri patted his hand. "One day you will have a strong son, mighty in the land."

He spoke with conviction, yet Sephil knew from others that Unniri's offspring stood high in the Khalgari court. "*You* have many strong sons and grandsons, remember?"

Lifting his head, Unniri turned his face toward Sephil and, for a moment, his eyes seemed to focus. "You will make a star," he said, "for the horsemen and the green land of rivers."

He is lost in his own mind. Carran, the eunuch who had been Sephil's childhood guardian, once mentioned the very old were sometimes capable of prophecy. "Those close to death's door see things you and I cannot," he said. Perhaps the elderly were very wise, but Sephil preferred to regard Unniri's mumbling as the fancies of a wandering memory.

"The gods made the stars," he said. "They are the tears of the Moon-maiden. Do they believe something else in Khalgar?"

Unniri smiled. "Your son will wear a crown of stars."

"I am not married."

"You will make a star," repeated Unniri, "for the horsemen and the green land of rivers."

Suddenly uncomfortable, Sephil looked away. As a prince, exiled from court and left to consort with the jaded sons of the nobility, he occasionally summoned fortunetellers to amuse him and his guests by casting the dice or reading palms. Words, their prophecies were but the words of charlatans who promised great wealth, power or renown to anyone foolish enough to offer coin, and Sephil gave them as much attention as he did those eunuchs who praised his wisdom and beauty.

Unniri, who spoke so softly his words seemed like cobwebs, made him tremble where the flamboyant sycophants of Shemin-at-Khul could not. *A son who will be king,* he thought. But no, that could not be, or rather, the words did not mean what they implied on their face.

It could mean anything, thought Sephil. One son who would wear a crown: it might mean his own offspring, or even Adeja, whom he referred to as his Sun. *No, I will not entangle myself in this web of meanings. To have a son, I must marry, and I will not do that.*

As a prince, even a disgraced one, a political marriage was an inevitable duty, and his father, seeking an alliance with Tajhaan against the Turyar, betrothed him to a princess whose lovely, kohl-rimmed eyes regarded him with disdain. But the kingdom whose laws dictated his world was gone, and his royal rank vanished with it.

Shaking his head, he stroked Unniri's hand and once again enquired after his health. He did not have the heart to tear away the old man's illusions by crying them false.

* * * *

Not quite perfect, judged Adeja, studying the result of his work in the atrium, but it would serve. If anything, his labors in the sanctuary were good practice for the stonemason's craft he meant to take up once he left.

And when will I do that? he wondered. Several times already Sephil gave him leave to go, even encouraged his departure, but Adeja judged it too soon. His health certainly presented no obstacle, for the wound he had received from the Turyar at Mekesh had healed cleanly.

Perhaps with winter coming it isn't so good a time for traveling. Adeja turned the thought over in his mind, accepting it as an acceptable reason for staying where he was, before brushing it aside as an excuse. Quite simply he had promised Sephil he would remain. Fragile and alone in the world, his family either slain or scattered to the winds by the Turyar, the prince needed a protector.

"But what can he possibly need protection *from*?" Adeja asked the wall. "Too many prayers, perhaps, or the dust he sweeps up each day in the courtyard?" In this place Sephil carried no title and, having renounced his claim to Rhodeen's throne, presented no threat to anyone.

A good idea at the time, it did not bear closer consideration. It was folly to expect a soldier to remain when he had no post to fill. No matter what he promised, Adeja knew he must soon leave or go mad in the piety and silence of the place.

Adeja took a brief rest, ate a few dried apple slices, and washed them down with water from a nearby well before returning to finish his work. Now that the grout had dried between the tiles, he could scrub away the residue. Even with the rags he tied around his knees they ached from the unfamiliar posture, and his back strained. Still, he gritted his teeth and continued with the task, knowing the work he meant to find in the cities would make this seem fair by comparison.

In the late afternoon, Sephil came to observe his work. For some time he stood quietly in the entryway, contemplating the damp tiles and the man at his feet before speaking. "You should be working in a palace or grand temple," he murmured, "not wasting your time here."

Adeja nodded at the compliment. "Your color is better," he said. "Have you been outside?"

Sephil looked at him, flushed, and dropped his gaze to the tiles once more. "It is lovely work."

"It'll serve." Adeja rose and unfurled his back, easing the stiffness from his tendons with an audible pop.

"If you are sore," said Sephil, "come to my cell tonight and I will rub ointment into your back."

Unless they came from a physician or a withered old mother who dabbled in herbs, such invitations could only lead in one direction. Adeja knew better than to accept, for it would persuade Sephil to believe that which was untrue. *With words he tells me to go, but with everything he does he wants me to stay.* A tactic employed by a desperate woman or a lover who could not decide what he or she truly wanted.

"You needn't bother," answered Adeja. "I can get ointment from the infirmary."

Sephil's smile evaporated. "I only wanted to do something for you," he said in a small voice. "I had no intention of seducing you."

We'll see about that. Adeja relented. "All right, you can rub my back and tell me about your dull day sweeping the yard and praying."

At supper they did not sit together. As a layman, Adeja must eat at the far end of the table, but like anyone who came into the sanctuary, he had to attend evening prayers. Adeja went through the motions, feigning interest while letting his mind roam. Abh was not his god, and the gods to whom he did pay reverence heard his prayers less often than they ought. It was, Adeja knew, a shameful lack of devotion from a man whose father had taught him better.

Afterward, the priests congregated in the halls, discussing practical and philosophical matters. Adeja slipped out, relieved himself, and washed before threading his way through the shadows to Sephil's door.

Sephil slept alone in a cell six paces across, on a cot furnished with a rough blanket. An oil lamp burned on a table, giving off enough light that Adeja could see the blotches on Sephil's cheeks and jaw. "What did you do to yourself?"

"I know you do not like the beard." Sephil put his hand to his cheek, careful not to touch the cut by his mouth. "I tried to shave, but it seems I made a mess of it."

Adeja stepped inside and closed the door. "The beard means nothing unless you planned to have me kiss you. I thought you said you hadn't any intention of seducing me. Did you lie?"

"I told you the truth," said Sephil. "I do not like the beard, either. I am not used to hair on my face and would not have grown the beard at all if I did not think that was how a proper man was supposed to look."

"You're never going to look like your brother," said Adeja, "or be him."

Sephil made no answer. Turning, he motioned to the bed, where a linen cloth and jar of ointment sat atop the blanket. "I did not lie when I offered to rub your back. I am not asking you for anything more, tonight or any other night until you leave."

"I never said I was going," replied Adeja.

"I know you are not happy here. This is no life for a soldier."

Adeja sighed. "It's not the fighting and marching I miss, that can be a miserable business. These priests just aren't my people. All this quiet and praying makes my head ache. Still, I did promise I'd stay, and when I give my word I keep it."

"You would be miserable keeping that promise," said Sephil.

This was not a conversation Adeja wanted to have tonight. Being released from his promise did not bring the relief it should. "It's the wrong season for traveling, anyway. But are you sure you want me to go?"

"I am no longer a prince to command you, Adeja," answered Sephil. "I know what you promised, but I would not have you remain and be unhappy just so I can feel safe. The world does not know I am here, and even if it did it would not matter. I am no threat to anyone." Turning aside, he patted the bed. "Come, I will do your back."

Adeja glanced around the cell. It was not the first time he had been here, but on all his previous visits he stayed only a moment. Aside from the table and bed, the cell's furnishings consisted of a stool and small chest for clothing and toiletries, nothing to recall the luxurious apartments that housed the prince in Shemin-at-Khul. "Where are your shaving things?" he asked. "If you're going to do this yourself you should learn to do it properly."

"Are you going to show me?" Sephil opened the chest and, from under a stack of neatly folded garments, drew out a razor and a little pot of ointment, which he gave to Adeja.

"You need a mirror," said Adeja. When Sephil presented him with a small looking glass, he took it over to the wash basin on the table and held it to the wall. "You need to hang it here. Tomorrow I'll get a nail and hammer and some string."

"I can do it," Sephil said softly.

"Yes, and you'll smash your thumb with the hammer."

"Then *show* me how to do it so I do not hurt myself."

He sounded so very much like a child demanding to be allowed to do adult things that Adeja could not help but smile. Among other things, it meant Sephil was emerging from his former listlessness. "All right, I'll show you tomorrow."

Adeja instructed Sephil to sit on the edge of the bed and dab the ointment over his lower face while he inspected the razor. "Make sure you keep this sharp," he said. Sitting down beside Sephil, he approved the young man's efforts, handing him a linen cloth to wipe his hands. "Clean your face in warm water first. It makes shaving easier. Now tilt your head just so and don't move."

Not once did Sephil close his eyes. Adeja felt his gaze, without malice or suspicion, as he began to repair the haphazard job Sephil had done, smoothing rough patches while careful not to touch areas where Sephil had nicked himself. "Have one of the priests watch you when you do this tomorrow. There, that'll do it. You're done."

Sephil went to the basin, rinsed, and dried his face. He returned, still holding the linen cloth. "Do you want me to do your back?"

"It's not necessary," answered Adeja.

Before the last word left his mouth, Sephil leaned across and kissed him. Adeja dropped the razor, heard it clink on the bare floor. His arms unfroze, came up to clasp Sephil around the waist and draw him deeper into the heat of the kiss before pushing him away. "We shouldn't be doing this," he breathed.

Sephil ducked his head, as unnerved by his actions as Adeja. "It was not supposed to be that kind of kiss. I just wanted to thank you for being so patient with me, but—I am so foolish. I should have just said thank you and left it at that. If you want to leave—"

Perhaps if he had not been so weary and hungry for sex, Adeja would have done just that, yet in their closeness he and Sephil seemed to generate a heat, an attraction that begged greater contact. "No," he said huskily, "it is all right."

The kisses that fell on his lips and jaw were tentative, asking a question only Adeja could answer.

How far Sephil wished to take things, he had no idea. Twice before, when the young man seduced him with his mouth and his body, Adeja had been passive, even though he was not accustomed to letting others take the lead. Habit urged him to pull aside their clothing, push Sephil down onto the bed and do as he pleased. With a male lover this usually meant turning the young man over on his hands and knees, spitting into his hand and inserting his cock. His partner's pleasure had nothing to do with it.

Now he held back, responding to Sephil's kisses and the tongue seeking entrance into his mouth when his body ached for more. When slender fingers slid under his tunic to explore his chest, he pulled off the garment, helped Sephil out of his shift, and tossed the jar of ointment, meant for his back and never used, onto the heap of clothing on the floor.

"I thought priests didn't do things like this."

"Other priests, maybe, but not here," murmured Sephil. "I can hear them through the walls sometimes."

Adeja licked his earlobe. "Is that why you want me, because it makes you hot?"

"I try to meditate and forget all such things—" Sephil grasped his left hand and moved it up his thigh to cup his buttocks. "Sometimes I feel nothing, and it is so easy to not want, but then I see you, hear your voice and then it seems I am not doing such a good job at being a priest."

Hands moved over his naked skin, lips traced his collarbone down to his left nipple. Adeja gasped, aware of that hot, moist tongue and the erection bulging against his loincloth, the only clothing he still wore.

If only the bed was not so narrow. In the prince's apartments in Shemin-at-Khul there had been a feather bed large enough for three to lay comfortably, furnished with silken pillows, coverlets and a golden canopy that trembled like a web in the evening breeze. Such luxury Adeja craved at this moment, for as they could not lay side by side it seemed he must push Sephil onto his back.

Sephil solved the dilemma by shifting onto his side, his back pressed to the wall. There was just enough room for Adeja to lie facing him. Still, the bed was too narrow, offering few options for pleasure. Had it not been so hard, and the night so cold, the floor would have been preferable.

"How do you want to—?" It was difficult to think with Sephil's lips tracing the line of his throat, and that pointed little tongue darting out to tease his collarbone and send currents of sensation to his groin.

The fingers that undid his loincloth and slid inside to grasp his cock provided him with answer enough. Adeja bucked his hips, grunting, quickening his pace until he shuddered and came in his partner's hand.

Sephil hovered beside him, lightly kissing his damp brow and rubbing a moist hand over his belly. From Sephil's subtle thrusting against him and the urgency of his kisses, Adeja remembered that his was not the only need. "Climb on top of me," he grunted.

"You are not hard." Sephil sounded wistful, while his fingers ghosted over Adeja's groin as though to tease his cock back to fullness.

"I don't need to fuck you to make you come," grunted Adeja. "Pull your leg over me. This bed is too small for anything else."

Once Sephil straddled him, Adeja ran a hand down his firm buttocks to slide up and over his thighs to caress him. Touching a young man in this way was not something he did often, for when a Tajhaani man made love to a youth, he did it strictly with his own pleasure in mind. Tender passions were reserved for women like the soldier's widow Adeja had comforted on his way north from Rhodeen, and whatever satisfaction his male partners had during sex usually came from their own efforts.

Sephil, neither woman nor male prostitute, fell into that gray nether region where Adeja rated sex with him as making love. For all that the prince had tarnished his military career and nearly gotten him killed for the sake of his own pleasure, Adeja did not know why he cared so much. *It isn't as if I can take him away from here and set up house in Bhellin or anywhere else with him as my wife*, he thought. *I should have moved on the moment I found him here. Staying doesn't do either of us any good.*

Adeja gripped his lover's slender cock and stroked, rubbing him the way he liked to be touched. The moans he received in response, and the way Sephil's tight buttocks clenched over his groin, were almost enough to make Adeja hard again. Sephil leaned over to kiss him passionately, muffling his cries in Adeja's mouth, and in the warm rush of fluid that spilled over his hand Adeja forgot how insatiable and difficult to satisfy Sephil could be.

Wrapping himself in his discarded robe, Sephil went to the basin and brought back a moist cloth with which he cleaned Adeja. "Perhaps we should not have done that," he murmured.

"Now isn't the time to be saying that." Adeja took the cloth from him and wiped the drying semen from his hands.

Sephil sat on the edge of the bed next to him. "It was not something I planned," he said.

Adeja thought hard. Conversation was not something he usually pursued with his lovers. Most of the time, he simply threw on his clothes and left. "Neither one of us planned this," he explained, "but here we are."

"Adeja, I was not trying to seduce you into staying. It was simply something I wanted to do."

For now, that made for a good enough explanation. Adeja, closing his eyes, shivered. Since he was not quite ready to leave, he shifted his body until he could get under the blanket. "It's cold and you're barely covered," he said. "Get under here with me."

Sephil appeared to hesitate a moment before extinguishing the lamp, dropping his robe and clambering over Adeja to take the side nearest the wall. Adeja pulled him close. "I will have plenty of lonely nights once you are gone," he murmured.

"Are you trying to make me feel guilty?"

"No, not that." Sephil nuzzled against Adeja's chest. "I was just stating a fact."

"I don't *have* to go—"

"But I know you want to," said Sephil.

Adeja was no longer certain what he wanted to do, except sleep. "Maybe, but spring is still a long time off," he mumbled.

Chapter Two

Adeja found a ready ear in Obiru, the man who guarded the gate. "Why do you stay here if you want a wife so badly?"

Although he spoke Khalgari fluently enough now to carry on a conversation, Adeja knew he did not always phrase his words correctly. It was the same dilemma he had faced years earlier when he first arrived in Rhodeen.

Obiru laughed, showing a mouthful of large yellow teeth. "Have to go to the nearest town to get one, and can't bring her back here. And who wants to stay in town and work, eh?"

In a proper stronghold, Obiru with his potbelly and slovenly ways would not have been considered fit to scrub the barracks midden. As for guarding the sanctuary gate, he did more sleeping and scratching than patrolling. Should the Turyar or any other enemy approach, Obiru's head would roll in the dirt long before he ever realized the threat.

Adeja thought it best not to mention that he was a trained soldier. There was no need to antagonize one of the few people who made life in the sanctuary bearable. "Hmm, that's wise," he agreed. "Now if I wanted a woman, where is this town?"

Obiru not only gave him directions but suggested by name one or two girls who would satisfy him. "Not much here—" He motioned to his head. "But here—hah!" Cupping his hands over his breast, he indicated precisely which quality he valued most in a woman.

For his part, Adeja would have preferred a wife, a good-natured, sensual woman to keep his hearth and welcome him home at night, but the priests frowned on women in the sanctuary. Adeja did not point out that in Rhodeen there were priestesses of Abh, or ask why it was different here. They would not welcome a wife, so he would have to venture out in search of prostitutes.

Adeja noted the information for future use and returned to work, a new project just outside the main chapel. Soon he would make the trip to Ivrish. For now, his own hand sufficed to relieve his need, and on nights when neither he nor Sephil wished to be alone, Sephil reminded him just how skilled he was.

Winter loomed over Ottabia's barren hills, bringing overcast skies and a bite to the morning air that did not dissipate as afternoon approached. Mist often blanketed the grounds, and when drizzle dampened the stones, Adeja could no longer work on the chapel walkway. Seneth, the priest who oversaw all labor in the sanctuary, gave him a new task filling in hairline cracks left over from fifty years of earth tremors, but made it clear that soon there would be no more work. Adeja would either have to find another way to make himself useful or go elsewhere.

His father found steady employment working on the High Prince's monuments, and from what he heard, the Khalgari king sponsored similar works to glorify his name. Because he could read and write, skills his father insisted he learn, Adeja thought he might be able to get work chiseling the texts that adorned Khalgar's temples, statues, and tombs. First, he needed to improve his grasp of the language, reason alone to delay his going until spring.

Adeja had not counted on winter's first threatening clouds and the restlessness they would bring.

Where rainfall scarcely touched the landscape the rest of the year, Ottabia rivaled Rhodeen in its damp winters. Downpours that lasted days turned courtyards into ponds and dry gullies into raging rivers. Adeja worked by candlelight, his senses lulled by the patter of rain in the overflowing gutters, and his memories took him back to his childhood in Tajhaan, where spring brought six weeks of rain, little sunlight and strained tempers.

"This weather makes me sleepy," murmured Sephil. Stretched out on his bed, naked but for a thin blanket, he presented a languid picture at odds with his apparent desire to renounce the world. Making love with him gave Adeja some ease, but not enough to sate his nerves.

"I need sunlight," he growled.

Sephil smiled and held out his arms. "Rain can be nice," he said. When Adeja sat down and embraced him, his tongue flicked out to tease Adeja's ear, promising more delights to come.

Adeja, however, was in no mood to play. His agitation craved relief, and he was ready to take it fast and hard. What he could not articulate he indicated through his rough caresses, until Sephil, understanding his need, obliged him by turning over on his hands and knees.

Positioning Sephil over the edge of the bed, Adeja rubbed his oiled cock between his buttocks and pumped him hard from behind. Afterward, realizing Sephil had not climaxed, he was contrite. "If you want me to do something for you —"

"No, it is not necessary," murmured Sephil, pulling on his robe. He said no more, and Adeja knew that in his haste he had smothered his partner's desire.

In the third week he recalled Ivrish and the brothel Obiru had described to him, and knew that if ever there was a time to visit, in spite of the weather, it was now. Adeja still had the money given to him by Zhanil, enough on which to reach Bhellin and live while he sought employment. While he had no intention of squandering it, he figured an hour with a woman would only cost him a few coppers.

Ivrish was half a day's journey northeast along a road that led to Bhellin. Adeja could easily traverse the distance, and a little rain would hardly bother him. He weighed his options, and knew he would go mad if he stayed pent up in the sanctuary until spring.

Sephil encouraged his visit. "Go if you must," he said, "but be careful. I have heard the priests say the roads have turned to mud."

Just before sunrise, his belly full of hot porridge and wrapped in a warm cloak, given to him in payment for his work, Adeja left the sanctuary. Knowing thieves plied their trade even in a small town, he armed himself and took only enough coin to buy what he needed, leaving the rest in Sephil's keeping.

The gate, which Obiru neglected in favor of his warm bed, stood barred. Adeja debated going to wake the man before deciding to get a priest to unlock the heavy access door that stood off to the side. He gave his request to a novice near the chapel, where the household, minus Obiru, gathered for morning prayers, before returning to the gate to wait in the mist and light drizzle.

From the mist appeared a bent figure. An elderly priest hobbled down the path on his cane, a key ring clasped in his talon-like hand. Adeja rolled his eyes, unable to guess how this man was going to assist when, it seemed, he could scarcely see the door, much less move it.

"Patience," said the priest, his voice so soft Adeja strained to hear it. As he drew near, he tilted his face to squint at Adeja. "Quiet your young blood, and return quickly."

Adeja all but snapped at him to hurry up. "Are you going to need help with that door?"

A wistful smile appeared on the priest's face. His skin, as paper-thin as an onion's, was crisscrossed with fine lines. "Do not stray too far from he whom you love," he said.

Stomping his feet in the cold air, Adeja glared at him. "Do you need help?"

Somehow, the priest managed to push the thick oak door open unaided. Adeja murmured his thanks and slid past, never giving answer to the old man's prying. Those soft words, however, left him with a chill of doubt he quickly pushed aside as he hiked up the road leading northeast from the sanctuary.

* * * *

Darkness came early with the season. Afternoon faded into a sunset that, through the clouds, cast a barely discernable smear of orange on the horizon. Before Adeja knew it, twilight descended on the land. Ivrish was a healthy distance behind him, the sanctuary on the hill before him dark except for the handful of lanterns indicating the life within.

With his exhaustion came the first flickers of apprehension. Not until now did it occur to him that the gate would be closed, the access door locked and no one on duty to admit wayfarers. Spring and summer saw supply wagons bringing beer, flour and cloth from the surrounding countryside and pilgrims traveling to various shrines throughout Khalgar. Only couriers and the occasional cart visited in winter, and by sunset all were safely indoors.

I shouldn't have lingered as long as I did. Ivrish was larger and more prosperous than Adeja thought it would be. The town's one brothel served the sour beer he had come to expect in Khalgar, and the prostitutes were plain and tired-looking, but after an entire morning on the road he had no complaints. After a meal and drink, he spent an hour with the youngest in a narrow room, sucking her nipples while she rode him and made the rehearsed noises all prostitutes made.

Adeja hardly cared what sounds the woman uttered as long as she gave him pleasure, and three times she managed to arouse him. Each time he took her in a different position, sating his restless hunger, yet as he thrust into her he could smell other men on the girl's skin, in her hair and even in her kiss. Not that he had never shared a woman, or thought a prostitute exclusively his—only a fool or a naïve boy in the first flush of love ever believed such a thing—yet what he never noticed before he now found distasteful.

Love was not what Adeja sought in Ivrish. A prostitute's mouth was best when wrapped around his cock, not plying him with false endearments or compliments. This one did her job well enough, and as he appreciatively slapped the girl's buttocks in farewell, he did not ask her name and she did not offer it.

Spending the night in the cold was not a prospect Adeja relished. As he came up the road to the sanctuary, he drew a deep sigh of relief to see a lamp burning in the gatehouse. In the darkness he found the bell, rang it and waited. And waited, stamping his feet on the threshold as his breath turned to smoke.

A thickset priest peered out from a window to ask his business. Recognizing Adeja's voice, the man let him in through the access door. "At least you didn't get caught in foul weather," he said. "We had another traveler pass through before, though I daresay he's gone now."

Adeja paid no attention to his chatter. All he cared about now was hot food and a warm bed.

Supper had been served an hour before in the communal hall, but he was able to wheedle some leftovers from the cook, a dour man who fed him disapproving glances with his stew.

"For your fleshly indulgences you should go without," said Tham, "and spend tonight considering a more spiritual path."

From what Sephil told him about what the priests did together in the darkness, Adeja nearly choked on his bread at the irony. "If you'd let me keep a proper wife I wouldn't have to go out of my way for a casual fuck, would I?"

Tham grew red at the insult, yet held his tongue. Adeja was able to finish his meal in peace.

His belly full and his body weary from traveling, Adeja craved sleep. Before he returned to his cell, though, he thought it best to let Sephil know he had returned safely and reclaim his money.

Taking a lantern from the kitchen, he threaded his way along the empty halls and colonnades toward the priests' sleeping quarters. As a novice, Sephil should have slept in the dormitory with the other novices, but as a prince he rated a private cell. With a chuckle, Adeja reflected that making love to him in the former would have been impossible.

As he rounded the corner, movement in the shadows made him pause. Holding up the lantern, he peered into the darkness that blanketed the colonnade and discerned a figure pressed up against the wall. Instinct and common sense told him something was amiss. A priest or novice would have simply kept walking.

"Who's there?" he asked.

Rather than step forward or answer, the figure darted away. Setting down the lantern, Adeja gave chase. He raced down the colonnade through an archway leading to a small courtyard that led nowhere. His quarry, whoever he or she was, obviously knew nothing about the sanctuary.

Without the lantern, it took Adeja's eyes a moment to adjust to the shadows. Then, crouched behind a pillar, realizing his or her mistake and trying to sidle past, the figure became visible.

"Show yourself," said Adeja. "I'm not going to hurt you."

No answer. Adeja feinted to the right, abruptly turning back to the left and lunging, grasping the intruder by one arm as he or she tried to escape; he felt solid muscle, and knew he dealt with a man.

The other arm came up, holding a knife that shone in the faint light, and slashed. Adeja ducked away from the blow, caught the man around the middle and tackled him to the ground. Whoever he was, the man was neither a priest nor an ordinary wayfarer.

Adeja tore away the man's hood before pinning him down. In the chaos he saw only a distorted face. Hard breathing and curses muttered in his native tongue. *He's Tajhaani*. Grasping the man's wrist, Adeja slammed it down hard against the pavement, forcing him to release the knife.

Priests, alerted by the noise, came running with lanterns. As the man tried to shove him off and run, Adeja seized him from behind and wrenched his head back. Bone cracked, and the man slumped to the ground at Adeja's feet.

"What is going on here?"

Adeja recognized the voice of the high priest, who strode over to survey the scene. Bedren drew his mouth into a tight line upon seeing the discarded knife and the man's broken neck. "Why did you kill him?"

Breathing hard, Adeja bent down and turned the corpse over to study the man's face. In the lantern light, he saw the man was dark, with features that matched his Tajhaani accent. "I didn't intend to, but he attacked me," he said, then explained everything that happened from the time he encountered the intruder along the colonnade.

One priest volunteered that Obiru earlier admitted a traveler who ate, rested, and left. As he gazed down at the corpse, the priest's brow furrowed at the realization that the man apparently had not departed. "He had a foreign accent."

"Like mine?" asked Adeja.

"Yes, like yours."

Adeja looked from him to Bedren. "This one's a long way from Tajhaan." His gaze fell on Sephil, who had come out with everyone else and now stood clutching his robe around him. "He was looking for something, or someone."

Bedren possessed enough sense not to question him in public. Quickly he sent a novice to wake Obiru while ordering three others to take the body away for burial. Everyone else was to return to their cells. When Bedren instructed Adeja to walk with him, Adeja seized the initiative and motioned Sephil to join them.

No one spoke on the walk from the courtyard to the high priest's office. Only when the door was securely closed did Adeja voice his suspicions. "This man might have been sent to kill the prince."

"How can you be certain?" asked Bedren.

"I can't think of any other reason why a Tajhaani wayfarer would be skulking around the living quarters in the dark with a knife."

Sephil sat frozen in shock. "Why would anyone attack me?"

"Why do you think?" asked Adeja. "Like it or not, you have enemies."

Looking away, Sephil anxiously chewed his lip. "How could they or anyone else possibly know where to find me? Only Zhanil knew about my being sent here."

"And whoever he assigned to accompany you," answered Adeja. "Any one of them could have betrayed you to the Tajhaani."

"You are making a serious accusation," said Bedren. Disapproval dripped from his voice. "No priest under my supervision would ever do such a thing."

"How else do you explain a man lurking in the shadows near the prince's room with a knife? We all know his cousin's taken refuge in Tajhaan and laid claim to the throne." Adeja felt his blood racing, chasing away his earlier exhaustion; he would get little rest tonight. "If Dashir sent an assassin to kill his cousin, I wouldn't be surprised." If only he had not killed the man straightaway, he might have been sure.

As Bedren started to speak, Sephil interrupted, "Dashir has no reason to kill me. My father struck my name out of the succession years ago. I do not even want the throne."

"Does *he* know that?" asked Adeja.

Sephil hung his head. "I do not think he cares."

"Brasidios never made public his decision regarding Sephil, so doubt might exist as to who is the rightful king. He did adopt Dashir as his son and appoint him Crown Prince when Zhanil died," said Bedren, "but again, from what I understand, he did not know his younger son was still alive. Whether this would have made any difference, no one can say. Whatever doubts he may have, Dashir has strong supporters in Tajhaan and should not have to resort to murder."

"Unless he thinks I mean to come out of hiding and claim the throne," said Sephil. "If I could just communicate with him—"

"That would not be advisable." Bedren opened a cabinet, withdrew a decanter containing a clear red liquid and a glazed cup, which he filled and handed to Adeja. "Drink this. It is Mittosian wine and will calm your nerves."

Although it could not seem to produce a palatable beer, Khalgar was famous for its wines, a reputation borne out in the richly flavored liquid in the glass. After the first taste, Adeja stared at it, amazed. Any wine he drank was the cheap kind soldiers could afford, but this was a good quality vintage that went straight to his head and made his nerves tingle.

Bedren poured a second cup for Sephil. "As I was saying, corresponding with Prince Dashir would be most unwise. I am certain he knows you do not intend to challenge him, but you could potentially become the pawn of a powerful rival. Simply by being alive you are a threat. Now that an attempt has been made on your life, you may not be safe here."

The cup quivered in Sephil's hands; he had not yet drunk from it. "What do you propose I do?"

"We could move you to another sanctuary," said Bedren.

"Dashir found him once," said Adeja, "and he'll find him again no matter how many times you move him. I still believe somebody here is sending information to Tajhaan. You don't send an assassin out to do a job without telling him where his victim is, and this man was too close to the prince's cell for it to be by chance."

"None of my priests—"

"Not *all* of the priests here have been under your authority," said Adeja. "You've got ten priests who came from Rhodeen with the prince, and who knows who they spoke to or what orders they were given before they left Shemin-at-Khul? I imagine Zhanil gave them instructions to evacuate his brother and look after him, but with the Turyar advancing I doubt he had time for much else."

"Prince Zhanil had time enough to write to me describing his brother's condition and ask me to shelter and train him in the priesthood," said Bedren. "Sephil already knows this. I showed him the letter as soon as he was well enough."

Going back to the cabinet, Bedren unlocked a drawer and drew out a small wooden box. "There is one other option." He set the box on the table and placed the key beside it. "In here are letters and tokens from Prince Zhanil. They were sent with his brother in the event they should be needed. The documents are all stamped with the royal seal. One is addressed to the king of Khalgar, the other to a maternal uncle a day's ride from here."

Sephil peered at the box, plain but for its sturdy lock, but did not try to open it. "Are you suggesting that I go to Bhellin?"

"It might be wise," said Adeja.

"Your brother clearly felt you might need to do so," added Bedren. "All I know for certain is that if your cousin intends to kill you, we cannot protect you here, and you will find no refuge with your uncle. Only the king can assure your safety."

Adeja drank from his cup again. "Something isn't right," he said. "Laban saw the man leave. How did he get back in with the gate closed? I don't think Obiru would have let him in."

His thoughts raced. Rope left outside to be used after dark, after the man studied the sanctuary, or a traitor from within who admitted the man through the access door. Tomorrow morning, assuming the weather held, Adeja resolved to go outside and examine the walls for traces of the former, while admitting he could do nothing about the latter.

"Laban did not have the watch the entire day, and Obiru is, I admit, not much of a sentry," replied Bedren. "I will have you assist him."

"He won't take kindly to it."

Bedren gave the slightest hint of a smile, the most Adeja had ever seen from him. "If we tell him that we have noticed his boredom and flagging spirits, he will welcome the company."

Whether Obiru would be so gullible, Adeja had no idea, and decided he did not care. He had kept watch with surlier men, and Obiru was more likely to fall asleep at his post than give him trouble.

"Sephil," Bedren was saying, "if you will accept my advice, I think you should seriously consider going to Bhellin to seek the king's protection. He is kin through your mother, and would not turn you away. This time you were fortunate, but there may be more attempts on your life. Next time you might not be so lucky."

"Ampheres will think I mean to announce my right to the throne," answered Sephil. "He will either kill me or use me as a pawn."

"That's ridiculous," said Adeja. "A kinsman is bound to shelter and protect you —"

Sephil slammed the cup down on Bedren's desk, sloshing wine onto his hand. "*Dashir* is my kinsman, too, and look what he has done!"

Bedren placed one hand on his shoulder while motioning Adeja to fetch a cloth from the cabinet with the other. "Calm yourself," he said. "Your cousin is an unscrupulous man who abandoned his family to death and capture—"

"I did the same!"

"That's different," said Adeja. "Zhanil sent you here for your own protection."

"Dashir has allied himself with powers who will not hesitate to use political assassination to their own ends," finished Bedren, "but you cannot assume this is the situation everywhere. Ampheres is a just and ethical man, and your brother apparently thought highly enough of his assistance to write to him on your behalf."

"You do not know what the letter says," Sephil said sullenly.

Adeja gritted his teeth. By now, a sensible man would have been on his horse and well away from the sanctuary. Sephil would hesitate so long that his cousin would not have to try very hard to have him killed, unless that was what he wanted; there was no telling whether or not his suicidal cravings had been excised. "Why should I need to read the letter? If Zhanil wrote it, he did it to protect you. Do as Bedren tells you," he urged. "He's giving you good advice."

Sephil looked at him. "It is still my decision."

"You're being stubborn."

"I do not wish to leave this place," replied Sephil. "I desire only a quiet life. If Dashir cannot see that I am no threat, then he is a fool."

"The only fool is you," said Adeja. "As a prince, you should know by now that you can't always have what you want."

Sephil clenched his jaw. "Do not speak to me as though I were a child," he hissed.

Adeja fought the urge to slap him. "Then stop behaving like one. Your cousin doesn't care what you want, and if he was here he'd kill you himself. If you want a long, peaceful life, you'd better start thinking sensibly and find yourself some powerful allies. Otherwise, I hope you're prepared to die."

Chapter Three

Sephil understood that Adeja and the high priest were impatient with him, and why, but held his tongue when it came time to explain his stubbornness. Never eloquent, he could not convey his need to live without the burden of his princely rank. If he left the sanctuary to appeal to Ampheres, he would find cold welcome in Bhellin. Surely his father corresponded with his wife's kinsman, and had spoken as poorly of his younger son as highly as he praised the elder. No matter what Zhanil wrote, Sephil knew Ampheres would despise him as weak and unfit to bear a royal title. As Brasidios had done, Ampheres would either lock him away or use him as a pawn in some vast political game.

Such thoughts filled him with despair. Death by an assassin's blade would be preferable to life as a royal prisoner.

It did not surprise him that his cousin attempted his life. If anything, Dashir would do it again. From Sephil's earliest memories, Dashir had always been malicious, shoving and teasing him whenever Zhanil was not looking. Maturity brought neither kindness nor wisdom, for when Sephil emerged from his long exile from court Dashir approached him and made his sentiments known.

"All these years we thought you dead," he drawled. "It is such a *pity* to find out otherwise."

Now that Sephil had time to consider Bedren's advice, he saw that writing to Dashir in Tajhaan would accomplish nothing except to confirm that he was, indeed, hiding among the priests of Abh in Ottabia. Bedren mentioned transfer to another sanctuary, but with a potential traitor selling information to Tajhaan, this option offered no guarantee of success.

Sephil grew wary, searching the faces around him for signs of treachery. As the days brightened with the approach of spring, he found it hard to dispel his personal gloom. Uncertainty dogged his meditations and studies as he tried to guess who among the Rhodeen priests would want to betray him.

At last, he decided Adeja must be mistaken, for there had also been several laymen on the journey from Shemin-at-Khul, men whose whereabouts were now unknown.

It is not fair, he thought. No matter what progress he tried to make, his family always managed to thwart his efforts. Just because his father was dead and his world upturned did not mean release from old constraints. More than once, he lapsed into petulance, sulking until both Adeja and Bedren told him to stop behaving like a child.

"A holy sanctuary is no place for a tantrum," said Bedren, "and such behavior does not become your station, either as a prince or a novice. If you aspire to be a priest, you must rise above this."

Sephil struggled to correct his behavior, but would not relent on the subject of going to Bhellin. Adeja and the high priest could accuse him of being petulant until the moon fell out of the sky, and perhaps they were right, but in some small way he *needed* to remain, to defy his enemies by insisting on his own path, even if it meant his death. All he wanted was for those closest to him to understand and let him be.

He also wanted to peer into the small box Bedren showed him and view the letters and tokens Zhanil sent with him, for although they were not meant for him, these were the only remaining mementoes of his brother.

I have not one word from him, not one relic. Adeja told him that from the moment the Turyar entered Rhodeen, Zhanil was preoccupied with the defense of the capital and outlying regions. He would have had no time for personal correspondence. "A good soldier focuses on what he has to do, not on being afraid or worrying about his loved ones," explained Adeja. "I doubt Zhanil even saw much of his wife or children in those last days."

And yet, Zhanil found time to write not only to Ampheres and their mother's brother, but to compose a lengthy missive to Bedren explaining the situation. More than once, Sephil pored over the letter, trying to pull from its formal language a personal message that did not exist. Zhanil spoke about him, but not *to* him, and he did not understand why.

That he had not known Zhanil better made Sephil's heart ache with regret. The most time they spent together were as children in the schoolroom, but Zhanil was seven years older, which meant he was far advanced in his lessons just as Sephil began his, and had his own tutors. Still, he was gentle, encouraging but clearly disappointed when he realized his younger brother would not match him in prowess or intellect. Their father demanded perfection from his sons, and he ruthlessly criticized Sephil for being a pale moon to Zhanil's bright sun.

Sephil spent his afternoons sitting under the shelter of the colonnade, his book forgotten in his lap as he watched the breeze stir the budding apple trees. His mind drifted, lingering over grim matters. The assassin's corpse had been taken away outside the walls and buried in an unmarked grave. While his life remained in danger, he need think no more on that particular man, yet the image of Adeja standing there in the darkness stayed in his head. Knowing Adeja had snapped the man's neck and expressed no remorse afterward made him afraid.

Why this surprised him, he did not understand, for as a soldier Adeja had killed many times before. Sephil told himself he was unnerved only because this was the first corpse he had ever seen.

But no, there was something more, and when he realized what it was, his apprehension only grew.

This time, he killed for me.

* * * *

"I am not trying to be difficult," murmured Sephil.

Adeja stretched his legs. Even with the blanket under them, the floor remained hard and the early spring evening was colder than he preferred, but the bed simply did not accommodate their lovemaking. "Difficult, foolish — it's the same thing."

"I will not be a pawn or prisoner of the Khalgari king."

"Your only other option is a corpse."

"I would prefer dying here than having to endure a living death in Bhellin," said Sephil. "Ampheres will be just like my father, and will shut me away or have me strangled in some dark corner to keep peace with Tajhaan. I want my last days to be happy ones."

Adeja found such fatalism foreign, even though part of him understood Sephil's desire to remain free. "You don't know that he'd do any of those things. Bedren told you he was a good man with a large family, and he's publicly expressed grief over the deaths in Rhodeen."

"What men do in public is different than what they do when others are not watching. I am sure people thought my father was a good man, too." Turning on his side, Sephil began to stroke Adeja's chest, drawing circles around his nipples with an idle fingertip. "Please, I do not want to talk about it anymore," he said. "Do you know it has been nearly a year since we first met?"

Women marked occasions like that. Men only noticed when their women shrieked at them for forgetting. Adeja wondered how a twenty-year-old prince could remain so sentimental and naïve after all he had been through. *I should've thrown him over the back of a horse three months ago and ridden for Bhellin.*

To avoid a scene, Adeja grunted acknowledgement. *I hope he doesn't expect me to give him a gift.* Women always wanted trinkets or flowers, and it would not have surprised Adeja to find Sephil desired the same. "Should priests be thinking about such things?"

Sephil kissed the skin just above his nipple. "I am just a novice, and the servants of Abh do not have to remain celibate."

Adeja squirmed as his lover began flicking his nipple with a pointed tongue. "Ah, so *that's* why you chose this god instead of some other!"

"You know that is not true!" laughed Sephil.

He knew all too well how to rouse a man's spent desire, a dubious quality in an aspiring priest. Under his skilled hands and mouth, Adeja quickly grew hard. In a very short time he had Sephil pinned to the floor and was entering him.

"And to think," gasped Sephil, wrapping his legs around Adeja's waist, "you were so reluctant in the beginning."

In response, Adeja thrust harder into him. *More fuck*, he thought, *less talk*. He spent so many nights sleeping in Sephil's cell that he hardly saw his own bed anymore. Bedren did not wholly approve, for while the priesthood of Abh did not mind occasional intimacy, they frowned on anything that could be construed as cohabitation. Not that Adeja cared what they thought. He was no priest, he liked sex, and as long as Sephil was willing so was he.

He took no more trips to Ivrish, instead spending his days watching the gate with Obiru, patrolling the outer walls and observing anyone who entered the sanctuary. With the arrival of spring, supply wagons were once again regular visitors, as were couriers bringing correspondence from Bhellin and other parts of Khalgar. The latter he watched carefully, noting which priests interacted with them, and who received letters or sent them.

In yet another show of disapproval, Bedren claimed these activities were intrusive even when Adeja explained that the assassin had not climbed over the wall but had help from within.

"You are making the brothers nervous," said the high priest. "I will not have it."

Adeja remained unflustered. "If they're nervous they may think twice before trying anything."

"This sanctuary is a refuge from such cares," Bedren said stiffly, "and it will not do to encourage this behavior. A far better course would be to remove Sephil to Bhellin or another sanctuary. Since you share his bed at night, I assume you also have influence over him. While you are pleasing yourself, you might take the opportunity to convince him."

Apparently he did not understand how naïve or self-absorbed Sephil could be, and Adeja never explained to him how their meeting came about as a result of the prince's selfishness. One could only speculate how different Sephil might have been had he received more responsible guardians, or not been locked away and ignored for three years.

Nor did Bedren realize that while Sephil might enjoy talking during sex, Adeja found it interfered with his pleasure. When he was hard he was more likely to silence his partner with a rough kiss than continue the conversation, and when he was done he usually fell asleep.

He climaxed into the shuddering body under him, panting into the lips that sought his. Sephil groaned, clasping him tightly as he writhed through his orgasm, then releasing him with a drowsy smile. "That was good," he murmured.

Adeja rolled off him. "No more, or I won't be fit for duty in the morning."

As Sephil rose from the blanket and moved toward the wash basin, in the darkness he stumbled over the sword Adeja left on the floor beside them. He hissed, cursing softly. "Can you not put this somewhere out of the way?"

"An assassin is hardly going to wait while I go looking for it."

Water sloshed in the basin. "I do not know that anything is going to happen."

Adeja sat up and took the cloth Sephil brought him. "A man doesn't try to kill his enemy and give up after the first attempt unless he didn't have much nerve to begin with." He tossed the cloth aside, fumbled for the sword and stood, wincing at his stiff joints. "I'm going to the bed if you want to come. This floor makes my back ache."

Once bundled into bed together, Sephil resumed the conversation. "You never told me why you became a soldier."

"Because I make a lousy stonemason," answered Adeja.

Sephil lightly punched his arm. "I am serious. I want to know. Why does a man choose to live such a hard life?"

"I *was* being serious. I can work with stone if I have to, but all the time I was in my father's house I wanted more, and the only way I could get it was by joining the army," said Adeja. "The problem was that the army in Tajhaan isn't what it used to be. There were no great wars to fight, no spoils to be won. I got tired of patrolling city streets and breaking up drunken brawls between neighbors, so I left. I hired myself out as a mercenary in Dhahar, and when I got tired of breaking debtors' arms for the moneylenders, I went to Rhodeen."

"You broke arms?"

"Yes, and kneecaps, when I had to. I was a debt collector, squeezing unscrupulous merchants and clerks for money they claimed not to have. I was rather good at it, too."

Sephil rolled over and peered down at him. "You enjoyed the work?"

"If you knew the kind of men I had to deal with, you wouldn't ask. Yes, I beat them, broke a few bones and told them I'd come back if the money wasn't paid, but I never threatened their women or children, not like some men did," said Adeja. "Go to sleep, Sephil. I'm not half the animal you think I am."

In the small hours before dawn, Adeja roused to the faint turning of the latch. On occasion, Sephil climbed over him to use the privy at the end of the colonnade; the jostling elicited grumbling from Adeja and threats to return to his own bed, which he never carried out. But no, his lover still lay pressed against his back, snoring softly.

Someone else was entering.

The door opened a crack. Adeja's hand crept down to the floor and quietly slid the short sword from its scabbard. Lying very still, every nerve poised to strike, through slitted eyes he studied the dark form that slid into the room and shut the door; it lacked the robed silhouette and unobtrusive movements of a priest.

Three months was long enough for someone in the sanctuary to communicate with Tajhaan, and for Dashir to send a second assassin.

As the shadow moved forward, it took on mass. Adeja heard muffled breathing, and could smell wool and leather. Closer it came, apparently not realizing that two occupied the bed rather than one, until in the thin moonlight coming in through the narrow window Adeja discerned the gleam of metal.

Throwing off the blanket and lifting his sword, Adeja sprang up from the bed with a shout that startled both the intruder and the sleeping Sephil. The man, cursing in Tajhaani, stumbled back into the wall. Behind Adeja, Sephil cried out as he bolted upright in bed.

"Adeja, what—?"

There was no time to answer. When metal jarred against Adeja's sword, he knew someone had warned this intruder that his intended victim was guarded. Compounded by the darkness and narrow space, Adeja could already see this would be no easy fight.

"Sephil!" he shouted. "Get your robe on and get Bedren—anyone!"

Behind him, he heard panicked breathing and shuffling. As Sephil bounded off the bed, the intruder lunged to the left to catch him. Adeja heard a cry half a second before he slammed his body into the man and sent him crashing into the wall.

No light to see and no time to ask if Sephil was hurt. The intruder lunged back to his feet, his sword swinging up in an arc that caught the moonlight. Adeja ducked and parried.

Off to the side, the door wrenched open and Sephil stumbled into the night, crying out the alarm. Once again, his attacker went for him, reaching the doorway before Adeja caught him. His sword came up, the flat of the blade striking the man's head with enough force to drop him to the ground. The man's blade clattered to the threshold after him.

Lanterns appeared along the colonnade. Roused by Sephil's alarm, priests emerged from their cells and novices, bleary with sleep, ran up from their dormitory.

In the light, Adeja saw the figure sprawled on the ground before him. The man was neither dead nor senseless, but moving, trying to crawl toward the priests. Stepping over him, Adeja smashed the hilt of his sword into the knuckles of the hand reaching for the fallen blade, and with his toe nudged it safely beyond reach.

He bent over the man and tore off the scarf the would-be assassin had worn to muffle his breathing. Jerking the man's arms behind his back, he bound his wrists. Seizing his prisoner by the hair, he then dragged the man groaning into the courtyard.

Not until a priest threw a blanket around him did he realize he was naked. As Bedren approached, Adeja turned to acknowledge him and saw Sephil at the high priest's elbow, wrapped in his robe and clutching his arm. Blood seeped through the wool. Shock painted his face white, but it seemed more from events than actual injuries.

"I've got him," said Adeja, "but I'll need a room to keep him." When his captive began to squirm and curse, Adeja kicked him.

After dispersing the gathered priests and novices, Bedren directed Adeja to a storage room far from any living quarters. Whatever was to occur, the high priest apparently did not want his household to be part of it. Sephil trailed along, until Bedren ordered him to go see about his wound.

Glancing down, Sephil noticed the blood. Bedren caught his other arm before he could faint and flagged down a passing priest.

"Go with Darinthes," said Bedren. "He will take you to the infirmary. Adeja, the storeroom is this way."

Once inside the storeroom, Adeja flung his prisoner into a corner and told Bedren to shut the door.

"If you intend to torture or otherwise hurt him," said the high priest, "you will have to do it outside the sanctuary grounds. The priesthood of Abh does not approve of such measures."

Adeja was in no mood to humor sanctimonious drivel and, binding the captive's ankles together with a length of twine, immediately ignored Bedren. "Well, dog," he said to the man in Tajhaani, "are you going to tell me what I want to know or do I have to hurt you?"

"Fuck you," the man hissed. He did not have the look of a soldier, but rather a back alley cutthroat whose knife was sharper than his wits. Such men exuded bravado, while true courage eluded them. A few blows, some threats delivered in the proper tone, the press of a blade against an artery at the right moment and the man would tell Adeja everything he wanted to know.

Adeja teased his jaw with the tip of his sword. "You might want to think about being a bit more polite," he said. "Tell me, how are things with the royal family in Tajhaan these days? I've been away such a long time."

When his query elicited no answer, Adeja jammed a fist into the man's stomach. Bedren blanched at the prisoner's gasping and retching. He moved toward the door. "I will not stay for this."

"He's not as tough as he wants us to think. It's not going to take much to get him to talk," replied Adeja, "and I think you'll want to be here for whatever he says."

"You will not cut him."

"Not in here, no, but what I do with him outside the sanctuary is my business, and if he doesn't give me what I want, I'm going to take him out and start carving him up." Turning his attention back to the man, Adeja lapsed once again into Tajhaani. "Now that we've made it clear that you're going to talk, why don't we start by you telling us your name?"

"Dhavi," growled the man.

"A nice name, Dhavi," said Adeja, "though I doubt it's your real one. No matter, though. I suppose you already know who I am."

Dhavi bared his teeth. "You're the soldier who fucks the prince."

"A pity you didn't remember that when you stole into his room," said Adeja. "Now tell me, how *is* the cutthroat business in Tajhaan? It mustn't be very good, if you have to look for victims all the way north in Khalgar."

"Why the fuck do you care?"

Adeja caressed his cheek with the sword. "Now, how are we to be friends if you keep cursing at me like that?"

"Why don't you just hurry up and kill me?" hissed Dhavi. "You're going to do it anyway."

Holding the sword tip steady over the pulsing artery in Dhavi's throat, Adeja smiled. "Ah, but there are ways of killing you, and then there are *other* ways, if you understand my meaning. I used to work for the moneylenders in Tajhaan, so believe me, I know all about pain. Now let us talk about the royal family, and the people who helped you."

* * * *

Though he did not want it, Sephil drank the syrup Darinthes handed him and let numbness overtake him as his wound was laid bare, washed and dressed. He winced and tried to jerk away as the healer applied a stinging ointment, but in his lassitude offered little resistance. Once the discomfort subsided, he felt nothing at all except the pressure of the dressing Varol wound around his arm. He could not even remember where he was or why.

As he lolled against the pillow, trying to remain awake, Darinthes stayed beside him to offer encouragement. "It is but a scratch, Sephil. In a few weeks it will be completely healed and you will never know it was there."

Muffled in the distance, Sephil heard the bell calling the sanctuary to morning prayers; he managed to open his eyes long enough to see weak daylight coming in through the window. *But it was night when I lay down*, he thought. Darinthes patted his hand, murmured something and left his side. A door closed, but like everything else it seemed very far away.

Sephil drifted in the heavy place between consciousness and sleep, heedless of the passing time. People moved in the background, going about their business, and unraveling threads of conversation which he could not follow for very long.

"…you give him so much for just a little scratch?"

Recognition made him stir, but he could not put a name to the male voice floating nearby.

"Vanol thought it best after last night's events."

Sephil forced his eyes open. The large room with its multiple beds momentarily confused him, until he recalled the word *infirmary*. Tightness around his arm reminded him why he lay in this bed and not his own.

At the foot of his bed stood a handsome, dark haired man, and next to him a tall priest. "Adeja, what are you doing here?"

The first man nodded. "How do you feel?" he asked.

His arm throbbed when he tried to move it, and for a moment he could not quite recall how he had been injured. Memory conjured darkness, a faceless attacker lunging at him before he could escape and raise the alarm. Another image came to him: Adeja standing naked over the man, pinning him down and binding him with his own scarf.

Sephil swallowed, licking dry lips. "What happened?" he rasped. His voice felt thick in his throat.

The mattress dipped as Adeja sat down beside him. His hair was damp, and he smelled freshly washed. "Someone tried to kill you again, of course."

Bedren hovered over Adeja's shoulder. "You are no longer safe here, Sephil."

"The brothers are getting your things together," said Adeja. "We leave for Bhellin in the morning."

"No, I do not—"

"You don't have a choice. Your enemies aren't going to stop, and I can't keep killing assassins like this."

111

The appearance of a novice healer with food and drink brought an abrupt end to the conversation. Both Adeja and Bedren stayed while Sephil choked down the porridge and ale. Vanol came over, inspected the bandage and pronounced him fit to leave the infirmary, which he did, wobbling on Adeja's arm. "I wish they had not given me so much medicine," he murmured.

All he wanted was to return to his cell and sleep, but instead Adeja led him to Bedren's office, where the high priest opened the cabinet, withdrew the wooden box and set it on the desk before him.

Inside were two sealed packets and a cloth-wrapped object. The high priest held up the packets. "One is addressed to your uncle Olmor, the other to King Ampheres. Zhanil said they are identical, and ask for support and protection. Your brother did his best to prepare for whatever needs you might have, Sephil. He could not foresee your cousin taking refuge with Tajhaan instead, and trying to kill you."

Bedren undid the velvet to reveal a golden seal ring. "Prince Zhanil sent this to help you. I am told it was his."

Sephil picked up the ring. The royal Sun of Rhodeen etched into the ring's sapphire cabochon mirrored the image impressed into the two wax seals on the packets. Although he had seen the ring many times before, he was never allowed to hold it. "This is the seal of the Crown Prince," he said softly. "Why would Zhanil send this with me when he needed it?"

"I don't know," answered Adeja, but his tone suggested otherwise. "You'll have to present it to the Khalgari king."

"I will have to accompany you," said Bedren. "Should you go alone, a young man and Tajhaani soldier traveling without an escort, I doubt you would make it through the palace's first gate, much less be received by Ampheres."

"How many priests do you intend to bring along?" asked Adeja.

"Seven of us will be sufficient, I think."

Bedren took back the seal and placed it with the letters in the box. Sephil wondered if he would ever see it again.

Able to walk unaided now, Sephil attended evening prayers before Adeja escorted him back to his room. No evidence of last night's struggle remained. "What did you do with the man?" he asked.

"I questioned him."

If that meant torture, Sephil preferred not to know. "Did you kill him?"

"Not yet."

"But you will?"

Adeja sighed. "What do you think, Sephil? I can't let him live."

Hearing the impatience in his lover's voice, Sephil felt foolish. After all, he himself was no innocent in such matters, having sent a previous lover to the forlorn stronghold of Mekesh where a Turya arrow ended his life. In his meditations, Sephil spent hours revisiting his transgressions, and though he could not say whether he consciously intended for Bedez to die, he knew must accept responsibility for that life lost.

How Adeja could kill without remorse, he did not understand. The military life seemed to strip men of their qualms. "Will you stay tonight?"

"I have business to finish before we leave. There are no strangers in the sanctuary now, and the gate will be watched through the night. You'll be safe enough."

"I did not think there would be another attempt tonight." Sephil swept the colonnade with his gaze, knowing tonight was the last night he would ever spend in the sanctuary. He could have easily spent a lifetime here, quietly studying, meditating and attending to the small tasks the priests gave him, but it was not to be. "I wish we did not have to go."

Adeja made no answer. It was not necessary. Sephil knew he would not miss this place.

* * * *

Adeja wiped the knife clean on the tarpaulin and returned to the access door where Obiru awaited him. "Nasty business, eh?" asked the guard. While Adeja hauled his prisoner to the gate and outside, an anxious Obiru stood aside for them. For all his talk, he had no stomach for violence, and did not watch Adeja slit Dhavi's throat.

When Adeja did not reply, Obiru filled the silence with more questions. "Are you just going to leave him out there?"

"For the night," grunted Adeja. Sensing his companion was about to speak again, he gestured for silence. "I'll send someone to bury him tomorrow."

After packing his few possessions and looking in on the sleeping Sephil, Adeja considered his next move.

From the beginning he knew it was a priest who opened the gate for both assassins. Now he had a name. That the man was from Rhodeen did not surprise him, or his proximity to Sephil, but the betrayal left a foul taste in his mouth nevertheless.

113

Bedren must be told, though how to tell him was another matter altogether. The high priest gave no weight to Adeja's suspicions, preferring to rely on the sanctity of holy vows to keep his priests honest.

Anyone, even a priest, could be bought for the right price, reflected Adeja.

He dozed for a few hours, and rose at dawn to wash and eat. Sephil met him outside the chapel, his belongings in a leather bag slung over one shoulder; his other arm he carried in a sling. "Vanol said I should wear this when I ride," he explained. "It seems a lot of fuss. My arm does not even hurt much."

"It will in the saddle," said Adeja.

A novice approached them with a message: Bedren awaited them in the outer courtyard by the gate. The high priest wore trousers and boots under a short, belted robe, and the six priests accompanying him were similarly dressed. Three of the four horses carried saddles. The other, a sturdy Khalgari pony, patiently bore the bundles two novices slung to its back. Most of the party, it seemed, would go on foot, an arrangement Adeja did not like at all. Priests were not soldiers. They were not used to marching, and it would take days longer than it should to cover the distance to Bhellin.

Bedren instructed a novice to take Sephil's bag and led him to the smallest mount. "She is old but fit and extremely docile," he said. "Adeja, you will ride the chestnut. I will take the black."

From the pensive look Sephil gave the mare, Adeja could see he was unaccustomed to riding. "It isn't as hard as it looks," he said.

"I know," answered Sephil, "but I have not ridden in five years."

Gazing past the mounts, Adeja studied the six priests. Against his advice, they included two men from Rhodeen. "Not them," he said, pointing.

"Kalion and Lathian are trusted—"

"Not this one." Before Bedren or anyone else could protest, Adeja crossed the distance separating him from the two men, seized Kalion by the collar and shoved him up against the nearest pillar.

Everyone in the courtyard paused. By now, he wryly reflected, the sight of him manhandling an enemy should have been commonplace.

"Adeja, let him go," ordered Bedren.

Adeja pretended not to hear. He did not have leisure to exercise tact.

Tightening his grip on Kalion, he asked, "Tell us, how much did the Tajhaani pay you to betray the prince?"

Chapter Four

"Adeja," Bedren said sharply, "I ordered you to stop."

"I don't take orders from priests, especially when there are traitors about."

Standing close enough to feel the heat of Adeja's anger, Sephil did not know what to think. That Kalion would betray him to his cousin was outrageous, but the sight of the priest shoved up against a pillar with Adeja's knife at his throat cowed him into silence.

Kalion appealed to Bedren with desperate eyes. "I-I am not—"

Adeja slammed him into the pillar hard enough to elicit a groan. "That's not what our Tajhaani friend told me. Why don't you tell us all how you let him in the gate after dark and told him which way to go?"

"He lies, I-I swear."

Sephil winced as Adeja sliced the top of Kalion's nose with the knife. *Not here, please.* "Let him down, please. You are hurting him."

"Let him down, Adeja, and put your weapon away," ordered Bedren, his voice filling the courtyard. "I will not let you treat one of my priests in this manner."

For all the acknowledgement Adeja gave, Bedren might as well have not spoken at all.

Blood streamed down Kalion's nose and chin to soak the collar of his robe. The terror in his eyes, and the cold fury with which Adeja threatened him with the knife tempted Sephil to run. The lover who held him with such care and passion could not be capable of such violence, though common sense told him it was so.

And Kalion, who watched over him in the worst days of his illness and nurtured his spiritual growth, could not *possibly* betray him. No, he could not believe that.

Swallowing his fear, Sephil took a step forward. "Adeja, why would Kalion hurt me? He has done nothing but look after me."

From the corner of his eye, he saw other priests and novices, who apparently caught word of the commotion, running up to watch. He heard their murmurs, then their exclamations at the sight of the knife in Adeja's hand.

"Traitors are found everywhere," Adeja said sharply. With the back of his hand, he struck Kalion across the face. Blood droplets flew onto the pavement. "How did the assassin know your name? Should I cut you again, or are you going to tell us?"

"I-I tended him when he came in. He—"

"Try again! He left before sunset, when somebody let him in. Are you going to tell us, or should I kill you here and search your corpse for the money the Tajhaani paid you?"

I have to stop him, thought Sephil, but the more he heard the harder he found it to move. Adeja did not invent tales, and someone from within *had* helped both assassins. That it might be Kalion made him ill.

Bedren moved forward to confront Adeja. "Enough of this," he barked. "I have said before that I will not tolerate bloodshed in the sanctuary. Unless you can prove these accusations, take your hands off him."

"Then search him, search his cell and his belongings," answered Adeja. "You should find at least three hundred *menar* somewhere among his things."

"Do it," said Sephil.

Bedren must have heard him, or wanted his own answer, for over Kalion's protests he ordered a search. Two priests forced a trembling Kalion to strip down to his loincloth and his traveling bag was emptied onto the pavement, while two others went to search his cell.

Sephil watched with growing anticipation, praying nothing would be found, but when a priest noted how heavy Kalion's discarded clothing was and tore open the seams to pull out the coins carefully sewn inside, doubt no longer remained, and no explanation Kalion gave could take away the sting.

"Was that all my life was worth to you, three hundred *menar*?" he cried.

"I meant no harm to you," said Kalion.

"You have a strange way of showing it." Adeja shoved him to the pavement and kicked him so savagely that Sephil thought he could hear the man's ribs breaking. "What do you want done with him? I've got a corpse outside that still needs to be buried. I say let him dig the grave, and we can bury them together."

Whether the question was meant for him, Sephil did not know, and did not trust himself to answer.

"You will not shed blood here," said Bedren.

"Then I'll take him outside and do it."

"No, he is under my jurisdiction and I will punish him." Bedren brushed past Adeja and, seizing Kalion under the chin, forced the man to meet his gaze. "Answer the prince's question: was money all that his life was worth to you? He trusted you. You betrayed him, and worse, you betrayed his brother who trusted you to look after him. Why in the name of the god would you do such a thing?"

Clutching his side in pain, Kalion gasped for air. "In Rhodeen, there were men who wanted to know where the prince was being sent. I saw no harm in telling them."

His words ended in a grunt as Adeja kicked him again. "And you saw no harm in opening the gate for a few *assassins* as well, is that it?"

Kalion hung his head and did not answer. Sephil wanted to grab him, shake him and demand an explanation, but was trembling so hard he did not trust himself to move.

Rather than force the issue, Bedren released Kalion. Turning and raising his voice so everyone present could hear, he announced, "Kalion will bury the dead with his own hands. Afterward he will be confined to a solitary cell for a period of three months, and until such time as we deem his penance done, he will keep a vow of silence. Kalion, get up and dress yourself. Your life belongs to the god now, and no man or priest may touch you."

With those words, Adeja sheathed his knife and moved aside. Obiru pushed his way through the crowd to lead Kalion back into the sanctuary while Bedren quickly made arrangements for another priest to take his place.

Sephil stood frozen until Lathian, another Rhodeen priest, took him by the arm and gently steered him to a place where he could sit down. A short time later, Bedren came to inquire after him. "I do not blame you for being upset, Sephil. I know what a betrayal this is for you."

"You should have made him tell you why he did it," said Sephil. "Three hundred *menar* is all I was worth to him?"

Bedren laid a gentle hand on his shoulder. "I will look into the matter when I return. Perhaps solitary confinement and enforced silence will persuade Kalion to speak."

At midmorning, they departed the sanctuary. Sephil averted his eyes from the barren patch of ground under the walls where Kalion, working under the watchful eyes of Obiru and four priests, scratched in the dirt with a shovel to bury the dead assassin. The sight merely reminded Sephil how wrong he was to place his trust in anyone.

I should ride off alone, he thought, *and find a place where no one knows me or has ever heard of Rhodeen.*

It was a wild notion which he quickly dismissed. He was no Zhanil, capable of finding his own way in the world when he could not properly wield a sword and had not ridden a horse in five years. The mare Bedren assigned him was docile, but he had never been an expert rider and was ashamed to admit that horses made him nervous.

Sephil spent his first journey through Ottabia lying semi-conscious in a covered wagon and saw little of the landscape. Now he marked the green shoots thrusting through the earth along the hills, transforming the countryside. Tiny flowers appeared amid the brush, and small streams followed the bending road. More than one priest told Sephil that other parts of Khalgar were as lush as Rhodeen, and that the sweetest grapes were grown in the lands east of Bhellin.

"What a marvelous city it is, Bhellin," said Shemil, who walked beside his mare. "There are grand temples and markets where you can buy anything you want, and everywhere it is so clean."

"Are you implying that other cities are dirty?" Sephil recalled what little he had seen of Shemin-at-Khul, which amounted to little more than the gleaming palaces, temples and pyramid platforms. Others told him about sprawling tenements, dusty streets and lively markets, but in his isolation, Rhodeen's ordinary people remained beyond reach.

Shemil nodded. "Some cities are filthy, yes. Your friend will take offense, I'm sure, but I found Tajhaan rather loud and dirty. Maybe I simply don't care for the desert."

"Have you been there?" If the priest could weave tales of his travels, Sephil would not have to dwell on the morning's events or how physically uncomfortable he was. Adeja was right to warn him about riding with his injured arm. The wound, which he initially thought was no more than a scratch, required twenty stitches, and would leave a thin scar once it healed. Under the bandage, soreness spread through his upper arm, but Varol assured him that as long as it did not become infected, the discomfort would pass.

Shemil did not disappoint him. "I was a cloth trader before I was a priest," he said, "so I've been many places. I did business for merchants, traveling with caravans and dealing wholesale in foreign markets. I visited Rhodeen many times to purchase silks and brocades from the warehouses there. I've been south to Akkil to buy fine Juvan linens and east to Thales for their cottons. I've been just about everywhere except Shivar and the Turya-lands. I don't know anyone who's been to the horse country and come back to tell of it."

Sephil would have liked to hear more about the Turyar than the biased fragments Adeja gave him. All anyone knew was they were persistent and merciless in battle, but surely any people who could harass the civilized world for centuries and conquer a kingdom like Rhodeen must be more than a mere bloodthirsty horde. Who were their kings and gods, he wondered, and what were their cities like?

In the early afternoon the party arrived at Ivrish. Because the day was pleasant, the party did not enter the town, but stopped to eat and rest under a stand of oaks overlooking the town and its fields. "Tonight we will stop in Yalaca," said Bedren. "It is only another five or six hours from here."

With his stiff muscles and bandaged arm, Sephil had difficulty dismounting. Adeja helped him from the saddle, but they did not speak to each other and the air between them felt awkward.

Adeja stayed long enough to make certain Sephil could walk unaided; he spent the remaining time tending to the horses and patrolling the hill. Sephil claimed a place under an ancient oak. With his good hand, he smoothed down the grass, and started at the brown snake that coiled and slithered out at his movements.

"It is harmless," said Bedren, seizing the reptile and tossing it aside as he approached. "In the House of the Snake Mother they keep deadly vipers for the oracles, but you will not find them in places like this."

In warmer weather, garden snakes sometimes crept onto the sanctuary grounds, where Sephil avoided them. He was more afraid of the rodents that scuttled about in dark corners, chewing everything in sight and leaving droppings that he and the other novices had to sweep up. Varol warned him that such creatures spread disease, and a bite from one could bring madness and death.

Bedren stayed close, sharing his bread, dried meat, and ale. Sometimes he spoke, but it was a long time before Sephil felt like talking.

"Why did he do it?" he murmured.

"If you are referring to Kalion, I do not know," admitted Bedren.

"But why would a priest need all that money when there is nothing to spend it on? Kalion spent all that time teaching me to renounce worldly things, and yet he could not even live by his own precepts."

"Men find it easy to preach, Sephil, but difficult to follow a virtuous path. We all have our temptations."

Sephil looked across the millet and wheat fields toward the town with its neatly laid out houses and streets. "I never did anything to him. Why should he want me dead?"

"I suspect Kalion harbored some ambition that drove him to betray you," answered Bedren. "If it is any comfort to you, I do not think there was any malice on his part. When I return, I will speak with him and see what I can discover. By then, Kalion will have had plenty of time to contemplate his actions."

"If my enemies could attack me in a sanctuary, how much worse will it be in Bhellin?" Sephil caught his lower lip in his teeth to avoid articulating his greatest fear: that Bedren was taking him to the Khalgari capital to sell him to his enemies.

Bedren nodded. "I cannot promise you that you will be safe in Bhellin. I only know what would have happened had you remained with us," he said. "Ampheres has not publicly stated where his sympathies lie, so we will go cautiously."

"And if he sides with Dashir?" asked Sephil.

"Then we will find some way to change your identity and hide you so no one ever finds you." Bedren paused, took a swig of ale from the jug next to him, and continued, "I would not be surprised if you told me you cannot trust anyone, even me. I do not blame you. However, there is still one person whom you know you can trust."

On the opposite side of the hill, Sephil spied Adeja sitting with Shemil and two other priests. "I do not like seeing him as he was this morning."

"That is what a soldier does, Sephil," answered Bedren. "Such violence is part of his world, and what he did yesterday and this morning was necessary."

"I thought you disapproved," said Sephil.

"I do not condone bloodshed within the sanctuary, but what happens outside the walls is another matter. Sometimes a man must walk a dark road to achieve a greater good."

"Eharideos states that a man cannot sacrifice his principles for his own benefit."

"Philosophy does not always mirror life," said Bedren. "Other gods are more exacting, but Abh understands that a man's morals may be fluid according to the situation if he acts without malice. Adeja's actions this morning were violent, but they were not evil because they were meant to protect others.

"I do not wish to belittle you, Sephil, but the truth is that you are still young and impressionable. When I was your age, I devoured books on philosophy and theology, and I thought I knew best how men should live. I thought I was pious, when in reality I was merely arrogant. Even now, I do not pretend to know everything.

"You must remember that scholars like Eharideos and Ulishban were old men when they wrote about the nature of the human soul and renunciation of all desire, and that it took them a lifetime of experience and contemplation to set down what they learned."

As Sephil pondered this, his thoughts turned to the circumstances under which he had been studying. Kalion had tutored him, and now Sephil wondered if everything he had learned was suddenly rendered invalid. Bedren could be playing the same game with him, pretending to mentor him while secretly preparing to betray him.

Once again, his eyes fell on Adeja, who realized he was being watched and acknowledged Sephil with a nod. *Perhaps he is the only one in the world who can be trusted*. The thought so depressed Sephil that he banished it at once.

"Let me caution you that once we reach Bhellin," continued Bedren, "you will have to be very circumspect in your dealings with Adeja."

Realizing the high priest was watching him, Sephil flushed and looked away. "I know you do not approve of the time I spend with him."

"If that were so, I would not have allowed him to stay as long as he has. I think his presence has done you much good." answered Bedren. "However, Bhellin is not the sanctuary. It may be that you will have to become a prince once more, and a crown prince at that. If so, your conduct must be beyond reproach."

"I have not led an exemplary life," said Sephil, "and Dashir knows that. He will slander me no matter what I do."

"I imagine that all princes and public figures must endure slander, even your cousin," replied Bedren. "All I can suggest is that you forget what happened in the past and remember what you have learned as a novice. I find that people respect priests even when they do wrong, and those who did not know you in Rhodeen will find it hard to believe such rumors if you behave as though you are still in the god's service."

Sephil privately thought the Khalgari court would see through the façade. They would point and titter at him as his father's courtiers had done. Taking their cues from their king, who ignored his younger son in public and openly criticized him in private, the Rhodeen nobles had compared Sephil unfavorably with his brother and cousins; they even jested that the late queen must have slept with one of her husband's catamites to produce such a pretty, but useless prince. Brasidios had stifled the gossip about his wife, but offered no word in defense of his son.

When the hour passed, the party resumed its journey. They passed through Ivrish rather than skirt around the town, where the presence of so many priests drew a few murmurs but no hostility; Shemil quietly explained to Sephil that the townspeople assumed they were on pilgrimage. A frail man on crutches limped alongside Bedren's horse to touch his robe and ask his blessing, which the high priest gave by wordlessly brushing his fingertips over the man's head; the scene repeated itself a few more times before the party left the town.

Unaccustomed to riding, Sephil preferred to walk with Shemil. Neither Bedren nor Adeja, who argued that it would be difficult to escape should an enemy attack, approved this move. Sephil thanked them for their counsel and insisted on walking. However, by the time they reached Yalaca, he regretted being so stubborn. At the inn where they would stay the night, he shared a hot footbath with two other priests, ignoring Adeja's good-natured barbs when the man brought him his supper.

That night, Sephil slept soundly. The next morning, after Lathian helped him change his bandage, he did as he was told and climbed up onto the mare.

Once they were out of Yalaca, Bedren rode up alongside him and Adeja to explain what would happen once they reached Bhellin. "We should be safe in the temple there. I know the high priest, and he is trustworthy.

"Since we do not know where the king's sympathies lie, you cannot risk announcing yourselves outright. Sephil, you will be Velath, a novice who has gone to Bhellin to seek further training. If anyone asks, you are riding a horse because you were injured climbing a tree, and you have an accent because your mother was from Rhodeen. Adeja, you will be Shamuz, a guard from the sanctuary who traveled with us for protection. We will keep it this way until we are certain it is safe. I do not think I need to point out that you should not be seen together."

At noon, they stopped for lunch along a shallow stream. Sephil used his free hand to splash water on his face, while Adeja led the horses to drink. A few priests took off their shoes to soak travel worn feet, while others looked for a suitable place to sit and eat.

Once he was refreshed, Sephil climbed back up the embankment to sit beside Adeja, whose hair and neck were damp from the water he sluiced over his head. "Should I start calling you Shamuz now or should I wait until we get to Bhellin?" he asked.

Adeja shrugged. "As you like," he said. "I've used my father's name so many times I'm almost as used to hearing it as my own name." He took the flat bread a passing priest gave him, tore it in half and gave some to Sephil.

Sephil gazed at the bread in his hand before biting into it. "Why did Zhanil send his seal with me? As Crown Prince, he would have needed it."

"I don't know," Adeja answered through a full mouth.

"Tell me the truth. Now is not the time to spare my feelings."

Adeja swallowed and said, "Zhanil wouldn't have needed it if he thought the city would fall. A man can't look at a Turyar horde coming at him and *not* think about dying." He drank from the jug of ale beside him. "Even outnumbered, they can be deadly. Their tactics keep changing, and they have weapons no one else has been able to duplicate: bows that can punch arrows through armor, and knives they wear over their hands and wield like swords. If I never see another Turya again, I'll die happy."

When Adeja handed him the jug, Sephil wiped the rim with the hem of his tunic before drinking. Adeja chuckled at his mannerisms. "You never told me how many times you faced the Turyar."

"Five times," said Adeja. "I was still in Tajhaan. We were sent north to keep the trade routes open. For what we put up with, the pay was lousy, and that's when I decided to quit the army once my term was up and look elsewhere. After Dhahar, I enlisted in Rhodeen and got a post in the capital. Even then, I knew the kingdom's defenses wouldn't hold if the Turyar decided to launch a full-scale invasion. Why your father neglected places like Mekesh, I don't know. He fought the Turyar thirty years ago, so he should've realized the mistake he was making."

Sephil shook his head. No one ever discussed military matters with him, which came as no surprise. What little he knew would barely fill a scrap of paper. "You never told me what happened at Mekesh."

"I didn't want to upset you."

"Was it really that horrible?" asked Sephil.

"I wouldn't want to repeat the experience. We did what little we could to hold the fortress, but the Turyar attacked in the dark, throwing scorpions, snakes and burning arrows over the walls. I don't know how many there were," said Adeja, "but once they started coming over the walls I ran for my life. I'm not ashamed to admit it. I'm no coward, but I'm not a noble fool either."

"You do not mean to imply that Zhanil was a fool, do you?"

Adeja frowned. "Sephil, don't put words in my mouth that aren't there. I think his honor was very important to him, but he must've known how foolish it was to ride out against the Turyar the way he did."

Why Zhanil chose to end as he did, Sephil could not say, and had no answer for Adeja. "I still do not understand why he would send his seal with me. It could not be because he wanted me to be king." Sephil's throat closed around that last word, as inevitably it brought the mental image of his father. He wondered if Ampheres would be like him. "Surely he must have known that I did not want the throne, and would not make a good king."

"Wanting has nothing to do with it," said Adeja. "Princes have to do things they do not want all the time. As for not being a good king, with the Turyar entrenched in Rhodeen, all this business between you and Dashir about who has the greater claim to the throne doesn't matter. I don't know that either one of you is ever going to see home again."

* * * *

On the fourth day, the travelers left the hill country for a flat green plain dotted with woodlands and farms. In the distance, shadowed against a hazy horizon, loomed Bhellin. Three more days passed before the travelers reached its gates.

Bhellin was an immense city whose ten-foot thick walls stretched a length of fifteen miles. "On the royal estate are farms which can grow grain in time of siege," said Bedren, "and there are underground cisterns that store enough water to supply the city for a year."

Every quarter of the city radiated bright color: bands of azure and ochre striping whitewashed tenements, statues painted to look alive, and gleaming tiles set into the city's many gates. As the travelers passed under the arch of the massive Arvatates Gate, Sephil craned his neck for a closer look at the glazed blue-green tiles glinting in the sun.

Shemil had been right in praising Bhellin's cleanliness. As they passed through the city, the priest elaborated on the city's complex drainage systems, and explained the lucrative business in public bathhouses.

Bedren took them through a walled park into the temple district. As in Rhodeen, Abh was but a minor figure in the pantheon, so the temple presented a modest face among the larger edifices and religious complexes, and only a few worshippers were on hand when the travelers rode in through the gate.

Having been briefed early that morning, Sephil anticipated what would happen next. Bedren gave their names to the porter, who arranged for their mounts to be stabled. A steward found them accommodations. As a layman, Adeja was restricted to the gatehouse, while Sephil was assigned a bed in the dormitory with the other novices.

Upon leaving his companions, Sephil saw a physician, who informed him that his wound was healing nicely and that he no longer needed to wear the sling.

"When it begins to itch," said the man, "rub this salve into the scab."

Sephil took the jar of ointment and followed a novice to the dormitory, where he set his small bundle of belongings on his cot and sat down. His escort pointed to a wooden chest next to the cot where he could keep his things, and the communal wash basin at one end of the dormitory.

"The privy's down the corridor," said the young man. "I'm Orin, and there are five others who live here. They're all at their lessons now. You'll meet them later."

Orin looked no older than sixteen. From him, Sephil learned that the other novices ranged in age from thirteen to seventeen. In Ottabia, everyone knew his name and why he received special treatment, but here it would be different.

"The steward says I have to take you up to the high priest's office." Orin gave him a suspicious look. "You seem awfully old to be a novice."

Sephil gave him the tale he had rehearsed on the journey. "My father would not let me enter the temple. He died several months ago when the Turyar invaded Rhodeen and took our estate. The temple was the only place left that could take me in."

Orin smiled. "You were a nobleman? I knew there was a reason you talked so stiffly."

"Not a very important one," replied Sephil.

"Then why does the high priest want to see you?"

For this question, Bedren had assisted with the answer. "Because I became a novice so late, and I am so far behind. The high priests want me to receive some private tutoring so I do not hold everyone else back."

Orin led him across two courtyards and up a flight of stairs to the high priest's office. "Do you think you can find your way back when you're done? You'll find it's not a very big place."

Sephil nodded and thanked him before rapping on the door. Inside, Bedren and Adeja waited for him in the company of a short, vigorous man Bedren introduced as Avorim, high priest of Abh in Bhellin.

"Welcome to our humble establishment, Prince Sephil," said Avorim. "Bedren and your Tajhaani friend here have been telling me about your situation. Rest assured that we will do whatever we can to help you."

"Avorim has connections in this city I do not possess," added Bedren. "As Sephil knows, one cannot simply approach a king."

Avorim nodded. "There have only been two official announcements from the palace on this matter: one condemning the violence of the invasion, and the other expressing sympathy for the lives lost in Rhodeen. Neither one gives any indication where Ampheres stands regarding possible claimants to the throne. I know that he has been approached by Tajhaan and certain displaced Rhodeen nobles seeking his support, but thus far there has been no word.

"The first thing we must do is make discreet inquiries through the Rhodeen embassy to discover where they stand on the matter. Their officials have access to the court, and if sympathetic, they can ease our way. Above them are officials who control access to the royal person. We may have to bribe a great many people in order to gain an audience with the king."

"And how do you intend to do that?" asked Sephil. "You will need money and gifts. I do not think the temple can spare either."

"You are right," said Bedren, "and you will not like the solution we propose. However, we must take advantage of whatever opportunities the god grants us." From his saddlebag he produced a canvas pouch which he opened to reveal a mass of gold coins. "Three hundred *menar* is a goodly sum in Khalgar."

Sephil did not grasp his meaning until Adeja burst out laughing. "If only your cousin could see this," he said.

"What do you mean?"

"Dashir's going to pay your way into the king's protection and he doesn't even know it."

Chapter Five

"This is blood money," protested Sephil.

"And if anyone is entitled to it, it's you," said Adeja.

Personally, he thought Sephil was being far too particular, especially when the prince had very little practical knowledge when it came to money. "These men have to be bribed and the money has to come from somewhere."

"I know that," replied Sephil, "but I do not like being reminded where the money came from."

"Actually, I think it's rather quite funny."

Sephil stared at him. "How can you say such a thing? They tried to kill me, and—"

"They tried to kill me, too, remember?"

Bedren gathered up the coins and dropped them back into the pouch, which he placed into a locked box alongside the royal seal and letters. "It is not sinful to bend evil works to good," he said.

Other than this, Bedren showed too much common sense to be sanctimonious about the matter. Adeja already regretted not slitting Kalion's throat. The only worthwhile traitor was a dead one, and he did not believe the strict penance Bedren imposed would do any good.

Because he could not enter the inner temple after sunset, Adeja spent his nights in the musty gatehouse with only a dour sentry for company. During the day he visited with Bedren and the other priests under the guise of receiving orders, and went through the motions of worship and meditation that were expected of a temple guard. Otherwise he had nothing to but wait and grow restless, especially when he learned that he could not visit the local brothels.

"Your movements may be watched," said Bedren.

"Who in this city knows who I am unless somebody told them?"

Bedren remained unmoved. "For your friend's sake, curb your appetite. Until it is safe, you must behave like a temple guard."

"And you're telling me that temple guards *never* have sex?"

The only answer he received was a raised eyebrow.

"I made inquiries today," continued Bedren. "The Rhodeen embassy has declared for Dashir. As for the exiled nobles, some favor Dashir, some are undecided, while most support the claims of a nobleman named Melin Wesares, who evidently has some royal ancestry."

Adeja glanced toward the door to make doubly certain they were alone. "Sephil has no chance against either of them. I say we get him out of here and find him a quiet place where he can live his life in peace."

Lifting one finger, Bedren indicated that he was not yet done. "That does *not*, however, mean the *king* acknowledges these claims," he said. "He is said to have doubts about both. This is a promising development."

"Promising for whom?" It seemed the best option at the time, but Adeja increasingly regretted urging Sephil to come to Bhellin. "You know he doesn't want any part of this."

"As a prince, Sephil knows he has certain duties. Even now, he is not a private citizen," replied Bedren. "He is an unlikely king, but he is capable of fathering sons who could be raised to the throne."

All Sephil wanted was protection against his cousin, not to be used as a dynastic pawn. "I don't like this at all," said Adeja. "Dashir is bad enough. We don't need two or three other factions hiring assassins as well."

Bedren nodded. "Which is why we are being exceedingly cautious. Believe me when I say I mean to keep Sephil from those who would do him harm."

That evening, Avorim examined the seal ring and Zhanil's letter to Bedren before reiterating his assurances that all precautions would be taken. "This business with the embassy is a disappointment, but we are not yet defeated. I have a few contacts at court who can help us circumvent the Rhodeen ambassadors and approach the king more directly," he said to Sephil. "Just be aware that I cannot promise anything."

"We have been making subtle inquiries without mentioning your name outright," added Bedren.

Over the next week, Avorim made small bribes to certain viziers at court while telling them he knew of a Rhodeen nobleman attached to the royal household who had crucial information for the king. "Of course, they are skeptical," he explained. "So many expatriates desire the king's time and money that he is weary of the business. If we wish to proceed any further, we will have to disclose the prince's name."

Bedren turned to Sephil. "It is your decision."

"Have I any other choice?"

Adeja found his listlessness irritating. "Yes," he said sharply. "We can flee now."

Sephil looked at him. "You were the one who urged me to come."

"I changed my mind. All this hiding and skulking about doesn't reassure me."

"I would prefer to leave," agreed Sephil, "but I do not think I would be safe anywhere, even with you to protect me. Whatever happens, it must be now."

Avorim placed a reassuring hand on his arm. "As I said before, we will do whatever we can to keep you safe."

"Words aren't strong walls or an army of loyal men," said Adeja.

Sephil shook his head. "You are a soldier. You put your faith in walls and weapons and men, but I cannot rely upon those things. I do not know where or what to trust, only that I cannot flee as you would like. If you want to leave, I will ask Bedren to give you a portion of the three hundred *menar* and you can go as you please."

Adeja grumbled, toyed with the idea of leaving the prince, and did nothing. Sephil represented a knot of contradictions, willful one moment and insecure the next, yet something about him compelled Adeja to stay. "This is madness," he grumbled, and said no more.

Within a few days, Avorim returned to court, sought out an influential vizier upon whose discretion he could rely, and communicated his need to secure safe passage for a member of Rhodeen's royal family. Although the vizier could not accuse a high priest of lying, when Avorim gave the prince's name as Sephil Brasides, younger son of the dead king, the man refused to accept it as truth.

Avorim returned to the temple with a full account, which he readily shared with Sephil, Adeja and Bedren. "'Surely you have been misled,' Cileil told me," he said, "'for if this young man is truly a crown prince then why does he not come openly with a full entourage and gifts for our king?' What he meant, of course, is why did I not offer him more money?"

"Did you explain that I am in hiding for fear of my enemies?" asked Sephil.

"I told him as much as was necessary for him to know: that you had come to Bhellin to seek the king's protection, and that you bore tokens and letters meant only for him. Of course, right away Cileil wished to see them—to verify their authenticity, as he put it."

Adeja snorted. In his experience, viziers and other courtiers occupied the same treacherous niche as eunuchs. None of them could be trusted. "For all we know, he'll burn the letters and conveniently lose the seal."

Avorim nodded agreement. "I told him he could not see what was not meant for his eyes, but to soften the blow I offered him more coin and a bottle of fine Besarian wine from the cellar."

Bedren widened his eyes in mock horror. "Surely you do not mean to let him have one of the temple offerings?"

Avorim appeared no more concerned over this ritual lapse than his subordinate. "It is all in the service of the god, my friend. Cileil at court has quite the taste for Besarian white. I have already sent him one bottle, with the promise of another to follow if he drops a word in the king's ear and something comes of it." He sighed and spread his hands on the table. "Short of publicly appealing to Ampheres and possibly risking the prince's safety in the process, it is the best I can do."

What influence the vizier Cileil wielded at court, or whether he ever approached the king, no one could say. No word came from the palace, and Avorim kept his second bottle of wine.

As Velath, Sephil lived in the dormitory with Orin and seven other novices, among whom he studied, prayed and worked undetected. While he appeared to enjoy the experience, Adeja preferred that he not mingle so much with the novices, who might learn more than they should and sell the information to the Rhodeen embassy or some duplicitous noble.

Even when Bedren explained that separating Sephil from the others would arouse suspicion, Adeja remained unconvinced. As he saw it, the situation called for armed guards and strong defenses. Bhellin was no more secure from potential assassins than Ottabia, and in many ways it was even less so.

Another week passed. During the day, Adeja stationed himself in the second floor window overlooking the main gate to watch the flow of traffic in and out of the temple compound. Since he took his meals in the kitchen, he recognized the servants making their daily rounds to the market. Worshippers entered with offerings of wine, cloth or sacrificial animals. Among them came supplicants visibly afflicted in mind or spirit who came to ask the god for healing.

Because the novices took instruction in accepting offerings and ministering to worshippers, Sephil could not avoid interaction with the outside world. Adeja cautioned him to say as little as possible, and forbade him to accompany the other novices on their occasional excursions to the bazaar. Anyone who inquired was to be told that he could not leave the temple until he mastered all his lessons and earned the privilege.

Sephil made a face when he heard this. "Back in Rhodeen, I would not even have to lie. My tutors never let me do anything amusing until I finished my work, and then it was always too late. I enjoy my lessons, and tending to the people who come here, but still, I would have liked to see some of the city."

"You would not have liked the bazaar anyway," said Adeja. "Such places are often quite loud and dirty, and attract cutpurses and other low people."

As Adeja continued to watch the traffic from above, one man carrying a leather satchel slung across his chest caught Adeja's attention. The deep red of his livery and the serpent badge on his arm identified him as a courier belonging to the palace.

Adeja crept downstairs to follow the man. The courier did not stay long, delivering a letter for the high priest and leaving without waiting for a response. Whatever the message entailed, it apparently did not involve sending for Sephil, and Adeja returned to the gatehouse to resume his vigil.

There were many reasons a royal courier might deliver a message to the high priest of Abh, he told himself, reasons which had nothing to do with a fugitive prince of Rhodeen.

That evening, Avorim shared the letter with him and Sephil. Word had come from the palace, but while the message confirmed Adeja's suspicions, it also provoked confusion.

"Ampheres is aware of your plight," Avorim told Sephil, "but he has not announced his intention to send for you, nor does he acknowledge your place in the succession. He says only that you are not to leave the temple until further notice."

Sephil looked at the letter, then at Adeja. Anxiety drew worry lines across his brow. "I do not understand what he means to do."

"No, it is not clear," answered Bedren, "but we should not assume the worst based on this vague reply. This is a delicate matter, and the king must proceed carefully. Granting you a royal audience, even in secret, implies his support. Ampheres will want to be certain before he takes this step."

"Then why restrict my movements?" asked Sephil.

Silence pervaded the room as the priests considered this question. Adeja tackled the matter from a different perspective, knowing that the best way to protect something was to confine it. He shared his thoughts with the others. "This isn't necessarily the right answer, just the one that makes the most sense." Since he did not know the Khalgari king, only that the man was Sephil's kin through marriage, he could only guess what Ampheres intended.

His assurances did little to ease Sephil's apprehensions. "Then why does the king not say that in his letter? Perhaps he wants me confined here simply so he can get rid of me without anyone knowing."

"Sephil," said Avorim, "letters can be intercepted. Ampheres would not commit anything to writing that he fears his enemies might read. And he may not wish to be specific about protecting you, since that would imply support for your claim."

"If he wanted you dead, he wouldn't do it here," added Adeja. "A temple is no place to shed blood."

Sephil glared at him. "Dashir had no problem sending assassins into a sanctuary."

"Your cousin is an unscrupulous bastard."

Bedren cleared his throat. "Strong terms, but I agree with Adeja. Ampheres respects the holy precincts, and he is your kinsman, Sephil. The importance he places on family bonds is widely known."

"I will make some discreet inquiries and see what I can learn," said Avorim, "though I must caution you that if he is acting in secret there will be little information to be had."

As Adeja expected, the high priest's sources had nothing to offer. Whatever the motives behind his peculiar instructions, the king kept his own counsel. Avorim took pains to reassure Sephil that Ampheres might simply be acting from a need to keep his Rhodeen petitioners from learning of the prince's existence.

Sephil turned to Adeja. "What do you think?"

"I don't like the secrecy or waiting," answered Adeja, "but I also think if he wanted you dead he would've seen to it already."

That evening, Bedren accompanied Adeja from the outer temple back to the gatehouse. Along the way, the high priest drew him into a shadowed corner and dropped his voice. "I did not wish to further distress Sephil, but I have reason to believe we are all being watched."

Adeja was not surprised. "How do you know this?"

"I suspected something two days ago," replied Bedren. "I did not tell you sooner because I am not certain that this is such an evil thing. I believe the king wishes to learn more about Sephil before deciding what to do about him."

"Or someone else might be trying to identify him among the novices before killing him," said Adeja.

Bedren shook his head. "The servants and priests have already had weeks in which to observe the novices. Sephil is the only one who is the correct age, and the only one with Rhodeen blood. As for rival claimants, from what Avorim tells me about them I do not believe they would trouble themselves with a young man quietly living as a novice under an assumed name."

"Dashir didn't see it that way."

"Sephil threatens his position as legitimate heir, and you must also consider that he is living under the protection of a Tajhaani prince who has no trouble murdering rivals, no matter how unassuming they seem," explained Bedren. "As for the other claimants, Avorim has been giving them a close ear. He tells me their debates over their claims to the throne do not include any mention of Sephil. I think they either believe he died in Shemin-at-Khul, or they have simply forgotten his existence."

Adeja was not ready to trust in that. "Do you want me to watch the servants?"

"Your movements would stir suspicion, and we cannot risk that," replied Bedren. "I will observe them myself, and restrict their comings and goings if I feel their dealings are with anyone other than the king, but I do not think it will come to that. However, as we are being watched, I must caution you not to do anything that would compromise Sephil."

"You know we haven't been together since before we left Ottabia."

"Then continue as you have been doing, and be certain that you do not make reference to any relations you have had. We do not know what information the king has, or what he may suspect, but we do not wish to give him any cause for concern."

Adeja retired to the gatehouse, uncertain whether or not to be insulted. Bedren ought to know by now that he was shrewd enough to realize his lover's precarious position, and that he had the decency to respect it. Still, being so close without being able to touch or speak openly to Sephil enflamed his desire, and he spent many a night stroking his cock in the darkness. A tryst was out of the question, or Adeja would have already had his lover in some dark, isolated storeroom.

Perhaps Bedren realized the difficulty. A week later he called Adeja aside and gave him two *menar* and directions to the temple of Shalath. "Now understand that I am not sending you to slake your lust at some mere brothel," he said. "This is a place of worship, and when you submit to the priestesses they will make certain demands of you."

This was all Bedren would say, and Adeja was not about to waste the opportunity by asking too many questions. He already knew from comments made by the other guard that unmarried priests and temple guards were not permitted to consort with common prostitutes. Any sex they had must come through the sacred prostitutes of Shalath, the Khalgari goddess of love and fertility.

Given that temple guards were also not allowed to gamble, curse or drink strong liquor, Adeja could not see why any man would elect to take such a job. As for the priests, he knew they bent the rules to their own whim by copulating with each other in secret.

When he presented his coin and explained to the temple officials that he was a newcomer to Bhellin, Adeja received such thorough instruction on the rules and procedures of the temple that he briefly forgot where he was. The priests assumed he desired a woman, for they did not offer a choice and not until later did Adeja think to ask if boys were also available.

First he was taken to a series of subterranean tiled chambers and told to strip down to his loincloth, after which he followed a priest into a sweating room where he was ordered to sit on one of the tiled benches that lined the wall.

"You will purify and prepare yourself," said the priest. "Should you feel faint, this will help you."

Adeja looked at the bundle the man gave him, brought it to his nose and recognized it as sage. A servant came in to add glowing stones to the brazier, beside which stood a basin and ladle. The priest dipped the ladle into the basin and poured water over the stones. The brazier sizzled, releasing a cloud of steam into the already-humid air.

"I will leave you," said the priest. Bowing, he closed the door, leaving Adeja to wonder how long the purification was to last. Sweat beaded on his forehead; he swiped it away with moist fingers. *So much fuss for a simple fuck*, he thought sourly. *I should have just taken the money, found an ordinary brothel and bought some good wine and two girls for the afternoon.*

Even with the sage bundle, he soon grew lightheaded. Memory failed him, and when the priest came to offer him a fresh towel and led him from the room, he forgot who the man was and why he had been sweating in the first place. He wobbled out on the priest's arm, into a second chamber where a servant waited to guide him into a plunge pool. The cold revived him, and when he waded out the servant toweled him dry and anointed him with oil.

From there, the priest escorted him into another series of chambers where he lit an incense stick as an offering to Shalath and received yet more instruction from a middle-aged priestess whom he seriously hoped was not going to be his partner.

"In the next room awaits the avatar of the goddess," she said, in so somber and sanctimonious a tone that Adeja had to restrain his laughter. "To achieve ecstasy and spiritual renewal, you must focus your efforts upon the avatar and bring her to bliss before you may claim your reward."

If this is how priests have to go about getting a woman in Bhellin, it's no wonder they fuck each other, he thought. Adeja cursed his ill fortune as he reviewed the instructions he had been given. He was not accustomed to using sex as a tool to achieve greater spirituality, he did not like to wait for his pleasure, and he did not like to go about it with so much ceremony and fuss.

The chamber into which the priestess ushered him was windowless, illuminated by glass lanterns that enfolded the space in a warm amber glow. From a nest of silken cushions rose a woman who undid her sheer linen robe, let it spill to her ankles and took his hand, urging him without words to lie down beside her. She was young and comely, and the sweet scent of her skin was enough to make him hard.

Had she been any ordinary prostitute, he would have pushed her to her knees and fed her his cock. *I would have given her pleasure afterward.* It was rare that he left a brothel without entering his partner, and the girls he always tried to please.

With an eager tongue, he kissed her and let his hands roam her supple curves. His fingers rolled and pinched her nipples until she gasped; he bent his head to suck on them, while letting his hands slide down over her belly to the moist slit between her thighs.

Not once did she speak, but with her fingers she showed him the hidden pearl that made her moan when he rubbed it, and how to use his tongue to give her pleasure. These arts he already knew, having learned in the embrace of a Tajhaani widow who, but for her reluctance to marry a young soldier, he would have made his wife.

Adeja did what pleased his partner while trying to curb his impatience. Her climax was not, the priests warned him, license to mount her and rut as he pleased. Any release he had must come through her agency, when and where she deemed it appropriate.

She spent considerable time teasing him, licking a trail from his nipples to the head of his cock, which she suckled without taking the entire length into her mouth. The stimulation maddened him, especially when it became evident that she knew a trick to keep him from coming. No one, not even Sephil, had ever been able to do that to him. Until now, he had not even thought it possible.

Without words, he could not comprehend why she made him wait when he had already pleasured her. An answer presented itself when, still licking his cock, she turned so she was straddling his chest. From his position he could touch and taste her, and as he let his tongue slide into her wet slit he realized he would not be able to enter her until she was ready for him.

From the noises she made and the way she moved upon him, he sensed she was close, but just short of her orgasm she drew away from him. Turning to face him, she guided his cock into her until he was fully sheathed. Slowly she began to ride him, meeting his thrusts, and when he placed both hands on her hips to steady her, she pressed his fingers to her slick folds.

Between his fingers he rubbed and flicked her pearl, drawing out the stimulation even when she began to squirm and shudder. Sensing his moment had come, Adeja rolled her over onto her back and thrust hard into her, neither knowing nor caring if this was permitted. As far as he was concerned, he had waited long enough.

When he climaxed, it was not the orgasm he experienced with a good healthy fuck, but an awkward mix of pleasure and pain that seemed torn from him. He rolled away from his partner and lay exhausted among the cushions, trying to regain his wind until a servant entered with his clothes and told him it was time to leave. As he sat up, he saw that the young priestess was already gone.

Exhausted, he emerged from the temple into the mid-afternoon sun. He returned to the gatehouse and lay dozing on his cot until the bell rang for supper and evening prayers. Afterward, he met Sephil on the stairs leading up to Avorim's office. To allay suspicion, he carried a temple guard's pike and adopted a sentry's pose, but anyone who ventured within earshot would have seen through the ruse.

Sephil gave him a playful wink. "Did you enjoy yourself today?"

"Too much fuss for a good fuck," mumbled Adeja. "Next time I'll leave the uniform behind and find myself a simple brothel."

Upstairs, Avorim awaited them with two packets, the seals of which had already been broken. "You have messages," he told Sephil.

"One is from Ottabia," added Bedren. "Kalion writes to you."

"I thought he was still confined," said Adeja.

"Yes, but he is permitted books and writing materials." Bedren slid one packet across the table to Sephil. "He wishes to make amends for his ill deeds."

As Sephil read the letter, his expression darkened and became strained. When he was done, he passed the letter to Adeja, who scanned the first few lines. *I do not know what evil made me do what I did. At first I saw no harm in giving information, for I did not know who would receive it or what evil they intended, but later when they offered money I confess I grew weak —*

Adeja snorted and held the letter to the candle. "He should've saved himself the trouble and just said he did it for the money."

Sephil snatched the smoldering parchment from him and put it out. A thin, pungent smoke filled the room. "I did not say you could burn it."

"Why would you want to keep it?" asked Adeja. "He doesn't mean a word of it."

"How do you know?"

"When you've lived with nine siblings, you just know. My brothers used to push and shove me, and when my father told them to apologize, we all knew it was just words. It was the same with my younger sisters. I used to slip lizards into their skirts and set fire to their dolls. I had to say sorry, but they were so annoying I never meant it," explained Adeja. "I suppose Zhanil never did such things to you."

Sephil shook his head. "No, never," he murmured.

"Kalion sounds like a priest dictated the letter to him. If he regrets what he's done, it's only because he was caught."

"I did not order him to write to you, Sephil," said Bedren. "As I said before, I will look into the matter on my return."

Avorim held up the other packet, turning it so the royal seal was visible. "I had word this afternoon that there is to be an audience. The four of us are to present ourselves at the palace tomorrow before noon."

"All of us?" asked Adeja.

Sephil reached for the letter and read it. "There are only three lines of text here, with our names and directions. Was there nothing else?"

"I am afraid not," replied Avorim. "Whatever the king intends, we will not know until tomorrow."

Adeja gazed over Sephil's shoulder at the letter, which consisted mostly of the king's titles and the formal salutations of the court. "I don't any of us is going to get much sleep tonight," he said.

Chapter Six

After breakfast and morning prayers, Sephil followed Avorim upstairs to the high priest's office and took the seat that was offered him. Adeja, freshly washed and dressed in a clean uniform, awaited him there.

Bedren, the fourth member of their party, was strangely absent. "He has gone to the bazaar to fetch something," said Avorim, "but he will return in time to accompany us."

"Whatever it is, could it not have waited?" asked Sephil. Since he was not permitted to attend his lessons with the other novices, he had nothing to do in the close silence of the office but wonder what ordeal the audience would be.

"Bedren assures me his errand is essential to your success," replied Avorim, "and he has promised not to dawdle. Once he returns, we can leave."

Sephil felt Adeja's hand warm and heavy on his shoulder; he tried to draw comfort from the gesture but could not. Half the night he lay awake trying not to imagine the worst. The only other king he had known had been his father, and the few times Brasidios received him were memories better left unvisited.

Their last meeting, which recalled Sephil from his long exile for political purposes, bore the cruelest sting of all.

"I have done my best to forget your existence," his father had said, "but political considerations have made recalling you to court an unfortunate necessity." Brasidios gave his appearance a long, disapproving glance. The dark robe Sephil wore lacked the severe cut appropriate for court, and with his long hair and lack of beard, he did not present an image worthy of the royal house.

"You have been keeping low company, I hear," Brasidios continued, "and I can see your effeminate ways have not improved. What the Tajhaani ambassadors will say when you are inflicted upon them, I do not relish hearing."

Intimidated by his father's presence, Sephil did not bother to point out that he had dismissed the dissolute young noblemen who frequented his household and tried to mend his ways. At this point, however, nothing he said would have made any difference.

The thought that another king might treat him thus was unbearable. As he dressed that morning, Sephil appraised himself in the little looking glass that hung over the dormitory wash basin, and did not entirely like what he saw. Although he had cut his hair to shoulder length and wore a novice's plain robe, he imagined his father standing at his shoulder to criticize his girlish appearance.

When he heard footfalls coming up the steps outside, it took all his nerve to remain in his chair and not rush to the door like a child.

Bedren entered, carrying a small parcel which he handed to Sephil. "This is for you."

Sephil fumbled at the ties with nervous fingers and drew back in confusion at the objects he uncovered. "You bought jewelry?"

"You will want to wear these." Bedren picked up one of the silver cuff bracelets and fastened it around Sephil's wrist.

Adeja picked up the second bracelet and looked at it before handing it to Bedren. "This is Tajhaani work. My mother had a bracelet like this."

Sephil needed no explanation for why Bedren thought the bracelets necessary. They would hide the scars on his wrists.

From the temple, they headed out into the city, skirting the bazaar at whose colorful stalls Sephil gazed longingly before turning onto the main thoroughfare that would take them to the palace.

Half a mile ahead, the street terminated in a gate whose deep red and blue tiles dazzled the eye. Officials, priests and petitioners passed through under the watchful eye of guards who stopped all newcomers. Avorim produced the royal summons for inspection. A guard inspected the document and seal, then waved the four visitors along.

The scene was repeated at a second, inner gate and twice more inside the palace before the four found themselves in an antechamber off the main hall. Sephil recognized the room as the sort of place where visitors might wait for an audience. On more than one occasion, his father had kept him waiting among the petitioners and lesser officials either out of spite or simply because he had forgotten he had summoned his son in the first place.

Sephil could not help but wonder if the scene would be repeated here. No sooner had he claimed a bench near the wall, however, than inner doors opened and a vizier emerged to escort them inside.

Beyond acknowledging them as the king's guests, the man did not speak. Following his lead, the four moved through two more antechambers and a short hall before coming to a room floored in green marble and thick carpets. Tall windows looked out onto lush gardens, but the desk and book-lined cabinets indicated that this was an office.

The vizier paused before the heavy desk, bowed to the man who sat there and announced the visitors. Sephil chanced a look at the man before lowering his eyes once more. This was a king, he knew.

Dressed in a robe of deep red wool, with jeweled rings upon his fingers, the king's dark hair bore threads of gray. Although he lacked the height and breadth that made Brasidios so imposing, Ampheres conveyed a stately air nonetheless.

With a gesture, Ampheres indicated the vizier should remain. Once again, the man bowed and withdrew to a corner of the room.

"I have received a petition from the high priest of Abh stating that a son of the late king of Rhodeen seeks my protection." Ampheres possessed a regal, quietly authoritative voice. Here was a man who, unlike Brasidios, had no need to shout.

"That is correct, my lord," answered Avorim. "I have with me letters and tokens sent with the prince by his brother, the late Crown Prince Zhanil Brasides."

"And I assume you have also brought Prince Sephil?" The slight lilt with which Ampheres voiced his question implied he already knew the answer. Sephil felt the king's eyes on him and cringed.

"Yes, he is here also."

"Then let us see the letters and the tokens you claim to possess."

The vizier stepped forward to take the seal ring and packet from Avorim. Sephil lifted his eyes to see Ampheres break the wax seal with a stylus, stand and walk over to the window where the light was better. Whatever Zhanil had written, it covered more than one page, and Ampheres spent considerable time reading and reviewing the words. With the seal ring he did the same, holding the jewel up to the light to study the engravings.

At last, he returned to his desk, sat down and looked directly at Sephil. "Delav, bring a chair for the prince so he may sit. The rest of you will wait outside."

Sephil chanced a backward glance at Adeja and the two priests as the vizier ushered them to the door. As they exited, a servant in red livery entered and pulled forward a chair upholstered in green brocade.

"Sit down," said Ampheres, "and kindly remove those unsightly bracelets."

With shaking hands, Sephil fumbled with the pins until the servant stepped forward to help him. He turned his wrists downward and concealed his hands in his lap while the king examined the bracelets.

"Cheap Tajhaani work," commented Ampheres. "Now let us see why it should be necessary for you, a prince and novice priest, to wear such ill-fitting ornaments."

Sephil dared not refuse. He sucked in a deep breath, turned his wrists over so the king could see his scars, and waited for a curt remark such as his father would have made.

Ampheres nodded, as though this was precisely what he expected to see. "Your brother indicated in his letter that you bore such marks, and why," he said gently. "You may conceal them now, if you wish. Were you aware that I knew your father?"

"No, sir."

"Brasidios and I fought together at the Irrend Pass some thirty years ago, when I had just become king and he was still the Crown Prince of Rhodeen. We expelled the Turyar from the western fringes of Khalgar, and to cement our friendship he married my kinswoman." Leaning back in his chair, Ampheres appraised Sephil for a long moment. "I see much of your mother in you, though not so much of your father."

"Yes, sir."

"For a prince in your predicament, you have remarkably little to say," observed Ampheres. "Do I intimidate you, or is it that you do not know what I intend to do with you?"

Sephil swallowed hard. "Both, sir."

"Brasidios occasionally mentioned you in his letters."

Now at last it would come: the cutting remarks, the criticism and rejection. Sephil swallowed hard. "He did not think highly of me, sir."

144

"No, indeed he did not. However, he had very exacting standards which I think few would have met," said Ampheres. "In time, I will judge for myself whether his opinion of you was accurate."

Sephil did not bother to point out that, strict standards or no, Zhanil pleased their father in every way. "Yes, sir."

"For now," said Ampheres, "you will remain here until I decide what to do with you. Your father did not see you often, but we will have many visits, and I expect you will improve your conversation."

Sephil viewed the promise of future interviews with apprehension. Ampheres would not waste his time without sufficient motive, and Sephil preferred not to contemplate what that might be.

"I suppose you would like to know what your brother wrote?" asked Ampheres.

Rather than offer him the letter, the king unfolded it and began to read sections of it aloud. "'*Sephil is young and impressionable, having had incompetent guardians. He has not been groomed for kingship and would, if raised to the throne, wear the crown with much difficulty. However, he has a good heart and should be allowed to live a quiet life, if you will but grant him your protection.*'"

Hearing these words brought a knot to Sephil's throat, so when Ampheres asked if this last thing was what he wanted, all he could do was nod.

"I have been watching you in the sanctuary and can see you have as good a heart as your brother says," said Ampheres. "Had it been otherwise, I would not have received you. For your blood ties to my house and the love I bore your late father, I will extend my protection to you, but you must understand that this comes with a price.

"Until now, I have managed to keep this matter quiet, but your presence here will eventually become known. By harboring you, I announce to the world that I am taking your part. That I have no intention of raising you to the throne makes no difference."

"I have no wish to be king," said Sephil. "I will say it before a thousand witnesses. I will sign a document stating it to be so."

Ampheres slowly shook his head. "Words are hollow things in politics," he said. "Had your father taken greater care with your education, you would understand that actions are what matter. As I have not yet acknowledged your cousin as the legitimate Crown Prince, my relations with Tajhaan are somewhat strained. Should your presence here become known, High Prince Armajid will regard my actions as hostile."

"Then do not tell anyone who I am," replied Sephil. "Send me to some remote, quiet sanctuary and let me live under some assumed name."

"If such a thing were possible, I would do it, if only to keep Khalgar out of this diplomatic muddle. However, your cousin and his protector already know you are alive, and it would not take much searching on their part to learn you had come to Bhellin. No matter where I house you, they will continue to search for you; that is how great a threat you are to them. And it is not only Dashir's claim that is at stake, you realize. His wife is with child."

It took Sephil a moment to realize Ampheres meant Terreh, whom Dashir had spirited out of Shemin-at-Khul and married. Despite the wordless disdain she showed him, Terreh had briefly been his betrothed. It now felt odd to hear she bore another man's child. "No, I did not know this."

"The child is due later this year. Should it turn out to be a son, you may be certain that his grandfather the High Prince will oppose any perceived threat, which includes you," said Ampheres. "It is better that you remain here, openly under my protection. As my guest, you may continue your spiritual studies under a tutor."

"I cannot return to the temple?"

"No, you will bid farewell to the priests and your bodyguard."

"I trust my guard." Sephil tried to suppress the emotion from his voice. "He saved my life twice in Ottabia."

"And for that we are grateful, but you will agree that it is prudent he not remain." The look Ampheres gave him implied things Sephil knew he could not possibly know. *There has been nothing been us since before we came here, not a touch, not a word. How* could *he know?* "I will assign you a bodyguard from my own household, a man in whose loyalty and discretion I place the highest trust. Delav, come here."

Ampheres gave orders to the vizier, who left the office to bring the man the king requested. Meanwhile, the servant brought wine and refreshments for which Sephil had no appetite. All he wanted was to return to the temple with Adeja and the priests, resume his quiet life of meditation and ministry, and forget this visit to the palace had ever taken place.

At length, Delav returned with a tall, broad-shouldered man dressed in red leather armor over his tunic and leggings. His only weapons were a dagger and short sword hanging from his belt. He saluted Ampheres, paying no attention to Sephil until the king indicated the prince was to be his new charge.

Ampheres turned to Sephil. "This is Melwas. He will stay by your side until death claims him or I release him."

Sephil looked up at Melwas, and did not like what he saw. The man's face was hard and blank, with none of Adeja's lively intelligence. Having him about would serve more as a reminder of his vulnerable position than as a comfort.

Once Ampheres gave him leave, and with Melwas shadowing him, Sephil went into the hall where Adeja and the priests waited to say goodbye.

"I cannot return to the temple, but the king will allow me to continue my studies," he told Bedren. Melwas stood at his back like a bulwark, prompting him to keep his voice low.

Bedren glanced nervously at the bodyguard. "That is good, Sephil."

Dropping his voice still further, Sephil asked, "I am very sorry I have to leave you like this. Is there any money left?"

"Yes, there is some."

"Will you give some of it to Adeja? I have no money of my own with which to pay him for his services and I —"

Bedren stopped his anxious flood of words with a reassuring hand. "Do not worry, Sephil. Avorim and I will see to it before I return to Ottabia."

Avorim offered a few words and a smile, nothing that prepared Sephil for the agony of facing Adeja. At that moment, he wanted nothing more than to fling himself into Adeja's arms and hold on, to pull his lover close and kiss him until they were both breathless, but mindful of the king's words and fearing Melwas at his back, he dared no more than a few colorless words and the promise of payment.

I am saying all the wrong things! He could see it by the way Adeja tensed and his eyes narrowed. *This is not my idea. I do not want you to go at all!*

"Then I suppose this is goodbye," Adeja said stiffly. "I wish you well, my prince."

Before Sephil could say more, Adeja turned and walked away, joining the priests and vizier who came to escort them back to the main hall.

Sephil's heart rose to his throat as he watched Adeja disappear around the corner. Footfalls receded against the marble floor. A distant door opened and closed, and with the sound came the realization that Adeja was gone from his life.

When Melwas addressed him, he did not acknowledge the man's rumbling voice, or the hand that gently prodded his elbow even when the man began to steer him toward another exit where Delav waited. Sephil moved numbly between them, hearing the vizier speak yet not listening.

Finally, they stopped in a corridor decorated with murals featuring lush water lilies and lotuses. Delav moved in front of Sephil, peered into his face and shook his head. "You have not been listening to a single word, my prince," he said. "I realize this is all very sudden for you, coming from a quiet sanctuary into the royal palace, but there is a strict etiquette you will need to master. The sooner you begin, the better it will be."

At the end of the corridor, Delav opened a door and ushered Sephil through. "Today we can leave off with formal instruction, but tomorrow we must begin in earnest. These will be your lodgings. Hauto will see to it that you have all you require."

Sephil followed him into a suite of apartments furnished in silks and dark, polished wood. Hauto, a heavyset man whom Delav introduced as his steward, bowed and uttered the usual assurances of comfort and exceptional service. Both he and the two servants who stood at the end of the foyer wore the same bland expression as Melwas, which did not inspire confidence.

All Sephil wanted now was the unadorned quiet of the sanctuary, and Adeja.

Dinner came in on silver and porcelain dishes, with two wines and a generous selection of sweets. In another room, the servants prepared a hot bath and fragrant oils for massage. Sephil hesitated at these luxuries, though he had known them most of his life. That such things were reserved for him alone seemed wasteful.

What he did not eat, he offered to the servants, who declined his gesture. He bathed and donned the clothes the servants laid out for him, while making sure they did not discard his temple robes.

That night, he lay down on a feather mattress in a bed hung with pale brocade, but sleep would not come. Such splendor felt cold, renewing his old fears of the dark.

For nine months he had freedom from his princely station and the constricting etiquette that accompanied it. For the first time in his life he had been content, finding purpose among the brothers of Abh, working with the destitute and hopeless, who taught him that he was not useless after all.

More than anything, it was a life to which he yearned to return, and his greatest fear was that, like Adeja, it was gone forever.

Chapter Seven

Sephil set aside his book to gaze down at his wrists. The inexpensive Tajhaani-work bracelets Bedren gave him at the bazaar were replaced by gleaming silver chased with little moons, a play on his name. Ampheres presented them to him two days after his arrival, and to please his host Sephil had worn them ever since.

The bracelets framed his wrists like manacles. In dark moments, Sephil thought of them as such.

Outwardly, he had no cause for complaint. His apartments were luxurious, and he had greater freedom than prior experience taught him to expect. Though his movements were restricted to the inner palace, where he would not risk being seen by the public, he could walk in the gardens, visit the king's private chapel and talk to anyone he wished. Melwas, however, discouraged socializing, so Sephil passed his days with little company.

Each morning, Delav came to instruct him in palace etiquette. A tailor brought fabric swatches and measured him for new clothes. When Sephil demurred, stating he preferred his temple robes, Delav pointed out that on certain occasions he would have to dress more appropriately. "Lean toward somber shades of gray, dark blue and brown, with a severe yet elegant cut," he said, nodding at the tailor. "You have a youthful face, my lord. Our efforts will enhance your maturity."

"Are these clothes meant for court?" asked Sephil.

Delav fingered a swatch of drab green velvet. "The king has not summoned you, but when you go out you should project the image of a prince."

"I am a novice priest."

"Yes, but you are not living in the temple and, as I understand it, you have not taken any binding vows," replied Delav. "One of the king's sons is a priest, but when he leaves the temple to visit his family, he does not wear his robes."

Several outfits were ordered, along with linen underthings, shoes and cloaks. As the tailor matched swatches with sketches,

Delav picked at the sleeve of Sephil's robe, fingered a swatch of fine ecru wool, and ordered a new robe as well.

Afternoons brought a priest offering instruction in theology and philosophy. While Sephil enjoyed these lessons, it was not the same as being able to work in the sanctuary. A priest of Abh's true work was among the poor and afflicted, and Sephil had taken comfort in the hours he spent ministering to the faithful. Isolation meant he could not follow the correct path, an argument against which his tutor had no easy answer.

Once a day, he spent an hour with the king. Ampheres offered him liqueur and delicacies, and spoke to him while browsing through the correspondence his viziers deemed was worth his attention. Mindful of what Ampheres instructed at their first meeting, Sephil did his best to uphold his end of the conversation. Mostly he listened, and learned things about his father that he never knew. He also learned about his mother, whom no one at court had mentioned after her untimely death.

"She was a lovely woman," said Ampheres. "I would have offered him a princess with closer ties to my house, but Brasidios would have no other but her. It was a sad day when he wrote to tell me of her death."

As his mother had died giving birth to him, Sephil had nothing to add. Once or twice, Zhanil commented that Sephil favored her in appearance and demeanor. These qualities, while desirable in a wife, were apparently unacceptable in a prince of Rhodeen.

Ampheres sipped his liqueur, a cinnamon-flavored concoction which Sephil found too strong for his palette. "I met Zhanil three years ago when he came to Bhellin on a diplomatic mission. He was an impressive young man, and it saddened me to learn of his death. Had he not been married already, I would have offered him one of my daughters. It is unfortunate that your father did not realize how exceptional Zhanil was."

"I think he knew," murmured Sephil. Such talk of Zhanil pained him not only because it reminded him of what he had lost, but also because it pointed out what he had not been able to achieve.

To his surprise, Ampheres laughed. "No, it was unfortunate that he did not see that neither you nor anyone else could be like Zhanil. I have six sons. Some excel in statecraft, others in theology, business or warfare. None are alike, yet I love them all equally."

As Sephil had not yet met the members of the Khalgari royal family, he could not comment. "My father also thought highly of Dashir and his brothers."

"I am certain your cousin can ride and wield a sword, but what I have heard about him thus far does not encourage me to acknowledge him as a potential king. A king must be ruthless when the occasion calls for it, yes, but he must also know how to be temperate and willing to compromise. This is not a quality I see in Dashir.

"I have said nothing to the Tajhaani ambassadors. Although you have not appeared in public, they are aware of your presence here. It will not be long, I think, before we must make an official announcement."

What that announcement would entail, Sephil neither knew nor wanted to know.

Nights brought old feelings of uselessness and desolation. Alone in his great bed, Sephil curled into a tight ball and tried not to think about the arms that had once held him and kept him safe. He did not want sex, although the king intimated that partners were available and would be discreet if he so wished it. Life in the sanctuary merely affirmed what Sephil already knew, and had known from the time he was old enough to confuse physical desire with his hunger for love; he did not need the former, but could not endure without the latter.

Fate conspires to take away those who mean anything to me, he thought. *Is it so much to ask to have one person — just one — to love?*

In the third week, Ampheres began to introduce Sephil to his family, beginning with his eldest son and heir, Ettarin. With each introduction, Sephil became more firmly convinced that Ampheres intended to use him for political gain. No doubt Ampheres expressed true sentiments in welcoming him as lost kin, but Sephil needed no explanation to grasp that his value rested in his proximity to the throne of Rhodeen, not in his tenuous blood ties to the Khalgari royal house.

Family gatherings eschewed politics. The king's two brothers, both influential members of the ruling council, his sons and nephews welcomed Sephil into their circle. "Soon," said Ampheres, "I will introduce you to my wife and daughters."

For the Feast of the Summer Solstice, which was a major religious holiday in both Khalgar and Rhodeen, Sephil remained at the palace while the royal family went in procession to the House of the Snake Mother. Delav explained that the omission was deliberate yet not malicious. "Appearing in the procession would put you on public display," he said, "and the king will not risk that yet. However, he sends an invitation for you to join him and his family for supper after the ceremony."

Sephil took the invitation, read it through twice, and sighed. Even before his exile, his father excluded him from public rituals as often as possible, explaining away his absence with the excuse of frail health. Once banished, he received news only through the servants or rare visitors. When Zhanil's sons were born, he received no word, no invitation to the name-day feasts, or any inquiry when he did not send a gift.

Although he understood why Ampheres could not include him, the invitation in his hand did not entirely erase the sting.

On solstice morning, breakfast came with the gift of golden bracelets etched with sunbursts: the emblem of Rhodeen's kings. Sephil studied the gift and the card that came with it until Delav urged him to try the bracelets on.

"You behave as though you have never seen jewelry before."

"I am not used to receiving gifts," he murmured.

Delav made a disbelieving noise and placed the bracelets on the night table to be worn that evening. During the day, as the distant sounds of festival reached him, Sephil walked in the gardens to remind himself that he was no longer a prisoner in his own apartments. Thoughts churned through his mind, returning often to the bracelets and the king's plans for him. Gifts came with attachments, and Ampheres had yet to reveal his ambitions.

That evening, he wore the bracelets to the private supper Ampheres hosted in the inner palace, thanked the king for his gift, and afterward locked them away with his misgivings.

A week later, Delav interrupted his religious studies with a message that he must attend the king immediately. Behind him trailed a servant bearing a robe of dark blue brocade. Sephil reluctantly dismissed the priest and allowed Piras to help him into the garment with its many fastenings.

When Delav brought him the golden bracelets, he balked. "Not those," he said.

"Forgive me, my prince, but the king specifically stated you were to wear them." Delav handed the bracelets to Piras, who removed the silver bracelets Sephil wore and fastened the golden ones in their place. "He also indicated you were to wear this."

Over Sephil's head he draped a heavy object on a gold chain. Sephil caught up the blue stone in his hand, and recognized it as Zhanil's seal ring, which Ampheres had retained with the letter. "Why must I wear this?" he asked.

"The king does not say," answered Delav, "only that you must." With a guiding hand, he nudged Sephil to turn toward the looking glass. "If you will permit me to say, my prince, you look very regal."

Regal was not a word Sephil would have used to describe himself. However, the deep blue of his raiment, the sunburst bracelets and seal ring gave the impression of regalia. For whatever reason Ampheres summoned him, Sephil knew that a public display would be part of it.

He followed Delav downstairs to a gilded chamber where Ampheres awaited him on a throne under a crimson canopy. With a gesture, the king indicated Sephil should take the chair to his left. Crown Prince Ettarin already occupied the seat to his right.

"We are about to receive petitioners you will find most interesting. You may be tempted to speak during the interview," said Ampheres, "but say nothing unless I instruct you."

Sephil swallowed the urge to ask what was going on. His father showed impatience with such questions, and Zhanil admonished him to be silent and observe before speaking. He could only pray that, whoever the petitioners were, Dashir was not among them.

When the doors opened, the herald called out several names. The six men who approached the dais wore Khalgari dress, yet by style of their names and their lighter coloring Sephil knew they were from Rhodeen.

As a group, they bowed to Ampheres. The king inclined his head and gave their leader, a stout, middle-aged man, permission to speak.

"Great King," said the man, "I thank you for your graciousness in hearing my petition."

"Given the noise you have been making these last two months, Lord Wesares, we thought it prudent to hear your case," answered Ampheres.

Gathering himself with what Sephil read as considerable self-importance, Wesares began his speech. "With the unexpected and most unfortunate fall of Rhodeen's royal line to the Turyar, those of us who have been displaced from our estates thank you for your generosity in these dark times. However, as we mourn our loss, practical considerations must prevail. Namely, in the absence of any direct heir, with reluctance I must draw attention to my own noble ancestry. My grandmother, daughter of Ardahir III, provides me with—"

"I have viewed your genealogy, Lord Wesares, and as substantial as your claims may be," said Ampheres, "descent through the female line is not recognized in Rhodeen."

"These are exceptional times, Great King."

"Still, there are those yet living who are closer to the throne, or have you forgotten the claimant in Tajhaan?"

Wesares made a dismissive gesture. "Prince Dashir Serrides is unwilling to give aid to the many exiles who have taken refuge here, he makes no assurances of future support in reclaiming our lost estates in Rhodeen, and worse, he has allied himself with Tajhaan's royal family to the point that he has chosen a Tajhaani name for his unborn son. He is the High Prince's creature, with no loyalty to his own people."

Ampheres nodded. "This may be true, but a claim exists that is even stronger than his."

Sephil tightened his grip on the arms of his chair, dreading the moment when this nobleman, who had thus far ignored him, became aware of his presence.

Wesares dropped an unctuous bow. "Then you will have to instruct us, Great King, for we are not aware of any such claimant."

"While we have no doubt that your mourning for the royal family is genuine, it seems that you have forgotten that your king fathered two sons, the younger of whom is still alive."

Wesares answered with a perplexed look. Nevertheless, he recovered his poise and within moments had a response. "Forgive my seeming ignorance, but we have had no word of the other prince. Surely he died some time ago, or perished with his brother's family in Shemin-at-Khul. Prince Dashir would not claim the throne if he owed allegiance to a surviving cousin."

The 'other' prince, thought Sephil. *He does not even recall my name.*

"You are mistaken," said Ampheres. "As a distant but beloved member of our royal house, Prince Sephil Brasides escaped Rhodeen just before the invasion and has been our guest for some time."

Sephil did his best to project an air of regal calm as Ampheres gestured to him, but beyond a moment's surprise and a slight flaring of the nostrils, Wesares did not acknowledge him. Instead, he bowed to the king and restated his case. "Forgive us for taking your valuable time, Great King," he said, "but nevertheless we urge you to consider our petition. Much effort will be required to reclaim Rhodeen from the Turyar. Its people, beleaguered and dispossessed, want strong leadership, and in the absence of Prince Zhanil, our influence over Rhodeen's many expatriates is considerable. Our claim is a worthy one."

"No petition worth hearing goes without consideration," answered Ampheres, "but given the situation, the answer you receive may not be what you most desire."

As the noblemen left and the doors closed, Sephil could not decide what stung more: being thrust without warning into public view or the complete lack of recognition from one of his own people. "I wish you had not done that," he murmured.

Ampheres displayed little sympathy. "What we do is out of necessity. As a royal prince you should understand that."

Sephil rose with the king and accompanied him and the Crown Prince into an adjacent gallery. "I cannot play the part of royal prince either," he said, "if the very people who should acknowledge me do not do so."

"As your father kept you from public view, it is an unfortunate reality. Melin Wesares desires the throne for himself, and as such will not acknowledge you. This will not be the first time you are slighted, Sephil, and I suspect that in time vicious slanders will be part of it," said Ampheres. "You have not always led a blameless life."

"You do not need to remind me."

"Whether you like it or not, I do. Perhaps now you will understand why I have permitted you to continue your religious studies. Wesares may not have acknowledged your presence, but be assured that he noticed you. He will spread rumors that you are immoral and have led a dissolute life, and that you fled for your life out of cowardice while your father and brother died defending Shemin-at-Khul. You will say nothing, but respond by showing yourself in the public areas of the palace and wearing the habit of a novice priest as you have been doing. We will counter any slander by demonstrating that you are very spiritual, that you were not in Shemin-at-Khul at the time of the Turya invasion because you were in retreat in Ottabia."

"That is not a lie," said Sephil.

Ampheres paused by a window. "It does not require a lie to bolster your reputation. An exemplary public image is a valuable commodity. Had your father not been so bitter over your mother's death and your failure to excel in the military arts, he would have realized the benefits of having a son in the priesthood."

From comments his father made over the years, Sephil knew he harbored a low opinion of priests. For that reason, and perhaps others, Brasidios would have scoffed at the idea of his younger son trying to lead a virtuous life as a priest of Abh.

"People always remember what they see as opposed to what they hear," said Ampheres, "and the sight of you as a proper novice visiting hospitals and shrines will bring you much credit."

Sephil found the idea of turning a genuine vocation into political opportunity distasteful. "You told those men I had a stronger claim to the throne than they, yet all along you have said you would not back me as king. If so, then why would you publicize my existence, or even take such pains to improve my image?"

Ampheres fixed him with so a hard look that for a moment Sephil regretted having asked. A moment later, the king's expression softened and he smiled, as though he found the question amusing. "In time you will understand these things. For now be assured that both your place in the succession and the image you present are important."

"Lord Wesares is already styling himself as king of Rhodeen," said Ettarin. "He has taken the royal name of Ardahir to remind people of his ancestry."

"He makes noise," said Ampheres, "but in the end his posturing will come to nothing. Rhodeen's military is scattered, either dead or paying allegiance to the Turyar. He will not be able to scrape together enough support to present a legitimate threat. Tajhaan will not back him, and he will find no aid here."

Sephil listened, absorbing whatever information he could before returning to his apartments.

His tutors gone and the servants quietly occupied elsewhere, he sat by the window with a book in his lap, unable to concentrate on Eharideos' treatise on correct thought and action. For all the threat he posed, Melin Wesares and his spurious claims could easily have been ignored, yet Ampheres chose not only to grant him an audience but use the occasion to divulge Sephil's presence at court.

What purpose this served, Sephil did not know. Ampheres insisted his claim was significant, yet in the same breath refused to make him king. Why go to such trouble validating one's right to the succession if nothing was to come of it?

Sephil looked out the window, and spied a young man and woman walking along a nearby garden path, their chaperone following at a discreet distance. As he watched them and pondered the etiquette of courtship, an answer suddenly came to him.

His claim mattered because, even if he did not take the throne, his right of succession would pass through him to his sons. And if he married into the Khalgari royal house, Ampheres would have a claimant worthy of support in the person of his own grandson.

No, he thought angrily, *I will not be manipulated.*

A moment later, he calmed down enough to reflect on the reality of his situation. Thus far, Ampheres gave no hint that marriage was on his mind. The possibility existed, however, and Sephil occupied such a precarious position that he could not risk alienating his protector and benefactor by refusing an arranged marriage.

Unlike Terreh, the Khalgari royal princesses were all pleasant young women, any one of whom would make an agreeable companion. Sephil understood this, yet the truth was he simply had no interest in either women or marriage.

* * * *

Neither an inability to swim nor his bodyguard's insistence that he remain onshore could keep Sephil from wading out into the surf after his companions. Strange and vast, the ocean drew him with its crashing waves and salt-tinged air. This, combined with freedom from the restrictions of court life, compelled him to pull off his shoes and follow the royal princes into the water.

Water surged around him, soaking his linen trousers to the knees. Despite his pleas to slow down, the two princes raced ahead of him, flinging themselves through the rising waves to reach deeper water. Sephil would never catch them.

Melwas followed like a shadow, his boots tramping through the salt water. "My prince, you must return to shore."

Sephil wished he would go away. "The water is only knee-deep."

"Yes, my prince, but it is not unknown for the sea to play tricks, to drag a man off his feet and under the water. Please, return to shore where it is safe."

With a last, longing glance at the two princes who waved to him from a distance, Sephil waded back, but did not leave the water entirely. Carrying his shoes in one hand, he walked along the shore, letting the surging foam play around his ankles as he pulled shells out of the sand with the other.

When he first arrived, one of the princesses showed him how to listen to the ocean by putting a shell to his ear. "Acoustics and air, my lord," said Delav.

"You did not have to tell me," Sephil replied sourly. An acoustic trick or no, the sound comforted him, and he liked the variations in shape, size and color among the shells he found. So did others, he realized, for in the summer palace were many objects decorated with shells.

Three large pavilions stood on the sand dunes above the beach: one for the men, another for the royal ladies, and a third where both sexes could mingle in the shade. Servants brought fruit, sweet bread, and chilled wine in addition to towels and ointments to protect against sunburn, a precaution Sephil ignored earlier in the week. Piras rubbed cooling aloe onto his reddened face and arms three times a day, while assuring him that his burn was not as severe as it might have been.

"In a week or two it will peel, my lord," he said, "and in a month you will not notice it at all."

High above the sand dunes, on a broad cliff overlooking the ocean, stood Adenna, the king's summer palace, where the royal family retreated when the heat in the capital grew unbearable. Messengers arrived each day with dispatches from Bhellin and other parts of the realm, but nobles and petitioners were barred from the residence. Unless the matter was urgent, Ampheres tolerated no interruption while at his leisure.

Here Sephil met the queen, a frail but good-natured lady whose many pregnancies had ruined her health. She made Adenna her permanent residence, where the physicians believed the sea air and the waters at the nearby shrine of Abh would invigorate her. Whenever Ampheres came to visit, he showered her with attention and many gifts.

As he continued his studies with his tutor and the local priests, Sephil accompanied the queen to the shrine and watched over her from a bench beside the mineral spring. She enjoyed conversation, a pastime which often left her out of breath, and took pains to introduce Sephil to her daughters, an unnecessary gesture he graciously accepted nonetheless.

While at the shrine, he tried the waters himself, as all novices and priests were encouraged to do. Wearing a linen shift, he stepped into the pool and waded to one of the submerged shelves where patients sat during their treatment. The water was warmer than he expected and, as it flowed around him, revealed a magical quality, stirring life into his limbs. For a moment, he thought of Adeja and how pleasant it would have been to share this with him.

For a moment, he smiled, then grew sad. However much he tried to achieve spiritual consolation through renunciation, he found it difficult to let Adeja go.

At sunset, servants brought torches down to the pavilions, and as the tide rolled in, the royal family dined upon mussels and fish caught that morning. Music and dancing followed the meal. Sephil did not know any Khalgari dances, and so had to rely upon the princesses to teach him.

Ampheres brought three unmarried daughters from Bhellin, with a fourth joining him at Adenna with her husband and infant son. "I would have liked to marry her to Zhanil," he said, "but he had already taken a wife. The gods were wise, it seems, for had things gone as I wished I would have been mourning her along with your brother. To this day, I do not understand why he did not send his wife and sons out of Rhodeen with you."

Sephil had no desire to revisit the tales of atrocities committed by the Turyar, and was grateful when Ampheres changed the subject.

With the king encouraging his attentions, Sephil spent time with the three remaining princesses. Though he was not a good rider, he rode with them along the beach, accompanied by Melwas and their chaperones, a middle-aged lady-in-waiting who did not know how to smile. With apologetic looks, the princesses endured her company and seemed to enjoy spending time with their cousin from Rhodeen.

Lissan, the eldest, taught Sephil how to dance, patiently correcting his steps when his feet became entangled in hers. Ketalya, the next-eldest, taught him to play cards, a game unique to Khalgar which he quickly grasped and learned to enjoy. The youngest princess, sixteen year old Naulia, had a lively sense of humor, but an annoying tendency to giggle when she saw him trying to dance with Lissan, who was taller than he.

Sephil could not guess which princess Ampheres preferred for a dynastic marriage, should it come to that. Naulia was too young, but both Lissan and Ketalya were pleasant. For a prince who desired a royal bride, either one would have been acceptable.

He might leave the choice up to me, thought Sephil. Zhanil might have found it an intriguing prospect, but for one who did not desire a wife, choosing a bride would be a grim task. All three were interesting companions, though Naulia was too young for marriage. The more time he spent with them, the more Sephil realized how little women had been part of his life. His only female relations, now captives of the Turyar, were a middle-aged aunt who regarded him as a nuisance and a cousin whose name he could not recall.

Having female friends was a notion both strange and intriguing. The princesses did not excite his sexual curiosity, but fascinated him in other ways, and it saddened him to realize marriage would ruin that.

"You are stepping on my feet again," murmured Lissan.

Coming out of his reverie, Sephil realized he had trod once again on his partner's feet. "Forgive me," he said.

"Your brother was the more elegant dancer, though Naulia complained that he was too old."

"Zhanil was better at everything, and your sister thinks anything over twenty-five is too old."

The next dance he gave to Naulia, who returned blushing to her mother's side as Ketalya claimed her turn.

While Naulia had been too bemused to say anything, Ketalya made conversation as easily as Lissan; the princesses, like most of the Khalgari royal family, were social creatures, bred to the rhythms and intrigue of court life. At times, they left Sephil grasping for a suitable reply. This evening proved no exception.

"Must a novice priest wear his robes on holiday?" she asked. "I thought Father had been quite generous in providing you with a wardrobe."

Sephil viewed such talk as a prelude to seduction, except in this case. Ketalya enjoyed teasing her companions, whether they were dancing or playing cards. "I wear them because I am accustomed to them."

"I know you visit shrines and spend several hours a day studying, but did not think you had a genuine vocation."

"I like to think I do," he answered. "Why would you think otherwise?"

"There are those at court who say you do this to show a pious face to your enemies so they cannot slander you," replied Ketalya.

Sephil smiled weakly. "It was your father's suggestion. Had it been my decision, I would have stayed in seclusion."

"Was the priesthood a path you chose for yourself," she asked, "or did your father dedicate you to the god? Two years ago, Father dedicated Teilan to the Snake Mother, but only because Teilan asked to become a priest."

"My father did not care much for priests or their teachings," said Sephil. "I went into retreat without his permission, and when the Turyar came Zhanil sent me with several other priests to safety in Ottabia. I decided then to dedicate myself to Abh."

At a pause in the music, Ketalya drew back, her playful smile subdued. "I would not say this if I thought it would offend you," she said, "but I thought your brother just a little *too* perfect."

Sephil could not recall ever hearing that criticism about Zhanil. "What do you mean?"

Ketalya's reply only added to his bewilderment. "They say one who stands too long in the sun is burned, and cannot be seen for the brightness."

Chapter Eight

The work was hot, dusty, and monotonous, once again prompting Adeja to wonder why he had not simply walked out of the quarry the first week and applied at the nearest barracks. For a kingdom not at war, Khalgar paid its soldiers well, and Adeja heard the rations were decent.

Too late now, he realized, and cursed his inability to act.

Bedren gave him twelve *menar*, what remained of the three hundred taken from Kalion. Combined with the money Adeja had brought out of Rhodeen, he had enough to live comfortably for some time. Leisure, however, did not suit him, and the same afternoon he left the House of Abh, he headed for the nearest stonemason guild to apply for work.

The masons to whom he spoke laughed outright at his presumption until they noticed his hand inching toward the sword he wore at his belt. Clearing his throat, the eldest mason took Adeja aside and explained that in order to do the elaborate carvings and inscriptions on monuments, one had to spend a lifetime working with stone, beginning with an apprenticeship under a master.

Because he had some training, Adeja was able to find work dressing the limestone blocks hewn and dragged out of the quarry. Although the job paid less than he would have liked, the foreman right away noticed his intelligence when he broke up a fight between two laborers. At the noon break, the man drew him aside and engaged him in conversation. Adeja revealed little aside from the fact that he was from Tajhaan, had been a soldier and was literate.

Unfortunately he also made the mistake of revealing that he had left the military because he wished to settle down and start a family.

The next evening, the foreman invited him to supper. Expecting a casual meal at one of the many shops near the public bathhouses, Adeja accepted. Lakhun, however, had other ideas and took him home, where a press of women greeted him with caresses and food as though he was a long-lost relation.

Adeja did not know what the customs of hospitality were in Khalgar, but he suspected Lakhun had more in mind than a simple meal. As he ate the food the women set before him, he studied them. Unless going to a festival or wedding, no woman he knew ever wore such brightly colored raiment or so many ornaments. And the way Lakhun was looking at him suggested a possibility Adeja would have found amusing were it not so startling.

What man brings home a husband for his sister or daughter when he's only known him eight days? Adeja shrugged, continued eating and enjoying the attention, and waited for Lakhun to broach the topic.

The foreman did not disappoint, directing Adeja's attention to his daughters in a painfully obvious manner that almost made Adeja laugh. "You see my girls there, eh? Such lovely little flowers, but Lahis, she is very special."

Considering how plain the young woman in question was, Adeja suspected her father did not regard her so much as special as he was desperate to marry her off. He grunted, nodded and waited for Lakhun to say more.

"She's a good cook. You liked the food, yes? She keeps house very well, and keeps her tongue, too," said Lakhun. "So she is not as pretty as other girls. A man is only asking for trouble when he takes a pretty girl for his wife."

Adeja again nodded, but said nothing. He would let Lakhun's tongue run itself dry and then see what he could make of the situation. The room he rented in the tenement block near the spice market was small, but he could not keep it himself.

Alternately anxious and encouraged by Adeja's lack of response, Lakhun continued, "You know, I'm not so young anymore, and a man could do worse than to have a son who can manage a crew and do figures. It's very profitable, this quarrying business, if a man has the right head for it, and you've told me already that stone is in your blood."

Soldiering is in my blood, or I would have stayed home and learned the trade. "The quarry is a big place," said Adeja. "You could pass the right man by and not even know it."

"Precisely!" Either Lakhun understood and chose to overlook the remark, or he misread it entirely; Adeja thought the latter. "Most men who work the quarry are dull, and too rough for a good girl like Lahis."

And you think a soldier is gentle? Adeja suspected the man wanted an ignorant foreigner desperate to make a good living in a new city, who would neither notice nor mind that his bride was formerly a widow. Lakhun had not mentioned this, but the women with their loose tongues let it slip while praising Adeja for being much handsomer than Lahis' previous husband. "Then perhaps you should look outside the quarry?"

Lakhun slapped his knee in agreement. "Exactly, my friend! I had no idea Tajhaan bred such fine men. I must marry all my girls to foreigners."

"But would you want a soldier for a son?"

"Ah, but you aren't in that business anymore, and who wouldn't want a son who can defend such a worthy wife?" answered Lakhun.

Even worthier was the money Lahis' husband had left her. It was not a large sum, but when added to her small dowry and Adeja's own savings, it made the deal more attractive than it otherwise would have been.

The wedding was celebrated on the next rest day. Lakhun led the procession to the neighborhood temple, where a priest of the Snake Mother joined the couple in marriage. A priestess rolled a scarlet egg over the bride's womb while chanting a fertility song whose words Adeja could not follow. Lahis glowed under her faded red shawl. Adeja drank more than usual. When she smiled, Lahis was almost pretty, but at that moment Adeja only hoped that under her voluminous skirts her body was not as thin as her face.

After a bridal feast at Lakhun's house, a second procession wound its torchlit way through the streets to Adeja's tenement, where the landlady and several neighbors complained about the noise. Adeja took his bride by the hand and led her up three flights of stairs to her new home.

"You'll cook and clean," he said, gesturing to the boxes and bundles Lahis' relatives brought upstairs that morning. "I expect everything kept orderly."

Their first night together was not memorable. Lahis knew what was expected, but she was nervous and could only lie there with her legs spread while Adeja went into her and did his business.

Before dropping off to sleep, he patted her thigh and grunted, "It will be better next time." Whether or not she heard him, he did not know.

Lahis spoke so little he initially wondered if she was mute. Through their interaction, he learned she was shy and had been taught to be deferential. About the latter he had no complaints, for a temperamental wife would have driven him insane, but he would have liked a more passionate bedmate.

She kept the house as he ordered, and each night had supper ready for him when he returned from the quarry. As the wedding feast resulted in copious leftovers, she did not have to cook for three nights, so it was not until the fourth and his first mouthful of stew that he realized Lakhun had duped him over one crucial matter: his bride could not cook.

"Woman," he grumbled, shoving the bowl away from him, "if I wanted to eat slop I would have gone to the local midden." In Tajhaani, he added, "I wouldn't be surprised to learn your first husband died of a stomachache from eating this poison."

Tears leaked from the corners of her eyes, and she pressed both hands to her mouth to keep her sobs from escaping. She could not have understood that last part, he knew. His angry tone and gestures had sufficed.

Almost at once, he felt remorse. "Who cooked the wedding feast?" he asked. "Come, woman, I know you have a voice. Tell me who prepared the feast. Was it your mother?"

She nodded haplessly.

"Tonight we eat out," he said, "and then tomorrow you'll go to your mother and have her teach you. When you do as I tell you and cook me a good meal, I'll buy you something pretty in the bazaar." Lifting his hand, he touched her cheek. "That would please you, yes?"

Upon later reflection, Adeja wondered if he should have bought her a trinket then, but decided it was better to be frugal. She did not know how much money he had, as each morning he gave her only enough to buy foodstuffs and other necessities from the bazaar; the rest he kept hidden in a hollow space in the wall behind the bed.

Lahis was still distraught when they returned, so that night Adeja took special care in his lovemaking. She did not climax, but he sensed she enjoyed his touch more than she had.

She must have told her mother the entire story, replete with tears, for two days later Lakhun greeted him with a hard look that conveyed his displeasure. Rather than apologize and try to ingratiate himself back into his father-in-law's good graces, Adeja stood his ground. Lahis was his wife, her father was not going to dictate what went on in his household, and there was to be no further discussion about it.

"I expect certain things from my wife," he said. "She will have to learn."

Lakhun frowned and grunted, but said nothing more on the subject.

As summer turned to autumn, Lahis improved her cooking to the point where Adeja kept his promise. On the next rest day, he took her to the bazaar and let her choose a new shawl. Purchasing trinkets for women was not something to which he was accustomed, but when, perhaps fearing to displease him by spending too much, she tried to choose a sober black, he stepped in and insisted she take the deep blue that originally drew her eye.

Domestic life was not unpleasant, yet there were times when Adeja missed being a bachelor. Some nights he preferred not to go home. To spare Lahis worry he sent a message telling her he would be late. Of course, he did not say he intended to have a drink at the corner wine shop, or wander down to the local brothel to enjoy the attentions of a comely boy or maiden, as she would not understand that, while he was not displeased with her in bed, sometimes he desired more variety than she could provide.

It was not yet dark when he entered the wine shop. Several men from the quarry sat together, including two who did not hold their alcohol well and would be next to useless tomorrow. Upon seeing him, they invited him to join them at their table, but, desiring solitude, he took his drink and claimed a corner booth.

After a few moments, he noticed a certain festival air in the shop. While it was not uncommon for patrons to toast each other over family births, weddings and other special occasions, Adeja rarely saw a celebration carry across multiple tables. Curious, he tapped a man on the shoulder and asked what the occasion was.

"A royal wedding," answered the man. He took a drink and wiped his mouth with the back of his hand before continuing, "One of the king's daughters married the Crown Prince of Rhodeen."

Adeja took his drink to the corner and brooded. There could be only one Crown Prince of Rhodeen in Khalgar, which meant it was Sephil's wedding everyone was celebrating. Why this disturbed him so, Adeja could not say. A wedding was a festive occasion, and from what he had heard of the Khalgari princesses, Sephil was very fortunate indeed.

"You should be toasting his health," he muttered to himself. He lifted his cup, but abruptly drained it before he could get the words out. Filling his cup again, he drank until he passed out.

He woke, fuzzy-headed and nauseous, in an alley behind the shop. His hand crawled to the pouch at his belt. The three coppers he brought with him were gone. *You drank it all away.* Turning, he vomited onto a pile of refuse.

Not knowing how late it was, he wobbled back onto the street and tried to recall what made him drink himself senseless. Then he remembered: it was Sephil's wedding day.

Staggering, his stomach roiling, he slumped against the side of the building, covered his face with both hands and wept.

* * * *

Sephil wanted it to be over: the endless ceremonies, the attention, and most of all, the ordeal of the wedding night. Although it lasted only a week, he had not forgotten his first betrothal to Terreh, the humiliating blunder at the ceremony, or his bride's reaction when she realized Dashir was not to be her husband.

May she find happiness in her choice. More than a year later, Sephil found he could reflect and wish Terreh well. She would have little happiness as Dashir's wife.

The prospect of consummating his marriage compounded his anxiety, for while he understood the basic principles of making love with a woman, he had neither tried it on his own nor had any desire to do so.

For his first betrothal, Zhanil had attempted to rectify the situation by sending a courtesan to instruct him. The tactic might have helped had the woman not told him that his bride, being a virgin, would not know what pleased her, and that he must be careful not to hurt her.

Thus far, it seemed this union would not echo the first. As a father, Ampheres desired a good marriage for his daughter, and was more considerate about the matter than he might have been otherwise. On their return from Adenna, he drew Sephil aside and explained the situation in plain terms.

"You must marry," he said. "I think you understand this."

Sephil nodded. "What do you intend to do?"

"At this early stage, one cannot build empires on sons that have not yet been born or shown promise. What is certain is that Dashir and his Tajhaani alliance must be countered. Your bloodline is a valuable commodity, and your ties with our royal house must be strengthened."

"No," said Sephil. "I want to know what you intend to do with me once those sons are born."

168

Such was his surprise that, for a moment, the king could not speak. At last, he found his voice and answered, "I do not know what worries torment you, but I mean to give my daughter a husband, not make her a widow. Now if you prefer Lissan, you have my blessing, but I have watched you with Ketalya and believe that you are well suited for each other."

Sephil lacked the nerve to voice his objections, so he meekly nodded his head and sat down to wait while Ampheres summoned his daughter. *I do not care for women. My heart belongs to someone else.* Ketalya deserved better than to be disappointed.

When she arrived and heard her father's decision, Ketalya turned to Sephil, smiled, and kissed him upon the cheek. Her easy acceptance led him to suspect the matter had been decided beforehand, and that his consent was simply a formality.

That evening, the family toasted the prospective couple over supper, and later in the drawing room kissed and embraced both parties. A complete reversal from the reception Sephil received in Rhodeen, for then his father had offered no words of congratulation, only a stern warning that the alliance with Tajhaan must be honored. From his cousins and aunt, there was only laughter.

Zhanil alone rejoiced, embraced him, and sent the gift of a jeweled dagger, which Sephil later used to end his ordeal. He did not know what Ampheres had told his daughter about her future husband, but he did not think she knew about his suicide attempt. All she saw was a novice priest who studied and visited hospitals and shrines to tend the afflicted.

The next afternoon, as they walked in the gardens followed by Melwas and a female chaperone, Sephil asked Ketalya her true opinion. "I imagine you would prefer a more impressive husband."

"Someone like your brother, you mean?" she answered. "You already know my thoughts about him."

"He was a good husband and father," said Sephil.

"That does not mean I would have been happy with him." Turning to him, Ketalya smiled. "Whenever you mention Zhanil, you always put yourself at a disadvantage. Perhaps he was a brave fighter and capable statesman, but that does not mean you are less than him, or that you would not also be a good husband or father."

At this, his heart grew heavy. It was clear she did not know him, and he could not explain without revealing all.

In Rhodeen, the wedding of a princess would have been a small affair, celebrated within the inner circles of the court but scarcely noted beyond that. Not realizing how the Khalgari seized every opportunity to stage a festival, pageant or procession, Sephil assumed his wedding to Ketalya would be an inconspicuous affair until, with much good-natured laughterAmpheres told him that there would be no such thing.

On a brittle autumn morning, the bridal couple rode in procession from the palace to the House of the Snake Mother for the marriage rite. Ketalya presented a radiant image in her gilded red silk veil and jewels, while Sephil wore the deep royal blue of Rhodeen. Zhanil's seal ring glittered on his right hand. It felt too heavy, and the golden circlet he was obliged to wear pressed against his temples, giving him a headache.

His recollection of the ceremony blurred into the long reception that followed afterward. A second procession took the wedding party back to the palace, where in a large, many-pillared hall Sephil and Ketalya sat in state to receive the gifts and congratulations of the court. Sephil did not know many of the guests, but did his best to appear intelligent and interested.

Halfway through the reception, Melin Wesares appeared at the head of the Rhodeen delegation. According to the king's informants, he continued to assert his claim to the throne while denouncing Sephil as an incompetent pretender. He honored the bride with a deep bow, yet acknowledged Sephil with only the briefest nod, and placed nothing on the dais alongside all the other bridal gifts.

Ampheres, seated on a throne at his daughter's left hand, answered Wesares with a curt nod before gesturing him to move along.

At sunset, a lavish wedding banquet awaited the couple in an adjacent hall. When Zhanil married, the festivities had culminated in a feast considered grand by Rhodeen standards, but fourteen year old Sephil saw little of it, and what he did remember did not match the silver-and-gilt splendor Ampheres had arranged on his daughter's behalf.

When the time came, Sephil had no appetite for the dishes the servants set before him. Not wishing to draw attention to his nervous state, he choked down just enough to satisfy custom, yet when he would have reached for his wine goblet, Ampheres cautioned him against it. "I do not think it will help you tonight," he said quietly. "A man should have a clear head on his wedding night."

MY SUN AND STARS

Sephil did not need to be reminded of the night to come. He tried to focus on the few lessons he had learned from the courtesan in Rhodeen, but as Ketalya was a virgin he had no idea how he would please her. Making love with a woman felt so different. What he liked, she would not, and he did not want to hurt her.

At the height of the banquet, Ampheres toasted the couple, hailing the wedding as a union between two kingdoms whose bonds of blood and friendship had always been strong.

Midnight came with dancing and revels, and at last with an announcement that it was time to put the bridal couple to bed. Sephil assumed that at a certain point in the evening, he and Ketalya would gracefully retire. Instead, the royal princes roused him from his chair, separated him from his bride and led him to a suite where they divested him of his wedding finery and dressed him in a plain linen shift.

Good-natured teasing and merrymaking accompanied him into a second suite, furnished with an elaborate curtained bed where Ketalya already awaited him. Her sisters and ladies of the court attended her, while off to the side Sephil saw the king standing with a priest and priestess of the Snake Mother.

The priest directed him to climb into bed beside Ketalya and lie down. Sephil tried to cover his embarrassment by avoiding the gazes of the onlookers, especially when the priest folded the coverlet back over his knees.

A tiny brass bell tinkled, bringing a hush to the bridal chamber. The next thing Sephil heard was a woman's voice chanting in a language he did not understand. Turning his head, he saw the priestess of the Snake Mother take swaying steps toward him, a red object cupped in her hands. When she bent over him to roll it over his belly, he realized the object was an egg, and when the priestess crossed to the opposite side of the bed to repeat the ritual over Ketalya, he understood that this was a fertility rite.

As the priest and priestess withdrew, the court took this as their cue to depart as well. Ampheres kissed his daughter on the cheek, followed by her ladies and other family members. Sephil received hand clasps and words of encouragement from his new brothers-in-law. Servants extinguished all but two lamps as they trailed out after the guests. The doors closed, the sounds of conversation and laughter dwindled, and at last Sephil and his bride were alone.

Ketalya sat up, drew the coverlet up to her lap, and heaved a great sigh. "I did not realize until now that it is better to be a guest than the bride."

"I have not been to many weddings," Sephil said quietly. He tried very hard not to think about what was supposed to happen next.

She smiled, then frowned as her eyes dropped to his lap. "Sephil," she murmured, "do you always wear your jewelry to bed?"

Sephil did not know what she meant until he followed her eyes and realized she was looking at his bracelets. "I always wear these."

"I have been wondering why," she said. "They do not belong to a priest of Abh's regalia."

Please, do not let her ask me to remove them. "They were a gift from your father."

Ketalya laughed softly. "I do not think he will be offended if you take them off tonight."

Had he simply refused, or pretended to be vain, she might have let the matter be, but when he tried to fold his hands under the coverlet, it only aroused her curiosity.

"Sephil," she asked, reaching for him, "what is the matter?"

"You would not understand."

Still, he did not resist when she drew back the coverlet, gently took one hand in hers and unfastened the golden bracelet. "I do not see what the fuss is about," she said.

Seeing there was no other choice, Sephil reluctantly turned his wrist over so she could see the scar. Then he undid the other bracelet to show her the matching scar.

Ketalya stroked the skin above and below the scar on his left wrist. "How did this happen?"

No one in the sanctuary or temple of Abh who saw his scars had ever asked him that question. Clearly she did not understand, and he did not know what else to say. "I did this," he murmured.

"Why would you do such a thing?" she asked.

"Your father told you nothing about me. I am not half the prince you think I am. I am nothing next to my brother. I was such an embarrassment to my family that my father wished I had never been born. I was very unhappy living in Rhodeen." Sephil sucked in a ragged breath, telling himself that he was not going to cry, not tonight, and not in front of his bride.

Ketalya lifted a hand to his cheek. "I do not believe that about your father, and I have told you before that you should not compare yourself with Zhanil."

"I am not exaggerating or trying to be dramatic," he said. "My father really did say that to me, more than once. I know he loved my mother, but I took her away from him by being born, and I brought him no joy in the bargain.

"I could not ride or fight, my tutors all thought me slow, and I did foolish things." Sephil glanced away to study the flickering shadows cast by the lamps before fixing his gaze on his lap: anything to avoid looking at Ketalya. "I-I do not know how we will do this. I have only been with a woman once. When I was to be married the first time, Zhanil sent a woman to show me how, but I did not enjoy it as much as he thought I would. She was a courtesan. I imagine he considered her very refined and beautiful, but I thought her vulgar."

"Well, I am not a courtesan," said Ketalya. "I am your wife. I imagine as a priest you prefer celibacy, but those who serve Abh are not expected to forgo sex."

Sephil shook his head. *How am I ever going to explain this to her? She will think I am unnatural and horrible.* "I did not say I was a virgin. What I mean to say is that I am *different* – that is the only word I know to describe it."

Ketalya made a show of looking him over before answering with a soft laugh. "You seem normal enough to me. I do not see what the problem is."

Her easy manner did not reassure him. "It is what I prefer in bed that makes me different."

"You prefer males?"

Sephil nodded. "From the time I was eleven, I had a guardian who did not want to be bothered with me, so when I was old enough to be interested in sex, he sent a boy to teach me and let me do as I pleased. I learned to enjoy making love with another male, or perhaps I was simply born that way. I do not know. Your father knows all this. Why did he not tell you?"

"Perhaps he did not think it such an impediment as you believe," she said.

Either she thought she could change him, or she truly did not understand. Sephil took a deep breath, wondering even then if he should say anything at all. "My guardian should have explained certain things to me, but perhaps he just assumed I knew. When I was sixteen, there was a man in my household, a guard, who was very handsome. I invited him into my bedchamber and let him do things with me that I was not supposed to allow."

Her indrawn breath told him that she had finally grasped his meaning. "Why are you telling me this now?"

What he heard was the *now*, as in: *why did you wait until we were married and I could no longer refuse?* "Maybe I should not have said anything."

"Well, now that you have, you had better tell me the rest," answered Ketalya.

"I told you because my enemies slander me," said Sephil, "and I wanted you to know what is true and what is not. My father was so angry with me for what I did that he shut me up in my apartments for three years, and the only reason he let me out was because he needed a son to make an alliance with Tajhaan."

"Did he really do that?"

"My family is not as forgiving as yours," he said. "I am sorry that you did not know. If you wish me to sleep in one of the chairs—"

"Do not be ridiculous, Sephil." Ketalya leaned forward and dropped a kiss on his forehead. "We have to consummate this marriage, or everyone will think something is wrong. Perhaps if we put out the lamps and take off our gowns and just lie here touching each other, it will come to us naturally. Surely we cannot be the first bride and groom to have had this problem."

"I do not want to hurt you when we—that is to say, when I go inside you."

She laughed softly. "Even if you were your mighty brother, you would hurt me the first time. Did no one explain to you that that is how it is with women? In the dark you can pretend I am a boy, and then you will realize it is not so terrible."

"I could not pretend with you," he said. "There are differences."

"I do not mean you should enter me like a boy."

Sephil could not believe what he heard. "I thought you were a virgin."

She rolled her eyes. "Only because I have not lain with a man, not because I am ignorant. I do not know what they do in Rhodeen, but here in Khalgar women do not send their daughters or sisters to the marriage bed without telling them exactly what to do or expect. Besides, it is impossible to live with six brothers and not know something about their lovers. Come, put out the lamp on your side and let us try."

Not knowing what else to do, Sephil let her direct him. He put out the lamp nearest the door while she extinguished the other, and in the near-darkness fumbled his way back to the bed to pull off his shift and burrow under the coverlet. The mattress shifted, and he heard the rustle of fabric as Ketalya climbed back into bed beside him.

When she touched his bare skin, he flinched.

"Does it bother you?" she whispered.

"No," he lied. Her hand felt soft and warm as it slid up along his arm, and she smelled pleasant, but he could not forget how much importance was attached to this one deed. *If only it did not matter so much*, he thought. "It is nice."

"Then stop breathing so hard and touch me back," she said. "You are not going to hurt me."

Ketalya proved far more brazen than he, wrapping her arms around him and, finding his lips with her fingers, kissed him soundly until he forgot to be amazed. Sephil touched her where her hands directed him to touch, and guided her when she asked what he most enjoyed in bed. How much she knew about men, he did not know, but he felt uncertain about showing her how to suck his cock. Adeja once told him that women did not always like it or do it properly, whereas other men just seemed to *know*.

Instead, he drew her hand to his groin and showed her how to stroke him, which she did, rubbing his burgeoning erection into fullness.

That night, she pushed him onto his back and mounted him, breaking the seal with her own body. So aroused was he by the tight heat that enveloped him that he forgot his fears, grasped her hips and arched up into her until he climaxed. Afterward, he was abashed by the thought that she had not enjoyed it as much as he.

"It is all right," she murmured, hushing him with a kiss. "We have time."

"Zhanil did not tell—"

Ketalya stopped his words with another kiss. "Sephil," she said sternly, "the next time you utter your brother's name, you *will* sleep in the chair."

* * * *

"Sephil, I would not have you enter into your married life with such misconceptions as you now hold," said Ampheres.

They sat at the table in the king's salon, leisurely eating lunch. Ketalya spent the morning away from her new husband's side, overseeing the removal of possessions and servants to their new joint household, while Sephil remained with his father-in-law, discussing politics and domestic matters.

"I do not understand," he replied.

Ampheres carefully set down his fork and removed a sheet of parchment from the correspondence through which he had been leafing. "You believe your father cared nothing for you. Perhaps it would surprise you to learn that you are mistaken."

Sephil could only wonder when Ketalya had found the time to pass this information to her father, and what else she might have told him. "I am not mistaken," he answered. "More than once he told me how he wished I had never been born."

"What men and women say in anger, they do not always mean," said Ampheres.

"He kept me confined for three years," Sephil replied tightly, "and expressed no remorse afterward. If he said he wished me dead, he meant it."

Ampheres nodded, but did not concede the argument. "I have here your father's last letter to me, sent to me just before he died. Since the messenger had to smuggle it out of Shemin-at-Khul, most of it concerns the Turyar, but your father mentions you as well. Would you like to hear what he said?"

Not particularly, though Sephil knew that would not stop his father-in-law. "I doubt he had anything kind to say."

Holding the parchment to the light, Ampheres cleared his throat and read: "'*Among other sorrows, it grieves me to tell you of the death of my younger son at his own hand. I have little time in which to write, so I will not burden your ears with the sad tale except to say that he should not have ended this way. Zhanil has reproached me many times for my harsh treatment, as have others, including you, yet not as I have reproached myself. I often wondered why I withheld my affection from Sephil. Some have said that it was because he was the living image of his mother who died, yet for that I should have loved him with a whole heart.*

"'*Now in this gray hour, as I mull these dark thoughts and bid farewell to Zhanil, who rides out against the Turyar – and whom I may never see again – I have come to understand that perhaps the gods never meant for me to grow old and cherish either son.*'"

Ampheres carefully folded the letter and set it aside. "It seems that your brother neglected to inform him that you were alive and safely on your way to Ottabia. The knowledge that one child survived him might have eased his last hours."

As Sephil listened, he distanced himself from the words, unwilling to believe they were anything more than a fabrication designed to allay old wounds. *My father would never say such things. He would never regret my death except to complain that it had not come sooner.* "It is easy to speak kind words of the dead," he answered, "when they can no longer disappoint or embarrass you."

"Your father did not mince words, but when he spoke he was sincere," said Ampheres. "When a man knows or believes he is about to face death, he does not lie. Had I known how heavily this matter weighed upon you, I would have shared this letter with you earlier. I know what you are thinking, but rest assured that my daughter told me only what she felt I must know. Otherwise, I would not pry into the private affairs of a husband and wife."

Once again, Sephil greeted his words with skepticism. From now on, whatever he said, did, or thought, there was no question his father-in-law would know about it.

Chapter Nine

When he entered the tumult that was his new household, Sephil learned that the first thing Ketalya had done that morning was dismiss his steward, Hauto.

"I do not find him trustworthy," she explained. "Varen has been my steward for years, and whatever he sees or hears he will not repeat to my father."

Sephil did not quite believe this, but for the moment he preferred not to cause strife by disputing her choice. Hauto had been as cheerless as Melwas, who even now hovered in the background like an unwelcome shadow. At least Ketalya did not dismiss Delav or Piras, both of whom Sephil liked.

As he wandered the apartment, he tried to assist Ketalya in directing the servants until she explained that as a Khalgari noblewoman it was her duty to manage the household. She would order the servants and keep the money, for which he was grateful since he had no head for practical matters. In Rhodeen, Nakhet had managed whatever funds his father allotted him, and in Ottabia he had no need of money.

The household encompassed two separate suites, yet in the first few weeks of their marriage Sephil and Ketalya shared the same bed more nights than he could count. This came as a surprise, for after that first, awkward night Sephil could not comprehend why Ketalya would wish to repeat the experience.

"How else will we have children?" she asked.

Sephil repressed the shudder of distaste he felt at this remark. He did not ask whether she spoke from a genuine maternal desire or as a mouthpiece for her father's dynastic ambitions; he preferred not to know the answer. "We do not have to have them right away."

Not only did Ketalya stay with him, filling the autumn evenings with her conversation and gentle caresses, but showed an unwavering desire to explore lovemaking with him.

Ketalya was soft where Sephil preferred hardness, and curvaceous where he was accustomed to sleek muscle, yet she did not repel him as the courtesan had. Her scent and even her taste pleased him, to the point where he wondered if he avoided women simply because he had never really learned to appreciate them.

Fearing her disgust and believing it should no longer have a place in his life, he did not confide in her his continuing desire for male partners, or rather, one male whom he tried hard to forget. As much as he wanted Adeja, and dreamt of him on those rare nights when he slept alone, Sephil knew that passion could never again be.

I would have liked one last moment with him. He quickly pushed the thought away. Ketalya told him outright that she would tolerate young men when she could not fulfill her husband's needs herself, and even admitted preferring that option to female concubines who might become pregnant by him. Had she known about Adeja, however, she never would have accepted him.

It is better this way, he thought. *I cannot cling to him like a child, and he deserves his own life. Perhaps he has even found a wife by now.*

One late autumn morning when Ketalya did not appear for breakfast, Sephil made inquriies only to learn from the servants that the princess was unwell. Alarmed to learn she was vomiting, he left the table and headed for her suite.

Despite his efforts, he got no farther than her bedchamber door. Amarno, the chief lady-in-waiting, stopped him with her considerable bulk. "The physician has been summoned, my lord," she said loftily, "but as the lady has no fever I do not think it is cause for concern."

Muffled retching from the direction of the privy told Sephil otherwise. Squeezing past Amarno, snapping at her when she would not move aside, he entered Ketalya's green-and-gilt bedchamber. Amarno followed, haranguing him as he entered the bathroom, and finally the marble privy where Ketalya, sweaty and haggard in her night shift, knelt over a chamber pot. A lady-in-waiting hovered anxiously at her side, bathing her brow with a damp cloth.

"What is the matter?" he asked.

She looked up at him, unable to speak before she turned and retched once more.

Sephil rounded on Amarno. "Why have you not called a physician?"

The good humor with which the woman answered him was intolerable. "My lord," she said, "I told you before there is no cause for concern. The princess has missed her monthly courses, and now we know why."

"What are you talking about?"

Ketalya lifted her head from the chamber pot and groaned, "She means I am with child."

He could not quite believe what he heard. "But you are sick!"

"Morning sickness is normal, my lord," said Amarno. With her hand on his arm, she firmly guided Sephil back to the sitting room where his breakfast was already growing cold. "I have already sent for a physician. He will explain everything once he arrives." With that, she retreated to her mistress' suite and shut the door, leaving Sephil to fret in stunned silence.

"How can she be with child?" he asked, fixing his gaze on Delav. "It has only been a few weeks."

"Such things can happen, my lord."

"Are women really supposed to be that sick when they are pregnant?"

"It seems so," replied the vizier, "though do not ask me why. The gods have not blessed me with a wife."

The physician, a kindly, middle-aged man who introduced himself as Ghanis, presently arrived and spent a half-hour closeted with Ketalya. When he emerged, Sephil was aghast to see him smiling.

"I hear your wife's ladies have already told you she is pregnant," he said. "From your reaction, my lord, I can see this will be your first child. Let me assure you that the princess is in excellent health, so at this stage I do not foresee any complications for her."

"I do *not* call what I saw before an example of excellent health," answered Sephil.

"Nausea is normal for an expectant mother at this stage," explained Ghanis. "As the seed takes root in the womb, the woman's natural functions are disrupted. The princess may be somewhat uncomfortable in the morning hours, but her nausea should abate by afternoon. Once the child quickens, her symptoms should disappear completely."

"You do not sound certain."

"Each woman is different, my lord, as is each pregnancy. The best thing you can do is remember that all of this is completely natural and remain calm."

It was good advice, yet difficult to put into practice. Sephil relaxed only when he was able to return to his wife's bedchamber and see for himself that she felt better.

Ketalya, bathed and dressed in a clean gown, greeted him with a tolerant smile. "Ghanis tells me I am to expect this condition in the mornings."

Sephil sat down beside her. "I am sorry."

"I do not see what you have to do with it."

"It is my child," he said.

"Yes," she sighed, "and sadly you cannot share in the joys of childbirth or letting out one's clothes." Then she laughed and patted his hand. "This was not unexpected, Sephil. My courses did not come as they ought, so I suspected it might be a child."

"Why did you not say anything to me before?"

Still smiling, Ketalya shook her head. "I wished to be sure. I will rest for a while and then see if I can eat anything. Meanwhile, you should go to the temple as you planned."

Sephil did no such thing. Through Delav, he canceled his afternoon appointments, sent a message to his father-in-law, then retired to the sitting room to await the king.

Ampheres arrived within the hour, visited with his daughter and congratulated Sephil. "Soon you will have to prepare your household for a son," he said.

With a polite smile, Sephil thanked him for the compliment, while secretly praying for a daughter.

* * * *

With his fair coloring and light brown hair, the youth resembled Sephil enough that when Adeja saw him, he paid for two hours in advance and took him upstairs.

Lahis was away tending a female relative in childbed, so the apartment stood empty, supper remained uncooked, and Adeja did not wish to be alone. He did not see why his wife's mother or sisters could not have gone in her stead, but as she seemed to want to go, he allowed her.

Winter brought rain to Bhellin. Building projects went on hiatus and all work in the quarries stopped. Adeja found temporary employment as a prison guard. Although less strenuous than finishing stones in the quarry, it was a grim task. Not only did he guard the cells and escort the menials who brought prisoners their meals, but he also had the job of accompanying the condemned to the scaffold.

Work and the wet weather made him sharp-tongued. On more than one occasion he found himself in the bazaar purchasing a trinket for Lahis, who bore the brunt of his ill temper, so when she wanted to visit her relatives he was not surprised.

After eating with other guards from his shift at a shop near the prison, Adeja braved the chill and drizzle to venture down to the nearest brothel. He did not know what he wanted, other than companionship.

As he walked into the establishment, he let his eyes adjust to the lamps and roam the main room, perusing the workers. Sometimes whores were so filthy or otherwise unappealing that he turned around and left, but so far that was not his experience in Bhellin.

Perhaps it would have been better if it had been. The moment the young man locked eyes with him and let his fingers trace an enticing path from his lower lip to his groin, Adeja he knew what he wanted.

Once the transaction was made, the young man twined an arm through his and led him upstairs. For his generous payment, Adeja rated a flagon of wine and a chamber with an actual bed, and the bedding was clean.

His partner lit a lamp on the table beside the bed. "If you prefer," he said, "I can put it out."

Adeja loosened his belt before pulling the young man into his arms. "What is your name?"

"Minare, or anything else you like."

In the half-moment it took Adeja to consider that option, he dismissed it. Minare resembled Sephil, with his enticing purr and promiscuous pout promising delights beyond anything a wife could provide, but the resemblance remained superficial. Adeja would not soil the prince's name by attaching it to this act.

As leaned in to kiss Minare's neck, his nose twitched at the overpowering scent the young man wore; it was cheap, and too much. "Wash this off," he said, sliding his fingers along Minare's throat.

At a corner basin, Minare dipped a cloth in the water and sponged his neck and shoulders, turning the motion into a slow, seductive act that could not fail to capture Adeja's attention.

Adeja came over, took the cloth from him, and bathed his throat and face, wiping off the kohl and henna that seemed to mark every prostitute he had ever fucked. "You're pretty enough without all this," he said. "You shouldn't cheapen yourself so."

Minare licked at the stray water droplets with a tongue that said he would do no less to Adeja's cock. Time enough for that later. For now, Adeja wanted to taste his mouth, slowly peel away his clothes and feel that slight, supple body against his.

"What is your pleasure?" murmured Minare.

Adeja slipped his tongue between those parted lips. "Don't speak," he growled. "I'll show you how I want it."

He spent his seed twice that night, letting Minare fondle and suck him to full bloom before spreading the young man over the bed and mounting him hard. Orgasm blunted his ache, but did not close the wound.

Through the dark streets he found his way home, climbed the three flights of stairs to his darkened apartment and fell into bed. Lahis still had not returned.

Tonight confirmed in his mind a thought that had been growing for many weeks. When spring came, it would be time to consider leaving Bhellin and putting distance between himself and what he could not have. Other cities in Khalgar held plenty of other opportunities, either in the stone trade or as a guard. Of course, Lahis would not like leaving her family, but he only knew that he could not continue as he was.

* * * *

Sephil relished the quiet of the sanctuary of Abh. Avorim welcomed him back, reintroduced him to the priests and novices, and helped him resume his studies.

"Bedren has written to me," said the high priest. "All is well in Ottabia. Kalion continues to atone for his actions."

"Unless he does it with a whole heart," answered Sephil, "he should not bother."

Perhaps Avorim conveyed these words back to Bedren, for Sephil heard no more about the matter. If Kalion repented, that was between him and the gods.

Sephil took his place once more among the novices, greeting old companions and weathering their amusement as they learned his true identity. At first, they addressed him by his royal titles, and expressed horror when he began ministering to the faithful as he had done before, but this treatment lasted no more than a few days. Although Melwas and another guard accompanied him, they remained at a discreet distance, enabling Sephil to work unhindered.

These quiet hours in the sanctuary, sitting beside the afflicted and destitute, serving them with his own hands and listening as they described their hardships, offered Sephil the sense of purpose he lacked elsewhere. He made one concession to his rank by wearing the royal Sun of Rhodeen on the lapel of

183

his robe. Ampheres took interest in his visibility for political reasons, but to Sephil it seemed more important that those he tended understand that he was both prince and priest, a living example that the royal house truly did care for those under its protection.

Ketalya took pride in his vocation. Oftentimes she asked what books he read, and wore around her neck a little silver reliquary filled with water from the Adenna shrine. She also wore the silver bracelets Sephil gave her to celebrate her pregnancy. With Varen's help, he found a jeweler to etch little moons around the bands, and presented them to Ketalya with much ceremony.

"In Rhodeen," he explained, "the king is the Sun, but the queen is *sepha rian*, the Moon."

Ketalya held out her wrist as he slid the bracelets onto it. "Then why did your father call you 'little moon?'"

"For my mother," answered Sephil.

With the announcement of Ketalya's pregnancy, relations grew strained with both Tajhaan and the Rhodeen faction represented by Melin Wesares; the latter cast such aspersions on the baby's paternity that he alienated the very king upon whose generosity he counted. Ampheres cautioned him to mend his words, which Wesares did only so far as the princess was concerned. Sephil, however, was fair game, and slanderous broadsheets continued to circulate in the city.

However much the family tried to prevent it, Ketalya saw several of these publications, with their crudely executed wood-cut caricatures of her husband in compromising positions. Sephil preferred not to look at them at all, instead taking his father-in-law's advice and treating the slanders as beneath his notice, even as he continued to visit hospitals and shrines.

"This is such tripe," said Ketalya, handing the latest broadsheet off to a servant to burn on the hearth. "Why anyone would believe such things, I do not know."

"I have not always had such a shining reputation," replied Sephil.

"Perhaps, but anyone who knows you can see these stories are false."

For his part, Sephil did not care to correct her by elaborating on how much of the slander was true, and how much was simply a distorted version of the truth.

Tajhaan provided a more substantial threat. Sephil sat beside his father-in-law in the audience chamber when the

Tajhaani ambassador delivered stern words from the High Prince, who chided Ampheres for endangering diplomatic relations between the two kingdoms by not recognizing the rightful king.

"Your prince addresses us as a brother," said Ampheres, "yet in his message we do not hear the language of a brother."

In his demeanor, Sephil saw that the ambassador plainly desired to be elsewhere. "Great King," the man answered, "my prince speaks only out of the highest regard and love for your person, and urges you to remember that brothers may occasionally exchange harsh words for good purpose."

When he would have continued, Ampheres cut him short with a gesture. "Spare us your mincing words. Do your duty and convey our displeasure to Armajid. Tell him if he desires a better answer, he would do well to remember our position. We are not subordinate, and will act when and in what way we see fit."

Sephil noted that in all this political wrangling, the princes, diplomats and statesmen of both lands continued to behave as though the Turyar did not exist. No official word had come out of Shemin-at-Khul, yet other sources confirmed that the Turya lord who had led the invasion had taken one of the captive royal women as his queen and was now consolidating his power, seizing estates from Rhodeen nobles who would not surrender and giving them over to Turya chieftains upon whose loyalty he could count.

Conquest did not involve decimating the general population, as commoners seemed unaffected by the change.

Ambassadors could pass back and forth as they liked, treaties could be signed and discarded, and insults doled out on both sides until Khalgar and Tajhaan stood on the brink of war, but nothing short of military action would dislodge the Turyar. Sephil, whose only concern at this point was his wife and unborn child, removed himself from the situation insofar as he was able.

Though two more months remained before the child quickened, Ampheres scheduled a visit to the oracle of the Snake Mother. Ketalya did not relish a visit to the oracle, and tried to persuade her father that it was not necessary. Without explaining further, Ampheres insisted and ordered her to prepare.

"I have no great love of serpents," she confessed to Sephil, "and do not wish to see some poor woman suffer simply to look into my future."

"What does the ritual entail?" he asked.

"Father will put a question to the oracle, and she will go into a trance after taking the bite of a poisonous snake." Ketalya visibly shuddered at her description, even as Sephil tried to picture the scene. "Her prophecies are supposed to be very reliable, but I do not want to see her ordeal. They say the oracles are chosen young, and die before they are thirty because they are bitten so many times."

She need not have worried. On the day before the visit, a priestess of the Snake Mother came to the palace to explain the ritual, as Sephil sat beside her to provide reassurance. "The holy oracle will place her hands on your womb and go to an inner chamber for the serpent bite and sacred trance," said the priestess. "Prophecy is the Mother's mystery, where even kings may not trespass."

When Ampheres came that evening to visit, he offered additional assurances. "All will be well," he said. "After your meeting with the oracle, you may return here and rest. Sephil and I will remain to await the outcome."

Had Sephil any say in the matter, he would have canceled the trip altogether. Ketalya clearly did not want to go, and he empathized with her reluctance. Whether the child was a son or daughter made no difference to him, and from what little Ketalya said on the topic, either gender would suit her as long as the child was healthy.

Late the next morning, they departed for the House of the Snake Mother. Due to her condition and the weather, Ketalya rode in a covered litter, while Sephil and Ampheres rode alongside. Twenty guards accompanied them, with Melwas riding behind.

Rather than approach the temple through the grand plaza, the royal party entered through an inconspicuous side gate and proceeded up a path that took them into a dimly lit vestibule. Sephil wrinkled his nose at the smell of mildew and old herbs, and Ketalya swaying, visibly nauseous.

Sephil placed a hand on her arm. "Do you want to sit?" he asked softly. "There is a bench by the door."

Gritting her teeth, Ketalya shook her head. "I want to go home," she whispered back.

Two priestesses emerged from an inner room and, after bowing to the king, approached Ketalya. For the occasion, her ladies had dressed her in a loose-fitting bodice and full skirt, which the priestesses undid just enough to expose her belly under the linen chemise.

MY SUN AND STARS

"All mothers know the blessing of the Snake Mother, who sheds her skin and renews the world," said one priestess, a formidable-looking crone who placed a hand over Ketalya's womb. Too early for the roundness that was the telltale sign of pregnancy, Sephil could not understand what the priestess expected to find.

As she spoke, four more priestesses appeared. In their midst stood a woman clad in white, small and on the gaunt side of slender. When she stretched forth her hands to lay them on Ketalya's womb alongside the crone's, old puncture marks stood out like bruises against her pale skin.

Ketalya said nothing during the examination, but Sephil sensed her discomfort. The woman's strange mannerisms did nothing to reassure him. Under her breath she hissed softly, and when Ampheres presented her with the gift of chalice filled with myrrh, her gaze passed through him. She was blind, or the effects of serpent venom made her appear so.

Once the oracle finished her examination, the priestesses rearranged Ketalya's clothing and released her. Ampheres nodded, and she left the temple with Melwas and and ten of the guards.

Temple servants brought food, drink and coal for the braziers. Ampheres did not appear impatient, for as he sat down on one of the cushioned benches, he confided to Sephil that he consulted the oracle about political matters he deemed especially important. "When the Turyar appeared on the borders of your father's realm," he said, "I put my question to the Snake Mother and learned that the head and star would fall, but not the body."

"That makes no sense," said Sephil.

"You might think so, but a prophecy bears much thought," said Ampheres, "and one must look outside the bounds of literal interpretation for an answer. Very often, one does not understand the truth of the Snake Mother's words until after the event has occurred. As king, your father was the head of state, and your brother's name meant 'little star.' Both have fallen as the oracle predicted, but the body, the actual kingdom, has remained intact."

If the truth could only be known *after* the event, then Sephil saw no practical value in oracles, prophets or other fortune tellers.

"It will take an hour or two for the oracle to finish her reading," continued Ampheres. "The viper they use for the ceremony is extremely deadly. The poison takes effect within moments, but I am told that the Snake Mother's message must be transcribed by the priests into a form we can understand."

Sephil wrapped himself in his fur-lined cloak and settled in to wait. Even with two braziers burning, the vestibule was cold and too dark for reading, so he put his book aside, concentrated on the sound of the rain falling outside and meditated. Time melted away, so it surprised him when when a priestess appeared in the doorway. Flanked by two priests, she swayed as she uttered the words of prophecy: *A son will ride forth, the sun at his back, the moon on his left and the stars on his right. Darkness wraps her cloak about him, war bathes him in blood, a crown of stars sits upon his brow.*

This was not the hissing oracle who had appeared earlier, but another woman whose words seemed rehearsed. Until now, Sephil had assumed the messenger would be a priest.

"These are the words of the Serpent," she intoned. "They may not be altered, they may not be circumvented. All shall come to pass."

Ampheres bowed his head to her. "We thank the Mother for her wisdom, and her servants for their tribulation."

While the king appeared satisfied, Sephil did not like what he heard at all. He wondered what gibberish the oracle had actually uttered in her venom-induced agony, and how much of it had been tailored by the priests to suit the ambitions of their royal patron. No matter what the truth; Ampheres would use the prophecy to shape his dynastic plans, and Sephil did not need such contrivances to know what that would entail.

A guard met them on the path leading down to the courtyard. Splashed with mud and droplets of what appeared to be blood, the royal escort did not recognize him as one of their own until he sank to his knees before Ampheres and blurted out his unit and rank.

He was one of the ten soldiers who had been assigned to guard Ketalya, and his condition told Sephil something was very wrong.

"What is the matter?" demanded the king. "Why are you not with the princess?" From his tone, Sephil knew he realized the danger also.

"Sire," gasped the guard, "we were attacked in the streets."

Sephil noticed how hard the young man was trembling and stepped forward to help him up. "Where is the princess now?" he asked.

The guard turned to look at him. A knife or other weapon had cut him above the left eye, leaving that side of his face covered in blood. "There were several of them, sir, maybe eight or ten—I couldn't count, they struck so fast. They cut down Melwas and overturned the litter. I heard the princess scream and went to help her, but they fell on us. The captain ordered me to come back here and bring the other guards."

Ampheres did not wait for the rest of the story. Shouting for his horse and his remaining bodyguard, he raced down the path ahead of Sephil, who instructed the priests gathered in the vestibule doorway to see to the injured man.

A crowd swarmed the street where the attack had occurred. Palace guards were already on the scene, dispersing onlookers while Ampheres dismounted his horse, shoved men aside, and bellowed orders. Still in the saddle, Sephil saw the wrecked litter and bodies strewn across the pavement. Melwas lay in a pool of blood beside the litter, his severed arm still grasping his sword. Sephil gagged and looked away, scanning the other corpses for Ketalya but seeing only guards and men wearing nondescript clothing.

Where is she? Fighting nausea and growing panic, he motioned to one of the captains supervising the scene. "I do not see the princess," he said. "I was told she was attacked. Where is she now?"

"Sir, I am not authorized to release information—"

"She is my wife, soldier!"

Saluting, the captain cleared his throat and answered, "Forgive me, sir. I didn't realize you were a prince. We arrived to find the princess bruised and disoriented, but otherwise unharmed. She was conducted back to the palace a short time ago."

Sephil breathed a sigh of relief at the news. "Who did this?" he asked.

"We don't know yet, sir." The captain gestured to the ruined litter and the nearby bodies not wearing the royal livery. "They were killed before they could be questioned. The guards took them down, and those that escaped them were cut down by citizens who heard the lady's cries and ran to help. Right now, we're doing all we can to find out more."

Seeing there was no more for him to do at the site, Sephil asked his father-in-law's permission to return to the palace. Ampheres dismissed him with an escort of five guards. "Go see to your wife," he said. "I will investigate this matter."

Chaos reigned in the household. The guard had been doubled, yet with Melwas gone there was no one to command them. Ladies and servants ran back and forth, carrying linens, smelling salts, and gossip, their frenzied activity unnerving the mistress who lay trembling in her bed. Sephil paused in the doorway, took in the scene, and ordered at everyone but the physician to leave.

Ketalya flinched at his commanding tone, which was harsher than he intended. Seeing this, Amarno attempted to evict him until he seized her by the wrist and shoved her out the door. "You are upsetting the princess," he said. "I will not have it." Before the woman could protest, he slammed the door shut in her face.

"I am sorry," he said, crossing the room to the bed. Ketalya's eyes, wide and dark in a pale face, never left him as he sat down. Scratches and a deep bruise marred her cheek, but Ghanis, who sat on the opposite side, assured Sephil that she was more stunned than hurt.

"She tumbled out of the litter," he explained. "When it toppled over, it shielded her from the brunt of the attack, and Melwas pulled her assailant off her before he could cause serious injury. However, she tells me that she witnessed much carnage, so it is understandable that her nerves are strained right now. I will give her something to sleep, but not too strong in view of her condition. As far as I can tell, the child has not been harmed."

Sephil stayed with Ketalya, holding her hand as she took the sleeping draught and slowly drifted off. Ghanis stayed a while longer, gently applying a poultice to the bruise and scratches, and prescribing rest.

Twilight darkened the gardens outside when Sephil rose from his wife's bedside. He tucked the coverlet around her, extinguished all but one lamp and stepped outside, softly closing the door behind him. All at once, the ladies-in-waiting accosted him, clamoring for information until he sharply gestured for silence.

"The princess is sleeping," he said, "and she is not to be disturbed. Amarno, you or one of the other ladies will sit with her through the night should she wake. I will not have all of you in there upsetting her with your noise."

Leaving the matter in Amarno's hands, Sephil retired to the sitting room where the servants offered him a meal he could not eat, and sent for Varen. "Until the princess recovers, you are entrusted with the daily operation of the household," he told the steward. "I will receive your reports in her place."

What he would do with those reports, Sephil had no idea. Management was not part of his upbringing, and he was content to let others delegate work and handle the budgets and endless paperwork. However, he knew he could not project incompetence and expect the steward to take him seriously. Necessity taught him that giving in to the panic he felt would only give his enemies the satisfaction they craved, and it would not help Ketalya.

"I will do all I can, my lord," said Varen.

As the steward was about to leave, Sephil suddenly recalled something. "Varen, who will command the household guard now that Melwas is gone?" he asked.

Varen turned from the door. "The appointment has not yet been made, my lord, but I am certain the king will appoint someone first thing in the morning."

That decided it. "No," Sephil said firmly, "this time *I* will make the appointment."

Chapter Ten

"My lord," protested Varen. "I am not quite certain this is permitted."

Sephil ignored him. "In the morning you will send messengers to the city's stonemasons and quarries and inquire after a man named Adeja ked Shamuz. When you find him, bring him here."

"Sir, if this man has some complicity in today's terrible events, the king should—"

"He is a soldier, not a suspect," answered Sephil. "Should he ask, tell him I wish to offer him a job."

Varen hesitated. "My lord, the king will want to make the appointment."

"As much as I appreciate the king's assistance, this is *my* household. The princess is *my* wife, carrying *my* child, and *I* will see to her safety," answered Sephil. His voice sounded harsh even to his own ears, but he did not soften his tone. "Is that understood, or do I need to dismiss you?"

Nakhet had not gone when ordered, and Sephil remained uncertain about dismissing a steward who belonged more to Ketalya than him. He softened his tone and added, "You do your work well, Varen, but right now your concern must be for the princess."

"Yes, my lord," replied Varen, "but there are certain protocols that must be observed."

Sephil took a chance, stepped forward and draped an arm about the steward's shoulder. Weeks of watching Zhanil interact with court officials and palace staff told him that self-assurance, not rank, was the key. Otherwise, the steward would never obey him. "You know I have only the best intentions," he said, "and the man I wish you to find is both exceptionally loyal and intelligent. Of *course* one must be proper about these things, but sometimes necessity dictates otherwise. You are simply following orders. Should the princess or the king express their disapproval, I will explain the situation to them."

At this point, Varen offered no further resistance and began making inquiries. Sephil did not inform Ampheres about his intentions, allowing the king to appoint a commander that, when circumstances allowed, he would dismiss.

Once alone, Sephil sat down and tried to focus his thoughts. The reality of the situation, bodies lying in the street and bruises on his wife's face, were too much to comtemplate. More than anything, he needed Adeja to place a hand on his shoulder and reassure him that everything would be all right.

I have overstepped my role, he thought. *The king will scold me for doing this, but what else can I do?* In their few weeks together, Sephil had watched Zhanil with his heavily pregnant wife and understood that a husband's role at such times was to offer support and protection. *How can I sit here and let others do everything? Everyone will think I am an incompetent fool.*

The investigation into the attack continued. Ampheres could offer little information, explaining how the officials charged with identifying and apprehending the perpetrators did not even know who the deceased assailants were. "They appear to be local men," he said, "but no one will come forward to claim the bodies and the witnesses say nothing."

"Why not interrogate them?" asked Sephil.

Ampheres gave him a questioning look. "Only a tyrant employs torture in that manner. Would an aspiring priest of Abh truly have us do such a thing to those who committed no crime?"

Abashed, Sephil said no more. That the perpetrator might escape punishment was a bitter reality he realized he would probably have to accept.

Putting a gracious face on the situation, he went down to the street where the attack occurred, met with the shopkeepers who had intervened, and thanked them for coming to his wife's aid. That evening, Ampheres approved his initiative, though Sephil did not seek such praise. He wished to atone for his earlier callousness, and hoped that his appearance would put a human face on the inquiries and prompt someone to come forward. On that point, his effort proved fruitless.

What time he could, he spent with Ketalya. Once she slept through the first night, she seemed calmer, but once in a while Sephil saw her stare at the wall, her eyes losing focus as though she was trying to recall something.

"Why would anyone want to harm me?" she murmured.

Sephil took her hands in his. Whenever he spoke to her, he tried to sound warm and reassuring, using the same tones he employed with those he tended in the sanctuary. "I felt the same when my cousin tried to kill me, and when the priest betrayed me in Ottabia," he said. "You know you were not the target."

"The baby has not even quickened," she answered. "It is not right."

"You will be safe here."

Ketalya leaned back against the pillows. Rain drummed against the windowsill and gutters outside. It was an afternoon for lingering inside with a warm fire and no servants. "What did the oracle say?"

"That it will be a son," he said. "I suppose we must decide on a name."

"I would prefer to wait, but if it amuses you, then go ahead."

Sephil sprawled atop the coverlet beside her. "Do you think he would like a Khalgari name or a Rhodeen one?" Sitting up on one elbow, he drew the cover down just enough to expose her belly, and addressed the occupant within. "Well, what would *you* prefer?"

Ketalya gently pushed him away. "Stop that," she said, smothering a giggle. "The child has not even quickened."

Propping his chin on his hand, he looked up at her. "Personally, I would rather have a daughter, but if it is a boy, I think he should have a Rhodeen name," he said. "Or we could wrap him in pink swaddling clothes, give him a girl's name, and fool everybody."

Ketalya took interest in neither his joke nor the business of naming. Her apathy baffled him, so when Ghanis made his next scheduled visit, Sephil drew the physician aside, explained the difficulty, and asked what was amiss.

Ghanis listened to his concerns. "I would not worry," he said. "I have observed with some mothers that they begin to take greater interest once the baby quickens. With the princess, it may simply be too early, or she may be preoccupied with what has just happened. Give her time, my lord, and all will be well."

Sephil decided to let the matter alone for now, especially with other, more pressing concerns to deal with. As the second day drew to a close, Varen still had no success in locating Adeja.

"My prince," he said, "I assure you I have sent out men to find him, but the stonemason shops have never heard of him and the quarries are closed this time of year. My men are currently making inquiries among the quarry foremen to see what they might know, but it is possible this man has found employment elsewhere, or left the city altogether."

"Keep looking," said Sephil. Should Varen's inquiries among the quarry foremen prove fruitless, he would have the steward widen the search to the city's barracks, for if Adeja did not go into the stone trade, he would probably return to the military.

Above all, Sephil did not want to contemplate the possibility that Adeja had left Bhellin.

On the fourth afternoon, a raging storm kept Sephil from the temple. As he read by the fire in the sitting room, Varen entered and announced his success. "I have brought him as you wished, my lord. He is waiting in the foyer."

Sephil nodded. "Bring him in."

Varen ushered in a man wearing an ill-fitting guard's uniform and an irritated look. Sephil looked up, recognized Adeja, and smiled. "Thank the gods you have come. I have been searching for you for days. Varen, have someone bring him a towel and something warm to drink. Adeja, please sit down."

Adeja took the cloth the servant handed him and wiped his face and dripping hair, but remained standing. "What do you want? I've no time for a social visit. If I don't work, I don't get paid."

"I would not ask you here if it was not important, and I will compensate you for any work time lost," replied Sephil. "My wife was attacked on her way from the temple of the Snake Mother. I need your assistance."

As he listened, Adeja's face changed. "I had no idea."

"She is pregnant, and I fear she will be attacked again," said Sephil. "Adeja, will you please sit down? I imagine you do quite enough standing wherever it is you work."

"I've taken a job in the local prison." Unpinning his damp cloak, which he let fall to the floor, Adeja sat down in one of the sitting room's velvet chairs. "I didn't know your wife was with child. Was she hurt?"

"She was more startled than injured, but most of her guards were killed," explained Sephil. "The king has already replaced them, and appointed a new captain. They are loyal, but I do not trust them to protect her or the child against whoever wishes them harm."

A second servant entered bearing a tray with goblets of mulled wine. Sephil took one and offered Adeja the other. "I called you here because I want you to take a post here in my household."

Adeja set the goblet down without drinking from it. His jaw tightened, and when he spoke his reply was a growl. "I'm not your fucking lapdog to come and go as you please."

"Mind your tongue," warned Varen, observing from the corner.

Sephil stilled his protest with a gesture. "Adeja, I would not have bothered you if I did not truly need you. You would be well paid, I assure you."

"I have a wife now," said Adeja, "and I'm certainly not about to leave her just so I can watch your door."

Smiling, Sephil offered his congratulations, but his joy was mingled with a disappointment he could not quite fathom. "I see no reason you cannot bring your wife with you," he said. "Many of the servants here are married and live together, and I am sure your wife would be pleased at the promotion. Work in the prison cannot be all *that* appealing."

Adeja threw back his head in frustration. "I can't just—"

"Who is this man?" asked a voice from the doorway.

Ketalya stood there, a velvet dressing gown thrown over her chemise, her hair loose and disheveled. While Varen quickly voiced his apologies, Sephil rose and went to her side. "Did I wake you, my lady?" he murmured.

"I heard an unfamiliar voice," she said. Peering around him, Ketalya looked apprehensively at Adeja. "Now answer my question: who is this rough-looking man and why is he here?"

"He is a guest. Come, I will introduce you." Sephil took her by the hand and, with some reluctance on her part, led her into the room. "My lady, this is Adeja ked Shamuz, my guard in Rhodeen and Ottabia. He is a man of considerable loyalty who saved my life more than once. I asked him here to offer him a position in our household. Adeja, this is my wife, Princess Ketalya kéya Ampheres."

Adeja made a short little bow. "He has offered, my lady, but I haven't yet accepted."

Even though Ketalya was courteous, Sephil could tell that she disliked both Adeja and the impromptu interview. Contrary to what he expected, her disapproval increased as he described Adeja's credentials. A moment later, he discovered why.

"Husband," she said, interrupting, "it seems this man is not a member of the royal establishment. Sir, you will have to forgive the prince. He means well, but it seems he does not yet fully understand our customs. In Khalgar, certain protocols must be observed in appointing guards or servants in royal households. You do not possess the proper credentials."

"Assassins care nothing for protocol," Sephil said tightly. He did not care for her patronizing tone, and would not suffer it in front of others. "Adeja has a long record of satisfactory service, as well as letters of credential from my brother. While I respect the customs of the royal household, I should also point out there are circumstances when one must go beyond what is proper. I do not see why our safety should be compromised simply because it is against protocol."

Adeja, now more amused than irritated, glanced from one to the other. "My prince," he said, "it seems you called me here without asking your wife first."

Sephil glared at him. "I did not wish to distress her anymore than she already has been."

"It is our task to appoint servants," said Ketalya. "We thank you for your trouble, but at this time we do not require more guards."

Tilting his head slightly to one side, Adeja drew a long breath and held it while he studied her. "I take it my lady knows who did this?" he finally asked. With one finger, he motioned to her bruised cheek. "In Tajhaan, we respect royal women. Any man who did that to a princess would be hunted down and killed at once."

His brusque, informal manner flustered Ketalya, who shakily repeated that an additional guard was not needed before withdrawing.

Sephil walked Adeja to the door. "I still want you for this position," he promised. "I will speak to her."

"Save your words," answered Adeja. "I wish you luck in catching whoever did that to your woman, but if the king and his entire royal guard can't help you, then I don't see what one lowly Tajhaani soldier is going to do."

"Why is it that we never part on good terms?"

"Because you're a prince and I'm a soldier, and when you don't need me, off I go like so much baggage."

"That is not true," said Sephil. "I have never sent you away."

Adeja donned his cloak. "You're right, but I doubt I'd be of much use to you."

He took the money Varen gave him, nodded farewell to Sephil and followed the steward out.

Sephil went to his wife's chamber and dismissed her ladies. Ketalya sat before the looking glass brushing her hair, which she continued to do even as the door closed.

"You were rude to him, and to me," he said. "I will not be humiliated that way in front of others."

Ketalya set down her brush and looked at him. "And you embarrassed me by insisting I meet that man when I was not properly dressed. Appointing servants is my duty," she answered. "Had you consulted me before bringing him here, there would have been no difficulty."

"You have no trouble allowing your father to appoint guards," he pointed out. "As your husband, I have the right to do the same. Why should I stand idly by while men threaten your life and the life of our child? I mean to pursue this."

"That man has not been trained by the royal establishment. He is not qualified to serve here."

"I do not see what that has to do with anything. I do not pretend to know much about these matters, but Adeja has served in a legitimate army and learned proper military discipline. I do not see what makes him different from any other soldier, except that he was born elsewhere." Sephil claimed the window seat recently vacated by one of the ladies; it was still warm. "Adeja has a long, satisfactory service record. He is capable, intelligent, and I trust him far more than I ever trusted Melwas."

"I am not going to make him captain in Branag's place."

"I never said anything about making him captain. Place him under Branag if it suits you," said Sephil. "I do not care as long as he is here."

Ketalya sighed. "I will think about the matter, but I am not promising you anything."

He rose, kissed her cheek, and left her to her toilette, informing the ladies on his way out that they could return to their mistress' side. There was still time to send a messenger after Adeja, but when Varen approached him with a missive bearing the royal seal, he saw he would have to postpone the matter until later.

'Come at once to the audience chamber. Wear your royal robes. Ampheres ké Eramen.' Sephil read the message twice, showed it to Varen, and sent for Piras to dress him. Within the hour, he sat at the king's left hand in the audience chamber, with Ettarin and an unknown chamberlain on the right.

"I do not expect you will find this a pleasant meeting," murmured Ampheres, "but it is one we have anticipated for some time. The Tajhaani ambassador will undoubtedly wish to address you, and you may reply, but I would not say too much."

Flanked by four attendants, the ambassador who entered was dark-skinned and as richly dressed as a prince. He offered a dramatic bow to each man on the dais, lingering on Sephil. "It is a pleasure to at last meet the royal cousin and pretender," he said. "Allow me to introduce myself as Fallaz ked Arbanu, envoy and humble servant of His Highness the High Prince, Armajid ked Jahzarin, may the Father keep him and bless him with a thousand sons."

Sephil answered this verbiage while overlooking the subtle insult the man had just dealt him.

"As you have journeyed a long way," said Ampheres, "no doubt you wish to deliver your message. We much desire to hear what our brother the High Prince has to say."

Fallaz dropped another deep bow. "Great King, our prince currently celebrates the birth of a grandson, Prince Ninarsha ked Dashir."

Sephil held his breath. So Dashir had a son. As his family increased, so, too, would his ambitions.

"Prince Dashir claims the title of Crown Prince of Rhodeen for his son," continued Fallaz, "and as such demands the return of the royal seal." His gaze darted to the ring on the chain around Sephil's neck. "This humble servant has been charged with carrying out that duty."

"An interesting choice," commented Ampheres, "giving a Tajhaani name to a prince of Rhodeen."

Fallaz smiled. "Our prince wishes to strengthen his ties with the royal house of Rhodeen."

"Nevertheless," said Ampheres, "as we have stated in our earlier correspondence, Prince Dashir does not hold the strongest claim to the throne. It would not be in our interest at this time to lend him our support."

"That is unfortunate," answered Fallaz. "You may perhaps recall that Prince Dashir's claim was recognized by the late king Brasidios, who adopted him as a son after the tragic death of Prince Zhanil." He glanced sidelong at Sephil, his lips curling into an oily smile. "As your brother, Prince Dashir bears you and your progeny no ill will, provided that you are agreeable in this matter."

Sephil found it inconceivable that Dashir, who spent more than a decade tormenting him, would suddenly express such sentiments. "As we are not sons of the same mother," he answered coldly, "Prince Dashir is *not* my brother. Go back and tell my royal cousin that had he not attempted my life in Ottabia, we would not have come to this situation, and I might have believed in his assurances of goodwill."

Fallaz's smile evaporated for the moment it took him to regain his composure. "That was an unfortunate misunderstanding, I assure you. Prince Dashir has come to regret his hasty action. He desires peace with the royal house of Khalgar and to see his son prosper. A gift of the royal seal would greatly reassure him that, as you say, you mean him no threat."

"And so Prince Dashir would make a gift of the seal to his son," finished Ampheres, "but that does not grant him a kingdom. The last we heard, the Turyar still hold Rhodeen and have made no offers to restore the royal house. Does the prince mean to raise Tajhaan on his infant son's behalf, or does he simply hope that the Turyar will plunder Rhodeen, retreat beyond the mountains to their own lands, and conveniently leave the throne to him?"

Fallaz shook his head. "Great King, the prince has not stated his intentions in this matter."

"Then this matter of the seal ring is a moot point," answered Ampheres.

"Consider it a symbolic gesture of peace and reconciliation."

"As my son-in-law has stated, it is a gesture that comes somewhat too late."

Turning to Sephil, Fallaz pressed his hand to his heart and molded his expression into a perfect, if insincere, mask of contrition. "The choice rests with you, Prince Sephil."

"I have already made my decision," said Sephil. Or rather, his cousin had made it for him by making two attempts on his life and, for all he knew, the attempt on Ketalya and their child. "Should Prince Dashir ever manage to cast the Turyar out of Rhodeen and make himself or his son king, then he may put the question to us again. Until then, the royal seal belongs to me and my heirs."

* * * *

Adeja scowled at the prisoners through the iron grille. It was just like Sephil to intrude when he wanted something, never mind that Adeja had a life and ambitions of his own. Lahis might not care for his working in the city prison, but the last thing he wanted was to join the royal household to work for a capricious prince who sent him away whenever he was not needed or for some snobbish princess whose only concern was that he did not have the proper credentials.

Fuck that, he thought. *I could take their guards and break them over my knee.*

A moment later, he admitted that Sephil was right. Nakhet had sent him away the first time, and Ampheres the second; the prince had no say in the business. *And he's got no say about it now, no matter what he claims. They might let me stay long enough to catch whoever tried to kill his woman, then dump me in the street again once they're done with me.*

Still, it irked him to see bruises mar the face of a beautiful royal woman. In Tajhaan, a man such as he would never be allowed to gaze upon a princess. Anyone who injured her in such a manner would meet a cruel death: flayed alive or impaled. When his anger cooled, Adeja agreed that Sephil should take severe measures to ensure his wife's safety, as her specially-trained guards obviously could not protect her.

In fact, Adeja took private pleasure at the change in Sephil. No longer a timid or spoiled child, the prince had handled the situation like a man, even if Adeja left the palace smarting at his preemptory dismissal. In Tajhaan, no wife would have gainsaid or embarrassed her husband in such fashion, but the Khalgari did not even have the wisdom to impose the veil upon their noble wives and daughters, or keep them safely sequestered in a harem. It was no wonder their women were attacked in the street.

* * * *

"Lahis," said Sephil, taking the young woman's hand and gently steering her to an overstuffed chair by the fire. "What a lovely name. Here, sit down and I will have the servants bring you something warm to drink."

Lovely as her name might be, Sephil was surprised to find Lahis plainer than he imagined. In her quiet, pliable manner, however, he could guess what drew Adeja to her. She said nothing unless directed to do so, and was clearly intimidated by her lavish surroundings.

Sephil decided that he was not disappointed but jealous. As he complimented Lahis on her dark blue shawl, he wondered how this could be possible. *She may be plain and simple, but she has Adeja*, he realized. *What right do I have to be jealous, when he was never mine to keep in the first place?*

L.E. BRYCE

Tonight he would meditate on the futility of possessiveness and strive harder to renounce his longing for Adeja. For now, he would do all he could to make Adeja's wife feel welcome.

Although Ketalya agreed to consider placing Adeja among the household guards, she made it clear that she was not going to make an effort to persuade him to take the post. And Adeja would not ask for the position however much he might desire it. Neither would risk losing face before the other.

Had Adeja not mentioned his wife, Sephil would have been at a loss on how to mediate between him and Ketalya.

When he smiled, drew her attention to his priestly robes and mentioned his vocation, Lahis began to relax. She found her voice long enough to tell him that she and Adeja had been married since summer, but froze again and turned pale when Ketalya entered the room, followed by two of her ladies.

"Piras tells me that you wish to see me," said Ketalya. Her eyes darted to Lahis, who nervously clasped her hands in her lap. "I was not aware we had company."

Sephil introduced them. "My lady, this is Lahis kéya Lakhun, the wife of Adeja ked Shamuz. Lahis, this is my lady wife, Princess Ketalya kéya Ampheres."

Judging from the withering look she gave him, Sephil realized that his wife was not pleased, yet could not understand why. Surely as a woman, warm and lively with her sisters, attendants and servants, Ketalya would warm to Lahis where she failed to welcome Adeja.

Ketalya seemed not only displeased at finding a common woman in her sitting room, but appeared to be under the assumption that Lahis came to plead her husband's cause. "If he desires the post," she said to the woman, "he may have it, but he must ask himself."

Seeing that Lahis did not understand, Sephil moved to reassure her. He took a porcelain cup from the tray, filled it with tea, and pressed it upon her before sitting down in the chair oppsite her. "I fear I must apologize," he said. "I did not tell my wife you were coming. My lady, I asked Lahis here so she might persuade Adeja to reconsider the matter."

Ketalya sat down, while one lady-in-waiting covered her lap with a velvet comforter and the other handed her silk floss and her embroidery hoop. "The man should not have to rely on his wife to do his speaking for him."

Sephil thought it unwise to point out how she occasionally did that very thing. Instead, he turned his attention to their

202

guest, who watched them both in bewilderment. Adeja clearly had not told her about his recent visit to the palace or the proposed job.

"Lahis," said Sephil, "we brought you here because we wish to offer your husband a position as a guard here in the royal household."

She stared at her lap. "He works in the city prison, sir," she murmured, "and for my father in the quarry."

"Yes," said Sephil, "but this position would pay very well, and you would be able to live here in the palace. You would like that, would you not?"

Her eyes widened in amazement, exactly as he had hoped. "Live here in the palace?"

Sephil grinned at her. "Of course," he said. "Adeja was our loyal bodyguard in Rhodeen and Ottabia, and we desire his service again. There is no one we trust more than him."

"But...live here in the palace?" she repeated. "We're simple people, sir."

"Our servants live here with us, Lahis. This household has more than fifty rooms." At one point, Varen mentioned the number, but Sephil did not recall. He appealed to his wife. "Is that not so, my lady?"

"Fifty-six rooms," replied Ketalya, intent on her needlework. Sephil wished she would say something to the woman, but the princess seemed determined to ignore her.

Lahis gaped at the number. Sephil seized upon her wonder and added, "Most of those rooms are for our servants and their families. You would find living here quite pleasant, and I am sure your husband would be happy to have a post where he does not have to work under the hot sun or in a prison."

"What would I do, sir?" she murmured.

Ketalya echoed the question in the look she gave Sephil: what *would* the woman do? Palace servants underwent the same rigorous training as guards.

"We will see what work best suits you," replied Sephil. "Can you weave?" He knew that the ladies-in-waiting passed their idle time embroidering, while some of the servant women wove linen and wool for everyday use. What they did not use they sold or bartered for other household goods. Perhaps a place could be found for Lahis among them.

Lahis softly confided that she spent her days shopping in the bazaar for food, doing laundry, cleaning, spinning and

203

weaving. Sometimes she also watched children belonging to neighbors or relations.

Before Sephil could question her further, Adeja stormed into the room, followed by a hapless porter who protested that all guests must walk behind.

"What is the meaning of this intrustion?" demanded Ketalya, half-rising from her chair. The comforter slid from her lap and the embroidery hoop dangled from her hand.

Adeja stopped, placed his hands on his hips, and glowered at her. "Maybe you should tell me, princess," he said. "I came home to find a guard at my door telling me my wife has been taken to the palace for questioning. Lahis is harmless. What could she have done that you'd need to haul her out of our home?"

"Mind your manners, soldier."

"I'll mind my manners when you tell me what all this is about."

In the coiled tension rippling through Adeja's frame, Sephil sensed a man prepared to do far more than violate etiquette if his wife was threatened.

With a smile, he rose and placed a reassuring hand on Adeja's arm. "I see the guard I sent to ease your fears has only increased them. Lahis has done nothing wrong. She has been my guest this last hour."

Adeja narrowed his eyes. "Your guest?"

"I confess," said Sephil, "when I heard you had a wife, I could not resist the urge to meet her. She has been telling me about all the things she does for you, and we have been telling her about the marvelous opportunities life in the palace can afford a family."

Adeja glanced over at his wife, who anxiously twisted her fingers in her lap, and glared at the servant who started to offer him a cup of tea; the man retreated to the sideboard. "Manipulating my wife won't do you any good," he replied. "I make all the decisions in the household, so if you've a proposal to make or anything else to say, you deal with me directly."

Ketalya arched an eyebrow at his commanding tone. "The position is yours if you desire it," she said coldly, "although I cannot fathom what my husband sees in you."

In the way Adeja clenched his teeth, Sephil knew he was swallowing a potentially cutting remark. "My service record speaks for itself, lady," he growled. "I can bow, spout 'my lord' and 'my lady,' and obey just as you please, but beyond that I was trained in a real barracks, with real soldiers. If all you care about is a guard with proper credentials, a pretty uniform and no brains to speak of, then by all means hire someone else."

"We may do that," said Ketalya.

Now deathly pale, Lahis drew a sharp breath.

Sephil lifted his hand to stop the argument before it could escalate. Though he was not accustomed to acting as a mediator, and dreaded stepping into a quarrel, he knew that if he did not try the tensions between the two would make a compromise impossible. "Please, there is no need for unpleasantness. Adeja, please soften your manners. My wife does not know what ordinary soldiers are like."

"Then you'd better educate her, my prince," growled Adeja.

Glaring at him, Sephil turned to his wife. "My lady, I realize that he is somewhat rougher than what you are accustomed to, but allow him the chance to demonstrate his competence."

"Husband, I was willing to give him the opportunity, but now that he has opened his mouth, I will not tolerate a boorish, insolent foreigner--"

"My lady," Sephil said sharply, perhaps more so than he had intended, "might I remind you that *I* am also a foreigner? My one concern is your safety and wellbeing, and that of our child. It is clear the guards the king has appointed cannot manage the task alone. Adeja has proven that he is a loyal and obedient soldier, and I see no reason why he should not continue to do so."

"He does not seem all that obedient to me."

"Under Branag's command, he will do as he is told."

"Since you are so intent on this course of action," said Ketalya, "do as you wish. As long as peace is maintained in this household, the foreigner may take the post if he wishes. However, if he does not do as ordered, he will be dismissed at once and there will be no more discussion."

Sephil cringed at her tone, and the uncomfortable scene that had already ensued; he dared not say more. Turning to Adeja, he tried to put a conciliatory face on the offer. *I beg you, say yes.* "It is your decision. Will you take the post?"

* * * *

Adeja stalked down the street, Lahis silently trailing behind. With his hands balled into fists at his side, he itched to hit something. The nerve of that bitch, insulting his honor and calling him an insolent boor when she knew nothing about making martial appointments, grated on him, as did coming home to find his wife taken to the palace for questioning. At least, that was how the guard phrased it, even if it turned out not to be so.

"Did they treat you all right?" he asked Lahis.

Wide-eyed, she nodded. "The prince was nice to me," she said softly.

"That's because he wants something." Priest or not, Sephil still knew how to manipulate others. Adeja wanted to throttle him for bringing Lahis into the matter. Some things a man just should not do, and playing upon a simple woman to get to her husband was among them.

"He wants us to live in the palace," murmured Lahis.

Adeja grunted, but said nothing more as they turned the corner, approached their tenement and climbed the stairs to their apartment. Because Lahis had no time to prepare a meal, they would have to eat out tonight.

On the stairs, Adeja sensed questions brimming on his wife's lips. She knew almost nothing about his military service, as before now she had taken no interest and he had not seen fit to enlighten her. Any other woman would have spent the walk home haranguing him about his connections to royalty and foolish reluctance to seize such a promotion. With Lahis, as long as he worked hard, brought money home and treated her gently, she was content.

Now, however, something awakened in her that had not been present before, and he knew who to blame for it.

Damn you, Sephil. Adeja paused on the landing, turned and sighed. "You want to live in the palace, don't you?"

Sephil knew precisely what he was doing. Between him and Lahis, Adeja realized that he stood very little chance of escape.

* * * *

The double strain of insecurity and her pregnancy was making Ketalya waspish. In public, she behaved as she had always done, yet in private, she alternated between irritability and inexplicable fits of weeping. Ghanis assured her that this was normal. Sephil did not see how this could be so, but he followed the physician's advice and tried his best to be patient and humor Ketalya during her outbursts.

Her behavior this evening, however, strained his patience to the limit. "That could have gone better," he commented.

"Then you should have thought more carefully about bringing that man here. He is the most uncouth creature I have ever met," she complained. "How could you even *think* of allowing him a position in our household?"

Sephil leaned against the back of her chair. "I would rather have a slightly rough, honest soldier watch over my family than some useless guard with perfect manners. And contrary to what you think, Adeja is not a boor."

Ketalya ran the brush through her hair once before placing it back on the vanity. "He was rude and defiant with me. A properly trained guard would never dare behave in such a manner."

Sephil was not about to point out that Ketalya provoked Adeja's temper by being short with him. "So he does not have credentials here. He still knows what he is doing. As for his manners, I am sure he seems rude because he is not accustomed to taking orders from women, but you saw how gentle he was with his wife. Obviously, he is not *completely* lacking in manners.

"You should not concern yourself with him. He will be under Branag's command, so whatever orders you wish to give, instruct Branag and he will see to it that Adeja does as he is told." He bent to kiss her temple. "It will be all right, you will see."

"But why do you insist on championing him so?" she asked. "There are plenty of competent, loyal men in my father's service. Why choose him, and not any of them?"

Sephil could not fail to miss her petulant tone. *If this is what pregnancy does to women, it is a wonder they want children at all. After this, no more babies.* "Because Adeja is one of the few people who has ever been honest with me," he explained. "Had I the same loyal and loving people in my childhood as you had in yours, one soldier would not matter so much to me, but I can count on one hand those who did not criticize, tease or lie to me."

"You should have told me you were going to invite his wife," said Ketalya. "I have no idea what I am going to do with her. She is not a trained servant, and I certainly cannot make her a lady-in-waiting. To tell you the truth, I find her somewhat simple-minded."

"Yes, but I am sure there are things she can do. I am sure she can weave and help carry goods from the bazaar and watch the servants' children. If you like, I will speak to Varen about it in the morning." Sephil dropped another kiss on the top of her head, anything to console her. "You will see that I am right, and then you will thank me for being so brilliant."

Chapter Eleven

"I do not question your good intentions in the matter," said Ampheres, "only your good judgment. The man does not have the proper credentials."

Sephil took a sip of liqueur to fortify his nerves. "No, he has not been trained to serve in this establishment, but elsewhere his service record and letters of credential would have been more than sufficient."

"Yes, I have reviewed those letters," said the king. "He has moved around quite a bit, never staying in one place too long. One has to wonder about that."

"I know his history," replied Sephil. "He completed his service in Tajhaan and chose not to reenlist there. He spent time in Dhahar and then enlisted in Rhodeen, where he spent several years. I know all of this, and as I told my wife, Adeja ked Shamuz is both loyal and intelligent, precisely the sort of man I want guarding my family."

Ampheres nodded. "That may be, but I am told that he is also uncouth and defiant. For a man who once worked as a hired thug, it does not surprise me."

Sephil was not surprised to discover that Ketalya had complained to her father about the arrangement. "You make it seem as though he uses foul language, has disgusting manners and is habitually rude to my wife," he answered. "His manners are better than you might think, and if he has snapped at Ketalya, it is only because he does not take orders from women. I have placed him under Branag. So far, the arrangement has proven satisfactory."

"So you say, though I would caution you not to put too much faith in this one man," said Ampheres. "Perhaps you would care to tell me how is it you believe he can do what our own specially trained guards cannot?"

"Adeja saved my life twice in Ottabia, and kept me from harm on several other occasions," answered Sephil. "I trust him to look after Ketalya and our child, however much she might not like it."

Nodding again, the king's lips curved in a smile hinting at things that Sephil would rather not discuss. "Yes, I *have* been wondering about his role in those two assassination attempts in Ottabia. Did you not tell me that in the second attempt, the would-be assassin actually entered your room and came as close as your bed before he was tackled? How would Adeja ked Shamuz know you were in danger, and yet not stop the assailant before he reached your room, unless he was actually *with* you at the time?"

Sephil stared blankly at him, his resolve crumbling, yet before he could find the words to counter the insinuation, Ampheres continued, "There are only two possibilities, and I very much doubt this man, Tajhaani though he is, was helping the assassins.

"That leaves the other possibility. Your father wrote to me on more than one occasion about your proclivities. Now before you try to defend yourself, let me state that what you may have done with this man in the past is not my concern. It is your judgment now that I question."

"I did not bring him into my household to conduct an affair with him," Sephil said weakly. If only he sounded more confident, but apprehension stunted his nerve. "He is a married man, and so am I."

"Marriage does not always guarantee fidelity," said Ampheres. "Of course, I have not said anything to Ketalya, as she does not need the strain at this time."

"You want me to dismiss him, or you will tell her, is that it?"

Ampheres slowly shook his head. "You misunderstand my intentions. Blackmail is not a game I choose to play. Should you dismiss this man too hastily from your household, Ketalya would become suspicious. Therefore, keep him in his current position if you wish, but be assured that I will be watching."

* * * *

"Sir, I had not thought to say anything, but—"

Considering how unusual it was for Branag, a middle-aged man with the imagination of a walnut, to be so flustered, Sephil immediately took notice. "What is it?"

"It is the new guard, sir, the foreigner," said Branag. "When he is on duty, he stops everyone: the servants, the stewards, messengers, anyone he has not seen before. Of course, I told him that anyone who is carrying the proper credentials or in uniform ought to be let through, but he does not listen."

Sephil set aside his book. Earlier in the day, one of the servants had complained about Adeja's activities, which Sephil had not investigated because he knew there must be a perfectly legitimate reason for the man to behave so. "Have you asked him why he does this?"

"Yes, sir," replied Branag. "He told me that anyone could get a uniform or forge credentials in order to enter and do you or the princess harm." His brow furrowed, as though the idea was either utterly foreign, ridiculous, or both. "I explained to him that all precautions have been taken, and that such things do not happen here."

"And yet the princess was attacked."

"Yes, sir, but that attack took place *outside* the palace."

"Neither the assailants nor their source has been identified," said Sephil, "which means another attack may occur at some point. I assumed you would have taken this into consideration."

"The princess has not left the palace since then, sir, and my unit is familiar with all those coming in and out. It is only the foreigner who has difficulty."

While Branag was not as dense regarding the situation as Sephil had initially thought, his adherence to protocol in the face of common sense remained less than satisfactory. "When the evening shift begins," said Sephil, "I want you to return and bring Adeja with you. We can discuss the matter then."

* * * *

Why Sephil permitted his wife to be present, Adeja did not know except to speculate that the woman had either beguiled or browbeaten her way into the sitting room. More likely the latter, he thought, for although Sephil insisted his wife had a calm, generous nature, Adeja knew simply by watching the two together who gave the orders in the household.

At least the princess did not insist on sitting among the men. Instead, she occupied a chair nearest the fire with her embroidery, with a lady-in-waiting to keep her company and attend to her needs.

"I realize you wish to perform your duties well," said Sephil, "but I should point out that there is a rather rigid protocol in place here that did not exist in Rhodeen."

That argument again. Adeja prayed that his time under the king's tutelage had not made Sephil as immune to common sense as the rest of the palace population. "Guard duty is the same no matter where it's served," he answered. "My job is to watch the door and protect the household. I've been doing that in one way or another for the last ten years."

Sephil nodded. "Your diligence is appreciated. However, there has been some concern that you are being *overly* vigilant."

Adeja did not have to think very hard to know who had complained. "With an active threat, there's no such thing as being too cautious," he replied. "Now you and the princess might know everybody, but I don't yet. Branag's introduced me to the servants and staff, and I know well enough to leave viziers and members of the royal family alone, but it's the others, the messengers and servants from elsewhere, who need to be checked."

"If they are wearing the correct livery," said Branag, "you can let them through."

Adeja distinctly remembered explaining his position, not once or twice, but enough times that it should have hammered a fist-sized hole in Branag's skull. "There have been attempts on both the prince and princess, and there are likely to be again. An assassin does not simply walk up to you and announce himself; he—or she—will hide in plain sight as a guard or servant and strike when least expected. Livery can be stolen, credentials forged."

"He makes a worthy point, Branag," said Sephil.

Branag remained unconvinced to the point where Adeja knew it would either take a royal command or an assassin's knife between his ribs for him to see sense. "There are strict checkpoints at all gates," the captain said. "If an assassin tries to get in, he will be stopped."

Stopped by whom, wondered Adeja, *your incompetent guards?* "An enemy doesn't necessarily need to get in to do harm. He or she can bribe someone within."

"That is inconceivable," said Branag. "All who work here are loyal."

"Don't be so certain of that."

"I do not know if you realize this, Adeja," commented Ketalya, pulling her needle through the linen garment on which she worked, "but every word you say casts aspersions on your own loyalty."

Adeja dared not hope that Sephil would banish his meddlesome wife to her chamber. "Perhaps," he answered, "but should anything happen to you, princess, I as a foreigner would be the first one questioned and probably the first one executed, whether or not I was guilty. Why would I take such a risk and ruin a promising career? I assure you, I have far more to gain by keeping you alive than seeing you dead."

Her silence satisfied him more than any insincere praise she could have heaped upon him.

"Even here," said Sephil, "we are still in danger. I would rather be overly vigilant than ignore the danger and suffer for it later."

On sleepless nights, Adeja had lain beside his wife contemplating what should be done, as he knew that with the impending birth of Ketalya's child, another attempt was imminent. "When I served in Tajhaan," he said, "I once had to take a message from the barracks to the palace. I wasn't allowed to speak with or even see the vizier who was to get the message."

"What does that have to do with anything?" asked Ketalya.

"Patience, my lady," he answered. "You will see in a moment. As I was saying, my captain told me this was common practice. He also told me that a servant would open the message, or any parcel that was sent. Poison is a favored method of death in Tajhaan. Sometimes a man's enemies can be very creative in using it. Since the prince has enemies among the Tajhaani court, perhaps he wishes to hear more?"

"Go on," urged Sephil.

"No stranger should be allowed near the prince or princess. Any unfamiliar person who is admitted must be searched for hidden weapons. Should —"

Branag started to interject that such precautions were absurd. In turn, he was cut short by Sephil, who gestured for Adeja to continue.

"Should any letters arrive that aren't marked with known seals, such as from the king, it must be opened by a servant. The servant doesn't need to read it, only to make certain that the parchment isn't laced with poison."

"I did not know such a thing was even possible," said Sephil.

Adeja nodded at him. "It isn't only possible, but I've seen it with my own eyes. In Tajhaan, new soldiers are often sent out to keep the peace in local neighborhoods. What one sees among ordinary people in a week would amaze you. One can soak parchment in poison so that when the reader does this--" Licking his index finger, he pantomimed turning a page. "When he does this, he will lick the poison. I've also seen letters or bundles of cloth laced with powders that will choke a man."

Branag turned a shade paler. "What else?"

"Should any gifts arrive, they must also be opened by servants, for the same reasons. You don't know how many tales I've heard of venomous snakes or scorpions hiding in chests or jewel boxes."

From the corner of his eye, Adeja saw Ketalya had stopped embroidering; she and her attendant stared at him in horrified disbelief. "If an attack in the street doesn't work," he told Sephil, "your enemies will find surer means to harm you."

Sephil looked over at Branag, who sat grim and silent in his chair, then at Ketalya. "We would be foolish to ignore this sort of advice," he said, "especially as the instigators of the most recent attack have not been found."

Branag slowly nodded, and Adeja saw the princess do the same. Reaching across the table for the decanter, Adeja poured a cup of wine for his captain and a second for Ketalya, only to pause when Sephil explained that her pregnancy barred her from drinking alcohol.

"Would the lady prefer to leave?" Adeja made the inquiry without malice. A woman had no business discussing such matters, and a pregnant woman doubly so.

"It is her decision," said Sephil. His voice conveyed a weight suggesting that he would like to command her, but lacked the authority to do so.

Ketalya refused to leave, just as Adeja predicted. "This concerns me and my child," she said. "I intend to hear it all."

Leave this to the men and go back to your women's quarters. Had she been his wife, Adeja would have gotten up, seized her by the arm, and forcibly led her back to her chamber. *I won't be blamed if you become upset and miscarry.* Instead, he shrugged and turned back to Sephil. "I thought the men who attacked your wife were all killed."

"They were," answered Sephil, "but we do not know who ordered the attack. No one has even come forward to claim the bodies, and the men were locals. Some say it was the Turyar, others that it was Dashir and the High Prince. Still others point to rival factions here in Khalgar."

Adeja drank from the cup he had meant for Ketalya. "I've never heard of the Turyar hiring assassins. They always attack openly."

"So you would discount them?"

"They've no need to kill a woman and child who don't threaten them," replied Adeja. "I saw the force that came to Shemin-at-Khul. It was the biggest army I'd ever seen, and I'm

213

sure by now more men have come in from the Turya lands. I don't know if it's even possible to expel them from Rhodeen at this point. They wouldn't have bothered with you or your wife, and I've got my doubts about your cousin and the High Prince, too."

"Dashir tried to kill me in Ottabia," said Sephil, "and he is the sort of man who would attack a woman and child if he saw profit in it."

Adeja did not disagree with him. "In Tajhaan, there's a very old tradition that says when a prince takes power, he kills his male relatives to secure his throne. You're an easy target, and I don't doubt that Dashir would strike at you, but he relies on his father-in-law for support. In fact, I don't think the man can take a piss at this point without Armajid's permission."

Branag cleared his throat. "Watch your language in front of the princess."

"You asked my advice and I'm giving it. Dashir isn't the source of your troubles, not now anyway. The High Prince controls things in Tajhaan, and he's going to think twice about attacking a pregnant royal woman whose father is a powerful king. He isn't going to risk going to war with Khalgar with the Turyar sitting on his northern border, especially when he isn't even sure the child will be a boy."

Chancing a quick glance toward the fireplace, he saw the princess had given up all pretense of doing her needlework and now listened intently. In another moment, she would probably get up and join them at the table.

"And when the child is born?" asked Sephil.

"If it's a boy, Armajid might consider doing away with him then," replied Adeja. "There's no prohibition against killing royal male children, only women. I know it's not my place to say, but if I were you and wanting to avoid bloodshed, I'd pray for a daughter."

The wistful look Sephil gave him suggested the prince desired that very thing. *I hope the gods hear your prayer.* Adeja anxiously cleared his throat. "I'm sure your father-in-law's officials know everything I just told you," he said.

Sephil poured himself a second cup of wine. "If they do," he said, "they have not passed the information along to me." He looked over at his wife, who shook her head as if to say that she had not heard anything either.

"Do you have any other enemies?" asked Adeja.

"Yes," answered Sephil. "There is a strong Rhodeen faction which has tried to discredit me. It is led by a dispossessed noble named Melin Wesares. He is descended from Ardahir III through the female line, and is using his ancestry to lay claim to the throne."

"Has he been questioned?"

"I am sure he has." Sephil rolled his eyes and sighed heavily. "Gods, I have no idea. I know that people have been questioned, but their names have not been released to me. I doubt the king would overlook Wesares.

"Adeja, I think I have heard more than I want to hear tonight, unless Ketalya wishes to know more. But before you go I have been wondering about that cut on your lip. Were you in a fight?"

Adeja looked over at Branag, who pretended not to notice. "Some of the other guards decided to test me," he replied, "so I did the same to them." He did not add how the two guards had harrassed his wife for marrying a troublesome foreigner, prompting him to confront them after their shifts ended.

With the long end of a spear, he had pinned both men against the wall and reminded them that Lahis was a good and honorable woman who deserved better treatment than she received. When released, one guard had answered with a blow that cut Adeja's lip. Adeja slammed the butt of the spear into the guard's belly and informed the man that in any other situation, he would be lying in an alley with a knife in his gut.

Branag shifted in his seat and brusquely assured the prince that such altercations were not uncommon, and order had been restored.

Palace guards worked six days, and rested two. Adeja rose an hour later than usual, ate breakfast in the household kitchen with another guard, and greeted his wife in the weaving room before deciding upon his course of action. Donning a plain gray tunic, he applied for a chit allowing him back into the palace compound and walked down to the street where the attack had occurred a month earlier.

Sephil had not asked for his help, but Adeja saw no harm in investigating on his own.

Consisting of a narrow thoroughfare, sparsely populated and lined with shops rather than stalls, the street seemed an unlikely place to stage an attack. Had he been asked to plan a public assault, Adeja would have selected a venue in which he could stalk his prey unnoticed, strike quickly, and merge back into a crowd whose numbers would cover his escape. This lack of forethought, coupled with their clumsiness in dispatching their target, confirmed Adeja's suspicion that the would-be assassins were amateurs.

Stepping into a wine shop, he bought a pitcher of Akkian red and a platter of flat bread and yoghurt, and sat near the counter where he could observe the owner. She was a pleasant woman once she saw he would not make trouble, and though she was too old for his taste, Adeja put on his best seductive smile and introduced himself as Shamuz, an employee from the local morgue.

"It's been an unpleasant morning," he said mournfully, shaking his head, "and not likely to get any better. My only consolation is good wine and a friendly ear."

Right away, the woman responded to his purring appeal. *Such* a handsome man, she said, and what an unpleasant job, working with the dead. She told him her name was Vanira and, leaning over the counter to flash him her wrinkled cleavage, urged him to tell his story.

"We've this body from a month ago," said Adeja. "His tag says he was killed right here on this street or thereabouts, but nobody's claimed the body. It's worse in summer, of course, but winter isn't much better with all the damp."

"Oh, you don't have to touch those *awful* corpses, do you?"

Adeja gave her a hapless look. "When we're shorthanded, yes. I wanted to become a carpenter, but my father made me get into the business. Said there was nothing shameful about working with the dead. He only had to bury them. *I* have to talk to the families when they came to claim the bodies, and try to find families when nobody comes." Wrapping both hands around his cup, Adeja gazed into its depths and sighed forlornly. "Gods help me, I'm past thirty and too old to find a new trade."

Vanira twined a strand of his hair around one finger and leaned even closer. "Is there *anything* I can do to help?" she asked.

The guffaws and comments behind him told Adeja that he had an audience, which was the last thing he wanted. Clearly the woman wanted him to bed her, which he could easily do. It would not be the first time Adeja had slept with a lonely wife or widow in exchange for something, but this time felt different. Lahis entered his mind and lingered, smothering his libido.

"I don't know," he sighed. "My boss wants the corpse gone by tomorrow and you can't just dump a body into a common grave without forms upon forms so we don't get sued later if the family comes forward. I tell you, we never had this problem in Tajhaan; after two weeks, we just dumped them in a hole in the desert. I mean, if the family hasn't claimed the body by now, they aren't going to, but that's not good enough for the boss. Either I find a relative to sign off or it's a pile of forms."

Glancing up at her, he offered a sheepish smile. "Look at me, boring you with all this talk of dead bodies on my rest break. I can't ever seem to get away from corpses. Why don't you tell me about yourself?"

Adeja continued to smile and make encouraging gestures as Vanira described her life as a shopkeeper. Twice a widow, she brazenly hinted she was more than willing to accommodate a third husband under the right circumstances. Adeja complimented her on her good looks and excellent establishment, but indicated that his break was nearly over. "I hate to leave so soon," he said, "but the boss'll give me no mercy if I'm not prompt."

Before he left, Vanira offered him an invitation to return after closing, as well as a name and address. "I'd *hate* to think of you slaving away under all those *bothersome* forms," she said, "but these are good people, you understand, and no troublemakers. With so many soldiers and officials asking questions, they've been too afraid to come forward. You'll make it easy for them, won't you?"

Assuring her that he would, Adeja leaned over the counter and offered a long, deep kiss as consolation for the return visit he would not make.

That evening, he put on his uniform and sought out Varen for permission to deliver a message to the royal couple. "It concerns the recent attack on the princess," he said. "I have information for them."

Sephil and Ketalya sat together by the fire, he reading and she working at her embroidery. The princess ignored him, while Sephil expressed his bewilderment at seeing Adeja in uniform. "I thought this was a rest day for you."

"It is, my prince," answered Adeja, making a little bow to Ketalya which she barely acknowledged. "I thought it might be better to dress the part when coming here."

"Varen says you have a message," said Sephil.

Adeja described how he spent the day, leaving out his flirtation with the shopkeeper. "I got an address and name, and went to investigate. Of course, the wife didn't want to talk to me at first, but when I assured her I worked for the local morgue she had a lot more to say. She told me how in the weeks before the attack a strange man often came to talk to her husband. She remembered overhearing several names in their conversation: *Ardahir* and *Rhodeen*."

Sephil immediately sat up in his chair. "Did she tell you who this man was?"

"I wrote the name down for you." Adeja passed him a rumpled slip of parchment, which he inspected before showing to Ketalya.

As expected, the princess expressed her skepticism. "Officials have combed that neighborhood questioning individuals and turned up nothing. How are we to believe that you could do in a single afternoon what they could not accomplish in a month?"

"Because I wasn't wearing a uniform, my lady," he answered. "When people see a uniform, they stop talking. I mean no disrespect to you, of course, or to the king's men. Khalgar has a strong army, and everybody knows that, but the problem is that everyone here is so *clean* and honest. But you see, even the most honest Tajhaani is underhanded when he has to be."

Ketalya raised an eyebrow. "And you do not believe that my father's men can be clever?"

"I didn't *say* clever, my lady. I said underhanded, as in, without morals or honesty," said Adeja. "The first thing a child learns in Tajhaan is that if he doesn't learn to use his wits, he isn't going to survive. A Tajhaani soldier learns the same lessons. You have good soldiers who know their trade, my lady, but they aren't prepared to take off their uniforms and do a bit of lying or arm-twisting."

"He used to work for a moneylender," added Sephil.

The princess nodded, but if anything, she appeared more uncomfortable than before. "Torture is not a legal means of acquiring information here in Khalgar."

"I didn't have to torture anyone, my lady," replied Adeja. "The shopkeeper was more than willing to help me, and the widow was very gracious once she saw I meant no harm."

Sephil stared at him. "Adeja, you did not—?"

"My prince, I'm a married man, and not without *some* scruples," said Adeja. "I don't dally with shopkeepers or widows anymore, no matter how buxom or accommodating they might be."

"Please, we do not need to hear about your sexual escapades." Ketalya took the note from Sephil and studied it.

"The king will wish to verify this information. It is a serious allegation."

"It makes sense," said Sephil. "Wesares has opposed me from the moment he became aware of my presence here. He snubbed us at our wedding and published ugly rumors about my character and our marriage, so it does not surprise me in the least."

* * * *

The courtyard was the last place Sephil wanted to be. A narrow space enclosed on all sides by high walls, it felt claustrophobic enough on an ordinary day, which perhaps was the reason the king chose it now.

A scaffold dominated what open space existed, and alongside it was a cordoned area for the witnesses. Ampheres would watch the proceedings from a balcony high on the north wall. On this occasion, he ordered Sephil to accompany him.

Sephil's attention strayed from the grim scene being played out below to the square of clear blue sky overhead. It was a beautiful spring day, one that should have been spent walking through the gardens or riding in the countryside around Bhellin. Now it represented the culmination of ten dismal days, beginning with the arrest and arraignment and ending with the execution of Melin Wesares.

For seven of those days, Sephil had observed the trial from the gallery overlooking the Great Hall. Delav sat beside him to explain the monotonous proceedings, while Sephil tried to curb his frustration at having to be present. "If this is all," he complained, "a secretary could have sent me a summary at the end of the day."

"I regret the inconvenience, my lord," said Delav, "but as this man is accused of doing injury to your wife and unborn child, and challenging your right to the throne, you must be seen to be present."

"Then why am I not seated down below next to Prince Ettarin?"

"Your brother-in-law is one of the judges," answered Delav. "Therefore he must sit near the king. As you have not had the requisite legal training and are not objective in this matter, you cannot sit among them."

Sephil countered his boredom by bringing a book to read whenever the proceedings stalled. However, he took note when Wesares was questioned, and when his wife was escorted into the chamber to give her testimony. Her appearance prompted

219

him to summon Delav for an explanation. "Why did anyone not tell me she would be called?" he asked. "I would have accompanied her myself."

"I apologize for the omission, sir, but if you will notice," said Delav, "there are many Rhodeen nobles in attendance, and your presence would cause tensions the king wishes to avoid. As you can see, trying Lord Wesares for treason is proving difficult enough."

Ketalya did not look up, and spoke in such quiet, measured tones that Sephil strained to hear her. Her injuries had faded, but as her pregnancy had just begun to show, she presented a sympathetic image to the court.

Adeja was not called as a witness, nor was his role in identifying the perpetrators mentioned, but the woman whose husband had been one of the assailants did speak.

Wesares did not stand trial alone. Four other men, labeled as his accomplices, were charged with him. Early in the proceedings, Delav had predicted that they would turn on their employer. "Men who commit such acts have so little moral backbone that betrayal comes easily for them. Observe and you will see for yourself."

As Sephil watched, each man shifted the blame onto Wesares and the other men, downplaying his own culpability in the incident.

For his part, Wesares did not deny instigating the attack. Instead, he attempted to use the court as a political platform. "Through my ancestry, I am the rightful king of Rhodeen," he said, "and I am only on trial because I refuse to recognize the inferior claim of a pretender who has insinuated himself into Khalgar's royal house."

Ampheres allowed him to finish speaking before giving his answer. "Your political views are irrelevant in this matter, Lord Wesares. You have been charged with treason solely for your unprovoked attack upon a member of our royal family."

"As a nobleman of Rhodeen, the court of Khalgar has no right to try me," said Wesares.

"The crime was committed within the jurisdiction of Khalgar," replied Ampheres, "and Rhodeen no longer exists as a state except in the person of its legitimate heir, whose wife and unborn child you stand accused of assaulting. You may protest all you wish, but your arguments are pointless. By Rhodeen's own laws, your claim is invalid, and as such we do not recognize it."

When announced, the verdict came as no surprise. All five men were condemned to death, the sentence to be carried out the following day. Only Wesares would receive a private execution; as a nobleman, he had the right to be dispatched by the headsman's sword. The others would be publicly hanged, drawn, and quartered.

Just before the execution, Ampheres received the condemned man's son in the salon overlooking the courtyard. Attended by Rhodeen's former ambassadors, Stavon Melines formally declared that he would not seek vengeance for his father's death, and renounced all further claims to the throne of Rhodeen. He seemed genuinely mortified by his father's actions as he acknowledged Sephil and asked his pardon.

"We wish health and long life to you, your lady wife, and heirs," he said. The ambassadors followed suit, each one bowing his head and murmuring similar platitudes.

Not knowing what to say, and apprehensive about the events yet to come, Sephil received these felicitations gracefully, bestowing the kiss of peace on Stavon's cheek. Later, Ampheres issued a decree requiring all expatriated Rhodeen nobles to renounce all claims to the throne or forfeit the right to dwell in Khalgar. Only a few families left Bhellin for other lands.

Melin Wesares went to his death impeccably dressed and groomed, and was allowed to bid farewell to his attendants at the scaffold steps. Less than thirty people came to watch him die. His son stood among his guards and servants, and the officials who had presided at his trial; the ambassadors did not stay.

Delav, who stood at Sephil's elbow, quietly explained that noblemen were granted certain rights in death. This included addressing the crowd. On this occasion, however, Wesares said nothing, but simply undid his collar and knelt in the straw.

Silence fell over the courtyard. Sephil held his breath and glanced away at the final moment. He knew the headsman, specially trained for the task, did his work in one stroke, for he heard the faint crunch of bone, a thud, and squelch.

Had Ampheres not nudged him, he would not have looked at all, and when he did, it was a moment too soon. As he took another steadying breath and gazed down at the scaffold, a macabre sight met his eyes: the headless torso kneeling in place as blood continued to pump through the severed arteries and spurt out onto the straw. Slowly, the trunk sagged and slumped over beside the head, which the dead man's attendants quickly covered with a black cloth.

Sephil felt his stomach roil. Suddenly the air was too close and rank, urging him to flee. Delav took his hand and squeezed it, while urging him to take deep breaths. "It is over, my lord," the vizier whispered. "He did not suffer."

Once the body was carted away, Ampheres withdrew from the balcony, signaling Sephil to follow. Leaving the salon, they strode down a long gallery, neither speaking to the other, until they came to an airy room where servants waited with cool cloths and liqueur.

The king took a glass from the tray and handed it to Sephil. "Drink this," he said. "It will calm your nerves. I can see that you have never witnessed an execution before."

Sephil sipped at the golden liquid, letting it spread warmly into his belly. His trembling gradually subsided, although the horrible images would not leave his mind. *Tonight I must pray, and ask the gods to grant me peace and him forgiveness.* "And I never wish to see another."

"Dispensing justice is the business of ruling," said Ampheres. "A king must be somewhat ruthless if he is to survive. Your father understood that, and so did your brother, but you have not had much experience in these matters. Remember the injury the men put to death today sought to do and be grateful. Go see your wife and spend the day in the gardens, or visit the temple and meditate. It will ease your mind."

"Does it not trouble you?"

Ampheres took his glass from the tray and, in a rare gesture, offered another to Delav, who stood behind Sephil's chair. "It troubles any man who has a conscience."

Once Sephil felt ready, he returned with Delav to his apartments. Ketalya had refused to attend the execution, but knew from the moment the trials began what ordeal awaited Sephil. "When I was fifteen," she told him, "I saw a man hanged for trying to poison my father. Father made me attend so I would understand how serious a responsibility it is to rule."

"But you were a girl," said Sephil. His father had never allowed him access to the ruling council, much less included him at public functions. Until that morning, he had never realized how traumatic an experience an execution truly was.

"In Khalgar, women can rule," replied Ketalya. "Father told me that one day I would become the wife of a prince or king, and I might need to govern on his behalf. I would need to know such things."

Before the tall double doors, Sephil spied Adeja on duty. Rigid stance, pike in hand, just as he had been in those early days in Shemin-at-Khul. Sephil paused beside him, opened his mouth as if speak, but remembered the eyes watching them. What he wanted to say, he could not confide in a mere guard.

Adeja did not turn his head; he did not seem to move at all save for the rise and fall of his breathing. Sephil started to look away when he caught the shift of dark eyes sliding toward him. Their gazes met, and worlds passed between them.

Chapter Twelve

Afternoon banished the fog, enabling Sephil to view the broad horizon beyond the shore. Salt filled his nostrils, and above the crashing surf he heard the cries of gulls. Spring at Adenna could be cold, misty and wet, but as summer approached and the household prepared to receive the royal family from Bhellin, the weather grew fair.

Sephil welcomed the reprieve from the capital, and knew that Ketalya, with her increasing girth and difficulty walking, was grateful that she would not have to give birth in Bhellin at high summer while the rest of the family was away. Now she could rest, visit with her mother, and take the waters at the nearby shrine.

Once the baby quickened, Ketalya's interest in its development and birth increased. While still in Bhellin, she oversaw preparations for a nursery, wet nurse and attendants with an energy that belied her physical discomfort. Her mother wrote to her twice a week with advice, and her siblings all suggested names.

Sephil laughed at her enthusiasm. "If it is a daughter," he said, "you should name her. If it is a son, I would prefer a Rhodeen name. He might need it one day." Other than this, he made no mention of the Snake Mother's prophecy, any possible threats to the child's life or any dynastic plans Ampheres might cherish.

Ketalya threw up her hands. "I would not know where to begin. There are so many suitable names I do not know what to do."

"If it is a boy we could call him Charnil. It is a royal name meaning 'little sun.'"

"Charnil ké Sephil?" she replied, trying the name on her tongue. "That sounds rather odd."

"Only if you say it in the Khalgari fashion, as you just did. In Rhodeen, you would say Charnil Sephides."

She nodded. "It seems I know nothing about Rhodeen names, so you will have to choose one for a boy. I will try to decide on one for a girl."

With all the preparations, there was one detail Ketalya overlooked, and it weighed on Sephil's mind as they made the journey to Adenna for the birth. She would not like what he proposed, and Ampheres certainly would not approve, but Sephil saw no other way.

"Not too close," he said to the man walking on the sand behind him.

Adeja, in uniform, stood two feet away. Branag and the other guards remained behind at the palace, leaving Sephil and his escort alone on the beach. "You want me to accompany you," he said, "but then you don't want me to walk too close. I hope this isn't some game you're playing."

"Adeja, it is impossible to have you under the same roof and not think about you."

"You said that to me once before, you know."

Sephil was surprised by the recollection. "Yes, but then I was trying to seduce you. This is not a game," he said. "We are being watched. The king knows about us."

"Did you tell him?"

"No, but he is no fool. I told him how you stopped that second assassin in Ottabia. I did not tell him you had been in my bed at the time, but he already knew about my sexual proclivities from my father and guessed the truth."

"Perhaps you should have another guard accompany you."

"I needed to talk to you," replied Sephil. "Tell me, are you happy serving in my household?"

Leaning against his pike, Adeja sighed impatiently. "You didn't bring me out here just to ask me that, did you?" he asked.

"No, but you can still answer my question."

"It's better than working in the prison or breaking rocks in a quarry," replied Adeja. "Now what's so important that you had to have me to follow you out here and couldn't tell me inside?"

For days Sephil had labored over what he would say, how he would explain his position to Adeja, then Ketalya and, last of all, to his father-in-law. All would object in some way, regardless of how ideal an arrangement it was. "If the baby is a boy, he will need a protector. Ketalya has arranged everything for him, even his toys and linens, but she neglected to appoint a nursery guard. Perhaps she feels the household sentries are enough."

Adeja frowned. "Are you asking me to watch the wet nurse change dirty diapers?"

"I wish you would not make light of this," said Sephil.

"Well, that *is* what you're asking me to do, isn't it?"

The words, so carefully rehearsed, fled Sephil's tongue. "No, it is not. Ketalya knows I would rather have a daughter, because if it is a son there will be attempts on his life. His grandfather will do whatever is necessary to protect and educate him, of course, except I do not necessarily trust the king.

"He tells me he intends to wait, to see if the boy shows promise, before deciding which course to take, but I know he will begin grooming my son to take the throne of Rhodeen as soon as he is able."

Adeja nodded at this. "I am sure your son will have an excellent education. The king fought the Turyar in his youth, and has several generals with similar experience."

"I am not concerned with my son learning how to fight," said Sephil. "Most boys learn to do that without much help. No, I need someone to teach my son how to *survive*. I do not know anyone better at doing that than you."

What Adeja thought, he did not reveal. "Your wife will hate the idea," he said, "and you don't even know if it will *be* a son."

"More and more I think it will be, regardless of what I want." Sephil hugged himself under his thin cloak, warding off a chill that went beyond physical. "The oracles have all said it will be a son who will ride into battle against the Turyar. Even if he does not, he will have enemies. Do you see now why I need you?"

* * * *

Adeja would not commit himself to the proposed post, leaving Sephil alternately frustrated and relieved. It struck him as inconceivable that Adeja could not realize how badly his services were needed.

At the same time, appointing him to a position that would bring him into the royal apartments, into daily intimate contact, made Sephil wonder what he thought he was doing. *At best, it is foolishness, at worst a disaster.*

Having Adeja at the door, so close and not being able to talk to or touch him was difficult enough. Now that he slept alone again, not a night passed that Sephil's thoughts did not wander to him. Oh, to be able to turn back time, to retrieve just an hour from those quiet, contemplative days in Ottabia, be held by strong arms and make love once again! Bittersweet memories led to furtive fondling under the blanket, but his own hand did not satisfy him the way Adeja could.

Those who knew might say otherwise, but it had never been about sex.

Ketalya sensed his unease, even if she did not understand the true reason for it, and arranged for a young man to come to his bed. Ceyath was lithe and lovely, a pleasure slave kept by the palace to entertain visiting dignitaries or nobles high in the king's favor, and for a few hours, his skilled hands and mouth brought comfort.

"Does something trouble you, my lord?" he asked, gently kissing the hollow above Sephil's collarbone. "If I do not please you, perhaps I could help you find another partner?"

Sephil found the tie that held Ceyath's robe closed and undid it, peeling the silk off the young man's shoulders. "No, I am not displeased with you."

He performed twice that night, and enjoyed the experience enough to summon Ceyath again, but bedding him was not the same as making love with Adeja.

Ceyath did not accompany him to Adenna, and once at the seaside palace Sephil tried to turn his mind to other things. In this, the king unwittingly provided assistance.

Upon being introduced to the Khalgari royal family, Sephil had neglected to inquire after his living maternal relations, who lived quietly on their estate in Ottabia. While they did not warrant an annual invitation to the summer palace, and had not attended Sephil's wedding, Ampheres arranged for his uncle and grandmother to come to Adenna for the birth.

Sephil was embarrassed by the oversight. He had not written to his relatives, and did not even know their names, while they welcomed him with gifts and praise. In particular, his grandmother Amenia could not stop hugging and kissing him, and exclaiming how much he resembled his mother.

Once she was introduced to Ketalya, his grandmother found a new outlet for her affection in fussing over the mother-to-be. "To think I am finally going to be a great-grandmother," she told Sephil. "Your uncle Olmor keeps promising to find a wife, but he is now so old the only thing he produces is gray hairs and flatulence."

Neither she nor Olmor mentioned Zhanil and his children, and Sephil did not have the heart to remind them.

While Amenia remained indoors with Ketalya and the queen, Sephil went riding with his uncle. Olmor projected a taciturn air. He was an able administrator of the family estate, but confessed to being more interested in philosophy and obscure texts than marriage. "Your mother did not care for book learning." he said. "She found words too dry, and your father had no patience for esoteric ideas or religions. I am surprised to find you so unlike them."

"I came to my vocation purely by chance." Sephil let his gaze slide down the grassy dune on which they stood down to the foaming surf. A cool breeze stirred his hair. He had left Adeja back at the house in favor of Branag, who rode a discreet distance behind. When Olmor inquired about the need for an escort, Sephil explained the attempts on his life and Ketalya's, but there remained certain things he did not want his relatives to know.

"Zhanil sent me out of Rhodeen before the Turyar struck," he continued. "I took refuge with the priests of Abh in the sanctuary in Ottabia, and found much comfort in their teachings."

"Is this the sanctuary near Ivrish?" asked Olmor.

"Yes, I stayed there for several months. Do you know the place?"

"Our estate is only a day's ride east," said Olmor, "and I have visited with Bedren on numerous occasions. Had we known you were there, we would have taken you in at once and spared you the threat of your cousin's assassins."

Sephil nodded. "Zhanil wrote to you," he explained, "but by the time Bedren decided it was best for me to leave the sanctuary, it was no longer safe for me in Ottabia."

Two weeks after the solstice, the king and his family arrived from Bhellin. The palace bustled with activity. Ketalya participated in the planned leisure activities insofar as she was able, taking short walks along the beach, attending music and poetry recitals, and dining in the torchlit tents, where she lamented that her girth prevented her from dancing. She played cards with her mother while Sephil danced with Naulia and Amenia, who at eighty-two was as energetic as a woman thirty years younger.

Time passed swiftly. Each day, Ketalya urged Sephil to place his hand on her belly to feel the child kicking in her womb. He did not know if one could tell sex by such movements, but they felt so vigorous it seemed they could only come from a boy.

A cradle stood in the room the queen set aside as a nursery, piles of swaddling linens and diapers had been prepared, and a wet nurse and midwife were ready, yet each day that passed without Adeja's answer heightened Sephil's doubts.

He will never answer, or if he does, he will say no. Sephil cursed the hierarchy restricting Adeja's potential. In Rhodeen, where men could join the military and rise no matter what their birth, Sephil could have made the appointment without having to defend his candidate's qualifications.

I brought him into my household once before. No one asked questions, and they should have. After the debacle resulting in his exile, Sephil still did not understand why his father failed to monitor his guards beyond appointing the uncomely but loyal Eumos. Perhaps Brasidios had no longer cared what he did, as long as it did not become a public embarrassment.

With the king and royal family present, Sephil could not approach Adeja as he wished. No more chance of solitary walks on the beach, or summoning him into a quiet office without arousing his father-in-law's suspicions. As even he did not trust his urges in a room alone with Adeja, the latter would have been out of the question.

Sending a written message would prove too risky. In his experience, messages were either intercepted or Adeja never wrote back.

In the end, with less than a month left before the birth, Sephil braved his wife's displeasure by confiding in her.

Her morning sickness gone, and stimulated by exercise and the sea air, Ketalya's mood improved. She also developed an appetite for exotic foods, which the cooks did their best to provide. Sephil took note of her preferences and set a scrumptious table on a terrace overlooking the ocean.

Once her moodiness abated, Sephil felt secure in teasing Ketalya about her cravings. "If you continue to stuff yourself, men will start saying I have two wives."

Ketalya made a face at him across the platters of oysters, crab cakes, stuffed mushrooms and pastries. "It will spare you the trouble of keeping a harem. I hear your cousin has taken a second wife, another of the High Prince's daughters. It seems Armajid will keep Dashir so busy breeding that he will have no time to plot against you."

Much to her amusement, he began nibbling at the delicacies alongside her. "Have you given any thought to who will guard the nursery?"

"There is no such post, dear."

"Perhaps we should create one," said Sephil. "Our enemies will not wait until our son grows up before making an attempt on his life."

Ketalya rolled her eyes. "Why must you spoil a lovely meal with such talk? You have already seen to it that no one can go in or out of our apartments without enduring the scrutiny of that insolent boor. We will be fortunate if the wet nurse can get through the door."

"When our son outgrows the nursery, he will need someone to watch his back."

"You do not even know if it is a son." Ketalya set down her fork and narrowed her eyes. "You do not seriously intend to appoint that man as our child's bodyguard, do you?

Sephil sipped his wine. "He is the most qualified man for the job."

"No, he is not. My father's generals will teach our son whatever he needs to know, and the household guards will keep him safe. Provided, that is, that we *have* a son."

"And who will teach him how to use his wits and survive?" asked Sephil.

"Adeja is more likely to teach him how to swear and scratch himself. The boy will come home insisting that his mother cover her head with a veil, hide indoors and keep her mouth shut."

"My dear, Adeja has never used foul language in front of you, and he only made that comment about wearing the veil once," said Sephil.

Ketalya speared a mushroom on her fork and bit into it. "It was insulting," she muttered.

"He meant to be respectful."

"I cannot imagine how."

Ignoring his wife's irritated look, Sephil helped himself to another crab cake. "He told me that in Tajhaan men hide what is precious. They do not want strangers looking at their wives and daughters and thinking unclean thoughts."

"If anyone is thinking unclean thoughts, it is him," grumbled Ketalya. "He is the most insolent man I have ever met, and it does not help that you are so fixated on him." She started to sip from her glass, then suddenly set it down and stared at Sephil. "Did you not tell me once that your father punished you for carrying on an illicit affair with a guard in your household?"

Sephil froze. While at some point he expected to have to answer the question, he did not think it would be now. "That was not him," he answered lamely. "I was sixteen, and I do not even remember the man's name."

"And you had no other lovers since then?"

"I had three other men, two of whom are dead. What I did with them before I came to Bhellin has nothing to do with any appointments I make now," said Sephil. "Adeja has a wife, and I would never do anything to—"

Ketalya drew a sharp breath. "I want him gone."

"Be reasonable."

"I *have* been reasonable," she hissed, "but you keep shoving him under my nose. It is intolerable."

"I am not going to dismiss him." Sephil realized he might not have a choice when Ampheres found out how distressed his daughter was, but for the moment he had no intention of backing down. "This is my child as well as yours. I have the right to appoint the guard of my choice."

"I will not share the same household as your lover."

"Adeja is *not* my lover," answered Sephil. "I brought him here to guard you and our child, and like it or not, that is what he is going to do."

"I will find—" Grimacing, Ketalya sat back in her chair, waving Sephil silent when he started to ask what was wrong. "Call Amarno in here," she gasped. "We can discuss this later."

Sephil hesitated, until she bit her lip and threatened to box his ears if he did not comply. "Is it the baby?"

"I do not know," she replied, yet her hard breathing indicated that she was in pain. "Something feels wet."

"Are you bleeding?" Sephil knew he should send one of the servants for Ghanis and the midwife, but he could not seem to make himself move.

"I think it is my water—oh, will you just *go* already?" Ketalya shooed him away with a frantic gesture. "You are no use sitting there like that!"

* * * *

Adeja had a distant memory of his mother giving birth to his youngest sibling, a girl who had later died. His father's household, smaller and far more cramped than the palace, swarmed with relatives, mostly female, who evicted the men into the tenement courtyard. Uncles had arrived with strong beer, and Adeja's father endured the long, uneasy wait by getting drunk. Adeja himself had spent the afternoon playing with his brothers and cousins, and slept that night at a relative's house.

Had he the freedom to leave his post and mingle with the royal family, he would have plied Sephil with alcohol to soothe his nerves. Instead, he watched from the doorway, amazed that neither the king nor any of the other men present had sense enough to get the expectant father a drink or whisk him away to a corner of the palace where he could not hear his laboring wife's groans.

Lahis was not among the serving women going in and out of the princess' chamber with water and clean cloths. Provision had been made for the guards and ladies-in-waiting to accompany the royal couple to Adenna, but all others had to stay behind. Before leaving, Adeja had soothed his wife with tender assurances that he would return safely in four months, and in a nearby town he bought her a pretty necklace. Such trinkets, however, were small consolation for the child she truly wanted and could not seem to conceive.

Several times, Sephil cast a desperate glance in his direction, but Adeja did not acknowledge the gesture. Nor had he given the prince an answer regarding his proposed promotion. Guarding the royal offspring was a responsibility other sentries might covet, yet not him. If Sephil's child turned out to be a daughter, a bodyguard would not be necessary. If it was a son, threats to the young prince's life would make the post no sinecure, from the assassins who would inevitably strike to the mother who would thoroughly loathe the idea.

Sunset deepened into a long twilight, and servants brought lamps into the sitting room. Night brought the changing of the guard. Adeja relinquished his pike to his replacement, went downstairs for supper, and then retired. For a brief time he lay awake on his cot, his thoughts lingering on the drama being played out upstairs, until he convinced himself that it was not his concern and closed his eyes.

Morning brought news to the kitchen that the princess still had not delivered her child but that it was expected soon. "I daresay the prince hasn't slept all night," said the cook.

After breakfast, Adeja relieved himself and went upstairs to take his post. From the foyer, he saw the doors to the princess' chamber standing ajar. Beyond that, he could not see through the press of attendants crowding the doorway.

Neither night shift guard left, instead joining the crowd in the sitting room. The silence was so palpable that Adeja wondered if something had gone wrong with the birth.

A moment later, he heard muted applause and sighed in relief. Everything was all right. The crowd parted, forming a ragged aisle down which Sephil shuffled, escorted by the other princes. Shadows bruised the prince's eyes, and a vacant smile hung on his lips.

As he approached the door, he stumbled. Adeja put out a hand to steady him. "Are you all right, my prince?"

Sephil lifted his head. His drooping eyes focused and, recognizing Adeja, his smile broadened. "I have a son," he said.

* * * *

Exhaustion dogged Sephil throughout the labor. Once the waiting was over, Olmor and two attendants helped him to his chamber and put him to bed. He woke hours later, still partially clothed, to a room darkened by twilit shadows. Faint, jubilant sounds reached him from a distant part of the palace.

As he wobbled out of bed and tried to flex stiff joints, a servant entered bearing a lamp. Sephil threw up his hands against the sudden glare until the man covered the light.

"I did not know you were awake, my lord," said Piras. "Everyone is downstairs celebrating. Do you wish to join them, or would you like to take your supper up here?"

"How is my wife?" Alertness gradually returning to him, Sephil recalled Ketalya, bathed in sweat and exhausted by her long labor, smiling up at him. Ghanis assured him that the delivery had gone well, but he wanted to be sure.

"The princess is resting, my lord, and the little prince thrives," replied Piras. "I will help you change your clothes if you wish to go down."

Sephil wanted to ask where Adeja was, for he had a vague memory of stumbling into the man at the door, but found it difficult to speak. Instead, he let his thoughts wander as he washed his hands and face, combed his hair, and changed his rumpled clothing for a robe of gray brocade.

I have a son. What his father would have said, he did not know. The teachings of Abh taught him to relinquish all regrets, which included his lifelong yearning for his father's approval, but it was difficult. Instead, he did his best to focus on his new family, whose joy on this day sustained him through his doubts.

"Piras," he said, "bring me the seal ring."

Opening the velvet-lined box, Sephil carefully slid the ring off its chain and onto his finger. The band was too large for him, and the stone too heavy to be worn by anyone but a prince whose hand knew the weight of a sword and could defend his people.

I am not the true Crown Prince.

Slowly, he removed the ring, placed it with its chain back into its box, and closed the lid. The revelation did not sadden him, only confirmed what he knew from the beginning. He could not take Zhanil's place.

One day, he thought, handing the box back to Piras, *my son might wear this ring. But I will not wear it again.*

He walked alone down the palace's grand staircase and onto the terrace where the royal family gathered to celebrate. As people noticed, they stopped to greet him. A brother-in-law pressed a goblet of chilled wine into his hand, while Olmor inquired if he had eaten anything.

"No, I only just awoke," replied Sephil. In truth, he could not remember when he last ate.

Olmor sent a servant to fetch a plate of food as Ampheres, tapping his glass with a spoon, called for everyone's attention. Sephil exchanged glances with his uncle and braced himself for the inevitable speech.

"Now that our beloved son is able to join us," said the king, "we may begin this celebration in earnest."

Sephil drank very little, and stayed long enough to mingle before retiring. A detour to his wife's chamber yielded a visit with Ketalya, who mumbled she felt fine even as she drifted off again. Her exhaustion did not surprise him. His own weariness might have led him to curl up alongside her had Amarno not insisted that the princess needed to rest unhindered.

Before the woman evicted him altogether, Sephil managed to look in on his son, sleeping peacefully in his cradle. The wet nurse dozed on a cot nearby. Adeja was not present. That would change, regardless of Ketalya's objections, and Sephil meant to see it done before they returned to Bhellin.

The following day he called Adeja into the sitting room and, with Branag as a witness, appointed him the young prince's bodyguard.

"My prince," said Adeja, "you offered me the post before. I never said I—"

"Soldiers are not supposed to question their orders," Sephil said sharply. "They do as they are told. You hesitated because you did not know if the child would be a boy. Now you know. I have a son, and he needs a protector. You will assume your post tomorrow. You will also work with Branag to select and train a guard for the night shift."

Adeja covered his surprise with a crisp salute and returned to his post. Sephil spent the afternoon with his wife and son. Amenia and the queen were also present, directing the servants while Ketalya rested.

"My dear," said Amenia, "you must hold your son."

Sephil recoiled from the swaddled infant his grandmother offered him. "I do not want to drop him."

"Do not be absurd," she laughed. "You will not drop him."

Rising from her chair, Amenia approached Sephil and directed him to hold out his arms. "Now when you hold him on your lap, you support his head with one hand like this, and his body with your other arm like this." She demonstrated, having Sephil imitate her until she was satisfied enough to ease the baby into his arms.

He froze in terror at the warm weight in his arms. His son seemed so small, so fragile, and should he move, Sephil knew he would surely drop him.

For some reason, the women found his dilemma amusing. "One can always tell a new father by how frightened he is of the newborn," said the queen. "It took Ampheres two months to hold Ettarin, he was so anxious, but when Naulia was born he wanted to dandle her in his arms before the midwife even cut the cord. Sephil, child, relax your arms before you get a cramp. You are not going to drop him."

He did as told, cautiously adjusting his hold until he found a more comfortable position. Right away, the baby began to bawl, his red face screwing up in displeasure. This, too, the women found amusing, while it mortified Sephil to think that his own son did not want to be held by him.

"Babies cry when they want something, my lord," explained the wet nurse. With an apology, she took the infant from him. "Maybe he is hungry, or needs to be changed."

"Or he does not like me," Sephil murmured, as he watched the woman carry his son out of the room.

"Nonsense!" said Amenia. "All he knows is that he is tired, hungry, or has a wet diaper, and as for not liking you, as long as you are warm or have a nipple, that is all that concerns him."

That evening, the king hosted a banquet in the palace's formal dining hall. Ketalya, having been admonished to remain in bed for one more day, did not attend, but Ampheres had food and rich red wine sent up to her chamber, and announced that she and Sephil would be his guests of honor at a second, more lavish banquet to be held in Bhellin upon their return.

During the second course, Ettarin's wife politely inquired what name Sephil intended to give his son. No one had asked after the birth, which Sephil found strange until Ampheres explained that naming was not done right away. "This will sound crude, I am sure," the king explained, "but announcements cost money, and we must make certain that the child will survive before committing ourselves to such expenditures. However, the little prince seems to be in excellent health, so I see no reason why we should not release news of his birth to the court by next week."

Revealing the name to his immediate family was not, as Sephil viewed it, an official announcement. Smiling at his sister-in-law, he replied, "His name is Zhanil Sephides."

Although the name was one among many he had considered, Sephil knew the moment he had placed the seal ring on his finger what legacy his son should bear. This Zhanil would be strong and wise and brave, as perfect a prince as his lost uncle, and all that his father could not be.

All eyes at the table turned to him, and Ampheres laughed. "Zhanil Sephides, it is then," said the king, raising his glass. "Here is to the young prince. Long may he thrive."

After supper, Ampheres drew him aside into his darkened study for a private talk. "Your choice of name does not surprise me," he said, closing the door.

Sephil refused the drink Ampheres offered him. He had drunk more than he intended the last two days, and felt lightheaded. "I could not give him any other."

"There are some who will not care for your choice," said Ampheres. "You may think it premature, but it might be prudent to proclaim Zhanil Crown Prince of Rhodeen as soon as possible."

In a box upstairs sat a ring the size of a newborn's fist, and far heavier. *He will wear it when he is ready, not before.* "I disagree," said Sephil.

"Do you, now?"

"You once told me that you would not build empires on sons who had not been born or who had not shown their promise. Zhanil is only two days old. For all you know he will turn out like his father: dull-witted and inept with a sword. Would you rest your ambitions on a potential weakling?"

"You make a valid point," said Ampheres.

"I will not have my son burdened with the title unless he desires it and is worthy of it."

Ampheres raised an eyebrow. "Desire has nothing to do with political necessity."

"The Turyar are entrenched in Rhodeen. They are not going to step aside so my son can assume the throne," answered Sephil. "Make no mistake: I am grateful to you for all you have done for me, but Zhanil is *my* son and I will not have him forced into a role he might not want. Train him for war if you must, but if later he desires a peaceful life, I mean to see that he has it."

Staring into his glass, Ampheres took his time about replying. "Your father thought you weak and effeminate," he said softly. "Regardless of what I told you, you still cling to these notions about yourself. However, you possess far more backbone and intelligence than you believe. I do not think your father would be displeased with you today.

"Having said that, I am not pleased by all the decisions you have made regarding this matter. For one, it remains to be seen whether you have shown sound judgment in appointing Zhanil's bodyguard."

"I have confidence in the man's abilities," said Sephil.

Ampheres answered with a long, probing look. "We will see how well he proves his worth. Ketalya does not care for the appointment. We both know why. I have assured her that your conduct in this matter has thus far been beyond reproach, and that you will continue to ensure it remains so.

"For now, we will respect your wishes and delay passing the title of Crown Prince to Zhanil until he is ready to bear it. However, you would do well to remember that your son was not born into a time of peace, and your enemies care nothing for your wishes or his. Like it or not, he must prepare for war."

Chapter Thirteen

"What's the matter?" asked Adeja. "Don't you like the necklace?" Women were such strange creatures, passionate one moment and crying the next. Earlier in the day, Lahis had flung her arms about him and kissed him in enthusiastic welcome, but now in the dark, when he draped the jasper beads around her neck, she burst into tears.

Touching the necklace, Lahis chewed her lip and kissed his cheek, yet she was still crying. Then she took his hand and placed it over her belly.

Adeja felt roundness where he did not remember any, just enough to make him draw back in amazement. "When did this happen?"

Four months ago, just before his departure. Lahis seemed reluctant to say more, as though her next words would be that the child was not his. Adeja, however, knew that was not so. "Why didn't you tell me earlier?" he asked. "This should make you happy."

"I wanted to be sure," she said, sniffling. "I didn't want to lose it like the others and make you angry."

"What others?" asked Adeja.

Lahis dropped her head so he could not see her face. "The ones I had before, with Chalak."

Had she possessed a sense of humor, Adeja might have made a jest about her first husband's lack of virility, but she was so distraught that he held his tongue. "Crying isn't good for the baby," he said. "Come now, dry your eyes, put a smile on your face and let me see how pretty the necklace looks on you."

* * * *

Ketalya showed two faces with regard to their son. In private, she was a loving mother, yet when it came to all official matters her smile vanished. She said nothing when Adeja assumed his post near the nursery, but her cold demeanor told Sephil that she did not accept the appointment. Sephil did not press the issue, trusting that in time she would see how suitable the arrangement was.

However, he could not contain his surprise when she revealed how much she disliked his choice of name. "Why did you have to call him after your dead brother?" she asked. "I thought you wanted to call him Charnil."

"I did," he said, "but when I finally saw him the name did not seem to fit. Why do you find my choice so objectionable? My brother was a good and honorable man."

"You do not understand," said Ketalya. "In Khalgar, mothers do not name their children after people who have died horrible deaths. I assumed you knew our customs. Do you think I want my son named after a man who rode out against the Turyar and came back staked to a pole without his head?"

Sephil was stunned that she would so explicitly remind him of his brother's fate when she scrupulously avoided all other mention of Zhanil. "I am doing all I can to ensure that our son does not suffer that fate. Why do you think I insisted on appointing Adeja as his bodyguard? I want him to have at least one protector who does not answer to your father, and who can teach him how to survive. My hope is that Zhanil will decide that he does not wish to pursue the throne."

"I do not see that he will have much choice," said Ketalya, "and by that I am not referring to whatever ambitions my father might have. What happened last week will happen again."

Somehow, the anonymous gift of a stuffed toy had found its way into the nursery, where on his daily inspection Adeja noticed movement under the plush velvet. Calmly instructing the nurse to take Zhanil out of the room, he speared the lion with his sword and bore it into the sitting room where he cast it into the fireplace.

Ketalya and her ladies, irritated by the interruption and the stench of burning velvet, scattered in horror at the dark shapes that writhed out of the burning pile. Adeja crushed two with his boot and speared another while calling for a guard to make certain the floor was clear.

"Scorpions, princess," he said, without looking at Ketalya. "It looks like a present from the prince's relations in Tajhaan."

An hour later, the entire household overheard Adeja berating the woman responsible for bringing parcels and messages into the household. She ran to the princess in tears, her cheek red from where Adeja had slapped her, but Sephil, who came straightaway from the temple of Abh upon hearing the news, had stern words for her.

239

"I do not care how harmless or cute it seems," he said. "Anything that comes for Prince Zhanil *must* go through the bodyguard."

Still weeping, the woman knelt before him. "But he shouts, my lord, and he struck me!"

"He will do much worse to you if this happens again, and I will not stop him."

Ketalya, still in shock, had nothing to say. She acknowledged Adeja's deed by formally thanking him, but did not warm toward him or Amset, the guard he had selected and was training for the night shift. Sephil meditated on the situation, and concluded that she did not like the perpetual threat to her son that both men represented.

"What happened will happen again no matter what name Zhanil bears," he said.

Naturally, the Tajhaani ambassador expressed horror at the incident and assured the king of his prince's good intentions. "After all," said Fallaz, "the gift came anonymously. Everyone knows the Turyar employ scorpions and venomous snakes in battle, so who is to say they have not done so this time?"

"The Turyar do not concern themselves with infants who represent no threat to them," answered Ampheres, "nor do they attack by such underhanded means. We know Tajhaan's reputation for poison and other nefarious means of death, and your custom of eliminating all male rivals, even the very young. Therefore, you would do well to hold your tongue and tell your prince that should such an incident occur again, he will not like our response."

Fearing another attempt, Ketalya insisted that Zhanil's cradle be moved to her chamber at night, and would not be deterred even when Sephil pointed out that the baby's crying would keep her awake. Her solution was to have the wet nurse sleep on a cot in the corner.

Some nights, Sephil slept beside her. Ketalya displayed no interest in lovemaking, which Ghanis assured him was natural following childbirth. "Give it time," he said, "and her desire will return."

Sephil knew his wife took herbs to suppress her milk, yet her scent, discernable even through the fragrant oils her ladies poured into her bath, aroused in him a fierce urge to protect her and the baby. Often he woke to find himself spooned against her back, his arms wrapped around her. Ketalya softened during these moments, when their world seemed no larger than the room, the bed in which they lay, and the infant she lifted out of the cradle and set on the coverlet beside her.

"He is such a beautiful baby," she said. "I almost wish he could stay like this forever."

"He will be tall," murmured Sephil, reaching across her to fondle Zhanil's tiny fingers, "and dark like you. And if he has your temper, his enemies had better beware."

She smiled and closed her eyes. "He will turn out as stubborn as you."

As autumn deepened and turned cold, Sephil called for Ceyath once more. Ketalya encouraged these visits, and even took a maternal interest in the young man, insisting that he eat and don a warm cloak before leaving. Sephil flushed with embarrassment at how easily she inquired if Ceyath satisfied him. She never asked about his life in Rhodeen or mentioned Adeja, yet beneath her solicitous interest he sensed unresolved tension simmering.

Could his desire be so transparent? He took care not to interact with Adeja without a senior member of the household present, and when he did the conversation was strictly impersonal. How could Ketalya know of his longings when he did his utmost to put them out of his mind?

One gray afternoon, Ketalya dismissed her ladies, instructed the nurse to bundle Zhanil in warm clothes, and announced she was taking him to visit Ettarin and his wife.

"Take Adeja with you," said Sephil.

Ketalya settled her mantle upon her shoulders. "Amset will accompany me."

Sephil started to protest that Amset was not on duty. Ketalya turned, spearing him with eyes that said she *wanted* Adeja to stay behind with him.

Even as he grasped her intention, he shook his head. "His place is with you and Zhanil."

"Whatever happens here while I am gone," she said coldly, "I do not want to know about it."

"I do not intend to—"

"I want this matter settled, Sephil. Do what you must, but I want it finished today."

Ketalya left the room, the nurse following with Zhanil. Sephil could not speak, and did not know what he would have said had he been able. *How can she expect me to do this when I have spent so long trying to denying these desires? For all I know, once I touch him again, I will not be able to stop.*

From the foyer, Sephil heard two male voices. One belonged to Amset. The other…. Only when he tried to swallow did he realize his throat had gone dry.

Adeja, wearing his red leather corselet, filled the doorway. Across ten feet their eyes met, an exchange brimming with confusion and longing. No words passed between them.

She arranged this, just as she might have arranged an evening with Ceyath. A wild thought, racing so chaotically through Sephil's head that he could not quite grasp it. At the same moment, memory took him back to the day when he first set eyes on the handsome foreign guard he had Nakhet procure for him, when he felt his heart race and desire stop his voice.

"You look like I just sprouted horns," Adeja finally said. He turned, closed the door and stepped forward.

Sephil blinked, and shook himself out of his trance. "Do you know why you are here?"

"Your wife told me just now. She thinks there's still something between us."

You say that as if it is not true. "Did she really say that?"

"Not in so many words, but I understood her meaning."

Adeja unbuckled his corselet, tossed it onto a chair and approached, so confident and delectable that Sephil yearned to embrace him, but the situation was so contrived it felt unnatural, very much like what he imagined a tryst in a brothel would be. "I am not so sure we are not being watched," said Sephil.

"She's dismissed everyone."

"The king also has spies."

Adeja smiled. "Yes, and I know who they are, too. They're also gone."

Drawn together by the heat of their attraction, their lips met. Sephil drank in the kiss, the tongue exploring his mouth and the hands running down his back to cup his buttocks and pull him close. All those lonely nights, this was what he wanted, needed, and he still could not quite believe that Ketalya was simply allowing him to have it.

His fingers found the hem of Adeja's tunic and drew it up, tugging at the cloth until Adeja acknowledged his need by removing the garment and tossing it aside.

Now able to touch his lover's bare skin, Sephil knew his desire should have intensified. He should have been pulling off his own clothing, fumbling at the laces of Adeja's leggings, drawing out his cock to fondle and take it in his mouth, all in a frenzy of passion. But the heat was not there, no matter how fiercely he tried to coax it.

Finally, he pulled away. "I cannot do this. It is not right."

With a sigh, Adeja released him. "Neither can I," he admitted.

"I *do* want you, but—"

Adeja bent to retrieve his tunic. "I know."

As he started to put the garment back on, Sephil spied an unfamiliar tattoo on his left bicep. Putting out his hand, he stopped Adeja so he could touch the design in blue ink. "This is the royal sunburst," he said. "I have never seen this before."

"I had it done a year ago."

A year ago, Adeja was working in the city prison. For all either of them knew, they had seen the last of each other. "Why would you do this?"

Adeja shrugged. "I don't know. It just seemed like something I wanted to do." Laughing, he pulled the tunic over his head and belted it. "It's a good thing I ended up in your service and not someone else's."

"You serve Zhanil now, Adeja, not me."

Adeja retrieved the corselet from the chair and buckled it on. "Lahis is pregnant," he said.

Of all the things he might have said, Sephil never expected this to be among them. "When did this happen?"

"Just before we left for Adenna," replied Adeja. "The baby's due at the end of winter."

"She is six months' pregnant and only *now* you think to tell me?"

"*I* only found out when we returned, and even then Lahis waited half a day to tell me. Besides, I had no idea you were so interested in the lives of your lowly servants."

His lighthearted tone and comical eye-rolling took the barb out of the comment. Sephil could not help but laugh.

"This means we have to celebrate." In a cabinet, he found a decanter of red wine and two glasses.

"I'm on duty," said Adeja.

Sephil handed him a glass nonetheless. "If you were on duty, you would be with Zhanil. One drink, Adeja, and then you can return to your post."

Adeja stared into its contents before drinking. "Your wife will want to know what happened."

"Then tell her the truth," said Sephil.

Once Adeja was gone, Sephil again became aware of the silence. This time, it was not oppressive, but serene, encouraging him to reflect. If she asked, Adeja would tell Ketalya nothing happened between them.

It was not entirely true.

Something had ended between them, yes, yet when Sephil closed his eyes and saw again in his mind the sunburst tattoo, he knew something far more profound had begun.

Facing the window, he raised his glass before drinking. "To you, my protector," he murmured. "And to you, my son, the most fortunate of princes."

About the Author

L.E. Bryce was born in Los Angeles, California and has never lived anywhere else. She has a Masters in English Literature from California State University, Northridge, and currently works as an English teacher. Her Jewish mother, two dogs and passel of cats help her keep her sanity. She is a regular contributor to *Forbidden Fruit* Magazine, and is the author of three other books, *Dead to the World*, *Snake Bite and Other Dark Homoerotic Fantasies* and *Those Pearls That Were His Eyes*. She maintains a blog at http://granamyr.livejournal.com.

Lightning Source UK Ltd.
Milton Keynes UK
05 November 2009
145880UK00001B/34/A